The Love Knot
'The author perfectly evokes the atmosphere of a bygone era
. . . An entertaining Victorian romance'
Woman's Own

The Kissing Garden
'A perfect escapist cocktail for summertime romantics'
Mail on Sunday

Love Song
'A perfect example of the new, darker romantic fiction . . .
a true 24-carat love story'
Sunday Times

The Nightingale Sings
'A novel rich in dramatic surprises . . . will have you
frantically turning the pages'
Daily Mail

To Hear A Nightingale
'A story to make you laugh and cry'
Woman

The Business
'A compulsive, intriguing and perceptive read'
Sunday Express

In Sunshine Or In Shadow
'Superbly written . . . A romantic novel that is romantic
in the true sense of the word'
Daily Mail

Stardust
'A long, absorbing read, perfect for holidays'
Sunday Express

Change Of Heart
'Her imagination is thoroughly original'
Daily Mail

Nanny
'Charlotte Bingham's spellbinding saga is required reading'
Cosmopolitan

Grand Affair
'Extremely popular . . . her books sell and sell'
Daily Mail

Debutantes
'A big, wallowy, delicious read'
The Times

THE BLUE NOTE

Charlotte Bingham

BANTAM BOOKS

LONDON · NEW YORK · TORONTO · SYDNEY · AUCKLAND

THE BLUE NOTE
A BANTAM BOOK: 0553 81274 2

Simultaneously published in Great Britain by Doubleday,
a division of Transworld Publishers

PRINTING HISTORY
Doubleday edition published 2000
Bantam Books edition published 2000

3 5 7 9 10 8 6 4 2

Set in 11/13pt Palatino
by Phoenix Typesetting, Ilkley, West Yorkshire

Bantam Books are published by Transworld Publishers,
61–63 Uxbridge Road, London W5 5SA,
a division of The Random House Group Ltd,
in Australia by Random House, Australia (Pty) Ltd,
20 Alfred Street, Milsons Point, Sydney, NSW 2061, Australia,
in New Zealand by Random House New Zealand Ltd,
18 Poland Road, Glenfield, Auckland 10, New Zealand
and in South Africa by Random House (Pty) Ltd,
Endulini, 5a Jubilee Road, Parktown 2193, South Africa.

Reproduced, printed and bound in Great Britain by
Cox & Wyman Ltd, Reading, Berks.

The blue note is the odd note: the one that seems to have a life of its own, and yet comes from nowhere. It cannot exist without the others, though, and needs the conventional notes to show up its oddness, its rarity. Sometimes it is a little sound, and strange; but it is always there, waiting to happen.

Afterwards they said there was never to be a time quite like it again. It was not just the exuberance, and not just the fun of it either; it was the sudden realization that they were actually *alive*. That despite the war, doodlebugs, rationing, dreary clothes and even drearier food, despite the A-bomb and the H-bomb, despite Korea and Malaya, despite Russia and the Berlin Wall, despite the terrible threat of Communism and Marxism, the Yellow Peril and the Red Peril, despite almost everything they knew or had been told about – against all those odds, against everything that everyone had predicted about the doom of days gone past, and the doom of days yet to come, despite all that – they were still living, and on this earth.

And what was more, and what was better, they were young, and some of them were not just young, but beautiful. Not that it mattered, beautiful or not beautiful, pretty or not pretty, handsome or not handsome; it did not matter a single, solitary little damn not once they came to and realized that after all that – all those dead people, all those fathers that had not come back, uncles who had never returned, mothers whom they had never known – *they* were actually alive.

But first – they had to grow up.

PART ONE

SOMERSET
1939

'There is no doubt that to our dying day the words salvage, war savings, herbs, hips and haws and meat pies will bring back poignant memories to all of us . . .'

Lady Denman, 1943

Chapter One

It would be not just their first wartime Christmas together, but their first sensations of the kind of childhood happiness that will always be remembered. Miranda's lasting memory would be of Bobbie crawling out of bed, once the red-dressing-gowned Aunt Prudence and Aunt Sophie had crept away, and staring into the woolly socks at the end of the bed. Teddy would always remember having a pillow put over his young face to shush him when he asked, 'Was that Father Christmas what just went out?' While Bobbie's memory would be of clambering to the end of her bed and reaching down into each of the socks by turn, and finding that unimaginable luxury, an *orange*.

'What is there?' Teddy demanded again in a gruff voice, only to be threatened once more with being hushed with a pillow, because Bobbie was sure that she could still hear their wartime 'aunts' creeping back down the bare-wooden-boarded corridor of the old rectory. 'What is *there*?'

Bobbie, small, brown-haired and always and

ever the eternal optimist, whispered gleefully as she felt down into the hand-knitted socks. 'There's an orange, and I think – something else as well – er – something woolly – yes, look, a pair of gloves. Navy blue, because of your father being in the Navy, Ted, I should think, and look – same for you too, Miranda,' she went on, staring at a pair of identical but much larger gloves knitted for his sister.

For one awful moment Bobbie thought that Father Christmas was going to have missed out on her stocking, and that there would be no gloves for her, because her father was dead. She suddenly could not remember whether he had been in the army, the Navy, or the air force, until, that is, she saw the colour of the gloves in her sock, and knew at once, the gloves being khaki, that he must have been in the army, because that was the colour the aunts knitted scarves and socks for soldiers, whereas for the Navy it would always be navy blue, and for airmen a sort of grey blue.

As she stared down at the small, expertly knitted gloves, for a few seconds Bobbie felt a single darting feeling of regret that her daddy had not been in the Navy, because khaki was not the prettiest colour, and blue would have gone better with the thick wool cloak that the aunts had found in the attic for her winter wear.

But there, she knew she was lucky to have any gloves at all, really.

Bobbie had been evacuated to the old rectory in Somerset via the WVS the previous September.

Before that she had been at a kind of boarding school for orphans where kindly relatives had paid for her but did not bother to come and see her. She was there until Lady Reading, who started the Women's Voluntary Service, had heard about her, probably because Bobbie's mother and Lady Reading had shared a mutual friend, so that was why Bobbie had been 'heard about'.

She would never forget that day, when Mrs Hervey, the headmistress, had read out her name and given her a bad look. Bobbie had been convinced that she was going to be *beaten*. Mrs Hervey always said *beaten* that way – 'I am going to *beat* you, Roberta. I feel you might not have told me the truth, so I am going to *beat* you!' Since, as soon as she saw Mrs Hervey, all thoughts except of extreme terror flew out of her mind, Bobbie never did find out why she was being beaten. But this time, just for once, there had been no beating, only what Aunt Prudence now gaily referred back to as 'rescue time'.

And instead of being beaten with the old hockey boot that Mrs Hervey so sweetly kept for that purpose, Bobbie had been marched out into the bitter wind in her thin clothes, and practically thrown into the back of Aunt Sophie's battered old pre-war 1932 Austin, and driven for mile after tortuous mile to Somerset, where quite suddenly there was a fire burning in the old rectory kitchen and the low murmur of the aunts' voices, and food on the table that was warm and tasted of all sorts of comforting things that were soft to eat. After which she had been put into a bed that smelt of lavender, between old linen sheets that felt cool but kept her snug all night, and when she had woken in the morning, she had heard birds singing, and there had been no-one waiting to punish her for something that she could not remember doing.

Since Bobbie's father and mother had been killed in a motoring accident before the war she knew she was officially an 'orphan', not just an evacuee or being paid for to be in a children's home. Being a proper orphan would have been really sad if she could have remembered her parents at all, but since she could not, and since she could only imagine them, they had become for her just like people in a story, people that she had read about, and she realized that it would have been much worse for her if she had known them, or been able to remember them, because she might not have liked them as much as she did in her imagination.

Of course Aunt Prudence and Aunt Sophie were only 'wartime aunts', not the children's real aunts, although since they were only in early middle age they could well have been. It was the same with Bobbie and Miranda; they were not related. Miranda had not been there long before the two girls began to try to pretend that they were sisters by trying to wear their hair the same, and not telling anyone in the village their real surnames – so much so that by now Bobbie had become all too convinced that her real surname was the same as

Miranda and Teddy's, and the three of them were really and truly two sisters and a brother, and always had been.

Somehow – and had they been grown-ups the children might have asked how – Aunt Prudence and Aunt Sophie were able to produce a small roast goose for Christmas lunch that year – a lunch which was placed reverentially into the lower oven of the once spanking cream pre-war Aga while they all went to church.

'A bomb hit the poor thing. How lucky that we found it!' was always Aunt Sophie's joke whenever they all sat down to a rare roast dinner in the rectory kitchen with its baskets of herbs hanging high up around the fire, and its blue and white cloth on the long, low oak table around which were placed oak chairs, which slipped a little when you sat on them.

Of course, seeing that they were living in Somerset, it was a bit easier for Aunt Sophie and Aunt Prudence to find food, much easier than if they had been in London, where Miranda said she thought her mother was still working in a place called 'Baker Street'.

'Right next door to Sherlock Holmes,' was another of Aunt Sophie's regular jokes, and although none of them exactly knew who their adopted aunt meant by this 'Sherlock Homes' person – Bobbie always imagined that he was perhaps some sort of relative – nevertheless they would all laugh uproariously, if dutifully, however often Aunt Sophie repeated her jokes, because she mostly made them when she was serving lunch or dinner.

The truth was that while Aunt Sophie's jokes were not at all funny, she was a perfectly marvellous cook, and Aunt Prudence a perfectly marvellous gardener who seemed to know where to find berries, or nuts, or any of the other things that Aunt Sophie would somehow make up into something which tasted, or just smelt, so good; so much so that for the three young evacuees from London it sometimes did seem nowadays, at mealtimes anyway, that there really was no war on at all.

'It's nice that it's Christmas Day,' Bobbie confided to Miranda as they struggled into two dresses that the aunts had unearthed from mothballs in the attic and adapted for their use over the holiday. 'I expect Hitler will stop bombing on Christmas Day.'

After which Miranda started to sing, '*Music while you work, Hitler is a jerk . . .*'

'Shshsh!'

Miranda had a really pretty singing voice but the sound of her singing made Bobbie feel suddenly and unaccountably sad, for no reason that she knew.

Miranda began again, her voice louder this time. '*You are my sunshine, my double Woodbine, my box of matches, my Craven A . . .*'

'Shsh! It's like a Sunday, we're meant to be specially good today.'

'It's all right – they don't mind! You know Aunt

Sophie's teaching me to sing. She says I should go far.' Miranda twirled suddenly, her arms above her head, her hands waving.

'I wish I could sing, Miranda.'

'I wish I could knit and crochet.'

'Do you think we shall have to do knitting and things today?'

'I hopes not.' Miranda spread out her old-fashioned ankle-length velvet party frock and twirled once more in front of Bobbie, her blond hair spinning, her slender childish form exactly suiting the elegant shape of the long Edwardian children's dress. 'I dunno. Do you think this was once Auntie Prudence's party dress?'

''Spect so, ducky!' Bobbie pulled a little face and rounded her forefingers and thumbs together, putting them either side of her nose, in a passable imitation of Aunt Prudence when she was wearing her specs. 'After all, they have always lived at the rectory. They knew my mother, you know. That is why I was sent here from the boarding school, because of my mother being a friend of a Mrs Harper person who is a friend of Lady Reading. She was killed – my mother I mean.'

Miranda nodded, and turned away suddenly. She had liked where she had been before, in Kent, by the sea, with Mr and Mrs Meades. But they had to give her up, send her back to London, because of the fear of invasion, or something like that. After being sent back to London to her grandmother, she eventually came down to Somerset with Ted, but no-one local wanted to take them, because they were too small and would be no use working on a farm.

She would always remember how she and Ted had stood and stood in the market square in Mellaston, from teatime until dark, getting colder and colder, and how Ted had kept crying, until Auntie Sophie came to the square, just by chance, and having first come over to them and tried to comfort Ted went and told Mrs Eglantine – who was very powerful in Mellaston because she was not just the WI Jam Inspector for the area but also the Billeting Officer – that since no-one wanted them Aunt Sophie was more than happy to take them back to the rectory with her and put them up 'for the duration if needs be, poor souls'.

Miranda remembered shivering and shivering, the cold almost seeming to become colder for just thinking that some time in the near future she and Ted would be less so, and how Mrs Eglantine had kept saying in a loud voice, 'But Miss Mowbray, I don't think so, really. I mean to say, these children are London children, you know. And such children, well, they really are quite a handful, I believe. After all, not even the *farmers* wanted them, so I am sure that you can understand from that, that they really might not be suitable for two spinst— two un-married ladies such as yourself and Miss Prudence to look after?'

'Oh, just so much tosh. They're just not old enough and strong enough for farmers to be interested in them. No use on the farm, just another mouth to feed.'

'I would warn you that children of this kind . . . their language, their bed-wetting, their nasty rough ways, can be daunting little people to take charge of, even for *married* women,' Mrs Eglantine had persisted.

But Aunt Sophie had cared less, scooping up Miranda and Ted's gas mask cases and their small cardboard suitcases and putting the cases under each of her thin arms she had given the two children one each of her mittened hands and stalked off in the chill evening air in the vague direction of the old Regency rectory which was her and Miss Prudence's home, and which stood, churchless and alone, on the edge of Mellaston. This was where once, centuries ago, there had been a small parish church, but it had long been swept away, the victim of some new religious movement. In its stead, some miles from it, the magnificent Mellaston Cathedral had been built.

Miranda and Ted had been freezing cold from hanging about waiting for someone to take them in as evacuees. They had no gloves, so Aunt Sophie's mittens seemed warming and they quite forgot how cold their knees were in contrast to their hands because she walked them along smartly until they reached the pony trap, as if, although they might have forgotten their bare knees, she had not, and could not wait to put the rug in the pony trap over their skinny, purple-patched legs, and herself sit up

11

behind Tom Kitten, her smartly turned out driving pony.

'Home, Tom, home,' she called to the pony, and they set off at a smart pace, the wind blowing hard, which made Miranda put out her arms to Ted and hold him close, because the little boy was hard put to stay on the seat of the trap, what with the smart pace of the pony, and his own short legs.

It was quite dark when they finally reached the old rectory, and saw Aunt Prudence shining a torch to greet her sister, the tiny beam of light glowing under the blackout material curtaining the old-fashioned Regency half-glassed doors.

As soon as Aunt Sophie introduced Miranda and Ted the tall, slender Prudence Mowbray put out her arms, and said, 'Come in, come in,' and brought them hot drinks of a mixture of fruit juices and some bread with stiff jam on it, and a spoonful of Virol which made Ted cry because it got round his teeth and he didn't like the taste.

After that they were put to bed, and in the morning Miranda woke up to find Bobbie at the bottom of their beds staring at them both, and asking their names, which Miranda told her were *Miranda and Ted Darling* but which their new aunts promptly changed to Miranda and *Teddy* Darling, for some reason that no-one else could imagine but which seemed to make the two spinsters very happy. All they told the children was that they had once had a cousin called Teddy, and they had liked him a great deal, a fact which the children accepted as easily as

12

they accepted that they should call their hosts 'Aunt' or 'Auntie'.

And so that had been the start of their friendship, and now they were all walking along towards the town, and as they walked the two aunts, who never believed in wasting a shining minute of any hour of any livelong day, span the wool which the children had collected during the week from the hedgerows, from field wires or off old gates and sticking-out nails in wooden stiles and fencing – from anywhere the sheep had rubbed or caught themselves and left precious wool that could go to make mittens and socks, or mufflers and hats.

The sun shone as they walked, and every now and then Aunt Sophie looked up and about her and murmured, 'It's not a bit like Christmas, is it, Prudence?'

At last they arrived at the cathedral after their brisk walk, the children a somehow strangely appropriate sight on Christmas morning, in their long old-fashioned clothes with their new knitted gloves, and feeling really rather thrilled at finding themselves arrived not just in good time, but early for once, joining the other morning worshippers outside Mellaston Cathedral.

Nowadays Prudence and Sophie Mowbray, having always attended church, found themselves regularly astonished, as doubtless was the dean, by the huge congregations that now followed their regular church-going example.

'Such a contrast to before the war,' Prudence

muttered, every Sunday, while Sophie hardly looked up from her relentless spinning.

Bobbie knew more of the people who made up the congregation than Miranda and Teddy, simply because she had been at the rectory longer than the other two. Of all the regulars she most dreaded seeing Mr and Mrs Eglantine, who were what Aunt Sophie, wryly called *very correct*, and had a habit of trying to pretend that the three children were not visible and saying things to Aunt Prudence like, 'And how are your little Cockney sparrows, Miss Prudence?' which made Bobbie squirm and Aunt Prudence turn away as if she had not really heard.

This morning, perhaps because it was Christmas, Mrs Eglantine came across to them and said, 'Happy Christmas, little people. I hope you realize that today is not just about presents and eating too much?' Then she stared down at Teddy in a particularly officious way, as if she suspected him of eating everyone else's Christmas ration, which made the little boy shrink behind Aunt Prudence, and stick a newly gloved thumb in his mouth.

'Well, well, the children look like some sort of illustration from an old-fashioned book, not like modern children at all, Miss Mowbray. Cloaks and hats, which really – well, I have not seen such cloaks and hats since I don't know when, really I haven't. And nor I suppose has Eustace, have you, Eustace?'

'Quite so, quite so, ahem.'

Mr Eglantine ran a thick, stubby finger underneath his moustache and nodded, lifting his hat as he did so to each and every lady who passed them, to some of whom he gave a second and more lingering glance, until his wife tapped him briskly on the arm and he followed her obediently into church.

'We do not want to sit near the Eglantines. It would not be wise,' Aunt Prudence said in a low voice to Aunt Sophie, and she pulled her feathered hat down firmly to illustrate her aversion to such a notion.

'We may not want to, dearest, but we may find we have to, because there is nowhere else suitable.'

Prudence Mowbray saw what her sister meant, for although they had arrived early others must have arrived even earlier, as they discovered when they entered the cathedral and saw that every pew was already taken up with churchgoers eager to pray for loved ones in danger. Since the start of the war everyone had come to cherish not just their church but a real church service, so many of the buildings having been already bombed to nothing but rubble.

In the event, the Misses Mowbray were quite happy to sit at the very back of the lovely old cathedral, in the last pew, and well away from the Eglantines, which was probably just as well, for Miranda had not yet *quite* mastered what could be called 'church manners', and Teddy could never be relied upon to sit completely still.

Having solemnly crossed herself, as she had only really just learned to do, Miranda looked up at Aunt

Prudence with her round, blue eyes and demanded in piping tones, 'Which is me bloody hymn book, Auntie Prudence?'

Aunt Prudence smiled.

'Now, now, Miranda dear,' she told her charge, in a gentle voice, ignoring the amazed looks from their fellow worshippers around them, 'never *me*, always *my*, remember?' and handed her the hymn book.

Mrs Eglantine was speaking for all the Mellaston Evacuation Committee, she said, when she sat down in the drawing room of the old rectory a week later and announced that she thought that Miranda and Teddy were really too much for the two unmarried Miss Mowbrays to handle.

'But they are very happy, and we are very happy with them.'

'But I understand from your laundry lady, whom I just happened to glimpse as I came up the drive and caught pegging out the laundry, that the little boy bed-wets, Miss Prudence. Surely it would be better if we at least took *him* and put him with a village family? After all, Miranda and Teddy do not have to stay together. The war has separated so many brothers and sisters. It is quite common to split up families.'

Outside the drawing room door the two girls stared at each other. Mrs Eglantine's voice was so loud that it carried all too easily into the hall where the children had been seated, waiting for some sort

16

of verdict from inside where the two Misses Mowbray were receiving their uninvited guest.

'I hate Mrs Eglantine.'

'Yah, she's an old cow, in't she?'

'No. I like cows.' Bobbie looked at Miranda, reproach in her eyes.

'She's nasty, then. She's like . . .' Miranda searched desperately in her mind for something she knew that Bobbie could not like. 'She's like Hitler.'

'She's a bad meat pie.'

'She's tapioca . . .'

'*Urgh.*'

They all started giggling, not because they were in the least bit amused, but because they were frightened, and seconds later Teddy clutched at the front of his trousers and rushed off to the cloak-room, because he still had problems.

Inside the room Sophie Mowbray was telling Mrs Eglantine in a firm voice, 'Lady Reading thinks that children should be kept together. And after all, they are brother and sister. Miranda is devoted to Teddy.'

'Lady Reading is a wonderful person, and you girls in green, you members of the WVS, are doing a grand job. All of us in the WI appreciate that, I am sure. But sometimes it is up to us as Christians, let us say, to come to the rescue of each other, and the committee feels that Teddy and Miranda are not really suitable for the rectory. Much better if they were with, say, my cleaning lady, some village woman. Besides, it would free both of you to do other war work, wouldn't it?'

Bobbie could hear the natural firmness in Mrs Eglantine's loud voice becoming more and more insistent, and her heart sank down to the bottom of her secondhand shoes.

Oh please, please, please, don't let her take Miranda and Teddy away from the aunts and me at the rectory, she prayed to God.

In her imagination Bobbie thought she could see the Almighty with His long white beard bending down from His great gold throne and booming to some angel who had just rushed her prayer in to Him: *Prayer granted to Miss Bobbie Murray! Let the Darling children stay at the rectory with the aunts.*

The children were still seated, looking outwardly a great deal more meek and good than they felt inwardly, when Mrs Eglantine walked smartly past them, her silk-lined skirt making a rustling sound so that despite her utter lack of lipstick, her tweed suit and pearl earrings, as the front door was closed behind her she left behind a distinct feeling of town-come-to-the-country.

'She is . . . she's a . . .' Miranda hesitated, and then leaning back against the hall chair upon which she was seated, and staring up at the ceiling, she said in resigned tones, to please Bobbie more than anything, *'meat pie.'*

After which for no reason at all, and despite being far too old for such girlish displays, Teddy burst into tears and Aunt Prudence took him and Bobbie to the kitchen for a glass of milk while Aunt Sophie beckoned Miranda into the drawing room and sat

18

down at the piano to play for Miranda to sing.

She had already taught Miranda hymns such as 'There is a green field far away' and 'The oxen with the lambs did lie', as well as songs made even more popular by wartime circumstances – such as Noel Coward's 'I'll See You Again'. After only a week or so in this vein Miranda was mastering 'If You Were the Only Girl in the World' as well as some of Vera Lynn's latest hits – 'The White Cliffs of Dover' and others for which they had the sheet music sent from Milsoms in Bath.

Miranda had proved extraordinarily quick at picking up not just the hymns but the songs, following Aunt Sophie faithfully and artlessly as if it was the easiest thing in the world not just to sing, but to hold a tune and never be behind or in front of her accompanist, and within only a few weeks to accompany herself on Aunt Sophie's piano too.

'She is a natural. She has only to hear a tune once on the wireless, and *voilà*, she can sit down and play it straight off. A complete natural, quite extraordinary, never known a child like it,' Aunt Sophie would murmur, filled with that particular kind of satisfaction that only the magic of discovering someone else's true talent can bring. 'She is such a natural that there is only one way she can go – right to the top. Mark my words, she will be at the Royal Opera House by the time she reaches her eighteenth birthday.'

'Now, now, Sophie dear, do not let us get carried away with such a notion. After all, there may not be a world at all by the time Miranda reaches her eighteenth birthday.'

This was usually said just before grace before meals, and could at will bring soulful tears to Miranda's eyes – for herself, of course, not for the world. The very idea that she would not reach her eighteenth birthday or the Royal Opera House was too terrible for her not to feel dreadfully sorry for herself, never mind the world.

Gradually, due to the singing, and the general feeling of refinement that necessarily pervaded the old rectory, the children started to change over the next months, so that by the time spring was about to creep through the hedges of the West Country and signal its arrival with hawthorn and with chestnut blossom, banishing the rust of the beech hedges to a conforming green, and Aunt Sophie and Aunt Prudence were talking about early potatoes and whether or not there would be any swallows coming back across war-torn France, Miranda was no longer to be heard coming out with artless expletives in the middle of matins, nor indeed could she be heard angrily comparing Mrs Eglantine to a farm animal with two horns and an udder.

Of course these were not the only changes in the children in Aunt Sophie and Aunt Prudence's care. During their first winter with the aunts each of the children had managed to fill out and start to bloom. Miranda's blond hair had been allowed to grow down and out of its hideous pudding-bowl cut and trimmed to a graceful shoulder-length mop, while even Bobbie's straight brown hair had responded to Aunt Prudence's constant rinsing with camomile tea. So much so that it now showed touches of red in the dull glow of the old yellowed wax candles that were the only form of lighting used on the upstairs floor of the rectory.

The first warm day of that spring Aunt Prudence insisted that photographs were taken of the three children on the lawn outside the drawing room windows. Miranda and Teddy were posed standing either side of the brown-haired Bobbie, their almost matching blond heads making Aunt Sophie murmur more times than any of them would *ever* care to remember, 'Not Anglos but angels,' leaving the children to wonder why she and Aunt Prudence thought this phrase so awfully appropriate whenever Miranda and Teddy were standing together.

Naturally Tom Kitten, the stout ex-milk pony who went between the shafts of the old Victorian trap, had become the focus of the children's attention, and once the worst of the weather had passed it was bliss for them all to climb into the back of the vehicle and sit up behind Aunt Sophie as they trotted off round the narrow Somerset lanes to collect for the Penny A Week fund that went to help the servicemen fighting all over the world. So marvellous were the rides in the pony trap that sometimes Bobbie would jump out of bed in the morning with only one thought in her mind: she might be going to be allowed to help with Tom Kitten's harness, or even, one day, take the reins.

'Your mother's coming to see you on the cheap ticket on Sunday.'

They were in the kitchen eating home-baked brown bread when Aunt Prudence announced this to Miranda and Teddy, and Teddy for some reason burst into tears as Miranda went quite pale.

'I don't think they, I don't think the Darlings, like their mother being talked about, dearest. It does always seem to make them very low, somehow. Brings back memories of their parting from her, one supposes,' Bobbie heard Aunt Sophie saying to Aunt Prudence while she went to find her coat and wellington boots by the back door. 'She is coming down to Somerset on the cheap Sunday ticket that is being so encouraged. The idea is to keep the parents from taking the children back to London with them, because what with the bombs and everything else – even shop windows being quite destroyed, I hear – going back to London is really not to be encouraged, I should not have thought. Although I believe that there is so much of that going on now, you know, children being taken back by their mothers, that one can only suppose they don't wish their children to be safe, dearest, that is what one can only suppose.'

Sunday proved to be a gentle day of sunshine and a light breeze which stirred all the trees and hedges a little, a day when all the West Country colours seemed to be at their Sabbath best. The pale greens and yellows, the daisy-strewn grass, the last of the primroses in the hedges, all seemed to be striving to look particularly welcoming for the visiting relatives of the evacuated children.

After church as usual, the children sat silent and thoughtful behind Aunt Sophie as she drove them smartly in the pony trap to the station. Miranda had hardly eaten since the announcement about her mother arriving, and Teddy had become tearful and sad by turns. Bobbie on the other hand felt only excited and envious, thinking that if the Darlings did not want their mother she might be able to have her instead, and that would stop her from being an orphan any more. She imagined the Darlings' mother would be pretty and blond like Miranda and Teddy, and kind, with blue eyes – just what she would like in a parent. Since she could not remember her own mother, it did not seem to her to be in the least bit wrong to want someone else's for her own.

There were other children at the station, and they all stood lined up outside the platform railings, waiting. All ages and all types of children, none of them holding hands or talking together, all of them standing quite alone, their eyes fixed on the track that led back to the train that they so hoped would bring their loved ones to them.

As if in respect of the hopes hanging on the arrival of the great black steam engine pulling the passenger carriages, the host families stood quite apart from the evacuees, chatting and gossiping among themselves as everyone waited for the train with the smoke puffing from it, to push its way at long, long last into Mellaston station. No-one expected it to be on time – not in wartime – and the station master and the porter could only nod and stare up the track, nodding and staring down the railway track a minute later, and then up the track again while still the line of children waited, their socks pulled up, their hair brushed, some of them longing so much to see their mothers that their knuckles were already white from clinging to the iron railings in front of them, as if just the very hope of the sight of a loved one was proving too much for them, or as if by holding on for all they were worth they could will the sight of those dear, familiar faces to appear soon at the windows of the longed-for train.

At last the news came, and it was not good. A bomb had fallen somewhere near the track in the early hours of that morning. There would be no train to Mellaston that day. Several of the older children burst into tears of sorrow at the news, and were led away by their host families to climb into the backs of dilapidated cars, or into dicky seats, or on to the seats of pony traps, and so be driven back to Mellaston and its environs to await another day when they might once more hope to catch a glimpse of their beloved relatives.

Aunt Sophie was not given to being sentimental, but on hearing that there would be no train, and no mother coming to see Miranda and Teddy, she hugged them both to her suddenly, and promised them 'double pudding'. Having dutifully allowed herself to be hugged, Miranda sang all the way home, and ate enough lunch for two, so hungry did she suddenly seem, while Teddy also found that he all at once had an appetite for the first time for many days. And after lunch they ran about outside in the rectory garden laughing and calling to each other as children will who have been let off some awful punishment.

'Why don't you mind your mother not coming to see you?' Bobbie demanded after Aunt Prudence had heard their prayers, checked the blackout curtain was in place, and blown out their bedroom candle.

There was a long silence, and then Miranda whispered, 'Promise not to tell?'

'Promise.'

As always Bobbie felt her heart sinking when she was about to hear a secret, because somehow a secret was so frightening, and you knew that it might come popping out when it shouldn't, or just when you thought that it might have stopped being one. But since she was six months older than Miranda, she knew she had to hear her secret, whatever happened. She could not be found to be a coward.

'I don't want to see my mother, because – well, she's my mother all right, but, see, she's not *Teddy*'s mother.'

There was a terrible wartime shortage of matches, but if there had not been Bobbie knew that she would have had to light their bedside candle and look at Miranda. Instead she sat up and stared down at where she thought she might be, in the next bed, but so dark was the dark in the country that she could not be sure.

'Why isn't she Teddy's mother?' Bobbie demanded in a voice that suddenly was far from being a whisper. 'Why hasn't Teddy got his own mother?'

Hearing himself talked about in such terms Teddy immediately burst into tears, which meant that Bobbie, whose turn it was, had to get out of bed before she could hear the rest of the secret and take him to the bathroom in case he had an accident.

Back in bed, although Miranda had lapsed into a strange contented sort of silence, Bobbie could not leave things be. She had to know more, but as Miranda answered her puzzled and disbelieving questions, she could not help marvelling at her friend's calm. She was as cool as Aunt Prudence's pastry-making hands when it came to explaining their circumstances.

'Well, when we was being evacuated, see, Ted, well he was in the orphans' bit, at the school where we were all being kept before being labelled and evacuated by these teachers and people, and he was crying his eyes out. And so when no-one was looking, because all the evacuees was in such a muddle, all of us just standing around at this

26

school, see, well I thought it was such a shame for him to be an orphan, and seeing as how I always wanted a brother. Well, that was it, see? I tore his label off of his coat, so when the lady came to take us down to the West Country she asked me who Ted was and I told her he was my brother, Ted Darling, because I always wanted one. And so – now he is, my brother, aren't you, Ted?'

'Ye-es.'

'And always will be, won't you, Ted?'

'Ye-es.'

There was a short silence after that, and then Miranda said, with some satisfaction, 'He knows I'll knock his block off if he says any different, don't you, Ted?'

'Ye-es.'

'But supposing someone finds out, Miranda? Suppose someone gets to know?'

'They won't.' Miranda slid down her bed and smiled in the darkness. 'Don't you know there's a war on?' she said, trying to mimic a well-known voice from the aunts' wireless and laughing suddenly and pulling a pillow over her face to drown the sound.

Bobbie stared ahead of her, but seeing only the dark, she quickly shut her eyes and thought of blue skies and the sun shining – things like that, things that were not dark, and made her feel warm and happy.

After the initial shock of being told such a big secret she realized that it was good, really – Teddy not being Miranda's brother – because it meant that she was now not the only orphan at the rectory. They were all 'pretend' brothers and sisters, so that now she too could share Teddy as a brother. He would be just as much her, Bobbie's, brother as he was Miranda's. This was such a cheery thought that Bobbie sighed with contentment, and before long was fast asleep, never even hearing the aeroplanes passing over the old rectory flying stealthily to 'somewhere in Europe'.

Chapter Two

It was time to go to the Clothes Exchange, also run by the Women's Voluntary Service. Bobbie found that she always dreaded these days, thinking that if only she was as pretty as Miranda it might be easier to find something to suit her, something that might not make Aunt Prudence sigh and shake her head before saying, 'I think we'd better go up to the attics at the house for something for you, Bobbie dearest. There's sure to be something there more suited to your looks, I feel.'

Aunt Prudence minded far more about how the three children looked than Aunt Sophie, who was more concerned about how they occupied themselves. Aunt Sophie liked them to be helpful, collecting hips and haws, and harnessing the pony, not to mention singing and playing the piano. They could all read all right, but Aunt Sophie said their writing was 'appalling' and she taught them all their loops and tails, as well as how to add up and subtract with the aid of onions and potatoes while they were helping in the kitchen. Thus, for Bobbie at any rate, mathematics were forever and always associated with the smell of flour, with the old tins and jars, with meat safes and cold larders, and with sets of old scales and heavy weights.

'Aunt Sophie likes to teach, I like to adorn,' was how Aunt Prudence put it before stalking ahead to the Exchange, one arm each round Bobbie and Teddy, while Miranda skipped determinedly ahead, thinking that if she arrived first she would find some marvellous frock or cardigan. The truth was that Miranda liked clothes as much as Bobbie loved Tom Kitten and helping in the stables, not to mention collecting the hens' and ducks' eggs for which the Mowbray sisters were justifiably famous in the neighbourhood, having always favoured the old-fashioned breeds of poultry.

Aunt Sophie had her own sort of walking prayer which ran: 'Never pick a bluebell for the house, it will wilt worse than a vicar's wife after the village fête. Pick rose hips for syrup, but leave the haws for walking the streets – well never mind anyway. On we go, more hips needed, ever more, and more again. There's a war on you know!'

Teddy was always being sick from eating too much of something, and just then, although he had not scoffed anything he should not, Bobbie could see that he might still be about to be sick, this time from the anticipation of swapping in his home-knitted jersey for another of a different colour. The excitement was almost more than he could take, coupled as it was with the humiliation of having his jersey taken off, publicly, and replaced with another, larger, one.

Meanwhile, Miranda, having arrived minutes earlier, was holding up a pre-war silk skirt against herself and twirling happily. Because of its being in the middle of the West Country, and remote from other places, the Mellaston WVS Clothes Exchange was always full of the strangest garments, so many being donations sent from the larger houses which were scattered about the countryside outside the town. On a good day there was everything to be found at the WVS Exchange, from black crêpe evening dresses with diamanté embroidery to seamen's sweaters made of oil-impregnated wool – and even, today, an old midshipman's coat which Miranda took down and stared at. It was made of doeskin and almost stood up on its own, as if it still had a person inside it.

'Won't cut down for Teddy, will it?' she asked Aunt Prudence with a grin.

'No, dear. But we will take it just the same, swap it in for my old fur wrap, and some of my pre-war shoes, because it will do very well for when Teddy's older, wouldn't you say?'

Bobbie stared at the coat and then at Teddy. She could not begin to imagine Teddy growing old enough, or tall enough, to fit the dark, doeskin coat, and it gave her an odd feeling when she tried. It did not seem possible for Teddy to grow so tall that he could wear such a coat as Aunt Prudence was holding. She smiled at him, suddenly protective.

31

After all he was her brother too, and so she had to look after him, make sure that he was not bullied too much by Miranda, because they shared Teddy now. He belonged to both of them, not just to Miranda.

Aunt Prudence smiled down at Teddy.

'That new jersey looks good on you, Teddy dearest. Very nice. Now let's see if we can't find you some sandals?'

It was almost too good to be true. Aunt Prudence pushed three old but seemingly unworn pairs of sandals, once belonging to goodness knows whom and only recently unearthed in the attic, towards the lady behind the Exchange counter, and after taking down and replacing pair after pair she found two new pairs for Bobbie and Teddy, as well as a pair of party pumps for Miranda, which were made of the most beautiful bronze leather, and had straps which went across the instep.

'They're not for every day, Miranda dearest, just for special days and Sunday, but seeing that they fit, and with some room to spare, we might as well – yes, I think we might as well indeed.'

Aunt Prudence smiled and watched as Miranda span round and round, her strange mixture of clothes looking odd and at the same time satisfyingly suited to Miranda herself. An old floral skirt, bronzed party shoes, a pink cardigan whose buttons were made in the shapes of daisies and 'hand-painted' the lady said – they all went into a parcel for Miranda, while Bobbie and Teddy walked ahead of her and Aunt Prudence, mesmerized by the sight of their new, secondhand sandals, and later by the patterns the sandals made on their bare feet when they ran about the fields and gardens over the following months, enjoying the gentle English summer. For them the war seemed hardly to be on, and had the aunts not switched on their wireless for the news the children might have indeed come to believe that the whole war was really somehow just some sort of grown-ups' fantasy.

In the event the longed-for train bearing Miranda's mother down to see her daughter in Somerset never did arrive. Instead, at the end of that summer, came that most dreaded of arrivals, a telegram from the War Office regretting that Mrs Irene Darling was 'missing believed killed while on active service'.

Miranda burst into tears as soon as Aunt Sophie told her, and Teddy did too, because the shock of seeing Miranda, who never cried, sobbing her eyes out was too much for a small boy. But given that Miranda's mother was meant to be Teddy's mother as well, the two girls were only too relieved that Teddy did cry, because, as Bobbie observed later, it would have looked rather strange if he hadn't.

It would be years before Miranda would eventually find out that her mother, by dint of having, it seemed, spent part of her childhood in France with a Breton great-aunt, at the outbreak of war had been recruited to work in something called Special

Operations Europe, the main headquarters of which was in Baker Street. French being her second language she had been dropped many times into France, and eventually killed on what was to be her last mission, taking vital information to the Free French. It would also be years before Miranda knew that she herself looked just like the dead young woman, tall, and slender, with blond hair and blue eyes and a way of suddenly laughing helplessly as if she could never, ever, stop.

Now, with Aunt Prudence standing looking sorrowful and Aunt Sophie the same, Miranda did not find it difficult to cry for a strange woman whom she could hardly remember. She really could not help crying because the aunts looked so very sad, and they were so sweet and kind and went and fetched sugar which they put in a twist of paper, and a teaspoon of honey which was put into a cup of mild herbal tea to soothe her.

'They are all orphans, now, and that being so we shall have to adopt them, dearest. It is the only way. And it being wartime, I am sure we shall have a good chance, because not many people want to adopt children of their sort of age, stuck as they are between babyhood and maturity. They are useful for nothing to anyone but ourselves – useless for anything, really.'

'Except to be loved.'

'Quite right, dearest, except to be loved.'

Aunt Sophie volunteered to go to London to see Miranda's grandmother, and find out exactly what should be done with Miranda and Teddy. She did not tell the children, because, as the sisters both agreed, if the Darlings' grandmother refused to let them be adopted by the Mowbrays it might prove to be a bitter disappointment to them. Bobbie still had Lady Reading taking an interest in her, so they judged her particular situation to be a little less urgent.

As always in wartime the journey was torture, and Aunt Sophie ended up travelling in the goods van, squashed between two Canadian soldiers and a fellow member of the WVS who was taking yet another small child back to London, but to who knew what fate, as her escort whispered to Sophie Mowbray.

'But the Canadians were ever so jolly, dearest,' she confided to Prudence on the telephone next day. 'Gave me some chewing gum. Imagine!'

'You didn't try it, Sophie?'

'No, dearest, of course not. Kept it for the littles when I get home. But London, dearest! It is just a sea of sandbags, but I have to say everyone does seem somehow better-looking, but perhaps that's uniforms – so well cut. Quite noticeable.'

At the rectory Prudence put down the telephone and frowned. She did so hope that she could rely on Sophie to conduct their business in London in an appropriate way. Really it should have been she who had gone to London to make their case for adopting Miranda and Teddy. Prudence realized that in many ways she was less shockable than the over-sensitive Sophie. On the other hand, the thought of leaving the rectory and the children in Sophie's sole charge was enough to make even Prudence feel quite, quite faint.

Sophie peered yet again at the piece of paper. The address in her hand declared itself to be in one of the poorer parts of London, and this was eventually confirmed when, having walked briskly through the narrow streets to reach it, she had to edge her way past miles of rubble, all quite carefully stacked, doubtless by the various authorities after the now all too frequent air raids on London. She walked on, bravely pretending that it was all in a day's work to find herself, a tweed-clad country spinster, in such an environment, until at last the number on the nearest house, still luckily standing, matched the number indicated on the piece of paper.

'Mrs Darling?'

The woman, older than Sophie, smiled brightly but did not reply. Sophie repeated her name, but when the smile stayed as bright as ever and no reply was forthcoming, Mrs Darling's visitor realized almost immediately that Miranda and Teddy's grandmother must be stone deaf, and had hurried to meet Sophie at her open front door without remembering to put in her hearing aid.

Sophie handed her a card which, since the Mowbrays had already written to the poor woman warning her that they might visit, must, Sophie felt, make some sense to the bird-like woman in the

36

flowered apron with the much-mended thick lisle stockings and strangely shaped lace-up shoes.

The woman looked up at her tall visitor but handed back the card with the same vague but agreeable smile, and promptly shut the front door. Sophie rang again and this time, with a polite smile, edged her way into the narrow, semi-detached house. The hall floor was covered in newspaper, the walls bulged with damp, and behind them, up the stairs, Sophie sensed there was someone very ill lying, quite alone. The old woman's milky grey eyes were turned up to Sophie's without the slightest comprehension in them.

'You don't know me, Mrs Darling, but I am here to offer to adopt your two grandchildren. Miranda and Teddy Darling.'

The old woman smiled again and nodded and Sophie realized with relief that it was all a bit of a wild goose chase. The two children had no mother and no father, only this grandmother whose reason had been overwhelmed by loss who was already wandering perhaps in those areas of the mind that are only open to the dead or dying, where the soul is drawn towards the light, and away from the darkness of human existence.

'I tell you what, I'll write out the necessary instructions regarding Teddy and Miranda, and you sign your name if you agree.'

In the end the old lady put a cross, and Sophie realized that the whole exercise had been a waste of time. As far as the authorities were concerned there was a war on, and they really could not have cared less what happened to Miranda and Teddy.

Bobbie did not want Miranda and Teddy to be taken away from the rectory, but young though she was she suspected that once Aunt Sophie had found the Darlings' grandmother – or rather Miranda's grandmother – the authorities would insist on taking them both from the Mowbrays and putting them in different homes. In the middle of the night she even began to imagine that Miranda would be put in prison for pretending that Teddy was her brother.

The following morning, while they were picking yet more sheep's wool from the hedgerows for Aunt Prudence, and building up their appetites for a well deserved piece of home-made brown bread and thick cheddar cheese, followed by a crisp apple, which was their standard picnic fare, Bobbie could stand the tension no more.

'What will happen?'

Miranda looked at her nonchalantly and her cornflower blue eyes, large and falsely innocent, stared into Bobbie's hazel-flecked orbs as she smiled mischievously.

'What?'

'You know – what will happen *when* . . . ?'

'What will happen when *what*?'

'When, you know—' Bobbie lowered her voice to a whisper. 'You know, when Aunt Sophie finds your grandmother and – and she finds that, you know – that she is not Teddy's granny, what will happen?'

Miranda shrugged her shoulders, and then started to laugh. 'Don't matter if she finds my granny. Don't matter two hoots.'

'Why not?'

''Cos my granny, she's not all there, see? She lost everything – twice, first because of Grandpa's losing all his money on the horses, and then when she lost both her cats and all her furniture 'cos of him – and now she doesn't know *who* she is. That's why I came here. And that's why no-one's come for us, 'cos Ted's an orphan, and my mum and dad's dead, and Gran's going to be taken to an asylum, one of these days, so, don't you see, no-one will ever know that Ted and I aren't brother and sister? Not ever, eh, Ted? Because Ted knows if he tells, a policeman's gonna come and take him away, don't you, Ted?'

She pulled him towards her and Teddy looked up at them and shook his head.

'Don't want to be your brother. I want to be Bobbie's brother.'

He pulled away from Miranda, trying to get back to the bush in front of which he had been standing picking everything but sheep's wool.

'Oh, blinking Ada, just look at his mouth. What you got in your mouth, you silly little squirt?'

Miranda unceremoniously stuck a handful of fingers into her self-adopted brother's mouth and pulled out some berries. They both stared at them.

'They might be poison!'

Bobbie shook Teddy. 'How many of them have you eaten? How many berries have you eaten, Ted?'

Miranda, who was taller, picked him up and started to carry him piggy-back across the grass.

'Supposing he's eaten poison? He might die!'

Bobbie ran ahead of Miranda, but although she was running all the time she felt as though her legs were not really working, as though she was really just running on the spot.

'Ted's eaten poison berries and we think he's going to die!'

Aunt Prudence turned from the stove and stared at Bobbie.

'Put him down on the chair, dearest,' she told the panting Miranda, who gratefully discharged the small boy onto the oak chair at the top of the kitchen table where he threatened to slip straight to the floor. 'No, hold him down, both of you. While I mix up an antidote to make him sick.'

Triumphantly Aunt Prudence watched the results of her quick thinking flush away down the old lavatory, still proudly dedicated to its maker Thomas Crapper.

'Well, that was good!' Aunt Prudence smiled round at the two girls who were both making *Phew!* noises. 'Do you know, Bobbie dearest, I have never known my home-made antidote to work so quickly? I really must make a note of it. Perhaps after the war I could even market it through Boots the Chemist, or some such? Now, Teddy, no more picking berries when you shouldn't, dearest. We really don't want to have to do that again in a hurry, do we?'

Thoroughly confused by the uncomfortable sequence of events, Teddy nodded instead of shaking his head, but finally said in a clear ringing tone, 'I promise always to be Miranda's brother now. Promise!'

For his pains he received a sharp, twisting little pinch from his 'sister', after which he started to cry again and had to be given some sponge cake freshly baked in the Aga and spread about with cherished butter and home-made plum jam. Miranda and Bobbie had the same, and as they sat on the old oak chairs a strange and marvellous peace settled around them. Miranda was thinking that whatever happened now nothing was going to take them away from the aunts, and Bobbie was trying hard to listen to the blackbird that was singing on the fence across the grass outside the windows, imagining as she listened that there was no more beautiful sound than that of a bird, not even Miranda singing 'The day thou gavest, Lord, has ended'.

That evening they all climbed up behind Tom Kitten and the sturdy little pony pulled them surely and fast, trotting into Mellaston, and so to the station, where they waited in some excitement for Aunt Sophie to arrive off the London train.

It was only an hour and a bit late, which Aunt

Prudence murmured with her usual stoicism was *surely a first for wartime*, but when Aunt Sophie was at last to be seen alighting from it, her small feathered hat slightly askew, the uneven hem of her dress trailing over her strap shoes with their black-eyed buttons set to the side, and her grey-pink stockings as always a little wrinkled, Aunt Prudence's hold on Miranda's hand tightened to a grip.

'Hal-lo, dearest! Had-doh! Cooee! Had-doh, evellybody!'

Aunt Prudence gave a quick look down at the two girls, and then, straightening her back, she walked up to her sister.

'Too much cough mixture again, Sophie dearest?' she murmured, taking her sister's small overnight bag, and swapping her grip on Miranda to her sister's arm. 'Too much cough mixture does seem to make you drippy, doesn't it?'

Aunt Prudence nodded sharply at Bobbie who darted to the other side of Aunt Sophie and took her other arm.

'What a business!'

Somehow they managed to stuff Aunt Sophie, there was no other word for it, into the pony cart, and the children, sensing public embarrassment, scrambled in after her. With a flick of the reins and a '*Yes, yes, yes,* Tom!' the pony trotted smartly out of the station yard, but not before the sharp-eyed Mrs Eglantine, seemingly ever present to meet her husband off the train, had seen Aunt Sophie's head lolling helplessly back against the black leather of the old-fashioned trap, and her hat, with an almost audible sigh of relief, parting company with her head and rolling into the road where it was left, Bobbie thought gazing back at it without regret, looking as if it somehow still had her head under it.

The next morning, to no-one's surprise, Mrs Eglantine called at the old rectory on official committee business.

'No sheets on the line, I see, so *someone*'s learning to control himself at nights, which is just as well considering his great age, I should say!'

There was a long and ghastly silence as the two girls, and their two adopted aunts, stared at Mrs Eglantine from the other side of the rectory drawing room, hardly able to believe that anyone could be so catty and unkind to poor little Teddy.

Of course Teddy, knowing at once that she was referring to his erstwhile bed-wetting, immediately turned scarlet and his eyes filled with reluctant tears. Miranda put her arm round his shoulders, while Bobbie stared in horrified hatred at Mrs Eglantine. Then, suddenly remembering something that she had heard someone's mother say at the boarding school, Bobbie spoke.

'What a vulgar thing to say,' she commented, unconsciously mimicking the patrician tones of the lady she had overheard. 'So vulgar. So terribly vulgar.'

Miranda at once twisted her mouth into a bunny

rabbit's mouth and wiggled her lips up and down, trying not to burst into her usual fits of giggles. The aunts on the other hand seemed at first to approve, because they merely continued to stare at Mrs Eglantine, a bit like two owls, unblinking, but determinedly silent.

The trouble was that Mrs Eglantine was so smartly dressed that she actually managed to look vulgar compared to the aunts in their faded pre-war clothes with their hair plaited and set over their ears in careful Anglo-Saxon knots.

'What is your name, please? Oh yes, of course.' Mrs Eglantine's eyes hardened and she took up her pen and wrote ROBERTA very large, as if she was determined never, ever to forget it. 'Well, Roberta, vulgar things do happen in wars, I am here to tell you. I am also here to tell your hosts – to tell you, Miss Mowbray and Miss Prudence – that alas the committee have come to the decision that they must, they really *must* insist that you keep only two rather than three evacuees. To be asked to look after three children is just not fair on either of you. The strain, I know, is telling on at least one of you.' At this she gave Aunt Sophie a *we all know what state you were in when you climbed off the London train* look, before continuing in her usual officious way. 'And as the children grow older, doubtless it will tell even more, perhaps even on both of you, and then where would you be? I would therefore suggest that you keep the Darling children, and let me find a new placement for Roberta Murray. There are plenty of kind families quite willing to take on someone like Roberta, I know.'

Mrs Eglantine looked pointedly over at Aunt Sophie, who was looking far from well since she was obviously nursing a quite terrible headache from *too much cough mixture on the train*.

Bobbie, whose feelings of indignation and fury at this horrible woman's having the beastliness to refer to poor Teddy's bed-wetting were still boiling over, now found that they had turned to a cold and awful dread as she realized with dawning certainty that her prayers for Miranda and Teddy to stay at the rectory with the aunts were indeed going to be answered. They were going to stay at the rectory; it was Bobbie who was leaving.

She saw the aunts' eyes swivelling from Mrs Eglantine's face to her own, and back again. She saw their doubts about the matter that was being put before them turning to compromise, and finally she heard Aunt Prudence say, reluctantly, 'Well, I suppose, since Miranda and Teddy are brother and sister, it *would* be better if they stayed together here, and Bobbie went to someone else in the town. After all, once there is a school again to go to, they'll see each other anyway, won't they? Such a pity, its being bombed like that, but still, better the school than the cathedral, I dare say.'

Before Bobbie was moved on to another home – whose location was yet to be announced, *although it will still be in Mellaston* – it seemed that they were all

45

going to make sure that Teddy had a birthday.

Miranda had announced this only seconds after Mrs Eglantine had been seen to the door by the Mowbrays, and during the time that the two sisters were heard to be talking in quick, low, urgent tones. To distract from the fear on Bobbie's face and in her eyes, Miranda had said quickly and loudly, 'It's Ted's birthday tomorrow. Let's make him something.'

Of course they all knew that it was not Teddy's birthday tomorrow. Teddy actually had no idea when his birthday was meant to be, and sometimes felt that he might never know now. Nevertheless, once Miranda had announced that it would be his special day on the morrow, he smiled at once. Teddy had a strangely affecting smile, so gentle and kind that it always made Aunt Prudence go back and give him another hug after lights were out, which in turn made Teddy rub his cheek with the side of his pillow as soon as her back was turned.

Next day there was a cake and candles, of varying sizes and quality, and they all sang, 'Happy birthday dear Teddy', and Bobbie gave him a drawing that she had done. It was Teddy standing by the old beech tree in the rectory garden with Aunt Prudence's tame magpie, and everything was just as it should be, perhaps even more so because they all knew that very soon it would not be like that any more.

Bobbie knew that it was useless to plead with the aunts that she did not want to go and live anywhere else in Mellaston. She knew this with all her heart and all her soul because she was an orphan. Orphans had no rights. They just got put where they were meant to be put, and they stayed where they were put until someone else came to get them, and then sometimes they were moved on and put somewhere else. There was nothing you could do about it, not if your parents were dead and you had few relations and no friends.

'Where do you think you're going to go, Bobbie?'

That evening Miranda had waited until the aunts were downstairs again and then had sat up and re-lit the old, thick, yellow wax candle before lying back and fidgeting in her bed under the window, her legs moving restlessly under the covers.

'I don't know. Don't care, really.'

'I expect we'll still see each other, Bobbie!'

Miranda got up and came and knelt beside her friend's bed, her pink bedsocks glowing against the old, dark, wooden floor, her eyes anxious.

Bobbie stared up at the ceiling for a minute, and then turned, wordlessly, on her side so that Miranda was faced with her back, seeing only her dark head against the pillow, the outline of her shoulder under the yellow knitted blanket.

'Once you get moved on, you don't see anyone from where you've been before. 'Member I was at that place where they beat you, and there were lots of other children there, and they never heard from people, not once they'd been moved on. That's what being evacuated is about, it's about being *moved on*, and no-one really caring where you are, not really, because there's a war on.' Bobbie closed her eyes, shutting them tightly, blocking out the light, the room with its flowered wallpaper, the moth that was flying nearer and nearer to the candlelight. 'I'm going to sleep now,' she announced.

Second later it seemed that she was, so Miranda blew out the candle and climbed back into bed. For once it seemed that even she had nothing to say. There was nothing *to* say. Bobbie was going.

Aunt Prudence was speaking slowly and precisely, as if she was thinking out the whole matter as she went along, a bit like the way she invented knitting patterns as the garment started to grow.

'How it is, Bobbie dearest, is that you'll be able to cope better than the other two. You see, if we adopt the Darlings first, then we will probably be able to have you back. Because once the Darlings are officially ours, Mrs Eglantine can't come round and tell us what to do. Then we can make a good case for taking in an evacuee, which can be you. But until then . . . well, as I say, dearest, you will be able to *cope* better than the other two. I mean you have already been to a beastly school, so you know that you *can* cope. And anyway I sense that you're more resilient than Miranda and Teddy.'

Bobbie did not know what 'resilient' meant, but she found herself wishing most heartily that whatever it was that she was meant to be more than the other two, she would really rather she had not been, given that this meant that she was the one whose number was well and truly up.

'Besides, I am quite sure that they will send you to a very nice family in Mellaston. There are so many, many nice families in Mellaston. There will be – I mean to say, I am sure that – that – well, that they will have a good choice of places still, Bobbie. And let's face it, you're never going to have to go to a farming family. You're too small and gently bred for a farming family to turn you into some sort of slave, there is no fear of that, Bobbie.'

Useless to say something like that to Bobbie, because fear was precisely what was eating her up now, daily, hourly. Fear of missing Miranda and Teddy. Fear of not being able to go out looking for wool in the hedgerows that surrounded the old house, of not being able to watch Aunt Prudence at her Aga with the pans bubbling and the toast being made in the special wire thing that went under the lids and had to be turned double quick to stop the bread from burning. Fear was what caused her to have cramps in her tummy at night when she thought of the school where her relatives had left her which had seemed to be filled with grown-ups who would beat little children and then laugh at them when they screamed and cried from fear and pain. And now, of course, because of how she felt, the days flew by and there just was not enough time to do everything that had to be done that one last time.

I will never ever run up to Aunt Prudence and give

49

her flowers again, because I won't be here. I will never ever see that sun setting just there ever again from this window, because I will never be here again at this age. I will never sit at supper and taste bread and butter puddings with cream and honey. I will never ever have a bath full of rusty water and steam that makes your hair curl, and a towel that is so big that it's like a blanket. I will never ever again have Aunt Sophie play to me on the piano. Or Miranda sing to me. Or Teddy put his arms round me and hug me goodnight. It is all going to go away for ever and ever and never come back.

And of a sudden the never ever time was over, and Mrs Eglantine was at the door, and smiling a sly kind of *just you wait* smile, because she knew just from looking into Bobbie's eyes that Bobbie was trying ever so hard not to look frightened and worried. So Bobbie put up her arms to hug Aunt Prudence, and they both smiled because it was better than crying. And then she put up her arms to hug Aunt Sophie, and again they both smiled, for the same reason. But when she turned to Miranda, she was gone. And only Teddy hugged her and whispered, 'Come back soon, Bobbie.'

After that she picked up her suitcase and marched bravely after the hated Mrs Eglantine, down the garden to the road that led back to Mellaston.

They walked along in silence, Bobbie pausing every now and then to change hands with her suitcase, until eventually they reached the old market place where now Mrs Eglantine stopped every other minute to greet the people they passed, and make remarks about Bobbie.

'Yes, of course, it was far too much for the Mowbray sisters. We, on the committee, could see what they could not, you know, so – yes, this is Roberta Murray and she is on her way to be placed. No, not with me, no, with the Dingwalls. It was the best that we on the committee could do for the poor girl. No, not entirely suitable, but there is a war on after all, and it is at least in Mellaston, we did promise them that. It was the best we could do, d'you see? The Brinkleys had offered to take her, so much more suitable, but the Mowbray ladies insisted she must stay in Mellaston, so the Dingwalls it has to be. One can, after all, only do one's best, as we have all agreed.'

Each time she stopped the conversation took the same course, although the words changed according to whom she was addressing. Sometimes the 'Mowbray ladies' were described as 'cracking under the strain of taking in too many evacuees', sometimes 'Roberta Murray' was a 'poor orphan', at others she was 'a little evacuee child, lucky enough to be going to be placed in a Mellaston family'. Whoever was the recipient of Mrs Eglantine's news, the words fell about Bobbie's young ears in a sad clutter of tawdry excuses, and after each stop, having changed hands, Bobbie would pick up her suitcase yet again and trudge after Mrs Eglantine with a leaden heart, all the time wondering where it was that they were going, where exactly she was to be left.

'So, Roberta, here we are.'

Still not knowing where she was to be left, or with whom, except that their name was Dingwall, Bobbie looked from Mrs Eglantine's face to the small gate that declared itself to be 'Rosebank', and from the gate up the garden path to the narrow, low door, which swung handleless and open.

'Mrs Dingwall, my charlady, has agreed to take you in, you lucky girl. They were the only family left in Mellaston with a suitable vacancy, and since Miss Prudence and Miss Sophie have insisted that you stay in Mellaston, this is all that is left to us. She will bring you to work with her every day, so we shall be seeing a great deal of each other. Now, off you go. Behave yourself, and don't cause trouble, will you?'

Panic such as she would never know again welled up inside Bobbie. Her eyes must have reflected her fear, not just of the unknown, but of narrow semi-detached houses that had no need of handles, or locks or bolts. She sensed that inside that cramped little house ahead of her, behind that dingy little façade with its careless exterior of weeds and half-hinged gates, lay a sort of hell.

Chapter Three

Mrs Eglantine liked to have breakfast in bed every morning, rain or shine. She sometimes murmured, 'You can always tell a lady because she breakfasts in bed,' as she stared at the tray that Bobbie had now been trained to place, soundlessly, on the luggage rack beside her bed.

Mrs Eglantine had a separate bedroom from Mr Eglantine, who did not breakfast in bed. He breakfasted, thankfully, downstairs in the dining room, a dining room filled with pre-war silver which Bobbie and Mrs Dingwall would clean every Thursday afternoon. Bobbie knew that silver now, after only nine weeks at Rosebank, as well as she knew her own face. She knew the newness of it. The blackness of the handles on the coffee pot and hot water jug, the shiny chromy look to the metal, so different from the dull, almost blue look of the silver at the old rectory.

The Eglantines' house was called Grass Mead, and it was set back from the road in one of the quieter districts of Mellaston. It was a large house designed and put up by a wealthy builder in the earlier part of the century for his son and daughter-in-law. The house was surrounded by a large garden, and a gate led through to what had once been the builder's own property, also a large square house, but of earlier origin. Bobbie hated Grass Mead as much as she had loved the old rectory. But she was thankful for it, for if it had not been for Grass Mead and the Eglantines' sometimes unceasing demands on Mrs Dingwall, there was no doubt that all of every one of Bobbie's days would have been spent at that hell of all hells – Rosebank. That place of smells and latrines down the garden that announced themselves long before you were upon them because of the swarms of flies in summer, and the burst and leaking pipes in winter. Grass Mead was a heavenly refuge after Rosebank and its realities.

As it was, Bobbie, having become a sort of servant to Mr and Mrs Eglantine, having joined the 'servant class' as Mr Dingwall would keep reminding her – 'You're one of us now, dear' – was only too grateful for Grass Mead and its claustrophobic practices.

She was even grateful to Mrs Eglantine for keeping up the old pre-war ways of going on, despite the shortages, for without them Bobbie knew that she would be condemned to weeding the Dingwalls' front garden, to digging their vegetable patches, or cleaning out their outside lavatory. Grass Mead had become a haven of decorous living compared to the terrors of life at Rosebank.

Of course she still hated Mrs Eglantine as much as ever, while at the same time feeling grateful for her, so that Bobbie's emotions whenever she saw her, which was far too much on some days, were always a complicated mixture, part of her wanting to kick Mrs Eglantine in the shin, and the other part of her only too willing to be sent to queue for something in the town, or set to clean her lizard-skin shoes and handbag. There were no such complications with Mr Eglantine, however, for after only a short time Bobbie discovered that Mr Eglantine had no redeeming features whatsoever to counterbalance a loud laugh and a way of looking at Bobbie which was not at all nice. It was as if, should they be left alone together, he was dying to share a secret with her.

Sometimes, if Bobbie found herself in the same room as him and, by some terrible misfortune, for a few seconds alone, he would immediately lean forward and whisper, 'Come and sit on my knee and we'll go riding together, Roberta. You know "This is the way the farmer rides", surely?' At this Bobbie would find herself dodging behind furniture and darting out of the door, while his raised voice could be heard following her, laughing and saying, 'You'll never make a farmer's wife, my dear, not unless you learn to sit to the canter the way the farmer does!'

Thank heavens he never issued his invitation to Bobbie to go riding with him when Mrs Eglantine was at home. Then he would stay in the drawing room, or in his study, usually standing in front of the fireplace whether a fire was lit there or not, and talking loudly at his wife while she sewed 'something for the war effort'.

And so when Mrs Eglantine took Bobbie out on what she called her 'rounds', visiting other children who had been placed by the Mellaston Committee in other households, Bobbie was yet again overwhelmingly grateful to Mrs Eglantine, so grateful that she quite forgot to hate her for a few hours. Indeed it was on these rounds that she learned what it was to be humble, and well behaved beyond any possible imagining.

Mrs Eglantine had devised the habit of introducing her to the different families that made up the more refined circles they visited together as 'poor little Roberta', whom 'we had to place with the Dingwalls' – 'Nothing else to be done. The Misses Mowbray insisted, and you know how it is with spinsters, they are quite determined when it comes down to it.' And while Bobbie sat as still as she could, trying not to stare at ladies in pre-war fashions who still sported hairstyles like the bob, or the shingle, Mrs Eglantine would set about loudly explaining her kindness to Bobbie to their various hostesses.

'She was an unhappy little thing, really. She was placed first of all permanently boarding, parents killed, long before the war, nothing else to be done. And then by the London WVS with the Mowbray sisters, and of course *they* couldn't cope. They've been single just too long. And so I volunteered to take her on, and now she's with my Mrs Dingwall, who *bless her*, has taken in the poor little mite. Of course we have to make sure she is given a good bath every time she comes to us, despite the soap shortages – otherwise the smell, you know, could be quite frightful or lice might happen – but really it's a small price to pay, really it is, in order to make a little child happy. Soon I hear the school will be found a new building, somewhere reachable so that Mrs Dingwall can walk her there, and she will no longer have to rely on myself to lend her such books as are suitable. But again, as I say, that is surely a small price to pay to make a little child's life better, really it is. And I know that.'

After one or another variation of this speech, Mrs Eglantine would pat Bobbie on the head and allow one of their many hostesses to give the 'poor child' a 'little treat' in the shape of a piece of Melba toast with a smear of much-revered W.I. jam on it.

It did not take long for Bobbie to appreciate life as seen through the eyes of a charlady's child. And after only a very few weeks she found she no longer resented Mrs Eglantine's insistence on taking her to those affluent houses in Mellaston, houses which, it seemed to Bobbie, appealed as strangely decorous after the eccentricities of the old rectory. It was as if everyone they visited was determined that nothing of the old world would change, as if the hands of their grandfather clocks had, by common consent, been set to stay at the same time of 1920. A time of flappers and cloche hats, of new slang, and left-over gaiety, of mad jazz patterns, and Parisian clowns, of love left too late, or arrived at too soon.

And so it was that in the many corners of the many drawing rooms they visited gramophones stood with handles unturned, the records in their paper sleeves in serried ranks beside them, and, like party dresses suspended from hangers in otherwise empty cupboards, Bobbie saw that they were now, without any doubt, sad tokens of a life that they were all pretending might come back, just as they were pretending that the dresses would be worn again, the rugs rolled back and the records played again, that perhaps if the ladies of Mellaston hung on to their hairstyles of former years, to the same vibrant colour of lipstick and the same slang, they might be able to will those days to return, and everything would be all right again.

Such was not the case with the Dingwalls at Rosebank. Mr Dingwall could not wait for the war to be over so that he could 'bring about a new order'. He wanted to lick Hitler, of course, and said so many times when he came back from the pub, but most of all he wanted to lick the people who kicked people like him about.

Whenever he declared his intention to do this Mrs Dingwall would wink down at Bobbie, then lick her index finger and point it in the air and say, 'I wonder which way the wind is coming from today?'

Mr Dingwall was a very small man, as small as Mrs Dingwall, which in a way was just as well since Rosebank had less space than half a cottage. Bobbie slept in the attic, what Mrs Eglantine – when she once visited Mrs Dingwall for a few minutes to make sure that she had delivered the jam to the WI – called a 'boxroom' and, having stared up the wobbly ladder for a moment, immediately declared to be 'very cosy'.

Mrs Eglantine was not entirely wrong. Bobbie's boxroom in the eaves of the semi-detached house was cosy to the point of roasting in summer, while in winter it was freezing and damp. The water tank opposite her bed leaked, and sometimes when Mr Dingwall climbed up the rickety ladder to find out why there was not enough water coming through to the kitchen he would fish out a dead rat from its murky depths, or on other occasions a drowned pigeon which had been causing the blockage.

Bobbie would never forget winter at Rosebank. How she would fix her mind on the cleanliness and warmth of Grass Mead. How she would look forward to that moment when she followed Mrs Dingwall through the tradesmen's side gate and round to the back door, how the Aga felt when she put her small, frozen hands on its smooth exterior, how her hands tingled and pained until at last warmth returned and she was once more able to pick up a bucket or hold a duster in the normal way.

Mrs Dingwall's hands were evidence of the harshness of her life. They felt, to Bobbie anyway, like sandpaper, as if they could usefully rub down the outsides of cupboards, taking off the old paint, preparing the wood for fresh. The state of Mrs Dingwall's hands started to obsess her guest. Why they were like that was evident: so much scrubbing with soap and ammonia, so much wringing of cloths and clothes, so much taking down and putting back again, water for rinsing, water for emptying, hot water, cold water, icy water, dirty water, water in cans, water in buckets, water poured into baths to make them hotter, water poured into old-fashioned jugs set about bedrooms in old-fashioned hand basins. Soft though water was it had made Mrs Dingwall's hands as harsh as Mrs Eglantine's voice.

After only a few weeks at Rosebank the state of Bobbie's own hands too started to become an obsession with her. She would wake in the night and place them against her face, not just to warm them, but to reassure herself that they were still as soft as when she had gone to bed. Sometimes when Mrs Eglantine was sitting at her dressing table putting on her moisturizing cream she would turn to Bobbie and rub some excess into the child's hands, an act of such unexpected kindness that Bobbie would feel like putting her arms round her neck and hugging her – not that she would dare to do such a thing.

'Bobbie has learnt to know her place in this life,' Mrs Eglantine would purr on their rounds. 'One day she will make someone a nice personal maid, or some such. Indeed, I shall miss her when she goes to school, when the school re-opens.'

Just that word *school* struck terror into Bobbie's heart. She had already been to *school* and she knew it to be a place of harsh beatings and children crying at night, sometimes all night. She hoped she might die before that day of returning to school arrived; and sometimes, during her first months under the eaves at Rosebank, when a rat ran across her face, or she could hear Mr Dingwall shouting at Mrs Dingwall and making her cry quite horribly, when her chilblained hands were cracked and bleeding from the cold and she could not even accompany Mrs Dingwall to Grass Mead because her shoes were at the mend, and she now had only one pair, she found herself lying in the upstairs loft of that cramped little half-house longing with all her might for death.

During that terrible winter with the Dingwalls, when there were so many shortages, and Mrs Eglantine was forever complaining about there being no stockings or lipstick, or Mr Eglantine came back from London having spent all night in an air raid shelter, Bobbie noticed that the Eglantines were quite able to ignore her. Even though she would sometimes take a long time to shuffle past one of them, a duster in her hand, a pair of mittens exposing her unfortunate fingers, the laces of her new secondhand shoes missing, they still did not appear to notice her. Even when they did, their concerns being quite other they only glanced at her briefly, and then would merely carry on, happy that Bobbie was busy with their dusting, and that despite the war they could be secure in the knowledge that at least Mrs Dingwall was attempting to keep up their pre-war standards of housekeeping.

And yet Mrs Eglantine must have noticed something, some loss of colour whenever she mentioned that 'Roberta will be going to school soon', because she said one day, stopping the small girl in the middle of polishing what seemed to be an endless array of fish forks and knives, 'I do think that it would be nice if you went to the rectory for Miranda's birthday tea party, don't you, Roberta? They asked if you might, when I visited them, only the other day. We might find out where they intend Miranda to go to school, and you might be able to go together, to the same place. I hear there is one for young girls opening up quite soon, in the cellars of the George and Dragon in the High Street. At least that is the rumour.'

Bobbie looked up at Mrs Eglantine, hope bursting through the expression on her small face, and it was obvious to them both that at the mere mention of Miranda and the rectory, it was as if Mrs Eglantine had held out a piece of hot buttery toast to a starving child.

'A tea party? You've been asked to a tea party at the rectory?'

Mrs Dingwall looked across at Bobbie. She could not look down at her, since she was hardly taller than a child herself. She put a small, brown hand to her throat and eased the collar around her neck as if the freezing cold of her little kitchen with its uneven floor had suddenly grown to tropical temperatures.

'Well, Roberta, we had better put your hair in papers tonight, 'adn't we, eh?'

Bobbie looked at her, startled. She did not know what was meant by putting her hair in 'papers', but a few minutes later she did, and after an uncomfortable night spent lying against the wretched twists she went downstairs to have them taken out.

As soon as Mr Dingwall saw her, coming in from the garden still doing up his trousers, he started to laugh. Since he had not yet put in his teeth to eat his breakfast, it was not a nice sight. Bobbie coloured scarlet when she saw the reason why he was laughing. The mirror in their small front room showed Bobbie just what she looked like. No wonder Mr Dingwall had laughed. Her hair stood out in a terrible bush of ringlets. Standing on a small leather stool Bobbie saw quite clearly that she didn't just look plain now – she looked worse. She looked stupid.

'What you done to her, Dolly?' Bobbie heard him demanding. 'She looks like an 'edgehog. She looks like Milly Molly Mandy. She don't look like herself. She looks like a comedian's joke, like something on the wireless.'

But Mrs Dingwall was proud of the way Bobbie's hair looked, so it stayed the way it was. Back in

London, where both the Dingwalls came from, a girl could never go to a party without her hair in ringlets, Mrs Dingwall told Bobbie as she dressed her in an old party frock that had once belonged to the Dingwalls' daughter – 'rest her'.

They walked through Mellaston that afternoon, but instead of stopping at Grass Mead and turning up the side to the tradesmen's entrance, they walked on to the outskirts of the town, and on up the narrow country road to the old rectory. This time Bobbie and Mrs Dingwall did not head up the side of the house to another entrance but walked up the old drive to the front door, and Bobbie found that she was in such a state of anxiety and excitement that she quite thought that she was going to be sick.

Using a strange sort of voice that Bobbie had never heard her attempt before, Mrs Dingwall announced, 'Roberta Murray come for the party,' in proud tones to a woman Bobbie did not recognize.

Bobbie obediently followed the primly dressed and hatted Mrs Dingwall through the familiar front door and into the hall, after which Mrs Dingwall made a strange little movement, a sort of feint, and whispered, 'See you later, dear. I'll come to the front door again, mind, so you'll be fetched same as how the rest of them are fetched, don't you worry.'

For a few seconds Bobbie looked up and around her. She could hardly believe it. She was home once more, back at the rectory at last. And for some few seconds she breathed in that special smell she associated with that dear house, the smell of wood smoke and lavender dried and placed in bowls, and she saw that the stairs ahead of her were still shallow and of polished wood, and there was the sound of a piano playing, and laughter.

And of a sudden there were Aunt Sophie and Aunt Prudence and they were both staring at Bobbie from the dining room door. There was a momentary pause, as she peered up at them through her ringlets, while they took in her second-hand dress of brightest pink and her angora wrap-over cardigan of brightest green and her ballet shoes, all of which had once belonged to Mrs Dingwall's late daughter. Bobbie smiled nervously and over-brightly up at them.

For a few seconds neither of the aunts said anything, but Bobbie thought that she would never ever forget the expression on the two women's faces as they stared down at her. Or the amazement in Miranda's and Teddy's eyes as they turned from the dining room table and stared across the room at her as she came in, pale-faced and dressed in her vivid hues. It was as if they simply did not know her. The terrible silence as she sat down in her strange ringlets and bright clothes patently and obviously declared to everyone, even to the children, that Bobbie was 'not one of them'.

As soon as she was seated all the grown-ups who stood behind the children's chairs, all the nannies and the mothers, started to talk at once, while the children looked at Miranda, the birthday girl, who sat at the top of the table staring at Bobbie, still at a loss for words. Only Teddy seemed not to notice and ran round the table and flung his arms around Bobbie's neck.

'I knew you'd come. Miranda said you couldn't because you were 'vacuated somewhere else, but I knew you'd come.'

It was not so for Miranda and Bobbie. Although it had only been a few months, there was now a yawning gap between the two girls. There had been enough deprivation, enough humiliation, enough change in Bobbie's life to have reduced her from being Miranda's pretend sister to being someone neither she nor Bobbie herself could recognize.

'This is our dear Bobbie, who used to live with us, and now is able to join the party.'

Aunt Sophie had murmured this, which was kind, because it meant that Bobbie could slip onto one of the spare chairs and pretend that she did not know that everyone was staring at her, as if she was a vision from hell. The old lace and old velvet of the other children's clothes, their beautiful clean, shining, brushed hair, their perfectly kept looks, declared them to be rectory children, or manor house children, while Bobbie was, as she saw too clearly, and as Mr Dingwall now kept reminding her, *one of us, now dear. Down at Rosebank you're one of us, and that means you must muck in and be like us.*

'Hallo, Bobbie.'

'Hallo. Happy birthday,' Bobbie replied with difficulty as she crammed some bread from the pretty floral and gold patterned plate in front of her into her mouth, because there was no-one to stand behind her chair and put tiny pieces of home-made brown bread with plum jam onto her plate.

Everyone else seemed to be waiting to play games, while Bobbie tasted Aunt Sophie's bread, and remembered the wonder of her cakes, and the delicacy of her fruit jellies. Despite the misery of her appearance, and the eternal pain that the memory of much happier days had precipitated the moment she walked into the old rectory, Bobbie could not stop eating. Here again she showed herself to be different, grabbing at the plates in front of her and stuffing bread into her mouth long after the others had finished, so much that the mothers and nannies could only stare and look away, and then, as if unable to help themselves, stare again.

'Do you like your new parents, Bobbie?'

Bobbie stared suddenly across at Teddy, who had asked her the question. A lull had fallen in the room, and of a sudden Bobbie's 'new parents' seemed to be of great interest to everyone, perhaps because of her strange, hungry manners.

Bobbie nodded slowly, her mouth still full.

'Do they give you jelly?'

Bobbie nodded again, finally finishing what was in her mouth, and adding shortly afterwards, 'And they have a toilet down the garden where there's a tame mouse and I take him crumbs.'

The other children's expressions were a mixture of envy at Bobbie's having a tame mouse and amazement that she had said 'toilet' at table, and in front of all the grown-ups.

'I wish I had a tame mouse,' said Teddy, and he quickly crammed the rest of his sandwich into his mouth.

'If you come and visit you could see him.'

That was all that Bobbie could find to say, because her whole concentration was on her plate, really. It was just so wonderful to taste Aunt Sophie's cooking after all those winter weeks of Mrs Dingwall's cabbage water and meat stew, often with caterpillars to be found in it, not to mention cardboard cake with hardly a twist of sugar and gone bright yellow from the dried egg wrongly mixed.

'I think we will wait for Bobbie to finish, before we cut the cake,' said Aunt Sophie, and she too stared in some amazement at what Bobbie had yet to consume. 'She had a long walk here which has quite obviously made her hungry.'

She did not mean to be funny at Bobbie's expense, at least Bobbie did not think so, but even so everyone laughed. It was half the laughter of relief and half the laughter of mockery, but Bobbie did not care. If only they knew just how that food tasted after Mrs Dingwall's cooking they would not laugh, not for anything. Besides, she knew she would feed off the memory of that tea for weeks to come. She knew just how she would lie in bed and dream about it, savour every little minute of it, so, laughter or no laughter, nothing was going to stop her eating.

Not that she did not care about other things. She cared terribly looking at Miranda who kept staring at her as if they had only just met. She cared that Miranda was looking so pretty, wearing her usual strange mix of clothes, part velvet skirt, part lace-embroidered blouse, her hair caught up in a decorous ribbon and looped prettily at the back. But she was looking at Bobbie as if she was a stranger, and the fact was that she could not be blamed. Bobbie was a stranger to her. She could see that. And not just a stranger to Miranda. She was a stranger to Teddy too.

She was not Bobbie their pretend sister any more, she was Mrs Dingwall's pretend daughter. She had arrived for the party from Rosebank and it was quite obvious that Miranda and Teddy both wished that she had stayed at the Dingwalls'. That somehow or other, since she was so very unrecognizable to them now, they really rather wished, for her sake and for theirs, that she had not come to the rectory, looking so different, not like their pretend sister as they must have remembered her at all, not like the Bobbie they had once known.

Happily, seconds later Miranda was called to help arrange the chairs for a party game and so Bobbie was able to go to the downstairs cloakroom and stay there for the next half-hour, her absence quite unnoticed. Eventually re-emerging she tried to join in the games, but everything overcame her, and what with her toes being chilblained, not to mention her acute embarrassment at her appearance, she ended up standing beside Aunt Prudence and helping to put on the gramophone records for Musical Chairs, while Aunt Sophie pretended to consult her about who she thought was the last to hit the floor during Musical Bumps.

Of course, anxious as she was not to let Bobbie down, Mrs Dingwall had to be the first to collect her charge, coming through the front door of the old rectory with her hat pinned on firmly, her eyes determined, and then hanging about beside the grandfather clock as if she was waiting to be paid. Bobbie really did not mind. She was actually only too grateful to see her. She did not care what Mrs Dingwall looked like to either the other mothers or the uniformed nannies, or to Aunt Prudence and Aunt Sophie, or to Miranda or to Teddy. She just wanted to go home with her and never, ever, see anyone at the rectory ever again.

She stopped by the front door as this thought came to her, and something inside her closed shut as she kissed the soft cheeks of Aunt Prudence and Aunt Sophie and then walked slowly and painfully after Mrs Dingwall on the long walk back to Rosebank, which was her home now.

Having thankfully removed what Mrs Dingwall kept calling 'yer party pumps' and stuck her head under the outside water pump and allowed the cold water to pour over the hateful ringlets, she climbed the rickety ladder to her little boxroom with its cold water tank and its mice and occasional rat and gratefully closed her eyes on the day. No matter that Aunt Sophie had taken her aside and tried to reassure her that she and Aunt Prudence would 'do' something for her 'soon' – just as soon as they were able. To Bobbie, now, that part of her young life was over for ever. She would never ever go to the rectory again. She would never see Miranda or Teddy again. She would rather die.

She was different now, and she knew it.

'She's got some sort of chest infection,' Dr Milton said, straightening up and looking round his immaculate surgery with its cream walls and its old sofa, part of his own house in Mellaston.

How Mrs Dingwall had saved up enough money to go to the Eglantines' doctor Bobbie would never know. But as spring beckoned, and the warmer weather was already on the way, out of tune with the season, Bobbie, having developed a cough, and lost not just weight but her appetite, had eventually been unable to go anywhere, and the panel doctor who would normally attend the Dingwalls would not come out to her, so Mrs Dingwall had decided to pay for the Eglantines' doctor to come to Rosebank and see her little charge.

It would have been a good plan only Dr Milton had no car, and no coupons, only his horse, as he had explained to Mrs Dingwall when she called on him, and showed him, by placing her money on his reception desk, that she actually had the money for a private call.

'He's just snotty,' Albert Dingwall said, shouting so loud that Bobbie could hear. 'He thinks we lives in a smelly slum so he don't want to come out, money or no money.'

And so, reluctantly, Dolly and Albert had taken Bobbie to Dr Milton, riding on Albert's bicycle saddle because Bobbie had been too tired from the coughing, and too feverish, to do anything else but cling on to them, one arm round each, as the two of them had walked along to Dr Milton's surgery, pushing Albert's bicycle, and stopping every now and then for Bobbie to catch her breath.

'How is her sputum, Mrs Dingwall?'

Mrs Dingwall reddened alarmingly, and Dr Milton could see at once that the mere mention of such a thing was devastating to a woman like Mrs Dingwall who prided herself on at least knowing about the niceties of life, if not always being allowed to practise them.

'She does cough a lot, I will say that, Dr Milton. It worries me terribly after losing our Marion to – after losing our Marion,' she murmured, straightening her hat and staring at the floor. 'And, same as her, she gets ever so hot. As I say, I brought her in to you straight away, soon as I realized that she weren't the thing, because we lost our Marion this way, see? She was only ten, you know, when she was taken from us, but that was in London. Before we come down here.'

Dr Milton washed his hands for a second time.

'Roberta will have to go to the hospital in Bridgetown for a chest X-ray, Mrs Dingwall.' Then, knowing that the poor woman's finances must be already dreadfully stretched, he added kindly, 'Don't worry. I have a colleague who occasionally helps me out in cases like these, children with no immediate parents, and I know he will help you. There will be no charge.'

Bobbie looked across at Mrs Dingwall. She had felt so ill during the past weeks that not even staying day after day in the freezing conditions at Rosebank had seemed to matter. She had known all the time, though, that she was very ill, because the Dingwalls would keep coming in and standing at the end of her bed and saying, 'You look 'orrible, really you do.'

And now as she saw Dr Milton stepping away from her, and Dolly Dingwall handed her yet another clean handkerchief to put to her mouth as she started to cough once more, it seemed to Bobbie that not even Dr Milton wanted to come too near her.

Indeed over the next few hours it was all too evident that no-one wanted to go too near her. Even the Dingwalls were only too thankful to leave Bobbie in the charge of a Bridgetown hospital nurse, who in her turn was quick to shut Bobbie in a side ward, and leave her, coughing and alone, to her own devices.

The chest X-ray confirmed what the grown-ups

had all suspected. Bobbie had tuberculosis. She was to stay in isolation. She was not to return to the Dingwalls. She was not to return to Mellaston.

'Where am I going to live now?' she asked the nurse at the end of her first week in hospital, during which time she had learned to fear needles and nurses, and the sound of hurrying shoes, more than even being alone with Mr Eglantine.

'I don't know, dear,' the nurse told her, backing out of the room. 'A Mrs Eglantine called, but she could not visit, because of infection. They're looking for some relative of yours to ask her what to do, I think. Don't worry, they'll find her soon, even if there is a war on. I am sure they will.'

Bobbie frowned, staring up at the ceiling. She did not really have any *relatives*. Yet it seemed that there was someone who cared whether she lived or died, because she wrote to Bobbie.

One of the nurses, having first carefully removed her mask, read Bobbie the letter out loud from a distance.

'My dear, I am a friend of your poor dear mother. We both worked with Lady Reading before the war, so I expect you know of me. I hear you are not at all the thing. But soon will be doubtless. I am suggesting that you be placed at Hazel Hill, which is by the sea, where you will be looked after by a really special nurse. Failing that there is Scotland, the Highlands – the snow, you know. It can be

74

beneficial, I understand, amazingly so for children like yourself suffering with poison on the lung. Do not worry, dear little Roberta. I will always follow your fortunes, if only from afar. This is because of the war, you know. It has made everything so tiresome, don't you think? I sign myself your Fairy Godmother.'

'Well, there we are, dear,' said the nurse, once more behind her mask, her eyes sympathetic to the small child lying, white-faced but with a high spot of colour on either cheek, on the bed in front of her. 'Everything is going to be all right after all. You're to go to breathe good air that will make your chest better, and quite soon you will be quite better, you see if you're not. You will be quite, quite better.'

The nurse's tones were so bright that not even Bobbie believed her, not that she cared. She only wanted to know one thing, and one thing alone.

'This place where I'm going, it's not school, is it?'

'Oh no, you'll never be going to school now, dear, I am afraid, at least not for a good long while, because of infection. But that doesn't mean you can't read books and learn things. No, it's not school. It's a special place for sick children. You're a lucky little girl really, having this fairy godmother. Some children who come in here don't have the chance to go to a sanatorium. So, you're lucky, really you are.'

*   *   *

All her life Bobbie would have a strange sensation, and sometimes at the oddest times. Sometimes she would shock people with it, and sometimes she would keep silent, yet all the time, whichever way she turned for distraction, she would be quite unable to avoid the truth of it. The first time she had it was when the Dingwalls came to see her off to Hazel Hill. She had to travel in a train, in a special carriage, and they stood on the station platform in Mellaston and waved to her. Bobbie could see Mrs Dingwall was crying, and waving her handkerchief, and that Mr Dingwall was jangling the change in his pocket and feeling embarrassed, because he kept looking away from his wife, and moving up and down the platform, and suddenly Bobbie felt that she would never ever see Mr Dingwall and his jangling change again.

Even so Bobbie waved to them both from the train carriage window. Mrs Dingwall had presented her with a teddy bear wrapped in tissue paper. It was a beautiful bear, but it was the wrong colour, a sort of pink, a colour that somehow did not seem right for a teddy bear, but Bobbie knew that she would have to forgive the bear for his colour, just as she knew that the bear would have to forgive her for her constant coughing.

Bobbie waved again, but the effort made her cough so that she was forced to press yet another handkerchief to her lips, unlike Mrs Dingwall, who was pressing hers to her eyes. The train started to move out of the station, and helped by the nurse who was accompanying her, Bobbie crawled back among the blankets that the hospital had sent with her for the journey. Seated in isolation, the rest of the train so crowded that people were staring resentfully into her carriage from the corridor, Bobbie clutched at her toy, and shut her eyes tightly. Miranda had used to call out, 'Scrim your eyes tight, Bobbie,' when they were out in the fields collecting wool and they came across a dead rabbit, or some such, and now Bobbie *scrimmed* her eyes tight shut in the old way, and saw colours and whirls of strange patterns, like peacock feathers and stars all muddled up.

But despite her tightly shut eyes, despite her efforts to avoid what she imagined to be the accusing eyes of the people in the corridor outside, and despite the nurse seated opposite her, Bobbie knew that she was quite alone now, and might easily die. She knew this as certainly as she knew that she would never see Mr Dingwall again, however much he had waved to her, however often Mrs Dingwall had said, in an effort to reassure her, 'You're going to a better place, dear, honest you are. It would be no good staying at Rosebank, not after this. We don't want you going the same way as our Marion, really we don't.'

The train journey involved many changes, and much stopping and starting, before an exhausted young woman and her charge eventually reached Hazel Hill. As soon as she had seen Bobbie into the hall of the country house, the accompanying nurse thankfully waved her patient goodbye and hurried off to spend the night with a friend, leaving Bobbie seated on a hall chair and staring round at her new surroundings, wondering if this was where she was being sent to die.

It was dark outside, and dark inside the house too, but Bobbie, although inwardly sick and fearful, and still clutching at her toy, could sense at once that this new place was somehow warm and calm. Once the muddle of women in front of her chair had un-muddled themselves, and she found herself staring up into a pair of friendly, humorous brown eyes, her grip on her toy imperceptibly loosened.

'You are Roberta Murray, no?'

Bobbie nodded.

'I am Marie-Helene, but all ze patients 'ere they call me *Marlene*, like Marlene Dietrich, it is easier for them, you know? It is very stupid, but now you are going to 'ave to walk through disinfectant, and then you 'ave some gargling . . .' the young nurse tossed back her head and made a gurgling sound to re-assure Bobbie that it was not difficult. 'And zen we will give you some supper, and you will 'ave a nice sleep, and in ze morning when you wake up, there will be nozzing to do but be 'appy and get better – no?'

Bobbie's intense gaze suddenly transferred itself away from the nurse. The journey had been so long. She had coughed most of the way, holding handkerchief after handkerchief in front of her mouth, but the nurse who had been charged with bringing her from Mellaston to Hazel Hill had seemed quite indifferent to her. More, she had seemed to be actually frightened of her – sitting far away and staring from her book to the countryside outside the window and then down at her book again, but never at Bobbie, as if the very sight, and most of all the sound, of the little girl was repulsive to her. And when she had spoken to her she had spoken as if Bobbie was quite different from the rest of humanity, as if, because she was sick, she actually needed to be addressed in a 'special' voice, the words slow and clearly enunciated, as if because she had a bad cough it was assumed that she could not hear either.

But now everything was different, and although Bobbie was exhausted, and the cough would keep coming, if only sporadically, as if it too was tired, suddenly there was this kind young woman with the dark eyes speaking to Bobbie in a normal way, not as if she was repulsive, but as if she was just a rather ill little girl. It was very nearly too much for her, but, because that door had closed within her, because she knew that she would probably never again go back to the rectory, or see the Dingwalls again, or Miranda, or Teddy, Bobbie was able, after only a few seconds, to look back into the young French nurse's eyes, and, swallowing away the lump in her throat, walk slowly after her towards the room where the buckets of disinfectant lay waiting for her.

TWO YEARS LATER

Chapter Four

Miranda had always known that she enjoyed none of Bobbie's finer feelings – why should she? Miranda was a survivor and she knew it. Of course she did *have* feelings, plenty of them, but because of the war and not knowing where she would be next she had long ago learned to suppress them – until, that is, she had seen Teddy bawling his eyes out in the evacuation centre. As soon as she saw the small blond-haired boy, tears dripping down his face, and no-one minding him, Miranda had known for the first time in her young life what it was to feel love for something or someone other than herself, and she had gone ahead and torn the label from his coat, and made him into her brother in a matter of minutes.

Here was someone as badly off as she was, and like herself quite alone, and so she had adopted him, in precisely the same way that she herself had been adopted and evacuated, and all the rest – arbitrarily, casually, and without consulting him.

She did not particularly think of any of this as

Teddy stood on the station platform that afternoon because Miranda was not given to that sort of thing, but she did think of how much she would miss him, and wonder how he would be without her. Would he be all right?

Certainly Aunt Prudence and Aunt Sophie seemed to have adopted them both with as little trouble as Miranda had adopted Teddy at the evacuation centre all that time ago. And not only had they adopted the two children, privately, but in doing so they had also changed their surnames.

'Very difficult for a boy to be called Darling at a boys' private school, dearest,' Aunt Prudence had told Miranda, very much *sotto voce* because she did not think that Teddy should hear about such things.

Miranda was not to be sent away to school. Girls were not sent away to school. Girls stayed at home and learned to sing and play the piano, and one day, Aunt Sophie told Miranda, she would be sent up to something called a music academy, and as a result would become famous, just as Aunt Sophie had wanted to become famous, until her father had put his foot down and she had been made to stay at home and help instead.

'Take care of yourself, Teddy,' Aunt Prudence told him, deliberately using a stern voice because a stern voice meant she was trying not to let the side down by being seen to be emotional.

'Yes, dearest, take care of yourself. If you have any kind of troubles, you write to us at once, and we will come straight to Herefordshire, won't we, Prudence?'

'Straight to Herefordshire, even if it means Tom Kitten trotting all day and all night.'

The words were meant to be reassuring, but although they were concerned, anxious and loving they were most definitely not reassuring, least of all to Teddy.

Seeing this Miranda leaned forward and pecked him suddenly on the cheek.

'Keep your pecker up, Ted,' she whispered, in their old London way, and before the sound of the train steaming into Mellaston station could drown her words. 'You know, keep your pecker up and don't forget to write me a card, eh?' Teddy nodded and gave his odd smile. He hated having to leave Mellaston, but the aunts wanted him to be a gentleman and become something important, Aunt Sophie had explained, and he could never be that if he stayed doing his reading and writing at the rectory.

Teddy stared ahead at the steam coming from the approaching train. He would probably be the only person on the train who was not a soldier. The WVS lady who was accompanying him to school nodded down at him at that moment as if to say, 'Now is the time to say goodbye, Teddy Mowbray,' and then, seconds later, the aunts were giving him a quick hug and he was on the train, with his trunk and his suitcase, and there was no time not to be brave, really, just time enough to look out of the window and see Miranda becoming smaller and smaller until the train rounded a corner and, of a sudden, she had vanished.

He sat back suddenly against the seat. Supposing he never saw her again? The train was hot and stifling, and full of soldiers and sailors. Teddy decided to try to count how many of each he could see, and before long, what with the heat and the sway of the train, and quite against his wishes, he had fallen asleep.

At last they arrived, after many changes, at yet another small country station. Climbing out after the WVS lady and standing on the platform with its blacked-out name Teddy had the feeling that he had come to a very pretty place. It was not that he could see much of it, but he could sense it, the way that children can sense the sea long before they reach it. Up until then he had thought that nowhere was prettier than Mellaston, but now he sensed that here was somewhere just as beautiful, and so, cheering up more than he would previously have thought possible, he picked up his suitcase, leaving his trunk to be collected later, and, following the tweed-coated lady in front of him, began the long walk to the school.

Taking it in turns to carry Teddy's overnight suitcase, they came at last to an elaborate pair of gates marking what the lady seemed satisfied was the correct place for them to turn, and from there they again walked for some good way up a long drive, grassed over now because of the war, the lady explained, where before the war there would have been gardeners to weed it. They walked on until they reached a flight of stone steps at the top of which was a pair of large, recessed, half-glassed wooden doors.

'Up we go,' the lady whose name Teddy had not bothered to learn, and now would probably never know, urged him.

The door at the top was opened by another boy not much taller than Teddy himself, but older in that particular way that boys who are the first to arrive at schools always seem to be.

'You're Mowbray, are you? I'm Rawlings.' He grinned. 'We're the first. We'll be able to get the best beds in the dormitory.'

He helped Teddy with his suitcase while the WVS lady went in search of a master.

'You'll like it here,' Rawlings told Teddy. 'It's smashing. You've no idea what we get up to when the masters aren't looking, but you'll soon find out.'

Teddy stopped, panting, at the top of the first great flight of wooden stairs and looked down. The lady who had brought him from Mellaston was hurrying across the marble-floored hall below him. He had not liked her particularly but now that she was going without bothering to say goodbye to him he would have given anything for her to have given him a quick hug, as the aunts and Miranda had done. It seemed to him that it was his fault that she was going without even a wave. They had hardly talked to each other.

''Bye,' he called down to her, but his voice was drowned by more new arrivals, by other people saying goodbye, by Rawlings calling from ahead of him, 'Come on, Mowbray, come on or you'll miss the bus!'

Teddy was lucky from then on. He was lucky in Rawlings who became his friend, and he was fearfully lucky because he was taller than all the other boys in his form. He rather looked up to Rawlings, and soon learned to sound like everyone else by imitating the way Rawlings talked. He also learned to play cricket and to swim, and to stand up for himself not just by being tall, but by being charming. He charmed the masters too – so much that no matter what escapade he fell into he would always get off scot free. Because of his charm, because of his quick wits, and because he was tall, most of the time he could look down on almost all the other boys in his class and drawl in his newly learned voice, 'Go away, squit.' He was also lucky, being tall, blond and handsome, since many of the men had been called away to fight, several of the 'masters' at the school were women. The boys still had to call them 'masters' and 'sir' but no matter, there they were, wondrous persons of the opposite sex, and some of them were even young and pretty, so that although in many ways school was not at all like being at the rectory with Miranda and the aunts, in other ways, what with so many adoring women around him, for Teddy it was *just* like being at the rectory.

Right from the start Rawlings took him home for many holidays, and so Teddy quickly grew out of the feeling that he must go home and see the aunts. Of course he wrote to them and to Miranda, at first, but because they wrote to him all the time he really did not feel an urgent need to write back to them so often. And there was so much for him to do at school, so much that he had to be good *at*, that the idea of sitting down to write a letter always seemed to come to him only when he went to bed at night.

He still adored Miranda, but when he did go home in the holidays he realized, time and again, that because she did not go to school, because she was all the time at the rectory being taught by the aunts, she really did not understand how things were at schools, and every time he tried to make her understand she skipped off to do other things, things that boys who went to school did not want to do, and probably would never want to do.

'The aunts hate it when you don't come home,' she told him, once or twice over the next year, and so when Mr Longman called Teddy out of his classroom one sunny afternoon and told him that he had bad news for him, those were the only words Teddy could hear in his head: Miranda's voice saying, *The aunts hate it when you don't come home for the hols*.

'There was a bombing raid in Sussex last night, and your guardians were both killed. They were staying at an hotel while visiting a sick little girl in Hazel Hill, and the hotel had a direct hit. No-one survived. I am sorry, Mowbray. You have only your sister now, I am afraid. But remember – that is after all something, to have a sister still.'

Teddy would always remember Miss Warninglid who accompanied him to the aunts' funeral at Mellaston Cathedral, and how beautiful she looked in her black coat and skirt with her blond hair neatly tied underneath a hat that sat to one side over her eye. It was dreadfully shaming, he realized afterwards, but he was really more preoccupied by being quite alone with his adored Miss Warninglid than he was by his feelings of sorrow for Aunt Prudence and Aunt Sophie.

Later, when he was older and looked back on that journey, Teddy was ashamed that he had not thought more about the implications of what lay ahead, about how sad it was for Miranda, and for him, that their adopted aunts had been killed. But the sober truth was that, at the time, all he could do was stare at Miss Warninglid and think of how much he loved her. All his thoughts were less of the sorrow ahead than of the wonder of her pretty face, and the smell of her perfume. He could hardly bear the idea that Miss Warninglid was rumoured to be engaged to the headmaster, and much of the journey to Mellaston was taken up with the idea that if he made a passionate speech to Miss Warninglid before the train pulled into Mellaston station, she might postpone her engagement to the headmaster until Teddy was able to grow up and marry her himself.

'Aunt Prudence and Aunt Sophie went to see Bobbie,' Miranda told him at the funeral tea afterwards, 'and the hotel was hit by a bomb. They didn't have a chance. What will happen now, Teddy?'

Teddy stared at his sister. What would happen? He had not thought of what would *happen*. He had just thought that he would go to the funeral, feel very sad, and then go back to school again with Miss Warninglid.

'What do you mean?'

'Well, you know—' Miranda tugged at his jacket sleeve, pulling him towards a corner of the old room, well away from the rest of the mourners. 'Mrs Eglantine has taken charge of us now, the way she did when we first came here, because you know she's always in charge of things like that.'

'I hate Mrs Eglantine.'

'I know, so do I, but what will happen, Teddy?' Miranda lowered her voice to a dramatic whisper. 'I mean someone's going to find out we're not really bro and sis and then they might put us in prison!'

'Course we're brother and sister. They adopted us, didn't they? I mean we're Mowbrays now. Mrs Eglantine can't do anything about that, can she?'

'I dunno.'

'We look like each other, don't we? I mean people always said so, didn't they?'

'Yes, but I heard the dean saying that the house is to be sold, and we're to be something called "wards" or something, until we're older, and

91

grown up, and that you're to stay at school, I mean the whole time, and I'm to go to a friend of the aunts in Norfolk. It's all arranged. Where's Norfolk, Teddy?'

Teddy frowned, and then eventually, with a vague gesture of one hand as if he was actually holding a map with the other, he said, 'Up there somewhere. It's on the sea. You'll like being on the sea.'

'You will write, won't you, Teddy?'

Teddy frowned and blinked, suddenly realizing that he actually loved Miranda even more than Miss Warninglid.

'Of course I'll write.'

'I'll send you the address. I'll send it to your school.'

'What about Bobbie? We must see her, mustn't we?'

'Bobbie's going to die, Teddy. I heard Mrs Eglantine saying that the aunts had gone to see her because she was "not expected to live".'

Teddy frowned, staring at the floor. It seemed that everyone they knew was going to die pretty soon. He looked up again and stared across at Miss Warninglid. He would not let Miss Warninglid die – he would kill anyone who tried to make her die.

'Shall we have to go to Bobbie's funeral soon, Miranda?'

'I don't know. I expect so. She's so ill she has had to be put in a special place, and there's no point in writing to her, because she can't write back. That is why the aunts went to see her.'

Miss Warninglid detached herself from one of the groups of mourners and came across to Teddy. 'We must leave and try to get back to school now, Teddy.'

'He's going to be staying at school, now, isn't he? Because of the house being sold and us being wards, he's going to be staying at school all the time?'

'Some boys do, and sometimes they go home with other boys, for holidays. It all depends,' Miss Warninglid said, looking pretty and kind, and yet somehow, because of that, less reassuring than if she was plain and cross.

'I want to go to school too, but they say I must go to Norfolk.'

'I say, do let's introduce ourselves. I'm Miss Warninglid, and you must be Teddy's sister, Miranda.' Miss Warninglid smiled her pretty smile at Miranda but Miranda, being a girl, was stubbornly unimpressed.

'Why can't I go to school with Teddy?' she demanded. 'I want to go to school with my brother.'

'Perhaps you will. We must see. In the meantime, Teddy and I have to catch a train, don't we, Teddy?'

'I want to go to school with Teddy!'

'I said we will see, really we will. I will discuss it with Mr Bratby, Teddy's headmaster, when I return. He might well consider making you an exception, Miranda,' Miss Warninglid repeated in a calming voice.

Not believing the teacher Miranda ran from the

room leaving Teddy staring miserably after her. The whole day had been really horrible. Seeing the aunts put in the ground of the churchyard and people crying, and then walking back to the rectory for tea, still expecting somehow to see Aunt Prudence and Aunt Sophie waiting for him, not really believing that they were back in the churchyard with the rest of the dead people, had all been too much for him. Of a sudden he burst into uncontrollable tears. Seeing his grief Miss Warninglid leaned down and put her pretty young arms around him in an effort to comfort him, but even that delight was not as Teddy had dreamed it might be, because her suit jacket was rough against his cheek, and her brooch scratched his ear, and when she straightened up and he had blown his nose, Miranda, his sister, was still gone. Through the drawing room window he could see her up the fields and far away from the house where they had once all played, he and Miranda and Bobbie – who was also going to die, like Aunt Sophie and Aunt Prudence. Suddenly his whole world was a sea of despair, and he no longer even wanted to marry Miss Warninglid, only to run after Miranda and for everything to be as it had been before.

'Now, Miranda, you're a very lucky little girl. One day, my dear, you will be a very rich little girl, but at the moment you are just a very lucky little girl, and I will tell you why.'

Mrs Eglantine put her heavily ringed hands

either side of Miranda's neck and pressed down on her shoulders, so that reluctant though Miranda was to sit down on the hated woman's sofa she was forced to do so, simply and solely because not to do so would mean struggling, or kicking Mrs Eglantine on the shin, or something.

'You are a very lucky little girl, Miranda, because the Honourable Mrs Sulgrave, who has always taken such an interest in helping evacuees, is a friend of . . .' She paused. '*Was* a friend of Miss Prudence and Miss Sophie, and as a consequence, hearing of your plight, and that of your brother, although she was not able to attend the funeral, she has asked for you.'

Mrs Eglantine paused again, and her eyes, never, even on a good day, a source of warmth, stared into Miranda's large blue ones seeking to find in them the same amazement that was reflected in her own voice.

Perhaps because she had been taught by Aunt Sophie to 'act' out her songs, not just sing them, Miranda knew that the time had come for some acting. She saw that it was necessary to assume, for Mrs Eglantine's benefit, an amazed, happy, and grateful expression. So she did this at once, obediently clasping her hands together in a manner of which she felt Aunt Sophie could only have approved, and at the same time imagining to herself that Mrs Eglantine was not a horrid lady whom she had always disliked, but a toffee, or a piece of chocolate.

'Oh, oh, oh, I am so-oo lucky,' she intoned,

knocking her tightly clasped hands slowly against herself as Aunt Sophie had taught her to do when coming to the end of 'Oh My Beloved Father'.

For a dreadful second Miranda thought that her acting could not have been as natural as it should have been, since Mrs Eglantine seemed unimpressed by her dramatic reaction. She was frowning, but then, perhaps remembering that the poor child had only just lost her two beloved guardians, she seemed to relent, and patted Miranda on the side of her head as she moved over to her small Davenport desk, with its clock resting on the top, and her diary beneath.

'Good, that is good. So long as you know that you are the most fortunate of children, then we may not need to say any more.'

She sat down at her desk, and taking a pair of pince-nez from one of the small drawers at the side she read out a letter which had been placed inside the diary.

Dear Mrs Eglantine, I would so like to help with the education of my late friends Prudence and Sophie Mowbray's ward, Miranda Mowbray. The Hall has been requisitioned for the duration, but we would welcome her here at the estate manager's house, and of course, will be responsible for her education in every way.

Yours sincerely,
Allegra Sulgrave

The pince-nez was now removed and Mrs Eglantine stared across at Miranda.

'You are to live at Burfitt Hall, in Norfolk. You are to live in one of the finest houses in East Anglia. You, who were once nothing but a London gutter-snipe. Well, well, well, the war has thrown up many changes, but surely few as extraordinary as this? Mrs Dingwall will accompany you back to the rectory and help you pack up your things, and then they are to send a car to pick you up. First you will go up to London, and then you will go to East Anglia.'

Miranda stood up. She was excited at the idea of not being with Mrs Eglantine for much longer, and at the same time she was horrified at the idea of being in a place she did not know. She had grown to know and love Mellaston, and now the house, as well as the aunts, was being taken away from her.

'What about Bobbie? Where is Bobbie? Is she coming?'

For a few seconds Mrs Eglantine managed to look embarrassed at the mention of Bobbie's name. The poor child, so ill, and all because of poor conditions. But still, the committee had done their best, and during a war what else could anyone do?

'No, dear, Bobbie is not a well little girl *at all*. Bobbie is in a place where they will try to help her to get better, but whether or not they can, I would not know. She is not at all a well little girl, I am afraid, Miranda. Besides, she is not a Mowbray. Someone else is looking after her, has made her her ward, a friend of her mama's, from before the war, a Mrs Beatrice Harper. When the war is over you might see each other again. Or, on the other hand, you might not. After all, there may not *be* a world in which to meet each other again, dear. Not unless we win the war. And even then, we may not be here. We may well all be dead, like your dear guardians up there in the graveyard. Dead, or under the boots of the Nazis. Don't forget that.'

Miranda stared at Mrs Eglantine and, sensing that she was really quite an accomplished sadist, smiled, slowly and beautifully, at the hateful woman in front of her.

'I expect *you* would like to be dead, quite soon, wouldn't you, Mrs Eglantine, because of Mr Eglantine? Because of his never having been in uniform, because of his making arms instead of using them? That's what Aunt Sophie used to say, wasn't it?' she asked, smiling sweetly, her cornflour blue eyes as innocent as her words were not.

Mrs Eglantine stared across at her in horror. 'I *beg* your pardon?' she said, sounding suddenly suburban. 'What did you say? Did you say you wished I was dead?'

'No,' Miranda replied, all innocence. 'No, I just thought you might feel the way Aunt Sophie used to say she would feel if her husband was not in uniform – that you might *like* to be dead, because of Mr Eglantine's not fighting like everyone else. That's what Aunt Sophie used to say.'

There was a short silence during which Mrs

Eglantine breathed in and out, and then, controlling her worst feelings and a deep desire to slap Miranda, she rang for Mrs Dingwall instead.

Mercifully Mrs D came to the door within seconds, far too few as a matter of fact. Mrs Eglantine realized this rather late. The charlady had responded to the bell so quickly that she must have been listening outside the door. Mrs Eglantine could see that the wretched woman was trying to suppress a quite beastly smirk.

'Miranda Mowbray is going to be picked up from the rectory by a military motor car. Some sort of American colonel or another is apparently to fetch her, some friend of her new host family, a Colonel Jennings, I believe. He is on his way to Norfolk and has volunteered to collect her and take her to London, where she will stay, the spoilt little hussy, at the Dorchester. The following day they will travel to Norfolk where she will be left at Burfitt Hall.'

Miranda was too proud to let Mrs Eglantine see her feelings, too proud to allow her to see what that one word 'left' did for her, the terror it gave her. She would never, ever, let anyone older see her feelings. She had never let anyone see how she felt, not since her granny went daft in the bombing, and took her to the first evacuation centre and *left* her with people who made fun of her. Not since she was first evacuated down to Kent and *left* to live with the kindly Meades. Not since they had to send her back to London, and her granny had again *left* her to be once more evacuated. Not since those days had she ever let someone older see how she felt, always suspecting that they would take advantage of it.

So, now, she left Mrs Eglantine's house without a backward glance, and walked along beside Mrs Dingwall in proud silence.

Inside of course she was terrified. She knew that once she went from Mellaston, she would become just like Bobbie, and no-one would ever hear of her again. She would be far away, and just a name, like Bobbie. Worse, she suddenly could not remember Teddy's school address because the aunts had always done the envelope for her. And she could not remember whether Teddy was meant to be coming home to Mellaston in the holidays, or whether Mrs Eglantine had said the rectory was to be sold, or had been sold. Fear and panic had sent everything from her mind, yet she must not show her feelings. One day she would be grown up, if Hitler did not kill them all, she would be grown up and no-one would ever leave her anywhere again. She would find herself a house, and she would stay there, and there would be sunshine, and she would have chocolates whenever she wanted.

All the time that they were packing up Miranda's strange selection of clothes at the old rectory, Mrs Dingwall kept saying, 'Nice for you, dear, going to London. Exciting too, really, to stay at a famous hotel. I love London, even now, even with the bombing, but I couldn't live there no more, not with our Marion being taken from us. No, we needed to get away, or it would never have left us, the sorrow of her, and I will say, as soon as we came here, my Albert did desist from some of his worser habits, I will say that for him.'

As soon as she had finished this speech, Mrs Dingwall would begin again, yet another version of the same speech, and hardly changing the words, so that very soon Miranda realized that she was like a singer with a successful song, quite happy to repeat, and repeat, and repeat, until such time as eventually she stopped. Which eventually she did, only to begin again after only a few minutes.

'She's daft like my granny,' Miranda told Colonel Jennings once she was seated beside him in the staff car, thankfully waving goodbye to the hatted and floral-aproned figure still standing outside the rectory front door, long after the staff car had turned and was heading back towards the gates.

Colonel Jennings laughed, and so did his young woman driver.

'That's British for "crazy", isn't it?' he asked the driver, and she nodded.

Miranda sat back, careful to keep to her side of the car, and stared out of the window. Mrs Dingwall had been so endlessly talkative Miranda had not really noticed that she was leaving the rectory for ever. She had packed up her few toys, her skipping rope, a teddy bear, and a few books and placed them in the suitcase with her clothes, and they had been taken and put in the boot of the smart military car, but she had not said goodbye to the old house, because of Mrs Dingwall talking, and talking.

It was raining outside the window. Miranda started to count the drops, and then to watch them racing each other. It was a strangely satisfying occupation, and took her mind off the car going further and further away from Mellaston, as those feelings, those *left* feelings, started to reassert themselves. They were like sharp, tangled wire in the bottom of her tummy. But if she watched that raindrop and made a bet to herself that it would be the first to reach the bottom of the window – or the next one – or *that* one – the feelings must go. She would make them.

Most of all she must not ever, ever think of Teddy, her brother, somewhere in Herefordshire, perhaps missing her, not knowing where she was going, because she knew without being told that Mrs Eglantine would never, ever tell him now, because of Miranda cheeking her, so she really might never see him again.

Instead she thought of him as he used to be, not at the funeral, but at the rectory, making her play cricket with him, bowling at her, far too fast of course – and how she would shut her eyes, and hope and pray that she would not let him down. And then she thought of him swimming, diving on top of her, making her scream, before they emerged muddy and weed covered from the local lake on a hot summer's day, and how the aunts would make *tiss, tiss* noises as they towelled them dry, all the time smiling because they had made sure to have them both taught to swim. For as Aunt Sophie used to murmur, 'Better to swim than to drown, dear.'

Miranda thought of all this on the drive to London, and sometimes she slept, and sometimes she woke as Colonel Jennings rattled his papers, or spoke to his driver, and once or twice they stopped at a place with what the Colonel tactfully called *facilities*, until eventually, after what seemed like days, but was only really hours, Miranda once again sensed London, and there were all the familiar sights of bombed houses, and sandbags, and she suddenly remembered being small there, and the bustle and the excitement of not knowing, ever, what was going to happen next. How people crowded past, and how little of the sky could be seen, and Mellaston was, of a sudden, just a memory. Like a postcard from a holiday place brought back, not written on, to be placed on a mantelpiece, or a sideboard, and every now and then picked up and stared at, only to be replaced again – just an un-addressed card from no-one to no-one, the sight of it bringing back that sense of how it had been, of sounds and people, of voices on summer air, of laughter suppressed, of a piano playing in the distance, its tune only now faintly heard – 'I'll See You Again'.

But the song was wrong. She knew now that she never would.

But then, not much later, it was no longer just London, but the Dorchester hotel, and Miranda was being helped from the car by the young lady driver, spanking smart in her uniform, and, although she did not know it, everyone was staring at this elegant child in her strangely magnificent clothes. Her long velvet skirt, her lace blouse, and her wool cloak with its red-lined hood made her seem like a child from an old portrait, stepping not from a car, but from another era.

'This is how she was delivered to me, I promise you, Pamela,' said Colonel Jennings laughingly, once they were all inside the lobby of the Dorchester. 'Just as you see her. A child from another age, I would say, but so *beautiful*.'

'Pamela' was also beautiful. Even Miranda, who was always reluctant to admit beauty in anyone but herself, could see that, so she graciously held out her small paw to the beautiful lady, and shook her ringed hand.

'Hayward Jennings, you have brought us a princess, you have – a princess.' Pamela bent down to Miranda and studied her quite perfect little face with fascination. 'Such colouring, such eyes! She will be famous. I predict it.'

Miranda stared into the green eyes that were gazing into hers, and a warmth such as she had never felt before stole into the centre of her being and then radiated outwards so that finally, inwardly, she gave a great sigh. It might have been mistaken for a sigh of relief at arriving, and indeed it was a sigh of relief and it *was* about arriving – arriving at the end of a long, long journey. At last someone had said out loud what Miranda had always known. She was going to be famous. She was going to be different from everyone else in Mellaston. They were going to be ordinary, but she was going to be famous. She was going to be famous and beautiful, and this beautiful lady knew it too.

Of a sudden Miranda was glad that she had left Mellaston, and even Teddy and Bobbie did not seem to matter so much. They would have to take care of themselves. Meanwhile – Miranda glanced around her, as Colonel Jennings and Pamela fell into animated conversation, quite obviously madly in love, looking at each other as if they were both ice creams on a hot day – meanwhile Miranda was going to make sure that she always stayed in places like the Dorchester, always, always, always.

'General Eisenhower was at Claridge's, but pink was not his colour, so he moved to the first floor here. Now no-one will dare bomb the Dorchester, for fear of Ike,' Pamela was telling Colonel Jennings, laughing, her eyes never leaving his, sending messages which Miranda could only guess at, knowing that they were quite untranslatable grown-up messages, but also knowing that they were to do with being beautiful and handsome, and staying at hotels.

Colonel Jennings leaned down to Miranda and spoke to her in his charming, joking, and completely kind way.

'I am not afraid of bombs, and I dare say you are

not either, so tonight we are going to have the luxury of staying in a proper suite, and leaving the rest of the scaredy cats to sleep downstairs in the Turkish baths and the corridors and so on, unless of course you are frightened?'

Miranda shook her head. Of course she was frightened, but since she was already passionately in love with both Colonel Jennings and his beautiful Pamela she had no intention of showing it.

'Follow me, Princess,' the Colonel said.

With that Miranda tripped after two of the most glamorous people she had ever met, and two of the kindest too, for they never seemed to even dream of leaving her in someone else's charge, probably because neither Colonel Jennings nor his Pamela knew anything about children or how to go on with them. Or it might have been because they liked everyone to enjoy themselves as much as they obviously did. Whatever the reason, nothing would do for them but to take their 'little princess' everywhere with them.

And so it was that after a long rest in what seemed to Miranda to be a great gold and red room, and a good wash in a marble bathroom, standing on a thick bath mat and sponging herself all over, Miranda was loaned a special little jewelled cape and a bracelet with small gold animals on it, and a jewelled clip was put in the top of her hair, giving her what Pamela called 'the Veronica Lake look, darling'. Although Miranda had no idea who 'Veronica Lake' might be, she knew that she must be someone beautiful, and for that reason she held her head high and followed her new heroine downstairs to the constant, magical life of the Dorchester hotel.

'Pamela has the *eye*, as my mother would say. It is quite wonderful, her taste, quite wonderful,' the Colonel said approvingly, as he held out his arm to Miranda. 'You look even more beautiful than you looked a few hours ago, and I did not think that was even possibly possible, my dear.'

The restaurant, Colonel Jennings told Miranda as they stepped formally and beautifully downstairs after Pamela, had been moved to the Gold Room and the Grill Room to the Ballroom Lounge.

'Which means,' Colonel Jennings joked, 'that lamb cutlets now waltz off the plate, and La Timbale de Petits pois quickstep off the trolley.'

He might as well have been talking Czechoslovakian, but Miranda was determined to laugh and smile as children must who are with grown-ups all the time and don't want to be left out.

'Because of security no-one here is allowed to be recognized, so I shall introduce you to anyone who stops at our table as *Her Royal Highness Princess Miranda*,' the Colonel announced as they sat down and perused the menu cards, which due to shortage of paper were precisely four and a half inches by six inches deep. 'There is no greater charge here than five whole shillings so I cannot order the world for you, but you might like a translation of tonight's menu, might you not? Pamela, will you do us the honours?'

Pamela read out the menu in a clear voice. '*Les Perles Grises de Sterle*, followed by *Le Fumet de Tortue au vieux Sherry*, then *Le Filet de Sole Riviera*, and finally *Le Blanc de Volaille perigourdine* with *La Timbale de Petits pois*.'

Miranda was determined to sit bolt upright, as Aunt Sophie had always instructed her. She could not appreciate Pamela's beautiful, refined, delicately accented French, as Colonel Jennings might be able to, but she would never forget that last big word *Timbale*. It was like her little jewelled cape, or the clip at the top of her hair; it was like the sound of the band slowly playing Aunt Sophie's tune – the one she always sang with tears in her eyes: 'I'll See You Again'.

'I can sing this,' Miranda told Pamela, in confidence, she thought, but Colonel Jennings had overheard and was beaming his now familiar confident smile.

'Then you shall do so. We will tell them to play it again and you can sing into the microphone, Princess Miranda,' Colonel Jennings joked.

'Of course! I shall ask Maurice to let you – but first we must try to eat out phoney caviar, and our sole Riviera, or the chef will be upset. Imagine what he has gone through to produce this. It hardly bears thinking of, does it?'

Years later Miranda herself would joke about that first moment when she discovered the power of the microphone. She would wonder aloud to friends how appalling she must have looked to anyone else.

'Can you imagine,' she would say, 'a child dressed as an adult singing "I'll See You Again" with a jewelled clip in her hair?'

But as it happened, at the time, she was only aware of singing to her two fans at the nearby table, not of how incongruous she must have looked in a wartime ballroom, singing what was already an old number to women in old-fashioned dresses and men in uniform, so, really, all told – really it did not matter. She cared only to sing to her hero and heroine, Colonel Jennings and Pamela, of spring breaking through again, and time lying heavy until they would see each other again. She put her whole heart and soul into it, as Aunt Sophie would have wished. Indeed, she pretended for the first few opening bars that Aunt Sophie was playing for her as she had used to do, so that her voice sounded as sad as it had ever done, because Aunt Sophie was now in heaven and not there to applaud her little star.

And so, following the warm applause, itself followed by air raid warnings which sent people in evening dress and military uniforms on their seemingly leisurely way to the Dorchester basement, to the Turkish baths beneath the ballroom – to anywhere else they considered to be 'safe' – Miranda forgot to be afraid. For a few sublime minutes she had held the floor, and had felt the power of one voice, *her* voice, coming from her small frame; and so she was able to follow Colonel Jennings and Pamela, not downstairs but upstairs, where they all retired to their rooms, ignoring the sounds of the air raid warnings, knowing that bombs were dropping but seemingly confident that because they were at the Dorchester, they could not be harmed. Buckingham Palace might be hit, but not the Dorchester.

Long after the sound of the All Clear, Miranda stayed awake, thinking of the fun that standing before a microphone had given her, dreaming of other nights when she would stand in front of an orchestra, perhaps on the wireless, perhaps singing to thousands of people at home. Pamela and Colonel Jennings also stayed awake, but for rather different reasons.

The next morning Miranda came to yet another new realization, namely that she had never seen a beautiful woman in her slip before. Hitherto her life had been filled with women such as the Mellaston aunts, practical women who could plait their long hair at the sound of a siren, quickly and efficiently, and usually at a moment's notice. As she stared at Pamela in her wondrous petticoat, Miranda did remember that she had once seen Mrs Meades too in a petticoat, but it had not been the kind that Pamela was now wearing, and even if it had been, Miranda was suddenly sure, it would not have looked at all the same.

Pamela had black hair, which was perhaps why the petticoat was trimmed with black, a white fashion slip gathered high around the bust with lace straps, but tightly fitted with two seams running in a narrow band to the hem, which was trimmed with black ribbon, beneath which was a thick frill. Not for Pamela the uniformed look of Colonel Jennings's pretty young driver; for Pamela the scent not of soap but of rare perfume. And not only was her petticoat elaborate, feminine and flattering, she wore real nylon stockings with seams. On the way to the Clothes Exchange in Mellaston, Miranda had often noticed that young girls they passed had painted their legs to look like nylons, but she had never before actually seen anyone wearing them. The aunts only ever wore much-mended lisle, and Mrs Eglantine what she called 'pre-war silk'. No-one in Mellaston had ever worn nylon.

Nylon made Pamela's legs look wondrously shiny and the lines up the back drew attention to their delicious shape and length, a length displayed to perfection beneath the pale blue spotted rayon dress that she now slipped over her head.

She turned to Miranda, who was seated on a small chair beside her dressing table.

'Do up my buttons, darling, would you?'

Miranda all but ran to help her push each of the covered buttons through the beautifully sewn loops at the back, after which she watched with adoring eyes as Pamela did up the belt for herself

111

and arranged the small, splayed bow at the front of the dress before pulling on her gloves, placing her tiny black hat with its spotted net to the centre of her head, and tucking a handbag under her arm.

'This is the way fashion is going, my dear, do you know? Colonel Jennings brings me back so much in the Diplomatic you-know-what from the States, and things – by that I mean coats and skirts of course – are going to be fuller once the shortages go away, really they are.'

She moved away from Miranda and as she did so the young girl's eyes fell upon the headlines of the *Daily Express*. Nighttime bombing had destroyed yet more of the East End. Fleetingly Miranda wondered if her granny was all right, but since Pamela was calling to her to come down with her, because the car was leaving, there was no time to go on trying to read the newspaper. Besides, her granny now seemed a remote figure, like someone in the Bible, not at all anything to do with Miranda Mowbray, nothing to do with the new life which Miranda now realized had adopted her so whole-heartedly. Indeed, as she effortlessly followed Pamela down the plush staircase to the rooms below, it seemed to Miranda that just as she and Teddy would never have recognized Bobbie when she came to her birthday party, now her granny would never have recognized Miranda in the sophisticated young girl who climbed once more into the military car – having first cheekily returned the salute thrown by the young woman driver as if she was military personnel – and sat cuddled between the divinely beautiful Pamela, and the still more handsome Colonel Jennings, all the way to Norfolk.

PART TWO

SUSSEX IN SPRING
1949

'Young man in a purple suit
doing a little business on the side
it was not for you my son died.'

Virginia Graham

Chapter Five

'Miss Murray! Your clothes! What would Mrs Harper say?'

Bobbie stared down unconcernedly at her new but faded brown corduroy plus fours, long socks, brogues and really quite smart green jumper, which she had bought only that morning from a local farmer's wife who supplied them daily with eggs and butter and home-made brown bread as nonchalantly as if she was actually helping to repay the National Debt, rather than breaking the law by supplying them with illicit produce.

'How about the hat, Miss Moncrieff? *Très chic, n'est-ce pas?*' Bobbie loved to use French to Amabel Moncrieff because she already knew that the poor lady was completely ignorant of even the teeniest bit of French, and so it was somehow marvellous to tease her. 'A trifle stylish, don't you think?' Bobbie went on. 'I bought these from Mrs Duddy, this morning. One of the land girls left them at the farm, and so Mrs Duddy passed them on to me. Even the wellington boots fit, with just a bit of scrunched-up paper in the bottom of the toes.'

'Oh, but Miss Murray, land girls' clothes, and someone else's too. Supposing Mrs Harper comes down and finds you like this, what will she make of it? And she will blame me, I dare say. She will blame me for everything.'

Miss Moncrieff did not add that Beatrice Harper always did blame her for everything, that being secretary to Bobbie's sometime guardian and self-styled 'fairy godmother' meant that she was really a whipping post for anything that went wrong in Mrs Harper's life.

Perhaps for this reason Bobbie now tried to look as serious as Amabel Moncrieff, because of course casting off Mrs Harper's old smart clothes, all of which had been retailored for Bobbie, and putting on corduroy knickerbockers and woolly socks and brogues, was, in Miss Moncrieff's eyes, tantamount to treason.

'Mrs Harper is not here, Miss M,' Bobbie gently reminded her guardian's secretary, 'so really – what does it matter? She is in London, and we are living in the Sheds, in the jolly old servants' quarters, so we don't need to pretend that we have to change into cocktail dresses for dinner, do we? Not really, not truly? Not even Mrs Harper would expect that, would she? I could hardly garden in one of her newest Mainbocher *ooh là là* suits, could I?'

For a second both Bobbie and Miss Moncrieff's minds flew to London, to Grosvenor Place, where

Beatrice Harper would doubtless be seated in her mock Strawberry Hill Gothick library at her eighteenth-century table with her all-important leather-bound personal telephone book beside her, wearing something new and striking, at the very least a little number with a roll collar by Schiaparelli, or a morning outfit with a charming Napoleonic collar by Piguet, paid for with heaven only knew how many clothing coupons.

'She might decide to come down. I mean. Dear. I mean, you do look like a land girl, dear, really you do.'

Miss Moncrieff's voice reflected the very real fear that Mrs Harper engendered in her employees, and indeed in her ward's heart.

'Well, of course I look like a land girl, these are land girl clothes, and if she comes down,' Bobbie continued, with sudden aplomb, 'which I doubt very much, seeing that the weather is turning so bad, I will tell her, you will tell her, we will both tell her, that I have to wear clothes appropriate for gardening.'

'Gardening.' Miss Moncrieff said the word as if it was a piece of cold cod on a plate that someone had ordered her to eat for breakfast.

'Out there,' Bobbie continued, waving a dramatic hand, 'out there is a wilderness that has to be conquered, Miss Moncrieff. For the moment I am afraid that we must forget my guardian—'

'We can never do that, Miss Murray—'

'—and tackle the jungle!'

'I just so miss my flat in Ebury Street,' said Miss Moncrieff in her usual dismal tones, before moving back towards the kitchen, and the old cooking range where, nowadays, she seemed to spend her days annotating little bills and writing home to her mother in Pinner. 'Have I told you about my flat? Quite pretty, really.'

'But I think it is delightful here. Can't you think of the Sheds as being really rather like having our own flat? It is really, don't you think? And we are so lucky not being at Hazel Hill any more. Well, not you, but me . . .' Bobbie paused, her mind stretching back over what now seemed to be the *forever years* of the war, years during which she had grown up, and been cured of 'poison on the lung' as polite people always seemed to call tuberculosis, years when she had known no-one of her own age, seen no-one of her own age, and worst of all not even had a letter from one.

Sometimes, feeling more lonely than she hoped she would ever be again, she had been forced to write to herself. These letters, which she called *Dear Bobbies*, were usually from imaginary Americans. It amused her to have them write things like, *Do tell me all about your situation in England. And if you would like a food parcel. And whether or not King George is a nice man?*

These pretend letters from people she named with startling unoriginality 'Frank' or 'Eunice', who did not and never would exist except in her own mind, meant that Bobbie could sit down at her window at Hazel Hill, with its view of sea and pebbled beach, and write descriptions of yet another imaginary life where she was living in a large house with lots of friends, instead of in a private sanatorium with no-one who really cared if she was alive or dead.

Being the only child growing up at Hazel Hill, she had not been allowed to mix with any of the older patients, some of whom sometimes died, and some of whom, on occasions, even married each other. Bobbie always heard of both these major events from the French nurses, but that was all she did hear, for the fact was that the French nurses only ever spoke French, and never really bothered much with English. Perhaps because of this Bobbie soon came to think of marriage and death as two states which were somehow inseparable.

This morning, as she tidied her room, an old piece of verse that she had written the previous year fell out of her diary and onto the floor, part of which ran:

> *She wrote in her books*
> *The things that she wanted*
> *Them to say.*
> *She wrote 'Dear me'*
> *And 'Ten today!'*
> *And 'How I love you*
> *More than I can say.'*

But now, today, of a sudden it seemed to be just that – an old piece of verse, for the fact of the matter was that the sun was shining and it seemed to Bobbie that she could feel its gentle warmth right inside her, and what with Hazel Hill and all its associations of lonely sickness being behind her, and the knowledge that she had a clean bill of health for the first time since she had lived with the Dingwalls at Rosebank, its intimations seemed to be quite passé, out of date, and thankfully gone for ever. No-one knew better than Bobbie how irritating a constant cough was to the sufferer, and all the more so for knowing that it was driving everyone else dotty as well. She had quickly come to accept this during the years that she had spent at Hazel Hill, as she had come to accept that her guardian must hate visiting her for this reason. And, really, Bobbie could not find it in her heart to blame her in the least. Beatrice Harper was a fashionable woman, who for many reasons could not risk being near someone who, as she elegantly phrased it, suffered from 'poison on the lung'. But although Mrs Harper had seldom visited her ward, she had always seen to it that Bobbie had an entirely private first floor room at Hazel Hill, well away from older patients, and that she could see the sea, and was occasionally visited by sweet and kindly but really rather frightened ladies who sat on church committees and undertook to visit the sick.

She also arranged for Bobbie to have private lessons. Sometimes these were from other patients, who were deemed to be on the mend and therefore in some way thought to be less infectious. Sometimes, as the months and years of the war crept by, she was taught by goodly women who came in from the small Sussex villages in and around Hazel Hill. These women were always single, but lots less gloomy than Miss Moncrieff. With their help Bobbie read every classic in the English language, learned History of Art, and was shown how to draw the view from her window, endlessly and sometimes to her way of thinking quite pointlessly, especially considering the wartime shortage of paper and pencils.

Finally, to Bobbie's amazement, the war had actually ended. She had really never thought that there would ever *not* be a war. Or if there was to be an end to it some day, she had never, ever imagined that she and the patients at Hazel Hill would be there to witness it. But somehow Victory Day had arrived, and the war had come to a halt, with a bang, as the atomic bomb was dropped on Japan.

At long, long last, with the war over, one by one the older patients had been moved out from Hazel Hill and returned to their homes or other places, while Bobbie had been deemed well enough to move to the newly vacated Baileys Court. Not to the main house, but to the old servants' quarters which directly overlooked the beach, up which the great sea would creep, or stumble, sometimes actually managing to pound on the one-storey building with its fists, at others quite content to *hiss* its presence, before backing once more down the sand.

Now Bobbie could not just see and hear what she

had come to regard as her old friend during the endless years she had spent at Hazel Hill; she could walk up to it and feel the water on her toes and stop and stare out over the grey-blue, blue-blue, white-grey, grey-white waters of the Channel, all the time wondering why it was that simply being on the beach was so satisfying, why staring at the sea seemed to be an entirely worthy occupation, as if looking at it made it seem more real even to itself.

It was shortly after Bobbie's arrival at the Sheds that she had been joined by Miss Moncrieff. But Miss Moncrieff was not impressed by the idea of a view of the sea. Indeed she had not been impressed by seeing the sea at any time since she had arrived.

'I just so miss my flat in Ebury Street,' she would repeat, every evening, before turning on the news, as if she was hoping that she might hear her own dear residence mentioned.

And she was far more interested in having Bobbie wind wool with her than in talking about the excitement of what might be happening outside the windows of their lodging, with its feeling of bygone grandeur and its old stone fireplaces. Indeed, it seemed to Bobbie that Miss Moncrieff had been made as miserable by her sudden change of address as Bobbie herself had been made happy.

Today Bobbie left the Sheds and in her new, secondhand, stout land girl shoes, she started to walk towards the tangled wilderness that surrounded the former monastery which was Baileys Court.

As she struggled past the walls of brambles that now swamped what had once been formal gardens, Bobbie tried not to notice the fallen trees with their rusting iron girders which littered the five hundred acre estate. But it was finally impossible, for they were everywhere, some cut into logs and then left, some just lying helplessly on their sides, bare roots exposed. It was the saddest of sights, and as she strolled past them, it appeared to her imaginative mind that they seemed to be silently begging her to turn them back to life and growth, beseeching her to restore them to the fine and beautiful sight they must have been before the war.

And where once fashionable ladies must have swayed down private walks to see the peach or orchid houses, now there were only weeds and broken brick paths, and stunted trees stripped of everything except their bare outlines, even those that had managed to remain upright were white and bare, strangely skeletal from the impact of the constant coastal winds.

Despite knowing nothing about gardens, Bobbie found even her normally high spirits inevitably lowered by the sight of endless broken fencing. As she climbed up and around the chaos of the deserted garden, she passed empty plinths that must once have proudly displayed statues of figures from the ancient world, but were now devoid of ornament. Overhead birds passed calling to each other, a sorrowful sound in such bleak surroundings. And despite the tangle of the brambles and the fallen trees, the wind too seemed to be calling to someone or something Bobbie could not see, making her turn to look behind her, fearing another human being and yet half expecting one too. And so, turning, and pulling her hat harder down over her long, brown, wavy hair, Bobbie headed back towards the outer edge of the small estate, which was itself bounded on one side by fields and a cluster of woods, and on the other by beaches and the sea.

Here she could walk without stopping every few yards to feel sad or to wonder at some empty sight or forlorn and broken wall or garden building. Here too she could be free of Miss Moncrieff and her dispiriting ways, her little sighs and moans – but most of all her knitting.

Living with Miss Moncrieff during the last rain-sodden fortnight, it appeared to Bobbie that the secretary was more than attached to knitting long brown stockings on very fine needles, she was positively dedicated to it. It seemed to Bobbie that part of the frustration of the poor lady's life was that the stockings never seemed to *lengthen*, and anyway what was the *point* of long woolly stockings, now that spring and summer were on their way, and the very thought of them, let alone the sight of them, was surely enough to induce an itch?

Of course Bobbie could hear the sea long before she could see it, as you always can, and so it was with a mounting sense of excitement that she kept walking, for this sea was very different from the one she had spent so many years facing from her sick-room at Hazel Hill.

But if there had once been well-worn paths to the beach from the outer edges of the garden at Baileys Court, they were now far too overgrown to be discernible, so it had taken a great deal of determination, in the last days, to make a path for herself through to the pebble beach. Yet from these forays into the undergrowth, from these lone expeditions, had arisen her determination that with this new life had come a need for new clothes. Useless really to wear a prim coat and hat, cast-offs from her rich widowed guardian's wardrobe sent to her from Paris, or New York, London or Rome. Bobbie knew that she needed wellington boots, and some sort of slacks, if she was to climb the fencing and barbed wire that lay strewn across the paths.

In fact, despite having already clambered past any number of obstacles already, at least a half a dozen times that week, Bobbie still felt amazed that, although the war was over there was still barbed wire on the beach, giant rolls of it – and to the left, further away, she could see evidence of defunct landmines, their weird shapes now much decorated by coruscations of barnacles and seaweed, just as when she turned back and looked up to the edge of the small estate, concrete 'pill boxes' from which soldiers would have been trained to shoot the Nazi invaders still stood sentinel.

She stared first at the grim evidence around her and then up to the now blue sky, at the seagulls that spread out their great wings and cried down to her, a lone figure on the grey-stoned beach, and it seemed to her that the birds overhead might be the souls of dead soldiers crying out for the waste of it all, and if she could have pulled at the barbed wire with her bare hands, or taken some dynamite and blown up the landmine or the concrete pill boxes, she would have done, but since she could not she picked up a pebble and sent it spinning across the suddenly mild surface of the sea.

She knew that her guardian had sent her and Miss Moncrieff down to Baileys Court for want of anything else to do with them. Bobbie had at last been given a completely clean bill of health, and Miss Moncrieff, although she had been with Beatrice Harper for years, was clearly no longer quite the right type to go with her employer's new and glittering image. For the post-war world had its stars, some of them still extant from the old world, others, like Beatrice, intent on rising to the height of the new social constellation.

Also, as Mrs Harper had put it, 'Now that I have purchased Baileys Court, we must keep a weather eye on it until such time as these stupid regulations have been waived, and we can get on with rebuilding.'

This of course would have been sensible if there had been anything for them to keep an eye *on*. The truth was there was not. In post-war England the Ministry of Works would not, and indeed dare not, issue building permissions for places like Baileys

Court without risking questions being asked in Parliament, and prosecutions of the most virulent kind were brought against anyone taking the law into their own hands and daring to build so much as a garden hut without a licence. In effect government rationing was not just on food and clothing, it was on everything, and while Beatrice Harper had snapped up Baileys Court for the proverbial song, restoring the former monastery to some kind of civilized state could take years, as Miss Moncrieff warned Bobbie daily, between the click of her four needles.

'I fear we could both be here in the Sheds until well into our dotage, dear, really I do.'

Much as she resisted Miss Moncrieff's doom-laden statement, Bobbie knew that this could be only too true, and her guardian could well leave them both at Baileys Court for the next five years, if such was her mind. They could be there for what used to be known during the war as 'the duration' – in other words until not just the building permissions were through, but every brick and tile was restored. And the truth was that, if this was so, there would be little that either of them could do. Bobbie at just eighteen and penniless, could be left with Miss Moncrieff for years, and years, until both their hair was white, while the regulations on building materials were still in place. It was just a fact.

But sickness and isolation had given Bobbie an attitude to life which at best could be described as courageous, and at worst, aggressive. Indeed, before Beatrice Harper had finally arrived in her life, Bobbie had long ago grown up. She had grown up in a way that children who are left by their parents to fend for themselves often do. She had appreciated that life was harsh, and that to survive she had to become determined. She was not like Miss Moncrieff. She would never show her real true inner feelings about anything, not to anyone, any more than she would grumble and moan as Miss Moncrieff did.

But Bobbie knew nothing about gardens. She had admitted as much to Miss Moncrieff after the poor woman had cooked them one of her far too early and perfectly inedible lunches.

'Do you know anything about gardens, Miss Moncrieff?'

At this Miss Moncrieff had looked immediately tired – as if Bobbie had handed her a spade.

'Oh, I don't think we need do anything at all, not until Mrs Harper comes down, or sends to tell us what to do, really I don't,' she said, sounding suddenly weak. Then she had pulled her home-knitted cardigan with its three-ply cuffs and collars closer to her, and sat down.

Bobbie walked back from the beach. Earlier she had found a bicycle, hidden at the back of what was once the stables, but was now bowed down beneath broken glass with saplings growing through it, the doors hanging to one side, sagging from rusty hinges that had long given up their onerous duty. By some miracle the brakes of the lady's bicycle

130

with its whitened straw basket and black chipped paint still worked, and so, having washed and polished it and pumped up its tyres, Bobbie set off, pushing it over the stony weed-ridden drive to the village.

Baileys Court was set well away from the village which boasted one store, one pub, and one all-important garage. First there was the drive down which she had to make her way, pushing in a stop-start fashion in order to negotiate the potholes and clumps of rough grass. In this way she managed to reach the tiny road past the woods, which finally finished up at the main road which led to the village.

At last Bobbie was able to bicycle, and the excitement she felt as she first wobbled and then straightened the bicycle and made it run in a straight line was intense. And there was a ridiculous and heightened sense of adventure in pushing the pedals down again and again, as round and round the wheels turned, and faster and faster she went, the still icy wind making tears of the water that ran from her eyes and down the side of her face.

The feeling of sudden freedom was intoxicating, so intoxicating that when at last she braked and came to an inelegant and necessarily sudden stop outside the village pub, she felt as if she had circumnavigated the world, not just bicycled two miles. And no wonder, for as she carefully dismounted from her bicycle, it came to her that this was the first time she had been really alone, quite alone, in her

131

whole life. Up until now, there had been nurses, and more nurses, and everyone either backing away from her, trying to pretend that they were not afraid of catching tuberculosis, or hovering around her. She had been a victim either of pity or of kindness, and both had been claustrophobic. Now, as she propped her bicycle up against the village shop window, after the past days of relentless rain, after the hours spent listening to Miss Moncrieff and sitting in stifling rooms filled with the smell of paraffin stoves, she felt as if she had been born again, but this time to a life that would be free of either pity or kindness. She had set off from somewhere to go somewhere, without being ordered to do so, and the feeling was out of this world.

The sign hanging on the door of the village shop proclaimed it to be shut even for the sale of Bovril, and so it was that Bobbie found herself on a late spring day, outside the pub, the garage and the village shop of Baileys Green with nothing to do but lean against a wall and watch the world go by as the sun came and went uneasily overhead.

She would have been quite resigned to sitting out the hour until two o'clock had she not been so thirsty after her bicycle ride. The sight of what seemed to be half the population of the village marching into the small inn prompted the thought – a thought which was enticing, insistent, and insidious – that she should follow their example, that she too should go in and have a drink.

She knew the very idea of someone like herself

going into a pub on her own would be perfectly shocking not just to her guardian, but to Miss Moncrieff. And yet she was so thirsty after her bicycle ride that she really thought she might not care too much. Not only that, but since being released from the sanatorium it seemed to Bobbie that she must never be afraid to do as she wanted again. She had seen death and faced him down after all, and now – well, walking into a pub was not about dying, it was all about living.

The Dog and Duck was necessarily old-fashioned. So old-fashioned that, because it was a bright spring day, the darkness of the pub's interior came as a shock to Bobbie as she pushed her way through the outer door. It was not just that the lighting, such as there was, was obviously dim, and of a very low wattage, but that the panelling, dating back perhaps two or three hundred years, was dark oak, as were the chairs and tables, and the faces of the working men and women, intent on relaxing for an hour before going back to their ploughs or their gardens.

'Major Saxby – how do you do?'

A gentleman on a bar stool, of military bearing, and a moustache of bright white that appeared even more so against a background of darkened cream walls and blackened wood, smiled at Bobbie and held out his hand.

'Bobbie Murray – how do you do?'

Bobbie smiled and, attempting a nonchalance she

133

did not feel, asked the barman for 'A beer, please.'

The Major smiled and interrupted her. 'Some beer, actually.'

'I'm sorry?'

'Some beer. You should always ask for "some" beer.'

He proffered a silver cigarette case which sprang open at a touch, and when Bobbie refused his offer promptly lit one himself, breathing in and then out with impressive gratitude.

'Thank God for a Craven A. What with no whisky, no cigarettes, no bread, and no blasted building permissions, England is worse off after the war than during it!'

Bobbie nodded understandingly, while sitting decorously on her bar stool and contemplating the half-pint of pale beer in front of her. She had never drunk beer before and as she raised the glass to her lips she was really very glad she had not, because it tasted perfectly horrible. Still, realizing that Major Saxby – judging from how many incoming locals touched their caps or greeted him with a handshake – must be someone who knew everyone, she determined on drinking the wretched half a pint, even if it took her all day.

'Bureaucracy!' The word sizzled, span, and shot across the old wood of the bar. 'Never has there been such a bad time in the whole history of England. Spivs abound! Spivs have become the heroes of the hour! Saint Crispin would be Saint Spiv in today's world!'

Bobbie looked impressed by this outburst. She liked people who fulminated. The French nurses at Hazel Hill had fulminated against everything. The Nazis, English food, English weather, the other nurses. Their black or brown eyes had been permanently fired up with indignation.

'Life nowadays,' the Major continued, 'is nothing but pettyfogging bureaucrats, pen pushers who only saw the war from behind their desks, and profiteers whose bank balances are overflowing with black market skulduggery. One wonders daily what is the bloody point? What? One gets back, there one is, back at one's cottage in Sussex, and one finds some jumped up idiot in civvies telling one that one can't rebuild the leaking bloody roof! I mean to say! Oh, *shut up, Gilbert*. What's the point? Just shut up.'

He shook his head and his whole body moved with the effort of it, as if he was some sort of damp gun dog shaking itself.

Since his tirade had come to a halt, at least for a few seconds, Bobbie said, 'I am looking for someone to help me in the garden at Baileys Court. I can dig and pull at things, and burn, and that sort of thing, but I don't know anything about gardens, not as such. You know, not as such.'

'Do you know that the other day a greengrocer was prosecuted, yes, prosecuted for selling a couple of extra pounds of potatoes that would have gone mouldy anyway? I mean what is this country coming to, Miss Murray? What?'

135

Bobbie shook her head, feeling suddenly miserable that the Major had not taken up her hint about needing help in the garden, but had thought fit merely to continue with his line of fire on the government.

'A chap in this village – *he* was prosecuted for killing one of his sheep a *day* early. I mean to say, *what?* The Nazis have not been defeated, they are still alive and running the councils, and the government, I tell you, they are. They are! *Shut up, Gilbert!* I mean, what is the point?'

'*This garden* . . .' Bobbie began again, determinedly. 'At Baileys Court. It is very difficult, because of the sea, apparently. Very difficult to grow anything by the sea, I read – almost impossible, it seems.'

'Bureaucracy breeds dishonesty, it is just a fact!' the Major went on, having paused to take a large gulp of his drink. 'You keep making tangles of everything, making people fill in forms, keeping bread out of their children's mouths, and what is the end result? *They start thinking of ways round it! There were no bread queues during the war, for God's sake!* It is just a fact. And now there are twenty thousand deserters alone living without ration books, did you know that? *Oh, shut up, Gilbert!* What is the point?'

Bobbie was just beginning to wish, and quite devoutly, that *Gilbert* really would shut up, and perhaps the Major too felt this because, of a sudden, there was a long, almost eerie silence.

'Now about this garden . . .' Gilbert Saxby smiled suddenly, and almost beatifically. 'I knew Baileys Court before the war, you know? My parents knew the Duffs who used to own it – you know both their sons were – you know, ahem? At any rate they could not bear to live there any longer, so they sold it on. But of course *they* had bought it from old Lady Bailey. Now she, poor lady, lost her three sons in the *first* set-to. But of course, before that, the Baileys had lived there since Henry VIII's time, and that was that, really. And so now you lot are there, are you? The Murrays, is it?'

'No, no – no, it's my guardian, Beatrice Harper, Mrs Harper, who has bought it, and we're living there – that is her secretary and I. We are living in the Sheds, you know, the servants' quarters? They have always been called the Sheds.'

'The Sheds. Yes, I remember them. Well, well, well. Lead the way, Miss Murray. You have quite whetted my appetite to see it all again. What's more, they have run out of beer and I have finished my lunchtime ration of one Craven A.'

Round and round the great tangles of high-grown weeds, fallen trees, and crumbling walls they walked, peering under shot saplings that had formed into a hedge, and over hedges of wild brambles that had grown as high as trees. Here they saw the remains of the great orchid house, there the remains of a greenhouse.

The Major grew more and more huffed and

puffed, but also more silent, and Bobbie too, as the vastness of the wilderness around them seemed to grow larger and larger.

'I expect you are completely put off?'

They were back by the stone-porticoed entrance to Baileys Court now, and Bobbie was looking cast down. The Major lit another Craven A and shook his head, not seeming to be able to find the necessary words to express his feelings. Bobbie had learned to be silent. She had spent weeks and months on her own for hours at a time, so silence was not intimidating to her – rather the reverse.

'No, I am not "put off", as you call it. What the devil sort of person do you think I am?' the Major demanded, frowning. 'Of course I am not put off. Far from it. As a matter of fact this is just what one needs at this moment. Something to get me out of the Dog and Duck, and a great deal better than waiting for some wretched little man from the local Nazi Party, otherwise known as the *council*, to allow me to mend my leaking roof! After the worst winter of this century, we are not allowed to even mend our own roofs. I must tell you that this is just what I need. Heaving and chopping, clearing and burning, I shall pretend it's them! Every time I chop something I shall pretend that it's one of those little Hitlers on the council.'

'You're very fierce, aren't you?'

There was a short pause before Major Saxby burst out laughing. He laughed so hard and so long that for a minute Bobbie thought that she might be going to feel insulted, until she realized that the Major's laughter was like other laughter that she had heard, from older patients at Hazel Hill. It was the laughter of someone who had not laughed enough; it was the laughter of relief; it was the laughter of someone who had laughed too little, and so long ago, that, like Bobbie and her bicycling, it had surprised him that he could still do it.

'Oh dear, whatever next!'

As soon as she saw Major Saxby and his scythe, Miss Moncrieff turned at the doorway of the Sheds, intent on going back inside. Bobbie looked out over her shoulder, already oddly excited at just the idea of somehow making the garden simply look tidier. It was as if, ahead of herself and the Major, was a kind of gigantic spring cleaning.

'Why not join us? You could cut and hack, you don't have to chop and hew.'

'Oh no, dear, I couldn't really, I couldn't. Gardening? No, dear. I do not have a garden in Ebury Street. No, dear. Not really. I wouldn't know where to begin. I am not suitable, really I am not.' Miss Moncrieff darted back inside the front door of the Sheds, pulling her cardigan even tighter around her large, low bosom. 'Besides, I am just coming round the heel of my stocking, always such an intensity of excitement.'

Bobbie shook her head, and frowned, and then bounced out towards the Major, the smoke from his Craven A already smelling somehow raffish and exciting on the cold spring air. Really, there was no dealing with poor Miss Moncrieff. She was so set in her ways. It was as if she had stepped in concrete and it had hardened around her lace-up chunky-heeled shoes and lisle stockings. Certainly there was no point in telling her that now the war was over no-one was going to wear stockings knitted on horrid little needles when they could dream of nylons. That despite the worst winter on record, most women would rather draw a line down the back of their bare legs, or rub them with gravy browning, than wear wool. It was just a fact. No point in telling her either that all the socks that the government had exhorted the women of Britain to knit for the men in the front lines had been warmly welcomed by the soldiery, and subsequently proved most useful to them – for cleaning their guns.

'I shall bring the Major back for lunch,' Bobbie called back to Miss Moncrieff. 'Mrs Duddy is bringing in eggs and brown bread, freshly made, and a little butter and cheese from under the counter, she said. And there are some onions I found in a jar, from before the war, would you believe? From before the war!'

'Oh well, if you insist.'

Bobbie rolled her eyes as she turned from Miss Moncrieff's aggrieved expression. Bobbie did not actually *insist*, as Miss Moncrieff put it, but she did think it was infinitely more exciting to be outside helping the Major to cut through the garden undergrowth, to be in the fresh air of the newly warm Sussex spring weather, rather than sitting listening to *Mrs Dale's Diary* on the wireless, as she knew that Miss Moncrieff would be looking forward to doing. *Mrs Dale* seeming, to Bobbie anyway, to be such a very ordinary kind of woman, always intent on leading the sort of life that Bobbie could never imagine anyone wishing to lead, ever. But then compared to the life that Miss Moncrieff had led, it was probably all too exciting.

Putting all thought of her guardian's secretary from her mind Bobbie ran off to follow the Major, and his Craven A, towards the main garden, the main house, and more specifically the old Norman chapel which before the war had been used for housing sheep, or cows, or some such. She was so pleased that the Major had turned up after all that she called 'Good morning' several times, long before she caught up with him.

They had arrived outside the main front door, and the Major was looking around him in amazement, as if he had landed in a nightmare, shaking his head, and pulling on his cigarette, when Bobbie realized, of a sudden, that it was really up to her to tell him what to do. She flushed with embarrassment at the thought, and looked about her as she did so, hoping that he would not notice. Perhaps he realized this for he turned back to her and said, 'I have brought my tools, don't worry. They're all in the back of my car. I hardly use it, so the coupons won't be a difficulty, not to begin with at any rate.'

He opened the boot of his old pre-war Riley and peering inside Bobbie saw that he had in fact transported what must be the whole contents of his potting sheds to the front door of Baileys Court.

'Bushwhackers, groovers, sickles and scythes, tampers, rammers and wimbles. Two in one for shears, fish oil to control scale, train oil against snail, turpentine against wasps, tobacco water against thrips, sulphur and carbolic. Enough to put a Nazi from the council off, let alone a red spider. Spades and forks all sharpened.' He looked round at Bobbie. 'Car's been jacked up on bricks until three weeks ago. No point in taking it out, not with the Dog and Duck so near. Not with the snow and the shortages, and petrol rationing and bread rationing, and everything else you can name.'

'You are kind, to bring so much—'

'Not at all. I only just got back from Burma last year, you know. I was so weak I could not have lifted my fork to my face, let alone put my foot to a spade, and of course the worst of it was, my wife died, just before I arrived home. So. You see – I kept myself together somehow, by cleaning this lot. It kept me sane, for a while, as you may imagine. Built up my strength too.'

Bobbie nodded, and there was an embarrassed silence as the Major's words seemed to hang on the air and she tried to think of the best thing to say, not the immediate thing, but the best thing, for the fact was the Major was still quite obviously not strong, having the pallid air of a man let out of prison only recently, despite the clean Sussex sea air, and the constant wind.

In the event there was nothing *to* say, nothing to add to his dreadful sense of loss, so she asked quietly, 'Do I see a dog in the back of your car, Major Saxby?'

It was his turn to nod, and opening the car door he let out a small pug dog who immediately sat down on his shoe and stared up at Bobbie, daring her, it seemed to her, to question his presence at Baileys Court.

'I would like to be able to tell you that this is my wife's dog – was my wife's dog – Miss Murray, but I do not like to lie, so I have to tell you that he is not. My wife actually liked retrievers, as a matter of fact. No, this is my dog. A lady's dog you might think, but you would be wrong. The rector who lived in the village had to go overseas, and so I inherited Boy here. And a better or more intelligent companion you would not find. As a matter of fact, as the rector told me, pugs have never really been ladies' dogs. They are Chinese, and came in on trading boats in the seventeenth century. Of course they were much taller in those days, and not so squashed in the face. Hogarth, you know, now he had a pug called Trump. Devoted to it he was. And with good reason: solid, intelligent, with sound common sense, that is a pug. Big dome, if you notice, plenty of room for brains.'

He lit another cigarette, as if overcome with the effort of such a long speech, as if it had taken a great deal of strength from him, after which the pug sneezed loudly.

'Sorry, Boy. I know.' He looked at Bobbie and shook his head. 'He can't stand my fags, you know. That's his way of telling me. He's no advertisement for cigarettes, I am afraid – sneezes every time I reach for the box.'

'You know you're going to have to be Head Gardener, don't you?' Bobbie asked him, at the same time leaning down to pat the still sneezing pug.

'Very well.' The Major cleared his throat again. 'Best if we start with clearing, I'd say. In the driveway, to begin with, or what was the driveway. We must begin at the beginning . . .'

'And go on until we stop,' they both finished together.

'I like a person who knows their Alice in Wonderland, don't you? Makes you feel you can trust them, I always say.'

There was no quarrelling with that, and so they both set to and for the rest of the morning the quiet of Baileys Court was broken only by the sound of the Major's scythe and Bobbie's fork, the pug snuffling and truffling around them, and the occasional sound of the Major lighting yet another cigarette followed by the inevitable sound of the pug sneezing.

Equally inevitably Miss Moncrieff, to fit in with her planned day around her wireless and her knitting, had announced luncheon to be at midday 'sharp'. Yards too early, Bobbie thought, but since the Major was grunting and mopping his forehead rather more than looked quite healthy, in the event midday turned out to be just the right time to stop for lunch.

Bobbie led the way back to the Sheds where she knew that Mrs Duddy would have managed to make up a small selection of things to eat, things that a farmer's wife had readily available to those persons who could be guaranteed not to betray her to the authorities. Since Bobbie had discovered that there was still heat in the old black stove during the night, between them they had devised a plan to make thrifty use of it, for the slow baking of bread, and other small necessities.

'What a place!' The Major stared round the Sheds in admiration. 'I say, Miss Murray, this place – it is superb, isn't it?'

The stone fireplace with the beam that crossed it, and the beamed ceiling above them, were dark and black with the smoke of centuries. The fireplace itself had a pair of old leather bellows hanging to the side of it, and the dogs and fire tongs were set to on its brick hearth. The walls of the sitting room were flush-beaded boards painted white to contrast with the blackened beams and fireplaces. The floor of the room, indeed the whole cottage, was uneven and made of brick, and the table upon which Bobbie now set out their communal picnic was made of country oak and rattled and wobbled as they both sat down to enjoy what there was.

Either from shyness or embarrassment that she had not been part of their gardening team, before they had even begun their repast Miss Moncrieff had already retreated to the scullery where the sounds of the wireless playing could be heard as the Major unstopped a bottle of pre-war beer which Bobbie had found among many in the back of the stone larder to the side of the kitchen.

As they ate and drank in companionable silence Bobbie wondered about the house, and eventually, her hunger assuaged, she asked the Major, 'I know the house is very old, but this place, although it doesn't look it, was all put together before the war, by the Duffs, wasn't it? Before they sold it, after . . .'

'My dear Miss Murray,' the Major said, a little thickly, 'you are quite right. This is quite new, as far as the main house is concerned. Mrs Duff, she had a really extraordinary attitude to Baileys Court. It astonished everyone. She brought everything in from somewhere else – from all over the country, like one of those film people, or that American press baron. Just imported everything. From everywhere. But you see, the strange thing is – never mind that people laughed at her at the time – the strange thing is, it works. I mean looking around us, it works, doesn't it? We would never really know that the fireplace was from Yorkshire, and the doors from the other side of Worthing. They're all in keeping. Which just goes to show something, wouldn't you say?'

146

Bobbie frowned. 'That fakes can be genuine?'

'There in one, Miss Murray. There in one. Fakes can be genuine.' He smiled at her with sudden warmth. Then he lit another cigarette and Miss Moncrieff suddenly appeared at the kitchen door and beckoned to Bobbie.

'A letter from London, dear. Mrs Harper. She is due to arrive here tomorrow.'

They both stared at each other, and then as one they looked around at the bare kitchen, trying, in their minds, to imagine Mrs Harper, French-scented, nylon-legged, her elegant figure clothed in some new Dior coat and skirt, or its equal.

'She can't come here, not now, not until we've made it better, not until we've done something to the garden,' Bobbie stated as if she owned the Sheds, and not her guardian. 'I'll ring her tonight, from the pub, and tell her. There is nowhere for her to stay. She has only ever seen Baileys Court in the snow before. She doesn't realize about the jungle that has grown up around the place since she first saw it. I'll telephone to her tonight and tell her.'

Miss Moncrieff stared at Bobbie, suddenly impressed by her firm tone, although quite obviously still panic-stricken herself; and for once Bobbie could not blame her in the least. For the truth was that the poor woman's face only reflected what Bobbie herself was feeling. The very idea of Mrs Harper staying at the Sheds was not only unimaginable, it was somehow appalling.

'Leave it to me,' she murmured to the obviously

frightened Miss Moncrieff. 'I'll put her off.'

She did not add 'I hope' but gave the poor woman an encouraging smile before returning to the garden.

As dusk fell the Major gave Bobbie a lift into Baileys Green.

'Come on, hop in, there's a good egg. Only twenty minutes till opening time.'

The sun was sinking, making a pink splash of waves and zigzags, and small dashes, such as some people put under their signatures, and with its final disappearance Bobbie climbed into the Major's car.

'Got a bit of a problem, have you not,' the Major stated, as he drove carefully around each pothole, over the humps of weeds, and every other kind of obstacle that lay across their path in the middle of the drive, until they reached the broken gates that led to the little road which itself led to Baileys Green.

'It's my guardian, Mrs Harper. She wants to come down this weekend. But she would not like it here, not now, not as it is now. It would be better if she did not come, not quite yet.'

'I know. The sort of woman who doesn't understand upset and discomfort? I know. Well, the best thing is to say that there is measles or mumps in the village or something like that. Women who dislike discomfort are usually most fearful of disease and that sort of thing. Dear me, yes. I know. The mater was like that. No. Disease is your best bet.'

The phone in the pub smelled strongly of cigarettes. As she asked to be put through to her guardian Bobbie imagined the very different type of phone that Beatrice would be putting to her ear, a new, elegant telephone with gold bits on it, possibly, or an old-fashioned one in two pieces – one of which would be held to Beatrice's brilliantly red lips. Whatever the type, Bobbie knew that there was no doubt at all that her guardian would be standing not on a cracked linoleum floor in a stone-walled corridor that led to a cellar filled with very old and dusty bottles from before the war, but on a piece of all-wool carpet, and her voice would sound dulled by the heavy silk or velvet curtains that would be at the long, floor length windows that lit her first floor reception rooms, and that as she spoke to Bobbie she would be turning at the same time to wave to a servant, or beckon to a friend, or stub out one of her American cigarettes, or watch a smoke ring that she had blown from those reddened lips lazily curling in front of her face, as Bobbie had seen her do on her few fleeting visits to the sanatorium during the war.

Such had been their relationship during the war that Beatrice Harper might, as far as Bobbie was concerned, have been a policeman checking on her, or an army official, or someone from one of the newly elected councils. Beatrice had been more than content to have telephone conversations with her self-adopted ward, Roberta Murray. To say that they had not been close would, Bobbie suddenly realized as she dialled Beatrice's telephone number, be to understate the matter. And nor had she ever had any idea why this wealthy widow should take an interest in her.

Of course she had been very busy with the WVS, as everyone during the war had been busy with something with initials – WRNS or WAAC or RAC or ARP. War children had grown up trying to muddle out which of their particular grown-ups had attached themselves to which set of initials, with only a very vague understanding as to what they did. They were just – busy. And not there. And that was how Beatrice was, or had been: very busy and not there. And quite honestly on the few occasions that Bobbie had met her, she had been really rather glad of her being busy, and not there.

'Yes?' Beatrice was always very brief on the phone.

'Measles in the village,' Bobbie said, consciously mimicking her guardian's manner. 'The charlady, everyone. Quite an outbreak.'

Beatrice Harper sighed. 'How dull.'

'Yes, it is, quite.'

'I shall have to cancel, of course. This ghastly winter, I suppose. Whatever people say about spring being here, I see no sign of it. It has brought these outbreaks, too awful. I can't think when there has been a worse winter. Not even the Savoy can produce much in the way of dinner.'

'It is spring down here, but still cold, of course.'

'I will make sure that funds are sent to the

village bank, as usual, for you, and of course Miss Moncrieff. How *is* the Bent Pin?'

'Miss Moncrieff is very well . . .'

'I must go, really I must, Roberta. Let me know how you are all coming along, and I will be down as soon as everything improves. Bless you. And don't forget to tell the Bent Pin the funds are in the bank.'

'Thank you.'

'And remember, I want the garden worked on, as much as is possible with these stupid regulations, and I want you both to keep the house as clean and tidy as possible. Have the Bent Pin sweep up the dead leaves from the halls and that sort of thing.'

Beatrice replaced the phone and Bobbie replaced hers too, neither of them bothering to say goodbye. Bobbie stared for a few seconds at the dirty walls of the corridor. For no reason that she could name she suddenly felt odd and sick, as if the sound of Beatrice's voice had brought on some kind of car sickness. Or as if her cool tones reminded her of someone or something sad. Or perhaps it was just relief that she had actually managed to put her off.

She returned to the private bar, and having been greeted with enthusiasm by the Major she sat on a tall stool and listened to him for some time talking of the good old days before the war, when the sun had shone every summer and ladies always wore lovely hats. Then, lighting her way with a torch, and feeling a great deal happier than she had when she first set out with him, she walked back to the Sheds to join Miss Moncrieff at supper.

The following morning found Bobbie watching at her bedroom window as rain swept across the Sheds and out towards the sea where it seemed to become lost in the grandeur of the waves, playing chorus to the main star, but not before it had impressed Bobbie with its insistent thrumming on the roof above her bed. Despite a remarkably congenial supper the night before, during which she had actually made Miss Moncrieff laugh, Bobbie now felt low. As low as she had felt when at Hazel Hill, for with the sudden worsening once more of the weather came the realization that there could be no gardening.

It was hardly a surprise, for it had rained all night, but this morning when she had peered out of the window she had seen that it was not just rain that was crashing around the roof and throwing itself against the windows of the Sheds, it was a gale of the kind about which the BBC would have sent out warnings on Miss Moncrieff's wireless, which now set Bobbie imagining what a comfort it must be to all the small boats out on the seas, fishing boats that had set out from harbours all around the coastlines, to hear a steady, calming, BBC voice warning them of the weather to come.

'I am going up to the house,' Bobbie told Miss Moncrieff after breakfast. 'I promised Mrs Harper that I would try to keep it swept clear of leaves and that sort of thing.'

'I dare say you can do as you say, but *I* really have enough to get on with here.' Miss Moncrieff looked distantly ahead of her at nothing at all, a habit of hers when she thought Bobbie might be going to ask her to do something that might mean venturing outside the Sheds.

'Oh, and by the way, Miss M. Mrs Harper said to tell you that your salary is being paid as usual into the bank at Baileys Green.'

Miss Moncrieff always blushed at the mention of money because it was so important to her. But the reminder brought on not just temporary embarrassment, but the inevitable ghost of Mrs Moncrieff.

'Mother, you know, dependent on me for everything. I have to send her an allowance every week without fail. A widow for so many years, without any support from my father's family, so difficult for her. Of course had I been the longed-for boy it would have been quite different, but, alas, I was not.'

'Had you been a boy you would probably be dead,' Bobbie muttered to herself, already moving away towards the start of a new day. She could not and would not, whatever happened, stay stuck in the Sheds, no matter what the weather outside. One cup of chicory coffee later and Bobbie was not only dressed, back in her green jersey and corduroy plus fours, but out of the door, hat pulled well down, dashing back up through the wilderness to Baileys Court.

*   *   *

Entering the walled garden through the side door, she paused before closing it with difficulty, the wind and the rain being still so strong. Then, head down, umbrella folded, for it was useless in the gale, she battled her way to the nearest wing of the house, reluctant to approach the main front door, which would, she knew from only a cursory glance inside, have meant pushing past leaking pipes and bare wires, stepping over puddles in the corridors and trying to ignore the sound of her own echoing feet.

Now she stood inside the entrance to the garden wing, and taking off her hat shook the rain from it, as also her old worn top coat, a fine navy blue wool garment with brass buttons that had a distinctly nautical air, but was lined, in typical extravagant Beatrice Harper fashion, with minerva – a kind of fine rabbit fur.

Bobbie had been told by the Major that, before the war, guests had used to stay in this particular wing in the greatest luxury, attended by maids and footmen dressed as medieval waiting women and pages, and indeed, as she stood there, for some reason quite unmoving, Bobbie was filled with the strangest sense that she was, despite the fact that the house was empty, actually trespassing – that all around, unseen , were people from the past waiting to observe what she was doing in *their* house.

'It's all right. I am not going to be doing anything that you would not like,' she said out loud, quite suddenly. 'I am just looking. I will not disturb anything.'

There were candles and matches left to the side of one of the windows, matches that proclaimed themselves to be from some pre-war nightclub. Bobbie picked them up and stared at the gold-engraved name on them in an absent-minded way – *Ciro's*. She slipped them into her pocket and stared round at the rest of the hallway.

Once Beatrice had purchased Baileys Court she had, with typical extravagance, the electricity in the main house and the wing turned on, but even so, after all the shortages of winter, Bobbie took the precaution of slipping some half-used candles left on a window sill into the pocket of her plus fours. Should the electricity fail, as it often did at the Sheds, she did not fancy coming down the winding, narrow, medieval staircase without any light.

She started to climb up the dark oak stairs, holding on to the dusty red rope that passed as a banister as she went. At the top of the first flight there was a narrow corridor. It was lighter outside now, the gale having abated a little, and so she pulled up the latch of the first round-topped oak door outside which she arrived, and stepped inside. It was a big, bare room with nothing in it except a strange medieval-looking wardrobe. There was no light switch, so she lit one of the candles and, curious to see the view of the gardens from above, walked across the bare, noisy boards and stared out of the window into the courtyard below.

It must have once had climbing roses and

155

old-fashioned planted borders. And although Bobbie knew that someone from the village had once been employed to try to keep the grass down during the war, they had obviously long ago given up the unequal struggle and left nature to its own devices, for the grass had been allowed to run riot, just as the walls which must once have been so solid had started to crumble with the impact of the constant gales from the sea, and the salty breezes. She had just started to imagine the garden as a place with wall fountains and sea shells set around the entrance and pots planted with bright flowers when the door of the room slammed hard shut, the latch catching and dropping, seemingly, of its own accord.

Bobbie jumped round, her hand flying to her cheek. She had no walking stick, nothing to hand, and so, for no reason she could think of, she lifted the candle and walked to the door, as if the light from it would somehow protect her from anything or anybody that might be on the other side of the round-topped door.

'Who's there?'

She called down into the winding stairwell, but there was no reply except the whistling of the wind, and the creak of other doors in other parts of the old house. Despite her determination not to show her inward fear, her inspection of the first clutch of rooms down that particular corridor became more perfunctory than it might have been, and she contented herself with standing at the entrance to each room and looking round before quickly closing the doors again. Open – shut – open – shut – and so she continued until she reached another round-topped oak door, up a short flight of stairs. Having climbed them and opened the door and looked briefly round, as with the other rooms, she just could not resist going right in, because the room was magnificent, and also strangely inviting, and unlike all the others it was partially furnished, which was surprising.

A red velvet curtain hung just inside the door, and at one of the Tudor windows was a dark oak chest, very large, and set about with brass fastenings. In the middle of the wall opposite the windows was a dark oak table bearing writing materials, a pen, some white paper and an ink well.

Bobbie, her imagination already thrilling to the idea, walked towards the oak table, curious to read the sheets of paper that were strewn about it, imagining to herself that there might be some last loving message left there from before the war by a guest, perhaps someone in love with his famous hostess, someone who had then flown off in a Spitfire, never to be seen again.

'I thought you might be put off when I slammed the door, damn it!'

Bobbie whipped round to see the vague outline of a tall, slender young man with a shock of blond – almost white – hair standing in the doorway through which she had just come. For a second time her hand flew to her cheek, but as ever when she was afraid she stood her ground. She lowered her hand, and feigned disdain as she looked at him, narrowing her eyes, and pulling herself up as straight as possible as she did so.

'What are you doing here, may I ask?'

'I said, I thought I might put you off, when I slammed that door down there! It puts off most people from the village! Damn it!'

'I am not from the village,' she told him coldly, her voice echoing in the gloom that surrounded them. 'I am not from the village. My guardian has just bought this house, and I am taking care of it for her. So will you please leave?'

The stranger stepped down the three wooden steps that led into the dark room, nodding his head agreeably.

'No, I know, I know.' He sighed. 'I know,' he said again. 'I should not be here, but there you are. It is so quiet, you see. And the house was empty all through the war, and so I am afraid I formed the habit of coming here because of its being quiet, usually so quiet, no-one around except myself.'

Outside the gale seemed to have returned with even greater force, slamming itself suddenly against the windows of the room as if it was trying to get inside, as if it was a wild, tormented person trying to gain entry and come between them.

Feeling distinctly affronted at his being there at all, Bobbie stepped back and away from the table as the stranger advanced, but at the same time she could not help feeling curious. He was very tall, and very pale, and his clothes hung off him, but they were obviously expensive clothes, or had been once, and he wore them with an oddly defiant air, as if he knew that they were strange, and did not care in the least. A cream silk shirt, black silk trousers, a deep red velvet jacket, slightly like the curtain which, Bobbie realized of a sudden, might actually belong to him, or it might be that the jacket had been cut from it, and finally, and most incongruously, on his feet he wore old, black, wellington boots.

He must have noticed her staring at his feet because he smiled.

'I wear these for trespassing through those underground corridors below,' he told her, smiling slightly. 'I wanted to frighten you off, you see.' He gave a little sigh. 'But you would not frighten, would you? I like that. I like people who are curious and not frightened, because I am always only frightened not to be curious. And frightened not to be passionate too. You know, about simply everything. I am frightened of that most of all.'

For a few seconds before he finally smiled, Bobbie had wanted very much to run away from this strange young man and his intensity, but then had come the smile. A smile which started in his large, blue eyes, and only at the very last dropped down to his mouth. As a person who has dropped from a height might find himself, of a sudden, in two minds as to whether or not to land on the ground below, so the young man's smile swung, seemingly undecided, for a few seconds between one feature and another, and it was only when it landed and his whole face lit up that Bobbie knew just where it was that she might have seen that smile before.

SUMMER FOLLOWING THAT SPRING

Chapter Six

Miranda had been expelled from her boarding school. She was most relieved. As soon as she was home she saw that her guardian, Allegra Sulgrave, was also relieved. The worst winter in anyone's memory had been followed by the hottest summer, and Allegra needed Miranda to put her gin bottles to cool in the stream that ran down the bottom of the garden. She also needed her to bicycle to and from the old ice house at Burfitt Hall, only recently vacated by the army, and left in terrible condition.

'The ice house was the one thing that they ignored, thank God,' Allegra muttered, her full lips closing over a Passing Cloud cigarette, her long-fingered hand holding its oval shape so elegantly that they all but concealed its presence, 'because the silly idiots would not know an ice house from a mad house, or a dolls' house, for that matter.'

They had returned to 'Burfers', as Allegra always called the fifteenth-century castellated house, surrounded by a moat, to take a closer look at the damage done by the now departed British army.

'War does not just kill people, it kills everything. Houses, wildlife, furniture, staircases – I mean did they really need to piddle down the stairs, one has to ask oneself? I mean was it too long a walk for the blasted idiots to make their way from the hallway to the loo? Really, the army – anyone's army – always do prove themselves to be such one hundred per cent *shits*.'

Miranda stared at the stairs at which Allegra was gazing, and then back again at her guardian's strangely affecting if ugly face with its long Plantagenet nose, its almond-shaped eyes set deep, and its general air of history preserved in one set of features – as if the face was in some way a living portrait. As usual Allegra was right. The marks from the urine had bleached a horrid little line, but that was not what was foremost in her ward's mind. What was foremost in her mind was that being brought up by Allegra had proved to be more complicated than either of them had at first envisaged. Not because they did not get on. It had taken only one look between Allegra and the tall, elegant, blond ex-Cockney child – delivered by Pamela and her American colonel that rainy afternoon what seemed like a century ago – only one glance, to confirm to the small, vibrant middle-aged aristocrat that they were twin souls.

No, where the complication lay was in the fact that Allegra, like so many patrician ladies, used the language of the barrack room and the stables as easily, and nonchalantly, as she smoked her endless

Passing Clouds in their pale pink boxes.

Miranda, under the influence of Aunt Sophie and Aunt Prudence, had learned to drop her Cockney accent and speak what they had always called *nicely*. Above all, not to use bad language, not at any time, or for any reason. In those days, which now seemed so far off, bad language had been 'bloody' and 'blasted' and 'damn'.

But then she had come to live with Allegra at the estate manager's house in Burfitt village, and bang, out went *nice* talk, and in came every kind of bad word imaginable. It had sent Miranda into great mental contortions, because if she did not use the same language as Allegra, her temporary, self-appointed guardian would not have understood her. In between 'cocktails' at lunchtime and 'cocktails' at six, Allegra spoke, rapidly and often, in a quite strange mixture of bad language and truly aristocratic, and sometimes Royal, references.

In this way it became quite natural for Miranda to grow up thinking and hearing that the Duke of so-and-so was an absolute unmentionable; or that Princess so-and-so had 'round heels' or that Mrs such-and-such was the 'by-blow' of a certain Royal personage. This did not matter at the Cottage – as the estate manager's house was known in the Sulgrave family – but it mattered terribly once Miranda had been sent to boarding school. It was only natural that, at moments of extremis, her 'Allegra-isms' *would* keep popping out. And so it was that, only recently, while Miranda had been trying to take her higher school certificate in an exam room which was actually an old air raid shelter and one of her carefully written papers had fallen to the really quite filthy floor, an extremely adult word had escaped her lips. Most unfortunately, quiet had fallen all over Norfolk at that point, and so Miranda, unsurprisingly, had been promptly and publicly expelled from her boarding school.

It had been a shame because she found school work very easy, and had really rather set her heart on becoming some sort of formidable bluestocking. Someone who would end up running a college at Oxford, firmly unmarried, tall and imperious, but just that one word, beginning as it did with the sixth letter of the English alphabet, had ruled out her academic ambitions for ever, and back she had come to Allegra, and Burfitt, and the Cottage, and all the other deprivations from which she had been rescued in a really rather comforting fashion by the strictures of boarding school.

But Miranda was nothing if not realistic, and the relief on Allegra's face when she opened the door of the Cottage had told her all. And when she had gone to the kitchen she had quickly realized that Allegra had been living off what looked rather like a form of cat food, and stuffing her soleless shoes with newspaper, rather than admit to Miranda that she could no longer afford to pay her school fees.

So, all in all, the naughty word that had escaped

Miranda's lips in the tension of the moment as she discoursed eloquently and beautifully on the dilemma of Shakespeare's Othello had been nothing but a blessing to the Honourable Mrs Sulgrave. As for Miranda, it had left her with a feeling of lingering regret, and a slight sense of having been arrested for a crime that she had not committed. But habit dies hard, and the truth was that Miranda's bad language was such second nature to her now that in moments of stress, such as an exam, or being stung by a bee, or a similar incident, the words popped not just up, but out. Besides, not to use the same language as Allegra would have been to alienate her guardian.

Not that they communicated in any particularly sophisticated manner. Their conversations were seldom of a beautifully eloquent nature. Indeed, such dialogue as they enjoyed would often be one of repetition.

This was most particularly noticeable between or after drinks time when, having drunk or smoked in silence, thankfully, for some few minutes, Allegra would, of a sudden, notice that her ward was still present – Miranda called it, quite privately, 'fire watching'.

'Don't you think that this government is one hundred per cent . . .'

Here Allegra would stop, suddenly searching wildly not just for another cigarette from the pink box beside her chair, but also for the word which would be most appropriate, all the while without turning to look at the cigarette box, but looking beseechingly across at Miranda.

'*Beastly*?'

Miranda would always start by trying something innocuous, hoping that it would be sufficient, but, like Allegra's drinks, a word like *beastly* was never strong enough.

'No!'

'*Ghastly*?'

'Miranda! No. You know. They are ...' She would click the fingers of the hand that was not holding the cigarette. 'They are – oh – what's the word! For God's sake! The government is – the government is – the government is ...'

At the inevitable clicking of her fingers, Miranda would have to give in and supply the word for which she knew her guardian was searching, experience having taught her that not to do so would mean that they would both be there all day – Allegra clicking her fingers, time and time again, and Miranda purposefully supplying every other word than the right one.

'*Shi*—?'

'That's it. God, these politicians are so – such – so – such – what was that you said? What? These politicians are ...' Click, click went the fingers.

'Idiots?'

'*No!*'

'Fools?'

'No, no, you know ...'

'Asses?'

'*Arses!* That's right. They are *arses*! Horses' *arses*! That is it, absolutely. You must admit. That is right! I mean to say! We have fought a war and we have won. But. What now? Things are worse than ever before. We never had any bread queues during the *war*. We never had such deprivations as we have now. But now. Now we have won the bloody war and what happens – no bread, nothing but rations, rations, rations. And no housing. Housing is left in charge of little Hitlers called *councils*, and *spivs* not fighter pilots are the heroes of the hour. It is not just preposterous, it is perfectly and absolutely *bloody*!'

Following these outbursts Allegra would promptly fall asleep with the Passing Cloud ash nearly a foot long, and dangerously close to setting her chair alight. In fact, once she was home from boarding school, Miranda realized that it was most probably just as well, for Allegra seemed determined to put danger first, and when she was not smoking and drinking, swearing about the government or driving her pre-war Austin 7 into a ditch, she was busy nearly setting fire to herself and the Cottage.

Even now, as Miranda turned round to see if she was all right, the ash of Allegra's Passing Cloud, as was her inveterate habit, was growing longer and longer, and longer. As long as the fingers that were holding it. And its oval shape, so admirably suited to the shape of a woman's mouth, was getting perilously diminished, so that very soon, it seemed to her ward, Allegra herself, or her deep red mouth, would become horribly burned.

'*Fire!*'

'Thank you, darling.'

They had developed this code for public moments, but now, since they rarely saw anyone, its use had extended to private moments too. Possibly because it was such an emotive word, Miranda had found that Allegra responded to it almost at once. In the same way that her old retriever responded to 'Hup!' and 'Fetch it!' his owner responded to 'Fire!' and would promptly put out the remains of her cigarette in a small gold box that she always carried in her old, worn, crocodile handbag.

'This is one of those moments.' Allegra breathed in and out very slowly, and then finally, and inevitably, started to cough. 'This is one of those moments when everything one has ever dreaded in life seems to have come to pass.' For a brief second, as Miranda, despite the heat outside, shivered in the cold and the damp of Burfitt's old kitchens, and heard the inevitable drip, drip of water leaking in a scullery somewhere, she thought she heard another sound too, that of Allegra's voice trembling, a bat's wing of a sound. But as quickly as the sound had escaped she had lit another cigarette, and they continued on. 'What will it take to bring this place back to life? And who will be able to do it for me?'

They had come to a standstill, unfortunately, because at these words Miranda's feet could be seen to be shifting uncomfortably. Was she meant now to be not just a 'Mowbray', which she palpably was not, but – a *Sulgrave* too? She prayed that she was not.

And yet, who else was there to help Allegra put the place to rights? Her brothers had both been killed in the First World War, and now, with the end of the Second, there was only Miranda left, for Allegra's husband had been killed in North Africa – *tanks, you know* – and her two sisters too had died in the war. One had been blown up in an air raid by a doodlebug, and the other while driving a Polish general somewhere or other – although where Miranda never could make out. Having been a favourite of her eldest sister, Allegra never mentioned her name without turning away and having a coughing fit, to cover the moment, perhaps, or just because she found the idea of her not being still alive so unbearable that even her body turned away from the thought.

'I can help you look after Burfers – if you would like?'

There, the words were out, and having uttered them Miranda felt terribly brave. She would, she resolved, take on Burfitt Hall, and help Allegra to restore it to its former glory.

'Don't be silly, Randy darling.'

Allegra gave her sudden and brilliant smile and turned away once more, shaking her head.

Having been very brave, and, as it were, volunteered her services, nearly dedicated her life to

Burfitt Hall, to be refused seemed suddenly insulting, and hurtful.

'I am not being silly. I will do everything we can – *I* can – to help you get the old place back on its feet again.'

'Miranda.' Having walked thankfully back into the sunshine again, Allegra sat down suddenly on the bench outside. 'Miranda, do you realize how big Burfitt is? No, of course you don't. No, so I will tell you, and then we can talk.'

She paused to light another cigarette, and as she began to talk again she puffed and puffed, talking between puffs, so that the general effect was of a steam engine at rest on a bench.

'Burfitt Hall is eighty foot high to its turret tops. It has two towers, as you may have noticed, it has a gatehouse, a moat which surrounds it on all four sides, and ten acres of gardens, not counting the walled vegetable garden. It has three kitchens, and seven sculleries. It is acknowledged as being one of the jewels of fifteenth-century architecture, and yet – it is untenable. I will have to sell it. The council knows this. I know it. But to whom, Randy darling? To whom can I *possibly* sell my old family home?'

'I will marry a millionaire and buy it for you.'

'Bless you, but you could not possibly take this on. Not even a millionaire would want it, darling. No. It has to be faced. It is an impossible house, and by the time the building restrictions are lifted it will be quite, quite unliveable, unrestorable – undesirable for anyone to live in, or buy.'

'I will marry a millionaire and come and live in it and you will too – live in it, I mean – and we will live happily ever after, as everyone must who lives at Burfitt.'

Miranda had made her little speech standing on the other end of the bench and poised as if she was about to take off like Mustard Seed, a part she had played in the Christmas production at the village hall. Now she lifted her bright blond head towards the brilliant sun. She was just about to go on, but on hearing a terrible sound she looked down.

Allegra, her head sunk in hands bereft of even a Passing Cloud, was crying not as if her heart would break, but as if it had long ago been broken and was quite beyond repair.

Miranda knew better than to try to comfort her. Instead, she reached into her guardian's crocodile handbag and taking one of Allegra's cigarettes she lit it and went for a walk around the moat.

Later, at drinks time, back at the Cottage, Allegra announced, 'Bless you for trying to think of things, Randy darling, but really, you will have to leave Burfitt and go to London. Not at once, of course – no-one goes to London in August – but once September is upon us, you must go, for the truth of the matter is that there is nothing for you here now. And let's face it, you are of an age to go to London. I am afraid doing the Season is out of the question, but I can have you lodged in a top floor flat, the lease of which we still own, near Cadogan Square.

A nice enough area, although not Mayfair. I can, at least, do that for you. Now, we must, I am afraid, call in some silly arse and ask him to value Burfers for us, and then up for sale it must go, poor old thing. Nothing else to be done. Top up the gin in this, bless you. I can't even taste it, darling.'

For a moment, as the train crawled, creaking and swaying, into the station, Miranda realized that she could not remember London. The last time she had seen it was from the window of the staff car that had been sent to fetch her and Pamela and the delightful American colonel, whose name she could not now remember, and take them all to Norfolk. Now, in the early evening light, Miranda began to remember. She remembered the sooty smell, and now dimly she recalled living somewhere very small, with her granny who had gone loony, and how she had then started to be left at different places, first by the sea with some people that she could not remember, and then in London again, and then with the darling aunts in Mellaston.

She turned away from that thought as she climbed out of the Ladies Only carriage. She had long ago decided to forget Mellaston and the aunts, and her brother, and Bobbie. Neither Teddy nor Bobbie had bothered to write to her, and although she had tried to write to Teddy, he had never written back, and so that had been that. She thought of him as dead. Which, the war being the war, he very probably was, or might be. And Bobbie too,

174

because Mrs Eglantine had kept saying *Bobbie is a very sick little girl*. She remembered that very well. Poor Bobbie. She must be dead, as so many people seemed to be.

She peered at the address in her hand. Number twenty-four Aubrey Close, it read. Nothing to do with Cadogan Square, for of course Allegra had managed to get that wrong too. Mrs Sulgrave's family had not owned any top flat, but in the event still had the freehold of this studio flat – or house or whatever it was – in Aubrey Close.

'Kensington, I am afraid, darling. Not at all chic or modish, but it will be a roof over your head, anyway to start with. When you have found your feet, or a millionaire, you can take it over, but until then I will be sure to have the trustees keep up the upkeep for you, or whatever it is you have to do in these circumstances.'

Allegra had no idea at all about money. It was just a fact. It was not something about which she ever talked, except in a quite roundabout way, and if she did it was always with a look in her eyes which said, 'This is disgusting.' Miranda had pretty soon realized that this was how she had to be too. It was sometimes confusing. If she came back from the village, for instance, and there had not been enough money to buy more gin from the black market man who supplied the whole countryside, if not the universe, Miranda quickly knew *never* to say, 'We did not have enough money for it today.' Instead she learned to say, 'They have run out of gin, I am afraid.' Although they both knew this could not possibly be true, it was an understanding, and the next time she was sent to the village Allegra would simply make sure to hand Miranda a purse with double the amount.

Now she climbed out of the taxi and stood on the pavement as the driver climbed out too and started to heave her trunk out of his cab. A passerby, seeing how large and heavy the old leather portmanteau was, stopped, and took the worn handle of the other end before Miranda could do so.

'Thank you so much! Thank you!'

The passerby touched his hat and walked on.

'That was very kind of him.' Miranda stared after the stranger.

'You're in Kensington now, miss. Most folk are kind in Kensington, I think you will find. It's the backwater, see – of London, that is. Not fashionable like Mayfair, nothing like that, but a nice place to live, I think you'll find. Particularly the park, and of course round here, well, it's really rural, isn't it?'

The driver looked round admiringly at the broad road and the trees that lined it, and then up again at the house outside which they were both standing.

'I am quite sure you're right, it is rural.'

Miranda too looked round, but of course to her, after the endless skies of Norfolk, after the marvel of seeing for ever, and sometimes farther than that, after the pretty villages with their neatness and air of prosperous calm, after the feeling that the sea was not very far, and then again, when she was on the beach, that the countryside was just near, Kensington to her seemed tightly packed, crammed with lamp posts, and almost airless. Where would she run about as she had done on the beaches in Norfolk? How would she see birds migrating, as she had done, or returning, which was always such a joy once spring was upon them? Of a sudden she wanted the driver to come into number twenty-four Aubrey Close with her, to stand beside her and reassure her that she was actually going to enjoy Kensington.

'Thank you so much.'

The door opened with difficulty, as all doors that have not been opened regularly seem to, and all at once the driver had gone, and the sound of his taxi was fading as Miranda searched and found a light switch, and turned it on.

What she saw around her made her gasp. It would have been a noisy, out loud kind of gasp, had she not been alone. Allegra in her usual fashion had said nothing of the kind of property to which Miranda was coming. She had said nothing about the rooms, or their disposition, but only, 'It's a family property, bless you. And you know, you will be quite safe there. There is nothing to worry about, and no-one to worry you either, because it's in a backwater. One of the old artistic quarters of Kensington. Lots of painters lived around there, and loved around there too, darling, but, you know, it is only Kensington, it's not Mayfair, I am afraid.

Your friends will probably have to pack their hotties into their motor cars and bring picnics when they come to visit, but that is the best we can do. My family has *never* been rich, but we do come up with the occasional property, darling, and old Aubers Close is one of them.'

'You are too kind to me, really you are.'

'No, darling, just bless you for not minding it's not Mayfair.'

Not minding it's not Mayfair! Miranda stared round. Not minding it's not Mayfair, wherever that was! She not only did not mind that it was not Mayfair, she could not have cared less, for, she realized, as the stood in the great room into which the second locked door had finally opened – she was in paradise.

Because it was entered from a narrow London pavement, with hardly a piece of railing or a strip of garden in front of it, because, at first, it seemed to have a façade only slightly different from any other façade in the street, the interior of number twenty-four Aubrey Close was all the more surprising. The windows that gave upon the road were not remarkable, for they were the windows of the upper bedrooms and the lower lobby. Where the windows became remarkable was where they gave upon the rounded, paved garden at the back, where they became decorative, colourful, and also, to an eye coming straight from the clear air of Norfolk, somehow claustrophobic in their vibrant colouring. Ambers, reds and deep blues coloured the feminine figures depicted in the glass of those great, tall windows. That they were without any doubt the work of some artistic genius was, to Miranda's eyes, indubitable, but that they were the vision of someone who saw women in some assumed, angelic, but trance-like state was also true.

As she stared up at them she realized that the women all had red-gold hair which they wore to well below their shoulders, and some of their heads were banded with gold; and their long dresses – they too were encircled with plaited gold belts that ended in tassels, and their feet were sandalled, showing toes that seemed, to Miranda anyway, to be more like the toes you saw on tombs than ones on real women. And when she turned from them she saw that the rest of the room was in keeping with the church-like windows. The fireplace was of dark oak, and a close look revealed it to be decorated with carvings of angels. The tiles beneath it were made up of dark colours, and obviously hand-painted so that few of them were the same. There too saints and angels predominated, their hands held together in a praying position, or holding thin gold trumpets ready to serenade the Lord should He appear to them.

From the bare essentials of the room Miranda now turned her attention to the furniture: tall pews in a light wood, hand-carved ends of complications which at first seemed merely to be linking scrolls and initials, but on closer examination proved to be birds and leaves, and tiny figures of angels.

Up one side of the great room ran a substantial staircase, and dark wooden bookcases, filled with books that glowed with the names of old authors and their works, telling of another age when there was time to examine the old truths. Miranda picked one small volume out, the essays of Joseph Addison. It was inscribed to a 'Maria', and the cover was engraved in a dull gold the initial M and in and around the corners of the book and on the back around yet another M were clover leaves delicately engraved. After a few seconds Miranda replaced the small volume and as she did so she realized with a start what the grand difference was between these books and the books at Burfitt – these were not damp and their pages not stained.

At the top of the substantial staircase was a wide landing. From it Miranda could gaze down onto the great room with its vast colourful windows below. In one corner were piled old trunks, which when she opened them she found to hold costumes of every kind smelling of lavender and mothballs, and wrapped in black tissue paper.

Ever since the days of the wartime excitements at the Clothes Exchange in Mellaston, there was nothing that Miranda enjoyed more than the glorious pursuit of beautiful or stylish clothes from another era. She sometimes thought she might faint away from the pleasure of finding a silver-threaded scarf, as she had just done, and placing it around her neck, as she was now doing. It weighed heavy and the silver in it was dully beautiful, the ends sewn in such a way that they were rounded.

Eventually she climbed down from her orgy of picking out and holding against herself the old clothes of beautiful young women from before both the awful twentieth-century wars, and feeling a little dizzy went in search of a glass of water.

Entering the small kitchen she could see that every jug and every cup, every kind of utensil, was old-fashioned or carved with strange symbols. Silver knives and forks in the kitchen drawers were wrapped in special cloths, and the glass she chose to drink her water from was engraved with a peacock, its great tail feathers fanning out from the bird to reach right round the glass.

From the kitchen Miranda went quickly back into the main room, the studio room – for that essentially was what it was – and stood gazing around her, yet again marvelling at the luck of finding herself in this strange paradise with its cornucopia of brilliant objects. The trunks with their yellowing labels which proclaimed that they had at some time or another visited Penang and Delhi, or Edinburgh, or Paris. The old engraved glasses filled with dust and not wine, waiting to be raised once again. The picture frames stacked one against the other, also empty, their old, gilded carving faded.

It was as she was still standing breathing in the dust-filled air that yet at the same time exuded that particular kind of fragrance that only comes from good, old, seasoned wood that her guardian's reticence, her reluctance to explain Aubrey Close fully to her ward, started to become clear. And it came to Miranda that the house must once have belonged to one of Allegra's sisters – perhaps her much mourned eldest sister? Or perhaps to the middle sister who was rumoured to have been, as Allegra always put it, *hopelessly artistic*? Whoever had owned it, it had been given to Miranda to live there until such time as she *found her feet*, which Miranda knew was Allegra's way of saying until such time as Miranda might decide to marry.

But Miranda knew what Allegra did not, namely that she did not want to marry, not ever, ever, ever. She had always known that she was not the marrying kind, and had gazed in amazement at girls at school as they happily spent hour upon hour designing their ideal wedding dresses, or talking about what good wives they intended to be. No, she wanted to be anything except just someone's wife – the *trouble and strife*, as her grandmother had used to put it when she was tiny. *I'm just his trouble and strife. I can't sign nothin' for you*, she'd tell house-to-house callers as Miranda clung to her flowered apron staring up at everyone from the Breton onion sellers to the shoe-shine men, or the knife grinders.

She gazed up at the windows again before turning to her own trunks and beginning to unpack, before going to find the bedrooms and doing all those statutory things, like bouncing on the beds by turn to find which one was most comfortable. Before all that she stood still, staring up at the saintlike figures that dominated the studio room.

She dared swear that those women portrayed up there had been, at some time, poor souls, a wife to someone or another. And where had it got them? Enshrined in a window, their bare toes peeping from apostles' sandals, their waxen fingers clasping lilies or held in praying positions. They were not women, they were saints and angels, nothing to do with glorious reality, or, more important, freedom.

Bobbie stared at the Major. He had just lit his tenth Craven A cigarette for that morning. She knew this, because she had made a bet with her new friend Julian that he would reach fifteen before they all stopped for lunch at midday.

The terrible thing was that once the bet was struck they had, inevitably, found themselves a great deal more interested in the Major's lighting up times than they were in helping him to chop and stack the fallen trees that littered the garden leading down to the beach.

'I dare say it is going to take us a good many weeks to clear this lot.'

'That's right.' Bobbie bent down to pick up and throw a piece of rusting metal into her wheelbarrow. 'It is strange, though, that all the trees fell over, because I mean to say, if you look at them, they really are quite old. At least they look quite mature, don't they?'

'It is because, before the war, they imported them all. You'd never find trees of this kind normally by the seaside. Look at the rusting girders. You don't see girders holding up trees as a rule, do you? Well, that is it, do you see, Bobbie? The family imported all the trees to look decorative and to make their restored monastery look acceptably park-like, and they put these girders round 'em to stop them falling over, and the result is they *did* fall over, once the girders had been eaten away with rust. Albeit it took them a quarter of a century *to* fall over, fall over they did.'

They all looked down at the rusted girder, and although it was summer, Julian coughed, and after that he laughed at some new thought, a habit of his. Sometimes, Bobbie had noticed, he laughed with an almost ecstatic happiness, as if he was hugging some wonderful notion to him, and finally she said, to fill in the moment, 'Tell you what I think. These trees are emblems, they stand for the aristocracy, don't you see?'

'No, I am afraid I do not, young Bobbie.'

The Major pulled heavily on his cigarette, and Bobbie wondered if she was about to lose her two shillings and whether he would light another one straight away, because it was entirely possible, considering the way he was smoking this one.

'Oh, they are emblematic all right, and I will tell you exactly why—'

'Sounds too damn intellectual for my tastes. Rust is rust, *if* you like.'

'Of course rust is rust,' Bobbie agreed. 'Rust is rust is rust is rust, *but—*' and here she opened her eyes wide and stared across at the Major before smiling in angelic docility. 'But,' she went on, dropping her voice, 'life is much more fun if we think of it as something *other*. It is just a fact.'

'Oh, very well, but if you ask me you'll be wearing a black beret and singing sad songs in a Parisian *boit de nuit*, some nightclub with black-frocked women, if all this goes on much further!'

'Are you ready, both of you?'

'Yes.' Julian smiled while at the same time he made sure to boss his eyes at Bobbie behind the Major's back to make her laugh.

'Get on with it, dear bean, really,' the Major begged, and then looking down at the pug he said, 'Boy old bean, better block your ears at this.'

'Very well, these trees,' Bobbie said, well pleased with the silence that now surrounded her, 'these trees, if you will imagine, if you would, please, that these trees, these trees – they are the *Normans*, because they do not, as we know, grow here of their own accord, they have been imported. They are the Normans, therefore, the invaders of plain, beautiful Anglo-Saxon England.'

'Fair enough,' the Major agreed, suddenly more interested, and lighting a cigarette.

'And the girders, they are the *law*.'

'Good,' the Major agreed. 'They are our impeccable legal system which has been in place since the Court of the Star Chamber, in good old Henry the

Seventh's days. Very well, dear bean, I get your drift.'

'Then we come to the *rust*. The rust is the two world wars we have suffered in the twentieth century. The rust therefore has induced the ancient, stable, Anglo-Saxon world, which has lasted nearly ten centuries, to fall over.'

The Major looked down again at Boy. 'It's all right, you can listen to this, old thing. Nothing too shocking for pug's ears here. As a matter of fact, old bean, I think you have a rather good thing here, in your emblem, really I think you have. Not as much codswallop as I imagined, dear bean.'

After which he smiled at Bobbie, and went back to his handsaw, while Julian too smiled, but only at Bobbie, opening his blue eyes a great deal wider than is normal.

It was at these moments that Bobbie realized what a mischievous look Julian had to his face. And not just his face – his whole aura was mischievous. He had long ago captivated Bobbie's imagination with his inventions, his dares, above all his ability to make a game out of nothing.

Julian's mischief was part of his permanent sense of *cocking a snook* at life – as Mrs Dingwall would often call it when Bobbie was living with her – and it was most particularly intoxicating to Bobbie. She really loved Julian for *cocking a snook* at everything. It made sense of him, and in a strange way it made sense of Bobbie too. It helped them both get by.

Of course at that particular moment, as she tried

to keep a straight face, Bobbie realized that she had really rather meant what she said, that, when you looked at it, it was like something in a painting, something that an artist would use as a symbol. All the fallen trees, the rusted girders, everything – it was very like England, with the fallen trees representing the old world of country house life, of servants and privilege.

And not only that, but, now she came to think of it, comparing the rust to the two world wars did seem very apt, because really, everywhere you looked in England now, everything did seem to be rusted through. Hardly a thing was not dull, or drab and sad, outside Baileys Court and Baileys Green, that is. The only way forward was to try to plant something different, something that would not need a great iron girder around it to keep it in place, something that would grow on its own, without support from outside.

'Will Mrs Harper have to import more trees again and hope that they will grow this time?' Bobbie asked, and this time it was she who bossed her eyes back at Julian, as the Major lit up his eleventh cigarette of the morning.

'Oh yes, thousands more. Well, anyway, hundreds. After all not even wild flowers will grow around here, only gorse and more gorse, and yet more – gorse.'

Julian laughed, mockingly, as always, and then, perhaps because the Major had lit yet another cigarette and the smoke smelt strong and acrid on the air compared to the subtle, sweet smells of wild flowers and the sea, he started to cough. Bobbie looked anxiously towards the Major, but if and when Julian coughed in front of him, the Major always seemed not to notice and would merely stroll off pulling on a cigarette, or whistling some tune he and his friends had whistled when they worked as prisoners of war on the Burma railway.

Often, at night – when they had all decided to stroll around the gardens together for what the Major called his 'last gasp' – Bobbie and Julian talked to him about *his war*, and he would tell them about the fall of Singapore and then Burma and the camps, and how he and all the other young Englishmen what he called *coped*.

Bobbie know that he did this to make sure that she and Julian understood how lucky they all were, to be there, to have freedom, to be able to work in a garden, or build walls as they were now doing, even if it was with cement smuggled to them by someone in the village, and sand the same, and bricks too. They were lucky, so lucky, because they were all still alive.

When Bobbie had first seen Julian standing in the great red-curtained room in the wing of Baileys Court she had, for a second, thought – no, that was really too weak a word – she had *longed* for him to be Teddy, all grown up, and come alive again in front of her.

It would be false and untrue to herself not to admit that there had been something about Julian's smile, something about his odd clothes, but most of all about his white-blond hair that had made her think for a few dizzy seconds that her wartime brother had materialized in front of her in that dark room. But of course he had not, and at that moment of meeting with Julian she had known suddenly that it was ridiculous to even think of Teddy again. Teddy was most likely, was almost certainly, dead by now. Shot, or blown up, something like that, because he was a boy, and that was what happened to boys, probably even before they were old enough to go into the army and be killed. It was the English way of life, one of the French nurses had explained to Bobbie – to bring up their sons to be killed for the Empire and England.

Of course as soon as she had realized that Julian really did want to live at Baileys Court all the time, for ever and ever, but would have his tongue cut out rather than admit to it, Bobbie had arranged with Miss Moncrieff to have him made up a bed in the garden wing of the house, in the room where Bobbie had first found him, and where for one glorious second she had thought he might be Teddy, come back to her, somehow finding her again – not in the bright pink dress and bright green cardigan and silver shoes of the much lamented Marion Dingwall, but in her own clothes, the kind of clothes they had used to wear in Mellaston, at the rectory – faded clothes of marvellous old-fashioned materials that had been softened by age.

Naturally, Baileys Court was different from Mellaston, quite different, and Bobbie very different too, thank goodness. For what with the marvellous hot summer, and the sea so cool to bathe in, she and Julian, between working in the garden and building walls, could wear practically nothing, and did. Even the Major now wore only shorts and a shirt and bare legs, uncaring how he looked. Only Miss Moncrieff remained in her twinsets, buttoned up and hatted.

At Julian's urging, Bobbie had asked the Major to come and stay in the old house.

'Too much for the old chap to be asked to drive in every day, what with petrol coupons and everything. And it'll kill him to keep bicycling in this weather. Let him come and stay in the house, but well away from me. He wouldn't want to be near me, especially not in the night when I prowl about, writing verse.'

It took little prompting for the Major to make his 'quarters', as he called his bedroom, on the ground floor of the main wing, near to where the old spider-ridden bathrooms, once used by the staff, were housed. The two men were so far apart from each other that the Major joked to Bobbie that he never met Julian in the house.

'Splendid chap, though.'

He always said that about Julian, and when he did an odd look came into his eyes and he patted Bobbie on the shoulder in a kindly way.

'I expect,' Bobbie said once or twice to Julian,

'you wish that the Major wouldn't be so marvellously nice to you. I know I do, often. It makes you feel all gooey, doesn't it? I am often fine, until I meet with the Major's kindness, and then whoosh, I feel sorry for myself. He really must stop being so nice, don't you think?'

At this Julian smiled, slightly raising his blond eyebrows, his blue eyes staring not at Bobbie but straight ahead to what Bobbie sometimes called 'our wobbly future', because they both knew that neither of them was quite as well as they should be, not quite. Getting better, but not quite the thing yet.

'Don't worry, though,' Bobbie went on bracingly. 'I'm so nasty I'll make up for all the Major's *gooeyness*. As a matter of fact I don't feel sorry for you in the least. Probably because I know you to be just a palsied poet of no fixed abode. I say – do you think that the Major's going to make an honest woman of Miss Moncrieff?'

They were walking down to the beach now with their picnic lunch, leaving the Major to wander off to the Sheds where he would be welcomed by Miss Moncrieff, who would serve him some form of the fresh kippers that he so adored for his lunch and some of Mrs Duddy's home-made brown bread, and even some butter.

'No, I don't think he is going to make an honest woman of her.' Julian sat down on the stones of the shore and stared out at the sea as if he could see far away to something that no-one else could, as if he was looking to something that was beckoning to him.

There were still fortifications left to rot at their back, but before them was sea enough and beach enough for them to swim and enjoy themselves at lunchtime, while the Major ate and drank with Miss Moncrieff, who, to the amazement of both Bobbie and Julian, seemed, under the Major's influence, to have taken up the last two habits with alacrity.

'The Major is not going to make an honest woman of Miss Moncrieff, for the good reason that he has not yet made a *dishonest* woman of her.'

As Bobbie unpacked their picnic they both started to laugh.

'I can't imagine them even holding hands—' Bobbie stopped, frowning. As a matter of fact she could not imagine *anything* to do with anything. She reddened slightly, staring at the silver salt pot in her hand. There was little use in asking Julian if he could imagine anything more, since he was a very ill boy and probably very ill boys did not even think of things like that.

'I think about love and passion all the time, do you, Bobbie?'

Bobbie looked up. 'I'm sorry?'

'I said – I think about love and passion all the time, but it's because of my condition, apparently, so you are quite safe with me, Roberta Murray of the long brown hair. Do you know that I have written a poem to your long brown hair, but you shall not read it until I am gone.'

'Oh, do stop talking about *going*,' Bobbie said, crossly. 'Besides,' she added with her usual show of pragmatism, 'you can't *go* until the garden is finished.'

They had become a little team during those early summer months, building walls, planting what flowers they could, hiding from the 'authorities' their newly built walls, draping them with fallen trees and rubble which could be removed the moment some spy or other from the council, or wherever, went away.

'I don't know why we bothered to fight the Nazis,' the Major would mutter after some new swoop from some new bureaucrat, 'it seems to me we've fought one lot and got rid of them only to replace them with a home-grown set. We have our very own Nazis in our midst now, and they've got us all shouting *Sieg Heil* with the rest of the mob – it makes you sick, really it does. The trouble with these bureaucrats is that they get everything so dead *wrong*. They simply can't see beyond their own noses. What is worse is that their thin skins and their prejudices are so apparent that they can put up more backs, cause more harm to the democratic way of life to which we all aspire, than a château filled with blasted Marie *Antoinettes*.'

After one of his long speeches the Major would usually stomp off to have lunch with Miss Moncrieff, leaving Bobbie and Julian together, nearly always staring after him in some bewilderment. They soon stopped worrying, however, and now, with the sun so hot, and the sea beckoning, and no-one else around to frown, neither of them thought anything of wriggling about under towels and changing into bathing things in front of each other. Probably because they were such friends, or perhaps because she had always 'shared' with Teddy and Miranda during the war, Bobbie found that they were not self-conscious at all. She at least thought nothing of changing in front of Julian, and nor it seemed did Julian.

More than that, they were, in so many ways, twin souls. They each knew precisely how the other felt, and the joy of this, the whole marvel of it, made Bobbie want to run up and down the beach shouting, just as they occasionally saw dogs running up and down along the shore, pretending that they were being chased by the waves which crept, or, on stormy days, cantered, up the shingle, before turning with the undertow, and following it back down again, barking all the time, just for the sheer joy of, the utter marvel of, living.

Sometimes, at night after dinner, and after they had walked from the Sheds across the garden, and then into the main house, dropping off the Major en route, Julian and Bobbie would walk arm in arm down the long thin underground passageway that linked the main house to the courtyard of the garden wing – a corridor built long ago as an escape route for the monks and left over from the days of the persecution of the Catholics. There in the wing, where Julian felt so at home, after a kiss of his

194

fingertips to her from the crooked winding dark stairway, he would disappear up to what he called his 'eyrie', leaving Bobbie to battle with a strong desire to follow him up and keep him company during what she knew might often be a long, wakeful night.

But knowing that Julian would not want that, that it would induce in him the kind of claustrophobia that she herself would feel when people were too kind to her, Bobbie would once more wander back down the secret underground corridor, imagining to herself the monks hurrying through that same passageway, their hearts beating with terror, fleeing from the sound of the soldiers of the government arriving to search the house, escaping from the men who were waiting to torture them. Thinking on these things she would climb back up the stairs into the main house, and eventually into the warm night air of the garden.

And so it was that, for most of the past nights, finding herself quite alone and filled with that particular sense of restless excitement that makes even the thought of sleep impossible, Bobbie would find it ridiculous to return directly to the Sheds and the gentle rhythmic snoring of Miss Moncrieff. She simply could not. She felt too full up with some emotion that she could not name. Instead she would walk across what had been, before the war, the front drive, to the hay barns that lay beyond, and pushing open the old, battered, protesting doors she would fling herself into the new-cut hay and roll about in it, hugging herself, filled with the joy of just knowing Julian.

After this she would lie for many minutes remembering various moments of the day that had gone, its colours and its pleasures running through her mind. The way Julian would boss his eyes at her behind the Major's back when the older man was lecturing them on some new subject. The way he would swim with her, read aloud to her from books by authors of whom she had never heard, and talk to her about the life of the spirit, making her listen with him to those sounds that can only be heard when, as Julian maintained, the soul is reaching towards unseen horizons, beyond the gross, greedy grasp of the material world, to where the rhythms of life make a music that speaks only of lightness of being, where there are only heavenly sounds.

Julian was not only Bobbie's first friend of her own age, for years and years, she was his too. And although they never spoke about the places in which they had both been incarcerated during the war, or about what it had been like to be a small child locked up for month after month with older people – older people who were often mortally sick and ill – Bobbie imagined that for Julian, as for herself, childhood must have been a kind of hell. Nothing but kindness, and pity, nothing but people pretending that he was not ill, that he would get better, that he was, one day, going to be just like other little boys and run about and play games and not have fevers and a never-ending cough.

For all these reasons Bobbie could never bring herself to go straight home to bed, but lay in the newly cut hay thinking that if she waited just a little longer she might hear the sounds of which Julian had spoken so often; but she never did.

Beatrice was speaking in her usual commanding way.

'Miss Moncrieff has written to me that you are very well, and she thinks you have grown this summer, and certainly look much better. Is there still measles about? I am off to the South of France to stay with Pansy and Mikey Holbrook, but when I come back I am determined that I shall come down to Baileys, measles or no measles.'

That dread of all dreads, a letter asking her to make a telephone call to her guardian, had Bobbie standing once more in the village pub at Baileys Green staring at the dirty cream-painted wall, looking towards the dusty barrel-filled cellars, hearing the sound of darts hitting a darts board, and male voices making speeches with ever mounting passion – against the government, against the council, against rationing and deprivation, the voices always wondering over and over what they had all fought and won the war *for*?

'I am also sending you a parcel of clothes,' Beatrice continued. 'The New Look should suit you, but of course there are other things too. I will require you to acknowledge their arrival, please, Roberta.'

Bobbie nodded silently into the phone which, as always, smelt dreadfully of cheap cigarettes.

'Thank you very much.'

'No need to thank me, Roberta. Just make sure you are wearing something that I have sent you when I come down, would you? It is always such a compliment, remember, when one wears something another has gifted to you.'

They ended their telephone call, as always, with a brevity of small exchanges that would have done credit to a Morse code message. Sometimes it seemed to Bobbie that the always beautiful, entirely competitive Beatrice was actually competing as to who could most swiftly put a stop to the telephone conversation.

'Is your guardian well?' the Major wanted to know, as Bobbie returned to the private bar to rejoin him and Julian.

'Very.'

'In that case why so glum, chum?'

Bobbie shook her head and smiled at Julian. She might look glum but she certainly was not going to go on feeling it. The truth was that she knew, logically, that she could put off being glum for quite a few precious weeks yet, weeks when Beatrice would be staying with one or another of her friends in the south of France, but after that Beatrice would be down, and Bobbie hated to think of how much that would change everything. It was not that she was not grateful to Beatrice, for everything, but when all was said and done – she was nevertheless *Beatrice*.

Certainly once Beatrice was down it would not be possible for the Major and Julian to stay on camping at the house. Nor would it be possible for the Major and Miss Moncrieff to continue to lunch together on the Major's smuggled gin and endless supply of cigarettes whilst listening to *Mrs Dale's Diary*, or whatever they enjoyed listening to together. All these delights would have to stop as Beatrice, seated on a great dark cloud of authority and possession, would descend like Cleopatra on Baileys Court, and Miss Moncrieff would once again be called into play to take notes and make telephone calls – for obviously Beatrice would immediately insist that the authorities install Mr Bell's famous invention – write letters and fetch and carry so hard and so fast for her employer that never again would she have the time or the leisure to round the heel of one of her famous knitted stockings.

That would be the *status quo*. Bobbie knew this from her guardian's past behaviour at Hazel Hill, where she would descend for what had seemed like only a few seconds, but was enough to ensure that the nurses were all running around her as if she owned and funded it, which perhaps she did. For Beatrice Harper's real enemy, even during the war, had been boredom. That terrible curse of the spoilt soul was always haunting her, snapping at her heels, and although Bobbie had hardly spent any time with her guardian she nevertheless sensed just from their conversations that her fatigue with life was even closer to her than her shadow. The inevitable *longueurs* induced by monied leisure hung over her, hovering like a bird of prey, and they were, it seemed, responsible for her all too tempestuous arrivals and departures. Often they would cause her to leave London suddenly for some unknown destination, New York, or Venice – Bobbie had gathered that it mattered very little where, really, just so long as Beatrice was moving on, restlessly, to some new playground. And if not to a city she would flee to one or another of the recently opened European resorts, some innocent spot, unmarked and unsung as yet, which the rich somehow always managed to find, make their own, and ruin.

So, if Bobbie, at Hazel Hill, had come to know just how painfully slow days could be, each second seeming to slowly, slowly inch its way on all fours through a whole set of sixty of the same, and another sixty, and another, finally making up, inch by little inch, the twenty-four hours that had comprised yet another whole day, then she realized that pretty soon – starting now – she would also be finding out the opposite. She would be finding out how tearingly fast the days could go.

The days to come, because she would go on being happy, she knew now would be more precious to her than any crock of gold at the bottom of any rainbow – and they would hurtle forward, refusing to slow down for anyone. Faster and faster they would go until quite unheedingly, not realizing just how unfair it was of them to be going at such speed, not realizing just how precious their cargo of happiness was, not realizing the effect on Bobbie and Julian, on the Major and Miss Moncrieff, on them all, they would crash to a terrifying stop. And gone for ever would be the happy hours that had made up all their previous days and weeks.

Bobbie also knew just how her guardian's arrival would be conducted.

First the car door would be held open by her chauffeur and out would step her maid, carrying the all-important blue leather, minutely monogrammed jewel case in one hand, the latest hat box from Paris in the other, a spare set of gloves for Mrs Harper tucked into her own handbag along with a bottle of Madame's favourite scent – ready to refresh Madame at any given moment of the journey.

Then would come Mrs Harper. First her long, nylon-clad legs, supported by beautifully shod feet, and then her tall, slender frame, dressed not to the nines, but to the tens, every hair in place, a piece of jewellery somewhere, quite prominent, perhaps a brooch, or a necklace. On her head a hat would be placed just perfectly, and on her hands, gloves, smoothly covering their long tapered shape.

Everything about Beatrice Harper would be so perfectly perfect that now Bobbie came to think of it, once she was dressed there really was nothing else for her to be except bored with life. When everything was perfectly perfect, time must hang so heavy.

'Time, gentlemen, please!'

Bobbie stared momentarily at the barman. To her he seemed to be calling, *Time, Roberta Murray, time,* and it occurred to Bobbie that his call must be directed straight at her because of a sudden there was so very little time left, so few days before Beatrice's perfectly shod foot came down firmly on the gravelled drive of Baileys Court. As soon as that foot hit the good Sussex earth they would all change. They would no longer be a strange little band, a comical team of incongruous friends. Nor would they any longer be comrades, shoulder to shoulder with hoe and axe, but just a pathetic assortment of beings whom, doubtless, Beatrice would dismiss within hours, bringing in instead some fashionable personage, some stranger to take charge of the gardens. And of a sudden the Major would no longer be heard whistling to his pug, and Julian and she would no longer be stepping, shouting and laughing, into the cold, often fast disappearing sea, and all the enchantment that they had sensed coming towards them from those slowly awakening places in the garden would disappear under the new people, and voices that were as sharp as the Major's axe would resound with new and modish ideas, and it would all be over. The happiest time of Bobbie's life would be quite over.

The lights behind them winked and blinked now the way they never had during the war, what with the blackout, the regulations, the fines if even a minuscule chink of electric or candlelight appeared beneath a blind, as the three of them walked along from the pub looking for fireflies, as they very often did after dinner and a visit to the pub.

'There's one – no, it's not, it's some kind of moth.'

'If you stop looking you will see one.'

'I know I saw one the other night.'

As bats swooped suddenly, making strange patterns against the luminously dark night sky, Bobbie stared up at the stars above them all. The beauty and distance of each one seemed to her, as always, to be so incomprehensible as to be almost comical. What on earth did any one of them matter compared to the stars above them? They did not matter, not even the tiniest bit. They were just specks of dust, one of a billion, billion dots that had sprinkled the earth since it had first exploded into life, and how they thought, how they acted, how they were, would affect no-one at all, not one person, not really, not finally.

'*When he shall die, Take him and cut him out in little stars, And he will make the face of heaven so fine That all the world will be in love with night, And pay no worship to the garish sun,*' Julian quoted as he wandered along beside her, his eyes, as always when he was happy, half closed, his smiling mouth giving him what Bobbie called his 'Cheshire Cat' look.

'Shakespeare has made people mind, and matter,' Bobbie remarked suddenly, her eyes once more on the road ahead. 'He at least has been, has become, is still, more than a dot.'

'We all make people mind and matter.'

'I don't think so. Or certainly not people like us. People like us – we are just dots. At least that is what I think we are, just so many dots – dot, dot, dots.'

The Major snorted lightly, ambling along slightly ahead of them in high good humour.

'What tosh you talk! But there. Perhaps you have to have been a prisoner of war to know what I mean,' he mused, and for a second the glow of his lighter illuminated his face in the darkness as he stopped and lit another cigarette. 'We all matter so much to each other at times like those, it's almost criminal.' The Major laughed, briefly, more a snort than a laugh really.

'You mean if you are in a camp or something, the little dots suddenly all become one big dot, all linked?' There was a pause as Bobbie considered this. 'You mean, like that painter Seurat, like *point-illism*, where all the little dots make up one marvellous painting and it all makes sense when you stand back from it? Like those little dots called stars that dot the sky above us – like those?'

'Yes, that is what I mean. We are like those little stars up there. Some of them may have already burnt out, but they stay twinkling away because they still want to matter. Like us. We want desperately to matter, but the truth is we don't, not really, not compared to the night sky, or the tides, or the weather.'

After she had finished speaking Bobbie looked up again at the stars in the clear Sussex night sky, at the wonder of it all, at the vast, far-flung, sometimes

204

midnight blue sometimes dark black silk sheet above them, seemingly so endless that it confirmed her view of life. But the Major was not happy.

'What tosh you talk, Bobbie, what complete tosh, you dear old bean. And I for one will have none of this mish-mash talk of whoever and whatever. Human beings must matter to each other or all is lost, and we will have fought and friends died for nothing at all. The world has to get better because of what has just happened, or at least *less* worse, or it has all been pretty bloody pointless, wouldn't you say?'

Another pause, and then Bobbie heard Julian laugh and say quietly, 'The trouble is, for me, it doesn't matter if it is, you know, if it is all pointless. It doesn't matter one of Bobbie's dots, not a single jot, and really, why should it?'

Julian laughed again, almost exultant, it seemed to Bobbie, at the idea that he would not have to toil through the usual three score years and ten like the rest of them, that he would not make old bones, but would, in some way, manage his escape to a better world before even the Major.

'We are none of us long for this earth,' the Major said, throwing his cigarette underfoot as they ambled along, while at the same time he smiled at Bobbie and Julian. 'I was like you, once, thought I was not going to last long, that I was sure to die a young, heroic death, but the Burma railway taught me different. Now, well, now I can't even see the morning light without wanting to burst into tears of gratitude that I'm here, and I bloody well wouldn't be if it hadn't been for one of those people Bobbie here calls *dots*. I tell you, I would not be. Dots! You dear bean, bless you, such tosh. Oh. *Shut up Gilbert!*'

After a minute the Major lit yet another cigarette and Bobbie watched its glow come and go in the darkness, thinking with regret that although it must be the Major's twenty-fifth smoke of the day, it was too late to win her bet with Julian.

'So what are we all settling for?'

Julian walked along without answering, staring ahead of him, his hands in his pockets, seemingly the epitome of relaxation.

'We are settling for making this world a better place to be in, dear bean,' the Major stated. 'We cannot settle for less. We have to help make this little jewel that is called England a better and more beautiful place. We must not have passed this way and left behind yet more rubbish or discontent. We must not leave behind a legacy of bitterness or hatred.'

'Easier said than done, Major.' Bobbie turned and looked at him gravely. 'I mean. Look at you. Can you forgive what happened to you?'

'I have, dear bean, I have. There was no other way. Can't forget, but I have forgiven or I wouldn't be able to go on, it's just a fact. Like Pilgrim, we must shed our burdens and look only to the day.'

Miranda looked at herself in the old mirror. She was wearing the New Look for the first time and as she stared at herself she could not help wondering why it was that it was considered so terribly, terribly shocking, which it was. Women passing other women in the street would berate them, or shout remarks as the long skirts passed them, or hopped up into a cab.

No amount of shouting in the street however had stopped Fenwicks advertising a *ballerina suit, with softly rounded shoulders, page-boy nipped-in jacket, gaily swinging skirt to give the new fashion look. Exciting colours and gay mixtures. 18 coupons. £5 12s. 6d.*

And of course, as soon as she had asked herself this simple question, Miranda knew that she already had the answer. She knew exactly why the New Look was shocking to people, and why women who wore it were frequently subjected to insults from passersby. It was because the New Look took up yards and yards and *yards* of material, so of course, in a time of post-war deprivation and clothing coupons, it was terrible to pass women in the street who were wearing more material in one skirt than most people would be able to afford, or obtain, in a whole year.

It had been easy for Miranda to avoid the coupons crisis that other young women all over London were facing when it came to trying to dress themselves as beautifully as they wished. Miranda had no need of coupons, she had simply to dip into one of the trunks on the landing above the studio. With a newspaper and an old sewing machine to hand she had created a wide-skirted summer dress for herself, made of old-fashioned sprigged muslin above a silk underskirt with a cross-over top. With long sleeves and a thin black belt it looked as if it had come straight out of Fortnum and Mason, not the trunks of Aubrey Close.

Her shoes were not so easy to pass off as modern, but with the aid of a large darning needle she had sewn the front of a pair of high-heeled sandals with bows to match her dress, bows that peeped out from under the full skirt. Her hat she had of course made herself, straw with ribbons and a tiny veil, and together with a muslin parasol that could pass as a modish umbrella she looked really rather shockingly fashionable.

There had been letters in the newspapers about young women and the New Look, about the fact that it was neither patriotic nor decent for a woman to be seen wearing a skirt which could reach nearly down to her ankles, but Miranda cared not at all. She was off to get herself a job, bent on securing a singing engagement. She had sung at the Dorchester when she was only small, and now, she determined, she would do so again. So there was nothing more important than that she should look not just up to the minute but *before* it, for she remembered the hotel, even during the war, as being filled with people like Pamela, still beautifully turned out despite the bombing and the deprivations. She had to look so fresh out of Paris, so devil-may-care, that whoever was in charge of auditions at the Dorchester would engage her straight away.

*   *   *

The woman at the side door of the hotel was ticking off names in her book.

'You are?'

'Miranda Darling.'

The woman stared at her. 'Well it's all in the name, dear, they do say.' She noted her name, ticked it off and nodded her in.

As soon as her feet hit the floor of the ballroom Miranda knew that her life was about to begin. She was going to be a singer. She was going to be famous. She would probably even be on the radio.

'Have you auditioned here before?' the voice from the first row of seats asked.

'No, but I have sung here. During the war. I sang to the orchestra that was here then . . .'

Suddenly it all came back to her. The room had been filled with diners, pretending to eat the strangest foods, which came wrapped about with French names and thin sauces. There had been Pamela and her American colonel. Miranda had seen that they shared a room together. First thing in the morning when she would not have been expected to be up she had seen Pamela slipping out of her colonel's bedroom and into her own, wearing his dressing gown. At the time Miranda had thought that Pamela might have left her dressing gown behind and was borrowing his, but not now. Now she knew all about people sleeping together, because Allegra had told her, and so she remembered Pamela in a different way, not so much as a

209

goddess who had encouraged her to sing, but as a woman who not only did not mind breaking the rules, but perhaps did not mind who knew. Looking back at that one wartime night in London Miranda realized now that it had changed her life for ever. It had sown the seeds of some divine restlessness, shown her that life was not always just about living, but could be exotic and dangerous.

Now, full of the confidence that Aunt Sophie had instilled in her, Miranda handed her music to the musical director, and with a swish of her skirt and a belief in herself that had remained unchanged since her days at the rectory, she started to sing.

The most perfect note came winging out, a note that began one of Aunt Sophie's favourite songs, 'Some Day I'll Find You . . .' She carolled, making round 'o's and crossing her 't's like mad, as Sophie had so assiduously taught her to do.

'Next please!'

Miranda could not believe it, she simply could not.

'What do you mean, *next* please? I've hardly sung a bar yet,' she protested to the musical director, who was actually only some few feet away from her.

'Sorry, dear, we are here to engage proper singers, not debutantes off to Ascot in the New Look.'

Miranda stamped her foot suddenly, which was very un-Allegra-like but, when it came down to it, very Miranda.

'I am *not* a debutante off to Ascot in the New

Look. My name is Miranda Darling, and I am here to sing and *you* are here to hear me out.' She stared across at the man.

'Oh, very well, dear, but don't be too long about it, will you? We've got another fifty behind you coming in today and it is still only twelve o'clock.'

With considerable aplomb Miranda flicked through the music in front of her, and having redirected the accompanist began again. This time 'Bye, Bye, Blackbird' soared from her slender throat and she was allowed to sing it all the way through, but the reaction from the floor was unmoved, and the expression on the musical director's face remained remarkably unenthusiastic, particularly considering that Miranda was quite certain that she was a genius.

'Thank you, we'll let you know.'

Miranda wandered out into Park Lane. After all that sewing and making herself look so up to the minute – so much so that even Christian Dior himself would surely turn to look at her as she passed him – after *all that* she was back exactly where she had started before the taxi had drawn up outside the wretched hotel. She was back amongst the crowd.

Feeling more disconsolate than she would have thought possible, Miranda wandered round to the front of the hotel. She would go in, she decided, and somehow once inside something would happen, she knew it would, for the truth was that she needed to work. It was no good just staying locked away in Aubrey Close. She needed not just a place to live, but money too, money to buy food and pay for taxis or buses. Her tiny allowance from Allegra – *Two pounds a week will be ample, bless you, won't it, darling?* – her silk stockings found at Burfitt Hall, left over from before the war, the marvellous clothes that seemed to spill endlessly from the old trunks at the top of the studio stairs, just as they had from the Clothes Exchange – they were all more than she deserved and she knew it, but the appalling fact of the matter was that she still needed money. She had to find a position some-where or her life at the studio would come to a shuddering halt.

For a second Miranda paused in front of the Dorchester. Judging from the flurry of activity in front of the hotel, it seemed that a great star was expected at any moment. She paused, partly out of curiosity, and partly out of envy. What must it be like to be a great personality of your day arriving in a limousine, the hotel staff ready and happy not just to greet you but to put you up – sometimes, she had read recently, for *free*. It was an intoxicating idea, most particularly because Miranda remem-bered her one night at the Dorchester with Pamela and the Colonel as being what Allegra would call 'heavenly'.

'A gin and it, please.'

Allegra always drank 'gin and it'. Miranda was not sure what the 'it' was really, but it sounded so right, she was really pleased she had ordered *it*. As she waited for the waiter to bring her the drink, she lay back against the plush of the chair and lit a cigarette, slowly and satisfyingly drawing in the smoke with evident and quite public enjoyment, once more feeling glad that Allegra, among many other things, had taught her to smoke, as well as not to cross her ankles, or say 'pardon'.

'May I join you, mademoiselle, for a drink?'

Miranda looked up. The owner of the voice that seemed to be so far above her was immaculately dressed in what she guessed must be English tailoring, dark suit, immaculate shirt, just the right kind of dark tie, but his voice had that faintly international twang that is acquired by the frequenter of exclusive bars in exotic places, attractive men in the diplomatic corps, foreign correspondents, and Americans living in Paris.

'I am sorry, I have already ordered. Besides, I am not in the way of paying for gentlemen's drinks.'

'Of course you're not,' he replied easily. 'A young woman as beautiful as you is used to having everything bought for her. So, obviously' – this as the 'gin and it' was placed in front of her – 'you are expecting someone pretty soon, I presume?'

'No, I am not.'

Miranda knew that if it were not for the fact that she was wearing a veiled hat, she would be looking confused and embarrassed. To cover her discomfort she quickly pretended to be Allegra, and stared at the man.

213

'Would it be presumptuous,' he asked, gently, 'if I asked you to expect *me*?'

'I'm sorry? Why should I *expect* you – you, if I am not mistaken, are already here, are you not?' A second later, she added, '*Bless you.*'

He lit a cigarette from a silver case and smiled with the kind of suavity that young women are always meant to find so fascinating in older men, but which, in reality, they find irritating and patronizing.

'Put another way, shall we, both, have a drink together, now?'

'Oh, very well. Bless you.'

Miranda's eyes, when she required them to, could look strangely hooded. She had practised using the hooded look in front of the mirror for many hours at the Cottage, usually to the sound of Allegra snoring off her lunchtime tipples. Now, however, she realized, the time had come not just to practise the look, but to use it on a real, live human being. And so she did. She stared at the elegant man who had seated himself, rather too promptly she thought, opposite her, and pretended to be a cobra.

'Is there something the matter?'

'No, why?'

'Nothing.' He blew out some smoke towards her, at which, not to be outdone, she promptly and swiftly blew some back at him. 'Nothing, no. I just thought you looked a little unwell.'

214

Miranda held out her hand as she said, 'Hungry actually. Miranda Mowbray – how do you do?'

'Sam Macaskie.'

'I actually sing under the name of Miranda Darling, but in private life I am just Miranda Mowbray.'

'You will never be *just* Miranda Mowbray, believe me. Take my word for it, you will never be *just* anything.'

For one tiny second Miranda had the worst idea, and it was the very worst, and it was that Sam Macaskie had guessed that she was actually not quite eighteen and that she had never sat drinking gin in the Dorchester on her own before – that, in fact, as far as London was concerned, she was more than a little wet behind the ears.

But then she remembered that she was a true blue Cockney, originally, and Cockneys did not scare or embarrass easily. They were born within the sound of Bow Bells, and they never grumbled, no matter what Hitler dropped on them, and so she raised her glass and sipped at the drink. Seconds later she stopped.

'You're not enjoying that one bit, are you?'

Before she could answer him he had leaned forward and, taking hold of her glass, had poured her drink into his own gin. Then, signalling to the waiter, he called for a lemonade 'on the rocks'. She looked momentarily shocked, so, perhaps to comfort her, he said, 'I never think that young women should drink gin anyway. Wine, but not gin. Gin gives them fat arms and a vile temper in the mornings.'

'I just thought it might be a nice change, you know, from – anything else. My guardian always drinks gin and it.'

'And does he have fat arms and a vile temper in the morning?'

'She. Oh no.' Miranda shook her head. 'But she does sleep rather a lot after lunch,' she added, after a few seconds.

'Speaking of lunch, I wonder if you would like to come up for luncheon? I am staying here for a few days.'

Miranda did not know where 'up' was but she guessed it must be to some luxurious set of rooms such as Pamela and her colonel had enjoyed what now seemed like a century ago.

'I *am* very hungry . . .'

'The Dorchester is beating the ration rap here quite brilliantly. The chefs are all back from fighting with the Free French in France, and coupons are not always asked for, I am happy to say.'

'Where are your – rooms?'

'Right at the top. You can see over the whole of London.'

'In that case I think I would rather eat down here, if you don't mind. I have no head for heights.'

'Of course, I don't mind at all.'

Miranda saw that he did mind, but thought that really, it was too bad. Allegra had never told her specifically not to visit a gentleman in his hotel room, but remembering Pamela in the Colonel's dressing gown, that quick glimpse of her wandering back to her own room from his bedroom, Miranda was suddenly not at all sure that she was really in the mood to break any rules, at least not quite yet.

Chapter Seven

Julian had told Bobbie a secret. It seemed that at long, long last the Major had made a dishonest woman of Miss Moncrieff.

'He has rounded off her stocking for her, and she is now a real woman,' he said, chewing on a long stalk of grass, his eyes as always half closed. 'He has made himself known to her, in the full Biblical sense.'

Bobbie started to laugh, rolling about in the thick-stalked grass that bordered the shore, running along the top of the beach before the line of over-grown hedges and shot saplings.

'Oh, no, please, Julian, don't say things like that,' Bobbie gasped, and stopped laughing, perhaps because she was laughing alone, but then she started again, laughing quite helplessly, because Julian's expression of Buddha-like calm was just so funny, and besides, the whole idea of the Major and Miss Moncrieff being Biblical together was even funnier than Julian's unmoving expression. 'I think you're wrong,' she said finally, and stopped laughing and stood up in front of the still seated Julian. 'I do think you're wrong,' she went on determinedly, brushing sand from her knees. 'You can't be right *because*—'

'*Because?*'

Julian's expression was suave to the point of urbanity and he lifted his damp chin from the sand and stared up at Bobbie.

'Because,' Bobbie went on, determined not to show him that she was in danger of bursting into another fit of helpless laughter at the sight of his sand beard. 'Because,' she said, breathing in, slowly. 'Because, because—' she cast around in her mind for the perfect reason why Miss Moncrieff would never, ever make herself known to the Major, in the Biblical sense. 'Because she has to think of her *mother*, in Pinner. She would never do anything to upset her *mother*, in Pinner.'

Julian looked up at Bobbie, his blue eyes solemn. 'I think you will find that when it comes to passion, mothers simply do not count, Bobbie. They just do *not*.'

'I never had a mother, so I shall never be able to prove you fearfully wrong.'

There was a short silence.

'Reasonably,' Julian announced as Bobbie sat down once again, and then eventually lay back in the blazing heat, giving in to the pull of closing her eyes and sunbathing, succumbing to the lazy, shimmering heat, 'reasonably you must have a mother, Bobbie. I mean, the Messiah had no father except

219

God, but the rest of us, Bobbie, even you, have all had a mother and a father, with the single exception of my grandmother's friend Mabel who had a virgin birth, because, so the legend goes, she and her husband simply did not *do* things like that.'

'Oh, you know what I mean. My mother and father were killed before the war, and I don't remember them.'

'Well, isn't that just too, too sad?'

It was Julian's turn to close his eyes and lie back against the sand. Bobbie had noticed that they always seemed to find it easier to talk quite frankly while lying down, side by side. However, today Julian obviously had nothing more to contribute to the subject of mothers, and since Bobbie would never dream of asking him anything that he did not wish to tell her, they lay for a while in silence, sweltering in the heat. The news reader on the wireless that morning had announced that England was enjoying the hottest summer of the twentieth century so far and just now neither of them had any trouble believing it.

By the seaside at Baileys Court, with the water running up the beach or receding out to sea, but constantly with them, the heat was bearable and enjoyable, and strangely marvellous after the freezing temperatures of the past winter. But in the cities Bobbie knew that there were no frigidaires and no ice houses, no cool streams and no sea. Those same people who had frozen in the winter now queued for coupons, for fish, for bread, for anything and everything that they could get, and if they could not get it they found themselves trying to buy it from a spiv in a pub, and all the while they stifled, for there was no air in the cities and the towns, and no coupons on earth, not even a spiv in a pub, could purchase air for them.

'Do you realize that somewhere, now,' Julian's sepulchral tones crept once more towards Bobbie, 'somewhere, nearby, the Major may well be *enjoying* Miss Moncrieff, Roberta? Do you realize that?'

Bobbie started to laugh again, uncontrollably. She did not bother to sit up, but just let the tears roll down her face into the sand.

'Oh, stop, Wretched Boy, stop,' she said, but the laughter became yet more uncontrollable, and she had to turn on her front and put her head in her hands, her shoulders shaking, a piece of towel to her eyes.

Wretched Boy was her new nickname for Julian because he had told her that when, briefly, he had attended a boys' boarding school, the headmaster had never addressed any of his pupils in any other way. Julian maintained that the poor man was a victim of the demon drink and as result never could remember anyone's name. All boys were 'wretched boy' and all the teachers 'Er Um'. He smelt so strongly of whisky before ten o'clock in the morning that someone's parents had, eventually, complained to the Board of Governors. As a result, in panic, or while still under the influence, he had

221

forced himself to drink a bottle of stale cologne, apparently in an effort to drown the smell before coming up before the said governors, and as a consequence died quite horribly.

Julian seemed to relish stories such as these, and he had a fund of them. He liked to quote Hilaire Belloc and his poems, and he liked to put on ghostly voices to frighten Bobbie when they walked under the house, down the long secret tunnel that linked the main house to the garden wing of Baileys Court. When he was not doing that, he loved to make up horrendous murder stories, relating them in a High Church clerical voice which he fondly thought made the item much funnier. *And after that he chopped and chopped until there was nothing whatsoever left of her except her little finger*.

But Bobbie eventually became inured to his stories, thinking of them as simply stories, just as now she could not believe that Miss Moncrieff had dropped any of her stitches for the Major, that it was not just another of Julian's inventions. And yet, as they walked back to return to their rebuilding of the old walls of the garden, to their discussions of where, eventually, the old roses would once more be planted, to their marvellous plans for making the grounds at Baileys Court a paradise, a jewel set beside the silver sea, Bobbie could not turn away from the realization that Julian might be right about her guardian's secretary.

To begin with Miss Moncrieff had changed her hairstyle of late. And what was more, she no longer wore her own hand-knitted stockings, but, also just of late, had affected a lisle pair, a really great advancement for her. Her hair too was no longer scraped back into a tight knot at the back of her head so that her scalp showed through pink and white – Bobbie flinched at the idea of sporting a hairstyle that must cause a kind of permanent headache – but arranged at the nape of her neck in a figure of eight wrapped around a piece of horse-hair. And then, too, instead of the eternal pre-war tweed coat and skirt, she had started to leave off not only her coat but her home-knitted cardigan with its three-ply cuffs and collars knitted in moss stitch. All this meant, to Bobbie, that Julian might be right, and by the time they both picked up their trowels and began work once again she had come to the same conclusion as Julian, Miss Moncrieff must now be leaving off not just her coat, but perhaps her skirt too.

The fact is that once an idea comes into someone's head, it is not unusual for that person to find that it simply will not be removed. And just as Bobbie always found that if someone thought her a bore she found it impossible to be in the least bit interesting, so too, now, she found that by the time she was handing Julian up the stones from the flower beds, and the Major and Miss Moncrieff were strolling back from lunch together in the Sheds, they presented themselves, to her eyes at any rate, as famously in love as any Antony and Cleopatra or Dido and Aeneas, or Daphnis and Chloe.

223

Julian nodded to her to hand up the next stone, and then winked largely and flamboyantly towards the Major and Miss Moncrieff, so that Bobbie would notice what must have been all too obvious all along. Miss Moncrieff was *wild* about the Major. She looked up at him for reassurance every two seconds, she ran to hand him his gardening tools, or his hat, she rushed back to the Sheds for lemonade, she darted to the stream for ice cold bottles of tonic once the sun had gone down below the yard arm and it was safe for any gentleman, or gentlewoman for that matter, to pour a goodly measure of gin into the bottom of a glass and sip contentedly together the just reward of honest toil.

The Major too had changed. His carelessness of dress had been replaced with a meticulous attention to detail, even in the boiling heat. So, although he still might be only in shorts, now he made sure that they were sparkling white, and he wore tennis shoes and socks with them, so that he looked more like a boy scout than an army major. He raised his hat to Miss Moncrieff at any moment that seemed appropriate. The moment she returned with the lemonade, up would go his hand. The moment she put the picnic basket with their lunch inside it down beside him the hat would be raised again, and the moment the precious gin bottle could be produced from the leather case with its silver-topped bottles and its glass casings, the courtesy was again performed, and the hat eventually replaced.

'It's all going to end dreadfully,' Bobbie

announced that evening as she and Julian strolled, side by side as usual, down the corridor under the good Sussex earth towards the garden wing. 'It's all going to end so dreadfully we shall be sobbing into large spotted handkerchiefs.'

'Why do you say that?' she heard Julian asking her, his voice sounding suddenly far away, so concentrated were her own thoughts.

Bobbie's voice sounded accusing, even to her own ears. 'Because the lives of people like the Major and Miss Moncrieff always do. They always end quite dreadfully in frustration and gin-ridden guilt. She will never allow him to marry her. The moment she sees her mother in Pinner again, the old ties will reassert themselves—'

'Doom, doom, doom, that is all you talk. You are the doomiest person I know,' Julian said, accusingly, and he fell back a few yards.

Bobbie wished that she had held her tongue as from behind her she heard Julian suddenly starting to cough, and cough. She knew he was suffering in the heat, and she knew just how, but there was nothing she could do. She had an idea that he was seeing a doctor somewhere, sometimes, because every now and then he would disappear for half a day, and return looking more cheerful, and she had noticed, over the past days and weeks, he did seem to have changed. He had filled out, and turned a marvellous golden colour in the intense heat of that particular summer. Not that she would ask him anything – not ever. Bobbie knew all too well what pity and concern in other people's eyes could do to a person. She knew how pity could make you feel more ugly than anyone could imagine, and how an outward show of concern could make you feel that your insides had turned to knots, and how, conversely, seeing the worry you were causing someone all at once made you feel that you would never, *ever* get better again.

'Nevertheless,' Bobbie continued, after, eventually, the coughing had stopped, 'it is true. Miss M will see her mother, her mother will moan and cry and never want her to leave Pinner again, not even to go to her flat in Ebury Street. Miss M will turn away from the Major and the Major will drink himself to death and be buried unmourned in the village graveyard with only the publican attending the obsequies, for he at least will have found that he has fond memories of him.'

'We won't let it all end that way, we just won't.'

'You will have to give in to the idea of fate. Fate cannot be stopped, Julian, ever. Fate will have its wicked way, no matter what.'

'I don't agree. I refuse to agree. I say we will stop fate. Like a traffic policeman we will hold it up, we will make it do as we wish. Just for a few days or hours we can turn the clock back, and make things better again.'

'But how can we?' Bobbie said stubbornly. 'We are mere mortals, just little dots. Not really mattering to anyone, anywhere, except perhaps to ourselves.' She was aware that Julian had stopped listening to her, so she quickly switched subjects.

'We will have to make a plan. We will have to talk to the Major, make him see that if he and Miss Moncrieff are to live happily ever after, he will have to, *have* to, run off with her. It is the only answer. We must at all costs stop Miss Moncrieff from returning to Pinner and her mother, or to London and Ebury Street. We must force her to run away and find a new life before even Mrs Harper comes down and starts dictating to her, in every way.'

Julian shook his head. They had reached the top of the secret passage. 'That would never work, Roberta.' He smiled down at her, suddenly and instantly sadistic, and Bobbie could only wait in awful dread, knowing all the time that he was about to make her laugh.

'Why ever not?' she asked, her own eyes now widening, returning the innocent look that Julian had managed to maintain, aware that she was falling into his trap, but utterly helpless to prevent it.

'Why ever not? Why ever not? Why, for the very simple reason, Roberta Murray, that the Major cannot run. He smokes too much.'

Bobbie whacked Julian on the arm.

'*Wretched* Boy, goodnight!'

Miranda was determined to keep Sam Macaskie from knowing her address. She did not want anyone visiting the studio for the minute, perhaps not ever – for the very good reason that she knew she had everything she wanted at Aubrey Close. Everything was arranged for herself, for her own return. It was her little paradise and she wanted to be alone in it.

Besides, she could, after only a few weeks, appreciate that there was something deliciously dominating and selfish about the atmosphere of studios. They did not ask you to be quite alone in them, they demanded it. In fact the studio at Aubrey Close did more than that for Miranda.

Every evening when she returned to it, it ordered her to dress up for it, to dress in some way that would please it and remind it of the old days, using any or all of the clothes in the trunks that still sat, old and important, on the landing at the top of the dark wood stairs. Once dressed up in some satisfyingly grand costume, Miranda would wind up the old gramophone and dance to it, quite alone. Or she would sit at the piano, and sing to the women with their gold headbands in the great coloured windows, or to the bust on the plinth beside the staircase, or to the dark-eyed woman in the red velvet dress who had been left, without a frame, somehow abandoned on an easel in one corner.

No, there was no question, there was no place for Sam Macaskie in the studio at Aubrey Close. There just was not, and to give him his due, Sam Macaskie did not seem terribly interested in escorting Miranda home, which was really rather a relief. Nor did he seem to notice that Miranda was reluctant to take a taxi cab in front of him, in case he heard her address. He was far too interested in asking her out to dinner that night.

'Oh, I don't think so . . .'

Miranda, still beautifully and perhaps, she realized of a sudden, a little eccentrically dressed, was now waiting with mounting impatience for Macaskie to go back inside the hotel. They had enjoyed lunch together; that was surely quite enough for two strangers. Why would he want to eat dinner with her too? Why would he choose to dine with her rather than any one of the older and more interesting women who had passed by his table?

The truth was that Miranda had grown up in only a matter of hours. She realized now that the life she had led in Norfolk with Allegra, which she had once thought to be so terribly sophisticated, was mundane and ordinary to the point of hilarity. Sam Macaskie's conversation, his whole approach to life, the people who stopped by his table in the dining room, were the opposite of everything she had known in Norfolk, or in Mellaston, for that matter.

These people were the epitome of sophistication. They had all to a person just come back from New York on 'the *Queen*', or were just going, and they made sure to tell Sam Macaskie this. Or they had just been to Paris or Rome. They dropped famous names, but not to impress, simply because they were friends, and friends do have names.

And then too they obviously knew him so well

that they laughed at 'in' jokes with him, speaking in a kind of shorthand – quite a different shorthand from Allegra's shorthand, but a kind of shorthand all the same. Whatever he was or was not, by the end of luncheon 'Sam, dear Sam' as one older lady kept calling him, laughing at his wry remarks while patting his cheek with her white-gloved hand, was obviously immensely popular.

What was impressive to Miranda about all the people who stopped by their table was that, beyond touching her outstretched hand lightly, they never once made the mistake of asking who exactly was, or why exactly their friend Sam was to be found on a sunny weekday in Park Lane seated with Miranda Mowbray.

It was as if they took it for granted that Sam would be having luncheon at the Dorchester with a young, pretty girl. To anyone less ingenuous it might have mattered not to matter to these worldly people, but to Miranda, it was somehow calming. And because she was not able to follow their conversations, not knowing those of whom they spoke, or about whom they laughed, it allowed her, seated silently opposite Sam Macaskie, to appreciate the women's clothes, their jewellery, their hats, and most of all their mouthwatering style. For despite clothing coupons, the summer heat, and the National Debt to America, style was back in force in London that year. White gloves worn to the elbows, and waisted, belted dresses, of silk chiffon and muslin, long and charmingly demure, some

230

almost to the ankle. Just watching the ladies who stopped at Sam's table made Miranda ever more aware of the improvised nature of her own New Look, for although she could appreciate that her hat was all that it should be, she knew that there were certain details of her home-made costume which were entirely and utterly amiss.

She had just decided to leave Sam Macaskie on the pavement outside the hotel while she nipped into a taxi and drove off, when he leaned forward and said, in a low but kindly voice, 'If not dinner, Miss Mowbray, how about shopping for some gloves, preferably white gloves to the elbow?'

As soon as he had finished speaking Miranda turned slowly and brightly red. She had so hoped that no-one had noticed her lack of gloves. If Sam Macaskie had noticed, then it was obvious that everyone else would have too. Perhaps that was why no-one had paid much attention to her? She had, from the start, been all too obviously *not one of them*, perhaps because of no *gloves*.

And Sam Macaskie had most probably noticed all along. All during the little matter of pre-lunch drinks, all during luncheon, he must have noticed that she was the only woman, young or old, in the restaurant without gloves. She had shoes, she had a hat, she had a dress and petticoats. What she did not have, and what her budget could not run to, were gloves.

All the gloves in the trunks at Aubrey Close were moth-eaten, or had holes, or were so stained that they were beyond even sending to a dry cleaner's. The only pair that she had been able to find were evening gloves made of fine kid, reaching right up to the tops of her arms, the buttons of which had taken her nearly a quarter of an hour to do up with a little tiny hook. When she had, eventually, done them up, she had been so pleased with the feel of them, the look of them on her long, slender arms, that she had gone back down the studio stairs again and danced in them, quite alone, waltzing around the studio, between all the old furniture, wearing only her underwear.

'Gloves.'

'I know a glove maker, very inexpensive, but we will have to go to his shop, in a back alley, around Soho. He makes up privately, for all the couturiers in Paris as well as London.'

Miranda hesitated. Out of the corner of her eye she could see a taxi cab waiting. She could see couples strolling towards the Park in their lunch hour. A man with a poodle on a lead being pulled along. She could see the trees nearby moving slightly in a sudden, thankfully cool breeze. What she could not see was that it could possibly be wrong to accept a pair of gloves from a man whom she hardly knew. She needed gloves, she wanted gloves, she had to have gloves. She just did.

'Oh, very well,' she said back, pretending to be Allegra. '*Bless* you, thank you. Yes, I would like some gloves as a matter of fact. Just until I go home.

I left mine at home, in my trunk, hardly unpacked yet, bless you.'

But life had a habit of not being quite as simple as Miranda wished, and even as she accepted the innocent offer of some gloves from Sam Macaskie she saw something that put her almost insatiable desire for gloves into true perspective.

She saw someone like the Pamela she remembered from long ago, a beautiful woman with auburn hair wearing a stunning dress in cerise pink which fell in tiny knifelike pleats so fine that they could have been in military formation. She wore the dress, together with a hat with a matching silk rose, tip tilted forward and shoes dyed to match, with such insouciance that for a few seconds Miranda could have believed it was Pamela – not because of what she was wearing but because of her sophisticated, carefree air. Watching her, Miranda felt that she knew just how the woman would laugh, how she would look, her eyes searching for, and always finding, amusement in something, if only the sunlight on the trees in the Park, or the man in the trilby hat who had just passed her.

Sam's deep voice penetrated Miranda's thoughts. 'I said – you would like to look like that, wouldn't you?'

'Yes . . .'

Now not just her lack of gloves, but everything about herself appealed to Miranda as being desperately home-made. The gloss, the patina, the ease of expensive clothes: everything about the woman who had just passed made her into someone quite different, someone that, of a sudden, Miranda wanted desperately to be. A *Pamela* of a person, someone who would look at ease beside this older man, this *colonel* of a person that Sam Macaskie seemed suddenly to be.

She was still looking back towards the woman sashaying down Park Lane when the American voice beside her was heard urging, 'Come on, then, Miss Mowbray, let's get gloving.'

Bobbie and Julian were seated with the Major between them in the private bar of the Dog and Duck discussing the finer details of the Major's plan to abduct Miss Moncrieff to Gretna Green. There he would marry her finally, and completely, and weeks before she was due to take her mother on holiday to Bournemouth, so that, as Bobbie pointed out in her usual practical way, there would be enough time for the new Mrs Saxby not only to become used to her new status, but to break it to her mother before all three of them went to Bournemouth.

'I don't suppose she'll mind her daughter being married, just so long as she knows that you will still holiday with her and share Christmas with her, and that sort of thing, I don't suppose Mrs Moncrieff will mind, will she?'

'Of course she will mind. If she was not going to mind Miss Moncrieff would have been snapped up and married years ago, wouldn't she?' Bobbie sighed.

The Major nodded and threw back his whisky in one before ordering another. 'The thing is, the thing is you're right, Bobbie,' he said, just a little fuzzily, 'we have to get under the wire, as we used to call it in Burma, before anything happens to induce "Bel" as I call her, to funk it. We just have to get under that wire, before her mother falls dangerously ill, or some other hazard. I would never get back in with her, because you know how it is with single women and their mothers. They have not remained single for nothing, they have remained single because their mothers don't want to be left on their own, so they stake their claim pretty early.'

Bobbie stared at her feet. She had suddenly found her feet extraordinarily interesting for the very good reason that Julian was bossing his eyes at her again. She knew that he was just as unable to think of Miss Moncrieff as 'Bel' as she was, and that, like herself, he was having difficulty keeping his face straight.

Yet undeniably they were both committed to helping the Major in his romance. More than that, they wanted to put their shoulder to this particular wheel most probably because it was like the Major's buying smuggled gin and defying the authorities. It was an exciting, spivvy, black market kind of thing to do, to help the Major elope with Miss M, help them get under the wire before Mrs Harper and Mrs Moncrieff discovered that poor Miss M was wild about the Major.

Indeed it was quite touching to see just how wild about Major S poor old Miss Moncrieff really was, seemingly happy only if she was following him around all day long, she pushing the wheelbarrow, he strutting ahead with his axe or his saw, once again a man in a woman's eyes.

'It's getting her things packed up, and, you know, rushing her, as it were, getting her under the wire before she thinks she has to tell Mother. And then again, getting her packed up before your Mrs Harper arrives and decides that she cannot possibly do without her for all the tea in China, that sort of thing. It worries the hell out of me, really it does. If she is made to choose between me and Mother she will choose Mother – no doubt about it, and she is not to be blamed. So. So this thing has to happen soon, because Mother telephoned again, didn't she, Bobbie? Last night, left a message here, so, if we are to be realistic, it's all ends to the middle, really it is, if we are to get under the wire.'

'I am afraid it was not only Mother who telephoned,' Bobbie said forlornly, 'Mrs Harper did too. Twice. So we have to get Miss M packed up and shut up, before either of them find out. Packed up and shut up,' she finished, in a determined voice.

'And into my old Riley, and off up to Gretna Green before she can think of some reason why she doesn't want to enjoy the rest of her days with me.'

'So tomorrow night had better be the night,

wouldn't you say?' Bobbie looked at her co-conspirators.

They both nodded their heads, both of them serious once again.

'Isn't it funny, they're both women, Mrs Moncrieff and Mrs Harper, and yet we're all frightened of them?' Bobbie stared at the Major, thinking this over, but the Major shook his head, and finally having knocked back his drink he said, 'Not funny at all, dear bean. Not funny at all. Some of the worst of the Nazis were women. Very frightening creatures, women.' He looked seriously at Bobbie. 'Just make sure you don't turn into one, that's all.'

Bobbie too frowned at that, suddenly knowing that the Major was right, that he had hit the nail on the head. Life was all about not just *becoming* something but also *not* becoming something. Whatever happened she must not turn into a woman; no sea-green change for her into some authoritarian with a foghorn of a voice and steely eyes.

'I,' she announced, thinking of something, her cheeks burning with the excitement of the moment, 'I won't. I promise, Major S, I will not turn into a woman, not ever, not for anyone, not ever, ever, ever.'

Julian gave her one of his quick, darting looks, looks that always acted like a pat on the back for Bobbie, but he was waiting, not quite believing that she could come up with something.

'What then? If not a woman, what are you going

237

to be, Roberta Murray, if not a woman?' asked the Major.

'A person. I think I'll just stick with that.'

Julian nodded, satisfied, and Bobbie knew at once that because he had said nothing, he had said everything.

'You know, Major, I am going to miss you. Julian and I – we're both going to miss you.'

As soon as Bobbie came out with that she realized that she quite felt like knocking back one of the Major's drinks, but instead she knocked back her lemonade and smiled, staring straight ahead at herself in the mirror behind the bar. The lemonade was having a strangely intoxicating effect on her, for some reason she did not really understand.

She had grown nut-brown and almost bonny-looking in the past months. As a matter of fact they all had, she realized, her gaze moving away from her own face to the Major and Julian. They all looked quite different from how they had looked when they had first come together in the spring, as a simple result of Bobbie's being too impatient to wait for the village shop to open, and thereby meeting the Major, and Boy, and all that.

'What about Boy? Will Boy go with you? Will Boy be able to get under the wire and go to Gretna Green?' She looked down at the pug, who was snoring noisily not beneath the Major's feet, but on them.

'Oh, he'll have to come too. You know how it is with pugs – they have to come too or they take fearful umbrage. It is "no speakers" for weeks and weeks if they're not allowed to join the excitement. Tails go straight, owner's life becomes completely intolerable, dogs throw asthma attacks, wheeze loudly in company, and generally make themselves repulsive – so repulsive that the message eventually gets through that pugs are *not* to be left behind.' The look on the Major's face was suddenly one of pride mixed with amazement as he went on, 'Besides, Amabel will never let me leave Boy behind. He's come to mean a great deal to her too. She has told me – and Amabel as you know is very truthful – she has told me that she never ever thought, never imagined that she would like a pug, but she has come to realize that she does now. In fact, quite frankly, she worships the little fellow. Can hardly bear it when his tail goes straight, as happened yesterday, when he thought he had been stung by a bee.'

After the Major had finished speaking they all stared down at the small fawn-coloured dog with the black mask and the curly tail. There was a few seconds' complete silence before, eventually, Bobbie said, shaking her head and sighing lightly, 'You know, Major S, if Miss Moncrieff actually likes Boy, then if you don't mind my saying yours really does have to be one of the great love affairs of this century.'

'I'm sorry?'

'This has to be one of the great affairs of the century, you and Miss Moncrieff. I mean if she worships Boy, snores and all, then she must really love you, Major S.'

The Major beamed at Bobbie. 'Get your point,' he agreed, proudly. 'She does rather like me, but the thing is – what we don't know is, does she like me enough to run off with Boy and me?'

For Miranda the whole shopping expedition had not stopped at gloves, and consequently had developed an unreal feel to it. 'Sam', as she now called Macaskie, did not bother with clothing coupons, nor did he seem to have any money problems. He merely took taxis, with Miranda seated primly some distance from him in the cab, to out of the way places, where doors opened immediately the vendeuses saw who it was with cries of 'Oh, Sam!' – as if they knew him so well that they were upbraiding themselves for not expecting him, as if a day when Sam Macaskie did not arrive outside their discreet doors was remarkable.

Miranda found herself mounting steep staircases which led to small, wooden-floored rooms which echoed so much to the sound of everyone's shoes that once more than two people moved around them, it was as if there was a ballet class in progress.

And then there were the vendeuses themselves, black frocks, discreet brooches, and tight, tight lips, like thin red lines of ribbon in their white, white faces – most especially when they stood back to view whatever it was they had just put Miranda into, carefully lifting the clothes over her head with wooden sticks, to avoid handling the precious materials.

Of course, because they worshipped at the feet of fashion, and doubtless at the feet of designers too, their manner was if anything more authoritarian than any police inspector's. And while Sam might lightly kiss the tips of their fingers in greeting, and they might smile at him with their lips, their eyes merely said, 'Ah, *bon*, *bon*, yes, it's you, Sam Macaskie, we allow you here because you pay cash, on time, all the time.'

They were not shy about mentioning money straight away either. As soon as he came into view, and even as they were appraising Miranda – her height, five foot eight inches, her waist size, twenty-two, her hips, thirty-four, her shoe size, five, her hat size, six, her glove size, seven – they rolled off figures and amounts of money at Macaskie. All the figures were spoken in French and very fast, so that Miranda started to get the impression that everything they tried on her, everything they showed them both cost '*mille cinquante*' something or another.

Yet between all the arithmetic, both physical and commercial, they repeated a kind of approving litany to Sam as their eyes flicked from him to Miranda, and from Miranda to the clothes being brought in by their assistants. It was a litany which had a delicate emphasis, overtones of congratulation mingled with vague amazement, as if they were saying, 'My, my, my, but how do you do it, Sam Macaskie?'

'Mais elle est si mignonne. Très, très mignonne, même belle, vraiment belle, vous avez raison, monsieur.'

If Miranda heard those words once that afternoon she must have heard them a hundred times, and each time they were said, Sam would smile, his eyes half closed, and laugh, and light another untipped French cigarette, and Miranda would stand as still as a statue as the assistants pinned and tucked the particular dress that the vendeuse, not Sam, had chosen, and then the vendeuse would turn Miranda, holding her firmly by the shoulders and, speaking rapidly in French, show her to Sam, who, eyes still half closed against the smoke of his cigarette, would nod approvingly, head on one side, while Miranda had the feeling that although he was in the room with them physically, mentally he was miles away.

The very first time Miranda was turned by her shoulders, and the curtaining behind which she had been almost forcibly changed flung aside, she did so to the accompaniment of a stream of voluble French. Although Miranda could not understand what the vendeuse was saying at all, she did recognize her tone as being cross.

'Sam, what is she saying?'

Sam smiled his slow, almost patronizing smile. 'She's saying you have the wrong underwear on for the cut of the dress,' he told her smoothly, and inevitably another cigarette was lit while Miranda blushed and Sam, pretending not to pay much attention to her sudden and quite evident embarrassment, gave her one of his reassuringly sleepy smiles before allowing her to be marched off to another room where the right underwear for her tall and slender figure was soon found.

The sensation of good underwear on her body for the first time was something that Miranda would never forget, most especially after wartime deprivations, after wearing whatever came to hand, in whatever fashion was easiest. It was not just the comfort of good corsetry, styling as it did her youthful figure into a particular shape, so that her young, almost angular body fitted every dress and costume that was produced, it was the actual feel of it.

And that was all before she stepped into a taffeta waist petticoat and swirled in front of the full length mirror. She did so spontaneously, arms above her head, petticoat flying, turning and turning so expertly that of a sudden the busy room in which she was being fitted, which normally did not stop for anything, not even the dropping of a bomb, suddenly did pause for a second, caught up in the sheer joy of the moment. Sewing machines ceased and pins were taken from mouths and stuck quickly back into pin cushions, as everyone laughed and applauded the sight of a young girl celebrating a moment that would never, ever come again.

And Miranda of course, knowing that all eyes were upon her, and loving every moment of it, having ended her balletic display with a creditable version of the splits was roundly told off, in fast, explicit French, by Madame la Vendeuse. And although Miranda understood not a word of French beyond *belle*, which meant beautiful, which meant herself, she understood only too well the message coming via Madame's boot-black eyes and wagging finger: that if Miranda wanted to do the splits she could join the Comédie Française or the Royal Ballet, but if she was going to be a mannequin she had to learn to take care of the underclothes, the dresses, the shoes – everything she was put in. They were not for her use, they were for her to make beautiful. That was what being a mannequin was about, making things look beautiful.

'That woman in there said I was going to be a mannequin.'

'But of course.'

'I didn't know I was going to be a mannequin.'

'What do you think this is all about?' Sam stared at Miranda, who was clinging to the passenger strap well away from him.

'Oh, I don't know. Bless you, I just thought we were having fun, really.' To cover her astonishment Miranda had suddenly reverted to Allegra's conversational style.

'Miranda.' Sam took her hand and gave it a light squeeze before quickly dropping it, and lighting yet another of his untipped French cigarettes. 'Miranda. You are only young, I know, but shall I tell you something? For absolutely sure, no man

244

goes to this much trouble over a young woman unless he is going into business with her. I am going into business with you, dear. You are going to be a mannequin, and I am going to manage you. I could not be certain of this until I saw you wearing the clothes, but now – well, now it is quite clear you are going to join the ranks of famous fashion models on either side of the Atlantic. Mention who you like, Miranda Mowbray is going to be up there with them. You have the cheekbones, you have the height, you have the measurements, but most of all you adore clothes. The moment you saw those gloves I knew and you knew you had to have them. Not for yourself – you had to have them for the clothes. You owed them to your clothes. We both knew it. You just had to have them. I am not saying you would have done anything to have them, but I am saying you wanted them very, very much. There really is no more to be said. Next week I will arrange for you to be photographed in some of those clothes we tried, and send the pictures on to Paris.'

He paused, smiling, and flicked her cheek with his free hand.

'I predict you will be over-employed within hours, but hours. The moment my friends in Paris see what you can do for their frocks that will be it, my dear, completely.'

He directed his eyes to the seats in front of him and smiled, staring ahead, obviously well satisfied with himself. As he did so Miranda realized that really she did not matter very much to him at all. Not the *Miranda* bit of her, anyway. Only her body mattered to him, her height, her shoe size, how she looked in the clothes in which he was making sure to see her fitted. She was going to be a means to quite another end: she was going to earn him a great deal of money. Perhaps she was also even going to earn money for herself?

Whichever way it was he was quite obviously not going to be her 'Colonel'. She was not going to be his 'Pamela'. Their relationship was not going to be like that. They were going into business together, the business of showing clothes to photographers, to fashion editors, to magazines, to Parisian or American designers, to anyone and everyone who was in the *business* of fashion. Her heart sank. It would not be how she thought of her clothes. It would not be like putting on something and dancing around in it. It would not be a love affair, quite private. No, there would be thousands of dollars at stake, and everyone would not be happy and at ease as she had been when she was dancing quite alone in the silvered scarf. They would be serious and demanding. From now on it would be just money, money, money.

She stared out of the window. The truth was, she could be just anyone to Sam Macaskie, any one of a hundred, or two hundred, young women. Miranda thought with sudden longing of the war days at the old rectory, when she and Teddy and Bobbie had seemed to spend hours and hours of so many days outside, gathering wool from hedges, until they had basketfuls of the stuff. And she thought too of how the aunts had given them blackberries in round blue and white bowls for their supper, and a strange kind of creamy stuff they called 'junket' to go with it. She remembered the way they had all used to rush out into the rectory garden as soon as lessons were over, and how they would then stand stock still. Longing and longing as they had to be away from lessons, once outside for a few desperate seconds they had not known what to do.

But then, as always, Bobbie would come up with something new, some marvellous game where they could all pretend, and if it rained they would go to a barn, and the pretence would start all over again, until it was time to go wool gathering, or walk down to see the cows being milked, or just lie in the long grass staring up at the sky half longing and half dreading to see an enemy plane. And sometimes they would hear one of the aunts calling to them from the house.

'Quick, quick, under the stairs!'

Somedays it was just a practice and at other times it was real, because the aunts would have had news of an enemy bomber from the village, and they would never risk the children, not at any time, because they had loved the three of them more than themselves, more even than their house.

'Is anything the matter, Miranda?'

Sam's voice interrupted Miranda's thoughts, and she found herself staring blankly at him, as if he, and the day, were not real, as if the only reality was in the past.

'I'm sorry, what did you say?'

'I said is anything the matter?'

'No, no, why should there be?'

'I thought you looked sad suddenly, as if you had heard bad news, that's all, dear.'

'Bless you, no. Why should I be sad? I have a whole new life in front of me, after all. A whole new life. I am as lucky as a sixpence. I am going to be a mannequin.'

'Yes, you are.'

Sam stared out of the window, and then back at her, the expression in his eyes quite determined.

'More than anyone I have met since the war, believe me, you have the quality to become a famous model,' he told her. 'It is not that you are the most beautiful young woman I have ever met, far from it, but you have the ability to make what you wear change into something a great deal more. Good gracious, you make *me* want to wear the clothes, for heaven's sake, and I, in case you have not noticed, am a man.'

He laughed a little sarcastically, which Miranda did not understand.

'It is not something of which you must become too aware, I think, but I promise you – and I really do know about this business – I promise you that you are one of those rare human beings who have the capacity to make clothes what we call in the trade *take off*. That is what all those women would tell you, if they spoke better English. It is not that the clothes wear *you*, far from it. You wear *them*, and make them enviable. That is what a great mannequin can do. She can lift the clothes to a great dizzying height of desire, so that every photographer wants to snap them, and every painter wants to paint them, and every duchess to wear them. It is truly a brilliant quality. You act your clothes, and that is perfect.'

'I shall have to ask my guardian if it's all right for me to go to Paris with you.'

'Of course you will. But first, my dear, I am here to tell you that you have to have lessons. In walking. You really must learn to walk.'

Miranda started to laugh. 'And to think I thought that at least was something I knew how to do!'

'You stand very well, but you don't walk at all well. I send all my young ladies to Mrs Kelso in Farthing Street. She has rooms above the fruiterers there. By the time she has finished with you, believe me, you will not be walking in your clothes, you will be floating in them, and they with you.'

Bobbie had quite forgotten one of Beatrice's most famous but least appealing habits. She either arrived hours and sometimes days late, or – which was really much worse – she arrived hours and sometimes days early. She was so notorious for this that it had even been written about in the newspapers and magazines like *Vogue*. Bobbie remembered the nurses at the sanatorium showing her little clippings about her guardian just after the war. They had seemed most amused about the famous Beatrice Harper, about her penchant for large French poodles, about her ability to arrive anywhere at any time, but never *on* time.

Tomorrow, she had just announced to Bobbie, she was arriving early, but since tomorrow was the day that Bobbie and Julian and the Major had decided was the best possible moment for the Major to elope with Miss Moncrieff, her decision was, in their joint opinion, less than welcome. In fact it was really very *un*welcome, so that a positive gloom had settled over everyone involved in the elopement plans.

'You will just have to go early, Major. Leave it to me. I will help Miss M pack, and Julian will help you to make all the other arrangements. We have bought lots and lots of extra petrol coupons from a spiv that we met on the beach of all places. We did not realize at first that he *was* a spiv, because he had no clothes on, not to speak of that is. But then when he offered me some nylon stockings, of course we realized at once what was what. And we managed to buy practically a sackful of petrol coupons from him, so I think you can get to Gretna Green and back now without any trouble at all. And we managed to buy some dress coupons too, so Miss M could have a white dress and a bit of veiling, and here it is, bought from Mrs Brewster. She is the mother of the hairdresser in Baileys Green, you know – *Rene of Paris and London* – and she has altered it for Miss M, and here it all is. I borrowed one of Miss M's summer frocks for the measurements and so on, so it should all fit all right. Of course it's not quite up to the mark as far as fashion goes, but very pretty.'

Bobbie handed the Major his box, and she and Julian stared in pride and wonder at the Major's face as he took it.

'Shan't take a peek at it because I have always gathered it's bad luck, isn't it, to see a girl's frock before the big day?' He cleared his throat, and looked down at the box, at which he continued to stare. 'But, at any rate. But at any rate. You dear old beans, really; you have been so kind.' He gripped Bobbie's hand. 'You have been more than kind, and do you know – I truly feel it is rather more than a chap like me deserves.' He cleared his throat again and turned away. 'You dear, dear old bean,' he went on, walking off.

Bobbie said later, 'Do you know, when we gave him all that – you know, all those coupons and the dress we found – I really think it must have been his best moment since the gates of the prisoner of war camp opened and he saw our chaps marching through. His whole face lit up. Like a torch . . . like a *beacon* . . .'

'Too big. I have always thought a beacon far too *big* to light up a face. A beacon would flood it.' Julian stuck his nose in the air, and squinted down at Bobbie. 'A face, a human face, is about right to light up like a *torch*.'

Bobbie frowned, suddenly feeling past caring, really. 'Still, he was pleased, wasn't he? And let's face it, it's a miracle we got them off the way we did, don't you think? I actually thought Miss M would funk it, that she would put off the evil moment, or the glorious day, whichever you like to think of it as, and just stay dithering, but far from it – it was the Major who went white as a napkin and had to be pushed into his car.'

'I just hope Boy isn't sick before they reach Scotland.'

It had been exhausting, the whole excitement of it, the planning of it, the execution of it, getting the middle-aged lovers off before Beatrice arrived. And now Bobbie and Julian were walking along the Sussex road feeling rather as if they had actually been to the wedding of those two old biddies, had just thrown the rice after the departing car, and laughed at the old boot banging along behind the old Riley, and the truth was they were now feeling rather flat, as if they had drunk too much champagne or eaten too much cake, neither of them quite knowing what to do now that they had actually brought off this big adventure for their elders.

In fact they both felt so flat that Bobbie found herself wishing they could go through it all again, just for something exciting to do. But if she was feeling flat now, it was not as flat as she would be feeling two hours later when Beatrice arrived, too early even for her, and certainly for her ward's peace of mind, or, worse, presence of mind.

*   *   *

The truth was that, ever since she had arrived at Baileys Court and found Julian using it for his own purposes, Bobbie had kept Julian firmly hidden from Beatrice. Now, faced with the formidable sight of the Rolls-Royce containing her guardian advancing up the broken-fenced, potholed drive to the front of the former monastery, she had no idea why she had actually kept his presence a secret from her guardian.

Why had she not told Beatrice about this strange young friend of hers with his tall slender figure, bright blond hair and permanent cough? It would have been much easier to tell Beatrice before she came down than once she *was* down, Bobbie realized of a sudden, and far, far too late.

But of course, faced with the sudden apparition of the chauffeur, with his jumping out of the car, and the sight of his hand reaching into the car interior so that the lead of Beatrice's huge white French poodle could be handed out first, all at once it came to Bobbie that the reason why she had not told Beatrice about Julian, why she had put the whole matter to the back of her mind, was because Beatrice was a hypochondriac.

Now Bobbie remembered that Beatrice had a quite famous fear of disease, a fear which was so all-embracing that she took care never to actually touch money, and not just money. She never touched public door handles, or people's hands; she never even embraced anyone, unless she was quite, quite sure that she knew them so well that they would have told her if they had a cold coming on. By way of greeting she would either crook one gloved index finger, or nod her head, briefly, in acknowledgement. It had even been rumoured by Miss Moncrieff that Mrs Harper wore white gloves at all times, whether or not she was actually in company, and kept dozens for her use in her houses and cars; and that she wore a mask if any of the staff presented themselves to her in what she suspected to be less than a fit state. Just the sound of a sneeze was terrifying to her.

All this came back to Bobbie with prismatic clarity as she watched the bright white poodle, the maid, and of course Beatrice, being decanted from the sumptuous motor car. Bad enough for Beatrice to know that Bobbie had been unwell. Bad enough having a ward with 'poison on the lung' as Bobbie's tuberculosis was always tactfully called. Indeed, as far as she could remember – and those endless days at Hazel Hill seemed so far off now as to be ridiculous – Bobbie could not recall ever really seeing Beatrice at all except from afar. She visited the sanatorium but she did not do much more than wave from the ground to Bobbie, standing high above at the balcony of her private room.

Perhaps realizing that the child might eventually notice this she had written to Bobbie quite clearly on the subject.

I will do my duty by you, and my dear, dear late friend your mother, but I cannot also be intimate with you,

Roberta. My own health has always been somewhat frail, and now, with the war, so many dead, it is not at all strong, not what I could wish, really it is not.

Of course Bobbie had quite understood, as children always understand that they have to accept a grown-up's wishes with good grace. Indeed, she had not just understood, she had actually sympathized with her. Even at the age of twelve or thirteen, Bobbie was quite capable of seeing that her beautiful, elegant guardian could not be expected to visit a sanatorium, however large the gardens, however far from infection she was placed, except very, very briefly, if at all.

'My dear, dear Bobbie.'

Beatrice, full of a kind of awe-inspiring authority, despite her use of Bobbie's nickname, held out her gloved hand to her ward, and shook the small brown paw held out in return. But she did not kiss her, and they both knew why. The dreadful fear of disease, the fear of contagion, still haunted her, and despite Bobbie's being really so well, for some years now, Beatrice still managed to look openly nervous of her ward. Her brown eyes were worried and narrowed behind the veil of her hat, as if she was waiting for Bobbie to cough, or look hot and feverish.

As Bobbie stared at her, smiling in admiration at the stunning sight she presented compared to Bobbie herself in her grey flannel shorts and her old gym shoes, one of Julian's old shirts and a home-knitted sleeveless waistcoat made for her by Miss Moncrieff, Beatrice's large diamond brooch flashed and caught the sunlight. It was all that Bobbie could do not to gasp at the extraordinary glowing muted light that was reflecting from it, the sun seeming to pick out all the secret lights hidden in its depths.

But even as Bobbie admired it, after weeks of being outside, of never really seeing anyone except Julian and Major Saxby, the brooch suddenly appealed to her as being not brilliant and beautiful, but hard and useless. Beside a rose a diamond was just a piece of rock. So it was that, with a strange sense of disappointment, Bobbie realized, of a sudden, that really diamonds were made for dark rooms and jewellers' windows, not for sunlit gardens.

'My dear, dear Bobbie,' Beatrice said again, her eyes swivelling helplessly back to her chauffeur, her maid and her poodle. 'What a lovely thing to see you again after all this time, all these years. I mean I know we have talked,' she continued, turning back to her ward, 'but that is not the same thing. You are much . . .' She hesitated. 'You are much *taller* than I remember. Well, I suppose you would be, considering that you are a great deal *older* than you were when I became your guardian. And you're very brown, fashionably brown, Chanel brown,' she went on, her eyes suddenly seeming to seize on Bobbie's slender, sandalled legs and become fixated by them. She continued to stare at the colour as if they were part of a piece of fine furniture she was considering acquiring. 'Very brown, indeed. Your legs are very brown.'

She must have seen the chauffeur too staring at Bobbie's legs, because she suddenly turned and snapped at him, 'Start unpacking the luggage and taking it to the front hall, would you, Davis? And Ward, you take Piaf for a toddle to tinkle round the bushes down there, would you?' She stopped once more before stepping into the hall, turning back to Bobbie as if it had only just occurred to her that she was one short of her usual retinue of personal staff. 'Oh, and by the way, Roberta dear, where is Miss Moncrieff, please?'

Bobbie had practised the lines. She had actually practised them over and over again, after having of course first tried them out on Julian. She had a choice of three versions of the same news to break to her guardian, and it had all seemed perfectly simple, until she started to try them out.

The first version was, 'Miss Moncrieff has had to leave in a hurry.' The second was, 'Miss Moncrieff has run off to Scotland with Major Saxby whom you haven't met, but he is very nice and they are probably now married.' The third was, 'I am sorry to tell you that Miss Moncrieff has run away with Major Saxby to Gretna Green before her mother could find out.'

Both Bobbie and Julian had managed to agree, while wiping away tears of laughter, that the last was probably the neatest and best, but now the time to speak the lines had arrived all Bobbie could do was stare at Beatrice, her brain quite numb.

For the truth was that Beatrice, in common with

so many rich people, came fitted with an especially powerful personality, a personality which, alas, neither Bobbie nor Julian had taken into account while Bobbie had been rehearsing how to break the news to her. After all that time spent trying out various ways to tell her frighteningly beautiful, dark-haired guardian that her secretary had eloped without asking her employer of fifteen years for permission, Bobbie now heard herself saying in a stammering, footling little voice, 'I, er, don't know, really. I don't know exactly where Miss Moncrieff is, exactly, I am afraid. That is. No, I don't know, I really don't.'

'I am sorry, what did you say?'

'I said I – er – don't know. I don't know where Miss Moncrieff is, exactly, I am afraid, that is.'

It was actually not quite a lie, not really. In fact it was a kind of half-truth, because Bobbie really did not know, and could not possibly know, where Miss Moncrieff was precisely. As far as Bobbie knew she might be halfway to Scotland, she might be actually at Gretna Green; or she might have changed her mind and stopped off in Pinner with her mother, or decided to live in sin with Major Saxby in Ebury Street. So, it was true, at that moment Bobbie did have absolutely no idea at all where Miss Moncrieff might be.

'You don't *know*, Roberta, you don't know *where* Miss Moncrieff is?'

Bobbie shook her head. 'She left the Sheds . . .' Bobbie was about to say *this morning* when another truth dawned: if she said Miss Moncrieff had only left this morning Beatrice might well think that they could all catch up with her. 'She left the Sheds *two days ago*, in the company of Major Saxby.'

Beatrice practically seized Bobbie's arm and marched her into the suddenly chill, stone-flagged hall, out of earshot of her chauffeur and her maid, and well out of the way of Julian, who was, Bobbie knew, hidden in some bush or shrub somewhere nearby.

Inwardly Bobbie sighed at the humour she knew that Julian would be finding in the situation. At how he would laugh at her, and not with her. He would split his sides at Bobbie's awkwardness, at her inability to come out with the lines required of her, lines that they had so carefully rehearsed together.

'What did you say, Roberta? Where has Miss Moncrieff gone? With whom did you say the wretched woman has absconded?'

Suddenly, staring into her guardian's narrowed eyes as they bored into her from under Beatrice's hat, Bobbie could not stand it any more. She was actually fed up with the whole business, if the truth were known. Fed up with Miss Moncrieff, with the Major, with Julian, with herself, with Beatrice, with the chauffeur, with the maid, even with the poodle, but most of all with life.

Why were people so difficult? Why could they not just be happy that some poor spinster in lisle stockings and a home-knitted cardigan had fallen in love and run off with the Major? Why was Beatrice looking like the wrath of God and taking off her hat and sticking her hatpin through it with such fury and force that for a second Bobbie had a sense of the hat's squealing in pain?

'Miss Moncrieff has gone off with the Major. Major Saxby, of the Pines, that is. It's a large house in the village with about half an acre of garden.'

'It's of no interest to me where the stupid man lives. He is obviously some fraud who has turned her head.'

'No, no, that's not it at all. You see, he lost his wife, do you see . . .'

'Stop saying do you see, Roberta. It's appallingly slovenly.'

'Well, he lost his wife, just before he got home from being a prisoner of war, and then he came here, to help in the garden, and you know Miss M was here and they were always having lunch together and listening to *Mrs Dale's Diary* and they, you know, they realized that they rather liked each other and as a result they, er, decided to – well, they decided to get married in a bit of a hurry, before they changed their minds, I expect.'

'And why, pray, did you not tell me before?'

'It's only just happened, really. You see, as I say, Major Saxby was helping with the garden. He was very useful actually, because he knew people on the council, and in the village, and he was able to get us sand and cement for the walls. Wait till you see them, I think you will be pleased. And then he was very, very sad, you see, because his wife had died, just as he came home from the Burma railway, and so gardening and building walls, or rather rebuilding them, well, they really cheered him up. And so he used to go and have lunch with Miss Moncrieff, because he didn't like being on the beach, we realized. And they ran off the day before yesterday, to Gretna Green, where they will be married, I suppose, very soon, and really it's very nice, because, I mean, they *could* marry. I mean neither of them are divorced or anything, so they could. Marry. I think Miss Moncrieff meant to tell you, but it was all so sudden, she probably forgot. Yes, that was it, she did forget, I think she said that. She forgot. And so did I, until just now. It didn't seem to matter, really. I mean they are getting married, and he is nice.'

'Nice!' Beatrice snorted the word. 'Nice? Miss Moncrieff would not know a spiv from a member of the Salvation Army. The woman is a complete and utter nincompoop! But that is not the point. The point is that staff are all, to a person, perfidious sneaks. After all this time to do as she has done, to skulk off without a say so, or a say why. After, it must be fifteen years? I think it is perfectly, utterly perfidious. She is a two-faced, perfidious sneak.'

Beatrice spat the words across the cold stone floor of the old monastery, and before Bobbie could say another word, or think of what to say next, her guardian went on, 'That woman has been *tolerated* by me for *fifteen* years, and now she chooses to walk out just as I *need* her to write letters, just as I *need* her to make telephone calls, just as I am opening up the *house* for the summer. I shall probably sue her. That is what I shall do. I shall sue her.'

Bobbie dropped her eyes to the floor. She had never heard anyone quite so cross, not ever. She had actually never seen a proper rage before. She had never seen a woman snatching at a cigarette from her handbag and stuffing it with trembling fingers into the top of her long, black cigarette holder, and now that she was a witness to this behaviour she could not help wishing that Beatrice's car had broken down on the way to Sussex. This perfectly frightful *woman* was not at all the kind of person that she, her ward, had always imagined Beatrice Harper to be, when she was growing up at the sanatorium in Hazel Hill and receiving parcels of dresses and coats and fine books with old bindings from her guardian.

'But you have another secretary, haven't you?'

Again Bobbie heard her own words rather as if they were being spoken by someone else. And she thought how strange this sensation was, this feeling that someone else was speaking through you, that it was your voice, but *not* your voice that you heard.

'Mrs Calder is my secretary for *London*, Roberta. Miss Moncrieff is my secretary for *Sussex*. *Was* for Sussex.' She stopped, and threw her whole cigarette, holder and all, on the floor and stamped on it, as if it was a stub. 'Well,' she went on, after a long pause, during which she breathed in and out in a way that reminded Bobbie of Aunt Sophie's pony Tom Kitten after some strenuous uphill work. 'Well, we will just have to make the best of it. We will just have to use *you* as my secretary, since you seem to have been in some way responsible for this. Encouraging the military to run off with secretaries is not a practice of which anyone should approve, Roberta. But there, it is done and cannot be undone, and you may now pay the penalty. You may now take up the very position which has just been vacated by Miss Moncrieff. You can be my country house secretary, my secretary for Sussex. You will need a role in life. Now I have found one for you. One door closes, you see, and another one opens.'

After this she stalked back into the sunshine, but as she reached the curved Gothic arch that made up the shallow entrance to the old monastery building she turned and with a cat-like smile, and, Bobbie could swear, a cat-like purr too, she called to her ward, 'I am afraid that from now on, Roberta, there will be no time for tanning yourself. Oh no, dear me no, no time at all. You will be inside, in the Sheds, from now on, and your tan will turn a pallid fawn, I am afraid. But never mind. You'll soon get used to it, I'm sure, and doubtless you too will, in your turn, become perfidious, like Miss Moncrieff and sundry others. But until you do decide to run off with some Major Saxby or another, congratulations – you have been found a new role.'

As she followed her guardian out into the sunshine Bobbie's heart, like the sun disappearing behind the clouds above them, was cast suddenly into the first shadows of many months, as she realized with dawning horror what her guardian's words really meant.

She was to be locked up once more, just as she had been at Hazel Hill, but this time it would be in the Sheds, and doubtless, as she must have done with Miss Moncrieff, Beatrice would throw away the key, and Bobbie would, again like Miss Moncrieff, turn to knitting stockings and wearing cardigans with two-ply – or was it three-ply? – moss-stitched cuffs and collars. And she too would become a prey to her nerves from not being able to run about. And her mornings would be full only of the doubtful delights of a warm cup of cocoa, or a bowl of Bovril at lunchtime with a piece of brown bread followed by an apple, because when you were sitting waiting for another to call you, sitting waiting to call or write to someone on behalf of someone else, sitting waiting for life to happen to someone else, those things were the only excitements to which your heart and soul could turn.

Suddenly, blind to the fact that she was not alone any more, Bobbie started to run and run, towards the sea, towards the stone-filled beach where the waves would be frilling and the seagulls dipping, towards what had been. But even as she began to run it was as if she was running towards a narrow tunnel, towards a pin of light which had already begun to shrink beyond any imagining, light that was already starting to pull away from her, so that she knew that in reality running was completely fruitless because there were hounds at her heels, and they were closing in on her, getting nearer and nearer, closer and closer, but they were not canine hounds but human hounds, and it seemed to her in her panic that she could feel their breath on her neck, just as it seemed her heart was going at a rate that was no longer sustainable, and that everything in her whole life was suddenly pointless, and black, and dark, until at last there was no longer any light at all.

Chapter Eight

It was the height of summer all over France. Despite the recent war families were holidaying at old châteaux in the Loire, or in farmhouses and villas in the south, or in small cottages by the sea in Brittany. Wherever they were, however, and whoever they might be with, they had, to a person, left Paris quite empty of anyone of any consequence, with the single exception of those who toiled behind sewing machines in the ateliers of the great designers, struggling to help produce the many and varied masterpieces of post-war fashion, masterpieces that would still be admired and talked about long after the fashion for them had passed and moved on, and would eventually stand behind glass cases to be admired by visitors to museums, and students studying fashion.

Miranda was now part of this great exciting climax that was slowly approaching the capital. She had been brought to Paris by Sam Macaskie as early as late July, to be walked through salons and drawing rooms, to be paraded in and out of back street ateliers, until he was well satisfied that everyone knew what a great beauty his new protégée was, how tall she was, how elegant, how beautifully she walked.

Of course, since Sam had taken charge of her life, he had changed her name. He had taken her original surname, her true surname, once he had discovered it, and found it most amusing to put it together with her nickname to make the entirely delightful Randy Darling. It was a name that, once he had thought of it, made Miranda wrinkle her nose and at the same time laugh helplessly, because she had to admit that Macaskie was right – it was not a name that anyone would be likely to forget. The French found it easy too, so that was good.

She, in her turn, not to be outdone, no longer called Sam 'Mr Macaskie', or even 'Sam', but just *Macaskie*, because after that first day when she had been foolish enough to be deceived by his intentions she had no intention of thinking of him in anything but a professional way. Sam was too informal, and Mr Macaskie too formal, and Macaskie seemed to satisfy him too, although he never referred to such things, seeming, really, only to be concerned that Randy Darling should make a name for herself, progressing to the point of international fame, after which, as he said, affectionately, 'You can take care of your good self, and I shall be off to seek another young woman. Although I doubt if I shall find her attempting to drink gin and it in the Dorchester. That is certainly not normal.'

'I told you, I was taken to the Dorchester during the war, by a friend of my guardian – a friend of Allegra Sulgrave. Bombs dropped all night, but we slept like tops. Anyway, I never forgot it, or Pamela, the lady who took me there.'

'I hear Chanel used to stay there, and that whenever she went down to the air raid shelter in the basement she was always preceded by her maid carrying her gas mask on a cushion. Now that is style with a capital B as in *beautiful* style.'

They were seated in one of those small cafés that have so few tables outside, and such a small bar inside, that anyone drinking there must have been forgiven for wondering at some time or another whether it could ever be worth the proprietor's while to try to make a living in such a small place.

Miranda looked across the street. An accordionist was playing on the pavement opposite. Two men, both carrying long sticks of bread under their arms, passed by wearing black berets and mackintoshes despite the heat. She watched them progressing slowly up the street, and as she did so it came to her that they would most likely have many stairs to mount before they reached their apartments, and that when they did reach them those same apartments would probably be damp, which might be the reason for their wearing mackintoshes on such a summery evening. Or it might be that they had no other decent clothes, that underneath those belted coats their other garments were so darned and patched, their everyday clothes were so impoverished, that their only shred of lasting dignity lay in their mackintoshes and berets.

She turned and looked at Macaskie, and was about to ask him whether he agreed when it came to her that a man like Macaskie would never think thoughts of that kind. He was just not that sort of person.

Miranda sighed, looking at his dark good looks as he smoked his usual untipped Gauloise in leisurely fashion, and read through the evening paper. She had done her very best not to fall in love with Macaskie, but since coming to Paris she had begun to find it more and more difficult, perhaps because she was lonely and spoke almost no French.

Or perhaps it was because it felt as if it was the right time to fall in love, that not to fall in love would be to miss out on the right time and the right place, and where could be more right, after all, than Paris?

It was not that Macaskie was more handsome than any of the other men she passed sometimes in the street, or saw arriving or departing from their hotels. It was not that he was the wittiest companion – he certainly was not that. It was, she had decided, when awake in the night and watching the occasional car light making shadows on her bedroom ceiling, his quality of aloofness, his ability to stand back and appreciate everything and everyone in his own particular way.

Yet it was not in a way that he would ever dream

of sharing with others, least of all, Miranda sometimes thought, with her. No – Macaskie was his own best kept secret, which somehow made him fascinating to Miranda, and to women in general, for she saw that, all too obviously, wherever she went, women were in love with Macaskie. Or at least, the women who knew him, married, unmarried, single, or unattached, all liked to imagine that they were in love with him. A certain soft, tender look came into their eyes the moment he turned the corner and they saw him, and that same kind of greeting that she had first noticed when they lunched at the Dorchester would be forthcoming – *Ah, Sam, Sam – how are you?* – and there would be much patting of his cheek with gloved hands, or kissing of that same smooth cheek with reddened lips that left a small imprint which had to be quickly removed with a lace-edged handkerchief.

The truth was that Miranda knew that she had about as much chance with Macaskie as any of the other women who knew him and loved him – in other words, she had no chance at all. Which was why she called him by his surname. It helped to distance him from her heart, to remove him from her feelings. He was not 'Sam' to her. To the others he might be, but not to her.

And she was not so stupid that she did not know that, despite all her youthful slender shape, 'Miranda' as a person meant little or nothing to him; to him her body was just something from which to make money. Of course the money that he would make from her was not just for him, it was for her too, but nevertheless over the last days, for some reason, as he took her from one photographic studio to another, it had started to feel more and more as if it was all for him – much less for Randy Darling, and much more for Sam Macaskie.

His preliminary plan had been all along, she knew now, for her to burst upon the fashion season well before it actually opened. He wanted his protégée to conquer the fashion press, even the dailies; to build Miranda's image as Randy Darling in such a way that by the end of September, by the time all the ballyhoo and the excitement of the winter fashion shows, in the magazines, even the newsreels, had calmed down, Randy would be *the* name of that season. That was the power, well known and apparently envied by his rivals, that Macaskie's interest in a model could arouse.

'Your whole life is about to change,' he announced after their first few days in Paris, and he stared out of the window and smiled at the rooftops opposite the atelier in which they were waiting for Miranda to be fitted with some new and exciting *toile*. Soon some new and exciting master would enter the room, and having turned and turned Miranda would – if the *toile* was right – smile and stand back, and call to his assistants to admire and gasp with him at his creation; or – and this had already happened many times – he would throw his arms in the air, a torrent of frustrated fury would escape him, and his assistants would all rush forward and start to unpin, or repin, or just take the offending garment tearfully away, before beginning on yet another potential masterpiece.

Again and again Miranda was witness to such scenes, and again and again, as the *toiles* were hurled back or greeted with ecstasy and sent on their way, as she saw them either fitted on her or repinned on a dummy, the awful realization would strike her that the clothes she was to model were, in every way, works of art, and it was up to her not to let them down in any way. They were the picture, she was the frame.

'Modelling clothes beautifully is as difficult as dancing beautifully,' her teacher, Mrs Kelso in Farthing Street, had told her. 'It requires a lightness of movement, an inner sense of beauty, an awareness of the moment, that has, to my mind, been sadly underrated. A bad model can destroy the artistry of clothes in seconds, as much as a good model can raise it to the point when the audience at that show will never, if they live to be a hundred, ever, forget the dress.'

It was fun, and yet it was not fun either, for standing for hours on end, not really knowing to what end some designer was working, required great patience. It required great patience, too, to wait for Macaskie to return to the hotel at dusk and take her off to the Ritz bar for a drink, and then perhaps on to some small café where he would let her drink red wine and nibble small portions of delicious food while he ate rather more heartily.

The difference in the ways of life enjoyed in France and in England was too strange not to be talked about, and the subject came up again and again, with Miranda protesting that it was unfair that the French, who had been invaded, had fewer problems after the war, or seemingly fewer problems, than the English who had actually repulsed the invader. The French had food, and wine, and gaiety, while at home the English could not even buy a piece of fish without queuing.

This particular evening Macaskie was in high good humour. Seated at their café table he insisted that he loved the English despite their way of life and because of themselves. He loved the French for their way of life and rather despite themselves, but whichever – he quite saw what Miranda meant.

In between taking small sips of anise he insisted, 'The British way of life is dour because they *like* it that way, believe me – nothing to do with the war. They like *not* to enjoy themselves. They like to sit out on hard-backed chairs while other nations dance. They like to keep Sunday particularly – a nice dark grey, no singing, no dancing, no markets, nothing but church, church and more church, and all before the weather turns nasty and they over-cook the vegetables. You know that Voltaire was once exiled to England?'

Miranda shook her head. She knew so little about Voltaire that quite frankly he might as well be a fashion designer, not a great writer.

'Yes, Voltaire exiled himself from France, in

disgust at the censorship, but after only a few months he came right back to France again – apparently he simply could not take all that gentility, poor fellow. And that was before he raised his fork to his lips and found out what the British did to food! Which reminds me that it must now be time for us to go to table, because I personally am starving.'

Miranda had spent four long weeks with Mrs Kelso in Farthing Street, and now, simply by standing up and walking ahead of him, she was able to make everyone stop talking and turn their heads as they passed. Despite the fact that she was simply dressed in only a dark coat, white gloves, seamed nylon stockings and high-heeled shoes, she registered with everyone that she passed. Not because the dark coat was anything special, nor because she was wearing nylons, and her blond hair was brushed up and back under her hat; it was because of the *way* she was wearing them. She sashayed ahead of Macaskie knowing that he was noting every one of those people turning their heads as she walked by their tables, that he saw how many of them stopped talking, even for a few seconds, and stared at her.

Miranda knew that, by the time they sat down opposite each other in the darker end of the restaurant, Macaskie would be yet again congratulating himself on his choice of model to promote that year. She knew without looking that he would follow her slowly into the restaurant, through the door which she was now pushing with her gloved hand, telling himself all the time that he had the golden touch, that Sam Macaskie had the eye that was needed to spot a fashion star, that no-one else had his flair, that photographers from all over would be queuing to use Randy Darling.

Once they were seated and had ordered, Macaskie, obviously bored by the discomforts of England, of life at its worst on the other side of the Channel, changed the subject. 'So, Randy darling, what, in your opinion, has been the best dress to date? Which one did you like best, would you like best to model?'

Miranda looked at Macaskie, surprised. 'Oh, you know what I'm like – I always think the dress I have just been fitted with is the one I love best. I have very little taste.'

Macaskie smiled. 'Well, never mind your taste. You know who wants you for his collection – so you had better change your tune, young lady.'

Miranda carefully blew some smoke into the air before saying, 'Who?'

'The Master himself. The Master has asked for you, Randy.'

Miranda turned and stared at Macaskie. 'But he has not even met me.'

'Yet, but he will, and he already knows about you. He has already been told about the new blond English beauty. He also knows that for the New Look to go on increasing in popularity those photographs in every newspaper and magazine all over the world are going to have to look more than marvellous, they are going to have to look stunning. Nothing else will do.' Macaskie reached under the table. 'Look, I had these developed for you to look at. Hold them up, and you will see yourself as others see you.'

Of a sudden, Miranda knew that she was about to change for ever; that seeing herself in those clothes, photographed by one of the world's most renowned photographers, she would fall in love with herself.

And she did.

She could not help herself. There she was, transformed from wartime orphan to a beautiful young girl dressed in a long, full-skirted, blue-printed organdie dress over a pale pink net petticoat, the whole strapless effect topped off by a dropped-shoulder bolero. And again, there she was in a faille silk and aubergine satin over-dress, holding a great bunch of dark-leafed flowers over her head while the strapless black velvet dress beneath the faille showed darkly against the pale blue studio walls. Schiaparelli's narrow suit with wide belt and peg skirt, hat pulled down, dark stockings paired with dark high-heeled shoes, gave her a mysterious look, as did a black faille suit with large sleeves and slim skirt.

'Now will you have your hair cut?'

It was certainly Macaskie's voice speaking, but Miranda could only stare at photograph after photograph of herself, not really recognizing this tall, beautiful young woman standing in clothes that were doubtless, according to the laws of fashion, already past it. She *was* beautiful. She could see that now. And she *had* always loved clothes.

Aunt Sophie had used to say, 'You have allure, dearest, such allure. Not many people have it. You must use it to get on, really you must. You mustn't be like myself, or Prudence. Don't just fester, make something of yourself, become famous, use your allure. Above all, keep away from making jam. People only eat your jam, and never thank you for it.'

'Sorry, Macaskie, what did you say?'

'I said *now* will you have your hair cut?'

'What? Oh, yes. Yes, of course I will.'

Despite rationing, fashion was back centre stage, filling magazines and newspapers with its peculiar importance. Hair was about to be worn short, and would be for some time, giving the demobbed hairdressers much-needed business. It also fitted neatly under hats, and hats were going to be just as important as the clothes themselves.

There would be chip straw hats worn with slender-waisted full-skirted dresses, or Venetian hats trimmed with silk worn with London coats, or hats that peaked at the front and were worn quite flat so that the wearer looked out cheekily, the hat nearly touching her eyebrows, the decoration, if there was one, worn to the front. Boaters too would be worn with white-collared Quaker dresses, and velvet cloches with many of the straight-fronted dresses – wing-backed, back-buttoned and reverse collared – but placed to the back of the head and finished with a bow in the same material.

The truth was that, loth though Miranda was to have her hair cut, she knew that in reality Macaskie was right: she would not be able to show off the coming seasons' hats well. For, with her long, full, thick head of hair, she would not be able to change them in seconds. Most of all she would not be able to look up to the minute. At any moment all hair was going to be short and curly, or short and tapered around the face. Not to have her hair like that would be to trail behind fashion. And yet her hair was so much *her*, or at least that is how she thought of it, the *her* of Miranda Mowbray.

Hardly had she consented to the whole tortuous business before Macaskie was steering her into a hairdressing salon. It was fashionably placed on the rue de Rivoli, naturally, but like the rest of Paris it was empty. Miranda closed her eyes. She did not want to see the hair falling to the floor, but she could still hear the scissors. Suddenly it came to her that all her life was in her hair. All her life she had brushed her hair a hundred times at night, all her life she had plaited it, and knotted it, put it into chignons, or ribbons, had it admired by her granny, or by the aunts at Mellaston. She had let Teddy ride on her back using her plaits as reins; every year at Mellaston she had been chosen as the Virgin Mary in the Christmas Story because of her hair. Her hair was her memories, her personality, her confidence.

After being pushed and prodded, and hearing the sound of 'ooh's and 'aah's from the other hairdressers who had come to watch the still unusual sight of the master cutting off this luxuriant hair to a length that was hardly longer than a boy's, Miranda opened her eyes. When she saw what the hairdresser had done, tears – tears that she had not shed for Aunt Sophie and Aunt Prudence, not for anyone or anything to date – started to spill down her face. He had ruined her.

Minutes later, when Macaskie arrived, he was unsympathetic. There was nothing to cry about, he told her, she looked better than ever; but his eyes, even as he spoke, drifted away from the shorn Miranda, and towards other models, being coiffed, or curled, or tonged.

Miranda stared at him, realizing suddenly that he did not care about how she felt, or how she looked. She was, she saw, just a girl to him. He was only interested in what she could bring to his bank. Deep down inside she felt desperate. She had to make him care about her, she had to make him mind about her more than anyone else.

'Sam.'

He looked bored. 'Yup.'

His eyes looked into hers, still bored, still longing to get on with something other than Miranda and her now very short hair.

'Let's go back to the apartment. I'll pull myself together, I promise.'

He shrugged his shoulders, his indifference

suddenly heightening her fascination. 'Yup. If you want. But it sure as hell won't help your hair to grow.'

'No, but – but you could make love to me.'

She did not know why she said that, or how the words, so alien to her, came out, all on their own, too. As if they were issuing from another person locked up inside her, as if that person had suddenly appeared beside her with an emotional begging bowl. Because without her hair, she was no longer Miranda Mowbray, she was a pathetic figure, without spirit, without shape.

'We'll see.' Macaskie turned away, still indifferent, still only interested, it seemed, in other models, other girls, girls who suited short hair.

In Sussex Bobbie was being lectured by Beatrice. Beatrice had decided to visit the Sheds. She wanted to know a great deal more about the estate. Bobbie must take her round. Bobbie stared at her dully, knowing that she should not feel this great lump of resentful dislike, verging on hatred, for this immaculately dressed woman who had saved her life, paid for her recovery from tuberculosis, altogether looked after her when no-one else cared to, and all because of some long forgotten promise to Bobbie's mother, made on the outbreak of war. But it was more than she could help, it was an uncontrollable dislike that had nothing to do with duty or gratitude. Deep down inside, deep in her secret heart, Bobbie knew that she hated Beatrice.

'You must show me round, Roberta, but don't come too near, my dear, you know, because of the risk of infection – my frail health, you know.'

Bobbie nodded, and picking up her coat she prepared to leave the Sheds and go outside into the wind and the intermittent sunshine of a day that already held a hint of autumn. Of course as soon as she was walking ahead of Beatrice and thinking about her guardian's permanently 'frail' health, the mischievous notion came into her head, and would not be dismissed, that if she wanted Beatrice to go away and not come back again, to return to London at once, she should really start to pretend to cough again. That way she would send Beatrice packing. But another thought came close upon the first one, and that was that this course of action would not only send Beatrice packing, it would doubtless mean that Bobbie would be sent packing too, but not back to London – back to Hazel Hill and the kindly French nurses, back to her room with its dull green institutional curtains, and its pale cream walls, and its far-off sounds of other people's sufferings.

That thought was too bad to contemplate. In fact it was so bad that Bobbie shuddered inwardly and put it away from her as being too terrible to think about, ever, even as she realized that her life was very far from being safe, or dull, now that her guardian was here. She would have to take particular care never, ever to cough in her presence, for to do so might be to invite a return to the sanatorium, to that other life that Bobbie had, recently, put so very far behind her that she had actually, until now, all but forgotten its realities. She was after all still under age, not yet twenty-one, so Beatrice was still her guardian, and could do as she wished as far as Bobbie was concerned: shut her back up at Hazel Hill, or put her to work down the mines. No, Bobbie was very lucky, really.

Yet still, she had not told Beatrice about Julian, nor Julian about Mrs Harper's hypochondria. She had said nothing to either of them that first day, hoping in some mad way to find an answer to her problems overnight, but the next day, which when it came dawned as fitfully as the previous one, she crept from the Sheds, and, avoiding the main house where Beatrice and her staff were camping in the drier more civilized rooms, dived into the underground passage and ran along it, hoping against hope that Beatrice would not find this secret corridor, at least not for months and months.

Climbing up the narrow winding stairway, she started to call.

'Julian! Julian! Julian!'

For a second as she knocked on his door, and then fought her way through the velvet curtain, she found herself imagining that he had gone, and she would never see him again. But, no, thank God, there he was and he was still as tall, and as oddly dressed, as always.

'Oh, Julian, there you are.'

'Yes, here I am, Roberta.'

She knew straight away from the expression on his face that he had heard what a rotten fist she had made of telling Beatrice about poor Major Saxby and Miss Moncrieff.

'You heard me telling her, didn't you? I knew you would. I felt you were nearby, I just couldn't see you, which was probably just as well, really, because I should have started to laugh, and it was bad enough anyway, without that.'

Julian stared down at her momentarily, his head on one side, a lazy affectionate expression in his eyes, and it seemed to Bobbie as she looked back at him that he loved her, but would never tell her so. She knew that he thought of her as a madcap but also that part of his problem was that she had changed so much since she had first stumbled upon his room in the garden wing. And of course she had grown up with him in the last months, it was only to be expected. Yet she had not grown *out* of him. Julian was still her best friend, her *fidus Achates*, everything that she could want in a companion.

Since she was a child Bobbie had always imagined having a friend of her own, someone to whom she could talk and confide everything that she had ever felt or thought. She had never thought of her future as one long enormous stretch of years, more one long enormous stretch of months, until Julian had arrived in her life and then, suddenly, she seemed to have a future, and there was always something to which to look forward – Julian arriving, seeing Julian, being with him.

And yet nothing stayed still, and she knew it. She could not ignore the changing weather, the way the waves were getting stronger, the winds around the Sheds noisier. Autumn will come and the leaves will fall, and there will be no more laughter, no looking for sense among the stars, no walking to the beach at lunchtime and stripping off and swimming all alone except for some figure miles off walking his dog. There will be no more of that, no more of the sunshine, and worst of all no more of the laughter. So, it is best if we treat the whole summer as being not like any other time to come and not spoil one lovely moment of it, remember it as it is, as it was, a sunny, happy, perfect idyll.

After that Bobbie said to Julian with her usual urgency, 'You see they don't know about the underground corridor that runs between the wings, and so you *can* stay on here, for the moment anyway. I know they will never, ever bother with this wing, not at the moment anyway. They're all too busy trying to make themselves comfy in the main house. Besides, I will tell Beatrice that this wing is dangerous, and damp, and so on, just to make sure. So you really will be quite safe still, here, until the building regulations are changed. And that won't be for years and years and years. You will be as safe as the mice in the attics, as safe as the stones on the beach, as safe as safe as—'

Bobbie could see that Julian was only half listening to her while in his imagination he, like herself, was wandering through the past months, laughing and talking, and, as always, Bobbie was *still* talking.

'So look, I'll come back here, with a picnic, because by dinner time they will all be past caring where I am, and then we can either go down to the Sheds, and picnic on the beach, or stay here. What do you say?'

Julian smiled his lazy smile at her, one last time.

'What a good idea, *dear bean*,' he said, imitating the Major. 'Come here, yes, and we'll picnic, by candlelight.' He gestured round to the precious candles of which they had only the other day found a quantity in the basement of the house. 'It'd be lovely.'

'Good, yes.' Bobbie turned, frowning suddenly. 'Sorry. Did you say "would be"?'

'No, I don't think so, why?'

'Nothing. I don't know why, I just thought that was what you said, that it "would be lovely" as if you were not going to be there. Because if you had you would regret it – Wretched Boy!'

She smiled across at him. 'Because.' She paused. 'Because . . . Mrs Duddy has promised to bring us *chicken*.'

'Chicken?'

'Yes, chicken.'

For a second Bobbie thought she saw the determination in Julian's expression waver. Chicken. No-one ate chicken nowadays.

'You must be her favourite person ever.'

'Of course.'

Bobbie hurried off, waving back to him from the courtyard below, and as she did so she imagined that Julian would turn away and start writing or drawing as it seemed he always did once he went back to his room in the garden wing.

Then she imagined how he would wait for her to come hurrying back down the underground passageway with the big, old-fashioned picnic basket from the Sheds. She delighted in the thought of his expectation of her arrival, of how he would hear her mounting the twisting stairway, each narrow step bringing her closer and closer to what she knew he always thought of as 'their room'. She thought of him imagining her pushing through the doorway, backing through it, as she usually did if she brought him a picnic.

Of course if he was not there when she returned, she thought suddenly as she went through the underground passageway, she would hate him for ever, and ever. She would hate him the way she knew girls and boys always hated each other when they had been let down so badly that they would never, ever forget, or forgive. But really, when all was said and done, that would be by far the best way, for her to hate him. It would be a far better ending to their idyllic summer. But not yet, she prayed silently, not quite yet.

After all, quite apart from the likelihood of his leaving now that summer was gone, there was also his incipient TB. They had both laughed so much about that word together. Why was TB always *incipient*, Bobbie had wanted to know, when nothing else was? There was no such thing as *incipient* measles, or *incipient* mumps, or *incipient* influenza.

'I tell you what – let's call ourselves The Incipients – you know, like a band, an American jazz band.'

Of course she had laughed and minutes later forgotten all about it, preferring to become engrossed in harmless gossip – like whether or not Miss Moncrieff had yet surrendered to the Major, or whether the landlord of the Dog and Duck was a black market spiv, or whether the Major was really a sham, and had never been a prisoner of war, and had made it all up in order to take Miss M's savings? Somehow it had all been talking. Even when they were swimming they had never really stopped talking, even if it meant swallowing mouthfuls of sea.

Necessarily, because they were always walking about or cutting things back, or digging, numerous fantasies had surrounded everything they did. All very harmless, but somehow, given the long, leisurely hours of that idyllic summer, the fantasies, the arguments, everything they talked about had assumed an enormous and engrossing importance. And that was before he had read Keats to her by candlelight, or walked arm in arm with her through the tunnel beneath the old gardens – or before she had returned to the Sheds and Miss Moncrieff.

And too, as summer had progressed, and he had seemed to become better and better – because of 'the sea air' as Bobbie had kept saying, so encouragingly – Bobbie had fantasized that they might be able to stay together, somehow, which was ridiculous, because they were both only young, and people like Mrs Harper never allowed their wards to stay with young men without futures.

And so now it was all over, and she knew that one of these days he would be going, without any doubt, moving on. It was perhaps because of this realization that she suddenly turned and ran back up the passageway again, only to find that he had stayed at the window long after she had vanished from sight, long after she had left the courtyard far below – long after that, Julian had stayed at the window, looking out.

Now he opened it and as he did so Bobbie kissed her hand up to him, in an exaggerated way, in 'their' way, and he kissed his hand back down to her, before shutting the window again, and going back inside the room.

'Wretched Boy!' Bobbie called up to him, but Julian was gone.

MEANWHILE . . .

'My eager feet shall find you again,
Though the sullen years and the mark of pain
Have changed you wholly ... '

Rupert Brooke, 'The Beginning'

Chapter Nine

Teddy had loved the idea of the army, until he joined it, that is. He wanted so much to join, and then the reality of it hit him, and another part of him, practically all of him actually, wanted it to go away and be something else, something which was less restricted. For, in his imagination, Teddy had thought that the army was going to be full of heroes in the making, and that he would become one of them straight away, the kind of person he had read about, seen films about, been inspired by. But the army was not like that at all. The army was like school. It was full of routine. And being in the army was like school, like staying with people's parents in the holidays, when you got close to it, it just was as it was, and could never be anything else except – the army.

Of course he loved the officers' uniforms, and of course he was grateful to Rawlins' father for getting him accepted into such a smart regiment, a regiment which was steeped in what seemed to be an endless history – Obdaman – Ratterspitz –

Constantin – the names of battles were written on the walls of the regiment's dining rooms, as well as on the minds of those joining it.

Oh, bravery, courage, taking a stand in some stinking hole, defending the King or Queen, and Country in some remote part of the British Empire, it was all there in the way that the officers walked, the way they talked, the way their dark blue coats swayed behind them on the Parade ground, the way their swagger sticks stayed under their arms, even when they lit a cigarette, it was all there, in the minds of those who had been elected to become part of this shining, brilliant elite.

It was there too in the impossibly matching horses, with their harness polished harder than the steel of the drawn sword that ended parade. It was there in the endless rehearsals of the military band, in the band master with his shining white moustache, in the music sheets so carefully annotated, in the sound and the sight of the blackened boots, each one of such a mirrored finish that they reflected the sun, before it moved on to silver spurs or horse bits, straps, or regimental buttons.

So why then, amid such beauty, was Teddy so relieved to break his back?

Why was it when the doctors, grave-faced and solemn, crowded around his bed to tell him he was to be moved to a specialist hospital, that Teddy Mowbray, who had so longed to join the army and become a hero, why was it that he felt so awfully relieved? Why was it that despite the gravity of his state, despite the sorrow reflected in the young nurses' eyes, despite his longed-for hopes for an army career, he felt nothing *but* relief?

I must be a coward, he thought, as he felt himself being lifted into an ambulance and driven for miles to the new hospital. *That has to be it. Without realizing it, I must be a coward.*

As the lights of the darkening evening flashed past the windows of the ambulance Teddy wondered whether or not his accident, falling from a high bar in the regimental gym, had actually been almost wilful? Perhaps, hating the army as he had from day one, night one, perhaps he had *caused* himself to fall? Not to die, of course, he would never want to die before his allotted span, but to fall – perhaps he had wanted that – falling was different. And now, it had to be faced, he would never ever be able to become an army officer.

Now, well now, now he would have to become something else, and that was, it must be said, more than a little depressing. He had never thought beyond the army, but if he should walk again, as the doctors had promised him that he would, he would actually have to *do* something. He would have to find a way to fill his days. It would not be enough to be an invalid with a small allowance, and most probably a limp, it would be less than enough, he would have to *be* something.

But what? What could he become? He had hated the army but it had, when all was said and done, actually been leading to something to which he had been able to aspire, a marsh light leading him on through his adolescence, but now the aspiration had vanished, he had to think of what to *be*.

But what, he groaned inwardly, *what?* He had been so lucky in everything so far. Lucky in a war that had plucked him out of the east end of London and sent him to the aunts at Mellaston rectory. Lucky that they had set about adopting him officially, practically straight away. Lucky in that they, being gentlewomen, had immediately set about sending him to good schools. Lucky that they had finally left him not just the old rectory in their wills, but half their money too, enough money to allow him to become an officer and a gentleman. Now, only the last part was open to him, because the first part, it had to be faced, was a gonner.

'Do it on purpose, did you?' the army doctor had wanted to know, but he asked it with such a twinkle in his eye that it made Teddy feel embarrassed for his lack of tact. Supposing it had been true, and he had?

'Of course!' Teddy had riposted. 'I love having accidents and breaking my back, and being in pain is positively spiffing.'

The truth was that over the next few weeks of recuperation, over the lying for ever as still as a dead leaf, over wanting to make love to all the pretty nurses that came to his bedside and knowing that he never would, the truth was that a new kind of truth was gradually dawning on Teddy.

This truth was – and he was too honest not to face

it – the truth was that he was not Teddy Mowbray at all. That was the real truth. He was no more Teddy Mowbray than he was William Shakespeare. He was *lucky* Teddy. He could be *lovely* Teddy. He could be *handsome* Teddy. But he could not, at any time, pretend any more that he was, actually, Teddy Mowbray.

Teddy Mowbray was the young boy that the aunts at Mellaston, his adoptive aunts, had invented because he had been the only kind of 'nephew' that could be acceptable to them. The reality was that he was actually Ted Darling, and even he was only what his so-called sister Miranda had created. Who he actually was he would probably never really care to know – it might be too off-putting. But what he did know, from being in the army those few months, was that he was definitely not a 'Teddy Mowbray of Mellaston rectory' kind of person, try as he might, and much as he would like to wear a smart regimental coat in dark blue with two regimental buttons on the half-belt and a great sway of cloth making up the main pleat at the back. He knew that he would look an idiot in it, because deep down inside he knew that he was just *not* that kind of person. And that was why he had not liked the army, because the person he really was would not like the army. In fact, he would hate it.

'I beg your pardon?' the chairman of the Army Medical Board stuttered, before following up his verbal astonishment with, 'I wonder if you would repeat that, if you would not mind? Did you say – did you say that you wanted to go to—'

'I want to go to art school, but not to paint, to study photography. I want to be a photographer.'

The gentlemen who made up the Medical Board now, to a man, stared at each other, and Teddy could see that in at least one pair of eyes his choice of training was confirming that they thought he truly must have broken his wretched back on purpose, and that now it was mended they should really have him shot.

'Gentlemen officers do not *usually* become photographers.'

'No, of course not,' Teddy agreed with his usual easy charm. 'But you see, now I am useless to the army, I don't suppose that matters as much as it would have done had I not been useless, as it were. Although,' he went on, the thought suddenly occurring to him, and the logic of it appealing too, 'Although, when you come to think of it, people like me – people with bad medical histories, we should be useful, if you think about it, because being so useless we could be the first to be shot, couldn't we? I mean really, when you think about it, it would be a better way, wouldn't it?'

There was a growing silence around him, and he sensed it, but he could not stop what he was about to say. He found it too interesting.

'I mean, the army could keep us crocks for everyday stuff, really, if you come to think of it, and save the fitter chaps for later, couldn't they? I mean

I always think it's such a waste really, putting really fit chaps, chaps who have taken months and months to get fit and are simply bursting with life and rippling muscles, into battle situations and then having them killed. I mean – having got them so fit.'

The dignified, respectable members of the esteemed Medical Board did not think this at all funny. In fact the grave-faced, unsmiling members of His Majesty's Army Medical Board, without saying a word, without looking either at Teddy or at each other, as one man, could be heard silently, and with relief, thinking, *What a mercy this fellow is being invalided out. What a blessing he is going. Better the Medical Board and a disability allowance than a court martial and a firing squad, because, with these ideas of his, that is where he would have undoubtedly ended up, being shot by us, and not by anyone else.*

There were some murmurings, some glances to and from the papers in front of them, and then the chief medical officer, the spokesman, said, 'Very well. If that is what you really want, if you are quite sure that you wish to attend an art school, to become a photographer, then that is what the army will pay for. You will be trained to become a – photographer. Perhaps you will be attracted to photographing war subjects,' he added wistfully, hope suddenly permeating his dulled, official tone. 'Perhaps you will be attracted to those subjects, with your – er – camera. Army subjects.'

Teddy shook his head, hating to let the poor man

down but now that the gates of freedom seemed to be opening up in front of him, he could not tell a lie. He felt too free, too much a soul at large, to be able to obfuscate. Besides, he believed in the basic tenets of beauty, truth and goodness, and that being so he had to tell the truth. It was the only way.

'I have to be honest, sir. I am afraid there is only one thing I want to photograph, really – only one subject that really interests me.'

The esteemed members of the Medical Board seemed to lean forward as one. Hope sprang up anew in their hearts, hope that a reprieve would be near, that this tall, charming, handsome young man would suddenly justify the army pension that he had just been awarded with some kind of decent attitude. Plants, animals, war, Africa, tigers, tanks, those would be the subjects to which a former member of the great, historic regiment of the Royals, would be undoubtedly attracted, surely?

'Women.' Teddy smiled just thinking of them.

'Women?'

'Women.'

The way the chairman said the word they could have been gorillas, or secret weapons, or foreign spies.

'Women.'

Once more the word span across the short space between Teddy and the board, span and span, round and round, repeatedly, until it finally lay flat, a brown, round penny of a word.

'Yes,' Teddy agreed, seemingly oblivious of the

consternation that one word had caused and the expression on his face becoming ever more dreamy. 'Beautiful women. I am going to photograph hundreds and hundreds of beautiful women.'

There was a sound. Not a loud sound, not a sound that anyone else would be able to identify, but it was a sound none the less. Certainly Teddy heard it. He had never heard it before, not even at school, but he did now. And if you can see a sound, which of course no-one can, Teddy definitely saw this one. It was large, and strangely shaped, like a doodlebug, growing in volume until, too late, it cut out and was upon you, destructive, final, fatal.

It was the sound of a body of decent, regular, church-going, respectable Englishmen giving up entirely and completely on a former junior officer of His Majesty's esteemed Royals.

But what followed was disappointing, for it transpired that there was no course for photographers at the art schools. No-one thought photography, still only a hundred years old or so, at all important. No matter that painters all over the world had been using photographs to work from, to paint from, to inspire them; art schools – those esteemed branches of the art world – still viewed photography as vulgar. And so, quite against his will, Teddy had pursued his art course, all the time moonlighting at a photographer's studio in Mayfair. Bicycling like mad, between lunch hours and classes, he began to learn what he really wanted to know, about lighting, about cameras, about what the magazines and the film companies, the theatres and Society, wanted from a photographer.

Flattery to begin with, naturally. (No-one wanted a photograph of themselves that did not tell them that they were yards better looking than they actually were.) That was to start with. Secondly they wanted something new. That also was hardly surprising. Thirdly they wanted it, whatever it was, yesterday.

Within a very few months Teddy had decided on his style. Dramatically, he would compose an entirely natural picture in an entirely unnatural way.

He would style his photographs the way stills of films were made, and he would style his sitters the same way. He would dramatize them. They would not stay stock still, characterless, just showing off their clothes – they would be *doing* something. Just as he realized that painters had worked from photographs, now he realized he could do quite the reverse. He could work from the ideas behind paintings and make beautiful photographs.

But London was just too drab. No matter where he went the underlying feeling of rationing and queuing, of a strange kind of defeat in victory, permeated everything. Society, the fashion world, the people he passed, whom he sometimes photographed, sitting on park benches or beneath some victory statue from yet another war. They had no life to them. It seemed that in the supreme act of repulsion had also come revulsion. The second great war of the twentieth century had taken its terrible toll on peacetime. It had been one war too many, even for the great, brave British. In defending their island they had surrendered their gaiety, seemingly, for ever.

And so the long holidays approached and not even the exotic and strangely un-Chinese Madame Yin, the photographer in Mayfair whom Teddy was now assisting, not even she, with her raised platform, her velvet drape, and her black backdrop, would stay – or worse, be seen – in town during August. With the closure of her studio for the month, Teddy packed up his old cameras, inherited from the aunts, his new lighting, bought with his allowance, and headed for Paris, and the apartment of a fellow art student much adept at faking Teddy's signature at the bottom of forms.

This was a really quite significant asset in any friend, particularly for Teddy. Dick Fortescue's ability to sign in 'Teddy Mowbray' was crucial when the real one was busy moonlighting with Madame Yin instead of attending drawing class or being set to copy, copy, copy, the old masters.

So, instead of copying an orchid, or staring disinterestedly at some nude woman in a life class, Teddy would be busy placing a single lily in a vase, or a vase of flowers on a fake plinth, before coaxing some middle-aged Society hostess into an appealing pose in the Grecian manner.

Dick could not understand the attraction of

photography, but since he was an easy-going sort of fellow he did not try to dissuade Teddy from his chosen route. Instead, he invited him to join him in Paris, cameras and all.

'Montmartre, dear boy. Nothing but steps, and far too many tourists, but once you're up them, you'll be pleased. Once you've lugged all your stuff up you'll find not just the view, but little cafés, little *boîtes de nuits*, little restaurants, great food. Oh yes, it will be worth it. See you there, if you haven't had a heart attack finding me.'

Teddy saw what Dick meant as he struggled from his taxi. If he had had to carry his stuff all the way up instead of coming round the back way, he surely would have had a heart attack, but as it was he had only two or three flights of steps before he was pushing open the door of the old, crooked apartment, whose floorboards were so uneven that for a minute they seemed to be imitating the steps outside.

'Welcome, dear boy,' Dick called to him, appearing from a doorway as crooked as the rest of the house. 'This is Maison Fortescue. Don't look at the wallpaper, look at the view.'

Teddy stacked his cameras and suitcases to one side of the largely unfurnished room, and turning saw immediately what Dick meant. The fact was the whole room was just one unbelievable view. Two large, floor length windows were wide open, and beyond them, set about with old chairs that had once been smart, was a balcony from which

302

stretched every rooftop in Paris, or so it seemed to Teddy as he stood there, breathing out and in with the marvel of it all.

Rooftop after rooftop, of every faded colour and patina, fell one after the other, seemingly sliding, sliding down and down until, inevitably, somewhere, beyond and out of sight, they were finally halted by the Seine.

Teddy stared. He could not wait to get out there, but it was already boiling hot, so he also could not wait to get down to one of the cafés below them and drink a beer at one of the tables, sitting under an umbrella and watching the girls whom he had already glimpsed sauntering by, some on the arms of men, some walking alone, some, tantalizingly, walking together, baskets on their arms, hips swaying, cotton dresses floating, hair shining. Long-legged beautiful women, women in smart clothes, women in expensive clothes, women in long dark clothes, student women, married women – they were all down there beneath Dick Fortescue's window, passing underneath his balcony. But first, he must drink a beer.

Of course Dick knew all the best places to go, and after lunch, long and leisurely and strangely filling after English food, despite there seeming to be considerably less of it, he took charge of the rest of the day.

'Come six o'clock I'll take you round to see that friend I was talking about. He's in the thick of it, do you see? Knows all the painters and the musicians, always in the Blue Note – you've heard of the Blue Note? It's on the Left Bank, always full of the best jazz musicians, and beautiful women singing sad songs, sirens beckoning us poor idiots into their webs before consuming us like dreaded spiders. Ah me.'

'Now, remind me.' Teddy frowned. 'The blue note in music, in jazz. It is the odd note, isn't it? The one between that doesn't fit?'

'Yes, dear boy. I will play it for you, *un de ces jours*. It is the quirky note, you're quite right – the one that comes between the two that fit together. Two are all set to harmonize, and then along comes the blue note *et voilà* – a kind of dis-harmonic harmony arrives, making a new kind of sound, but not the kind of sound that is expected. Beautiful, but completely unexpected, almost uncalled for, like so much that is interesting or worthwhile.'

Dick rolled his eyes, and, what with his freckled face and red hair looking, as it did, somehow incongruous beneath his navy blue Gallic beret, he made Teddy laugh at him, which was what he was aiming to do, for Dick was never, ever serious about anything, least of all art, which he took too seriously to be serious about except, as he said, when he was quite alone.

'Art is decoration, amusement, entertainment. It should never be political, or try to change the world. It can change the world, but if it does it must only be by chance.'

This statement – which he all too frequently

repeated in front of a set of extraordinarily serious, unentertaining, entirely politically minded fellow students – had landed Dick in more trouble than any politics. Better for him to have been a Communist, really. But of course as soon as he had realized how wonderfully inflammatory his statement was, Dick had been quite unable to leave it alone, and had repeated it as often and as publicly as possible. Which of course was where Teddy had come in, also all too frequently. Teddy had stepped between Dick and his enemies in bars and pubs, in clubs and cafés, and despite his only recently mended back had been quite prepared to take on all comers for his friend, for Dick had that effect on people. Teddy thought sometimes it was because he was so droll, or so nonchalant, or so sunny natured, seemingly uncaring, full of optimism and loving life, that he earned people's undying devotion or their undying enmity.

'What are you thinking of? You have your submerged expression, dear boy.'

'I am thinking of photographing everyone I meet in the Blue Note. I am thinking of all the beautiful women, all the beautiful girls, I shall meet there.'

'In that case, stop thinking.' Dick shook his head. 'There are never, ever any what we would find *beautiful* girls in the Blue Note. There are singers, and deadbeats, and Existentialist women with long black hair, but no beauties. Beautiful girls are not attracted to the Left Bank. If you want beauties you want to go to the sixteenth arrondissement, not the sixth.'

'But there will be women with long, black hair.'

'Women with long black dyed hair.'

'Ah yes, of course. That is all the rage, long black dyed hair.'

'And they will have dangerously loose morals.'

'Of course, dangerously loose morals.'

'And strange habits.'

'Those too?'

'Some very strange habits . . .'

Teddy sighed, already delighted beyond his own imaginings. 'I can't wait to photograph them in a dim light, their white faces lit by a Gauloise cigarette, their waists nipped by a large black belt, their long black skirts showing their womanly shapes.'

And now there they all were, just as Dick had described, except more dangerously feline and more svelte than Teddy had dared to imagine. There they sat, among the tables, listening to the jazz, some with a drink in front of them, some talking, despite the music, some smoking, some waiting to stand up and sing, if and when the opportunity offered itself.

For that was part of the attraction of the Blue Note, as Dick had carefully explained. It found new people for all the people who had already been found to admire, and they in their turn found new people, and so nothing stayed static, for obvious reasons.

And there was a great turnover in human beings

– musicians, singers, customers – due to the late night, and other, habits of the clientele and performing artists. There was much talk of smoke, and dope, and drink, and other things that went on there, Dick had said.

But, on the surface anyway, it was, Teddy thought as he looked around, a huge outward success, being far more like the popular conception of a jazz club in Paris than anything he himself could have imagined. The atmosphere was loosely held by something unseen, some kind of commitment to that oddity to which perhaps only a thousand or so souls are linked at any one time, that gossamer thread that makes a sound that certain souls know and recognize to be the blue note of life, something for which they are searching.

All this was fine and exciting to Teddy, to find a place to be a cliché of itself was not to be disappointed. And as his eyes wandered to and from the incoming people, the departing people, the dark-clad legs of the girls, the striped jumpers – obviously a must – the black, black everything black, eyes, hair, clothes and even faces. A new set started and he began to listen to just some of the inspired music which was played there every night of the week.

It happened just as a lone pianist had started to improvise brilliantly. A girl at the far end of the room stood up and started to sing, drunkenly, wantonly, perhaps imagining in her drunken state that she too was improvising. She sang in a horribly

dissonant drunken way, her black hair and white
face somehow grotesque against the walls, so fearfully drunk that as the other people around him
started to catcall, and some to laugh at her, Teddy
turned his head away. He hated to look. There was
something particularly upsetting about a girl who
was drunk and making a fool of herself. Besides,
he was still old-fashioned enough to think that a girl
getting drunk was pretty terrible.

'Taisez-vous, enfin! Partez, enfin! Trouvez votre mec
et partez, mademoiselle!'

'That is not a blue note that girl is making,' Dick
commented, turning his attention away from an
extremely beautiful woman at the next table, and
bossing his eyes at Teddy. 'That is a *screwed* note. Sit
down, mademoiselle, sit down and let us enjoy the
music peacefully!'

Teddy shook his head, still turned away from the
sight.

'Sit down, you stupid tart!' someone else called
to her in French.

But the young woman at the far end of the room
continued to sway, trying to sing too loudly and too
long above the sound of the slow, sexy music, one
hand holding on to the checked tablecloth beside
her.

At last the man she was with stopped laughing
at her, and pulled at her hair suddenly and
viciously hard, forcing her to sit down. Teddy had
turned just in time to witness this yet more upsetting sight, and of course he stood up at once. As

Dick said afterwards, 'Being English, he would, wouldn't he?'

'That's going too far,' he announced to Dick, but even as he started to walk across the room Teddy heard Dick behind him urging him to come back.

'Dear boy, this is not Frimley, this is not Tisbury, this is the Left Bank in Paris, and here you would do well to mind your own business, really you would.'

Teddy ignored him, of course, for the simple reason he was none too sober himself. He walked between the tables towards the girl, whose black dyed hair now touched the red and white tablecloth, waving one finger side to side in that well-known international gesture which said to the hair puller, 'No, no, no. Drunk she may be, singing like a banshee she may be, but hair pulling is just not on.'

The man, suddenly seeing Teddy making so purposefully towards the table, quickly stood up and left the club. The music went on playing, cool music that Teddy was just beginning to appreciate when he bent down and said in fractured French, 'Are you all right?'

''M all right – 'm all right – kind of all right – just a bit.'

Her voice tailed off and she relapsed into unconsciousness. It was as if Teddy had been hit. Not just because the voice was English, but because he knew it so well. He stared down at the collapsed girl in horror. The dyed black hair, the white face, the dark clothes, none of it was finally a disguise.

'Oh, my God! I say! For God's sake!'

He turned and beckoned frantically across the room to Dick.

'Over here,' he called in English. 'Quick, over here. I need help with this girl. We must take her out of here. She may need to go to hospital. She's very ill.'

Dick arrived slowly and reluctantly at his side and he too stared down at the girl collapsed over the table. It was a very unattractive sight, and although Dick thought that Teddy might be right, and she might be ill, what he said was, 'You want to be careful who you pick up in here, dear boy. Some of them have rather large men attached to them, business arrangements, you know the kind of thing.'

'Never mind that. You've got to help me.'

'Oh, very well, but this girl is, I have to tell you, dear boy, hardly the kind of girl that your mother would want you to bring home.'

'That is not quite true, actually, Dick.' Teddy's expression was grim as he tried to rouse the girl. 'Help me, would you? Take that arm.' He draped the other around his own shoulder and Dick followed suit. Teddy started to drag the unconscious girl towards the exit. 'You see,' he went on, as they inched their way towards the door that led to the Paris street outside, 'this girl is actually my sister.'

*   *   *

It was winter now, and Bobbie was permanently sheltered in the Sheds. She kept telling herself that at least she was not in London with Beatrice, at least once the winter started to bring what winters tend to bring – rain and sleet and hail – Beatrice would visit Baileys Court less often, and then only at the weekends. But even this did not do very much good. Why would it? She was in the Sheds and all alone, and not able to be anything else, really. She was at Beatrice's beck and call, a minor, as Beatrice kept reminding her, and a minor for some years to come, and likely to be left in the Sheds until such time as she reached her majority and was able to free herself from her guardian and her seemingly endless, and very often pointless, demands.

The autumn had been terrible. She had never before had any real opportunity to get to know Beatrice, but now she had, she devoutly wished that she had not.

Beatrice, Bobbie discovered, could not have anything tomorrow, she had to have it now, this second, not even this minute. And Beatrice trusted no-one, which was not just tiring, it was exhausting, and then, worst of all, because she was so beautiful, because she could never, ever bear a hair to be out of place, her clothes to be less than perfect, she was always in perpetual fear that they were, in the same way that because she enjoyed perfect health, she lived in terror of disease.

Sometimes Bobbie found herself wishing that Beatrice would actually be ill. That she would contract something mildly terrible which would allow her to concentrate on just one thing that was wrong with her, instead of fearing a hundred. It would make life so much simpler for everyone if Beatrice was surrounded by real doctors and nurses, instead of by unknown terrors about which nothing could possibly be done.

I am hoping that and here she wrote *she* only to rub it out again and leave a blank, *I am hoping that   will go away soon.*

Bobbie wrote this in her diary. That was all she wrote and she was careful not to date it because she knew without being told that Beatrice would be the sort of person to read her ward's diary, and any more would incur terrible retribution. For besides her fears about her health Beatrice suffered the usual fear of the very rich – she was convinced that no-one liked her for anything except her money.

'Your mother was one of the few people I really trusted. She saved my life once, from drowning, I was drowning in a swimming pool, and she dived in and rescued me. I had fainted, it seemed, and was going under, and staying there, and she dived in – just like that. So brave. It was then that I said I would do anything for her. Anything at all, but of course, I never realized that she would take me at my word and leave me her daughter.' Beatrice had laughed humourlessly at this, as she did at so much. 'Life can be funny like that. You will find that out, Roberta,' she would add, her eyes flicking backwards and forwards from some magazine which would be also being flicked, endlessly and restlessly. 'You will, in time, find that life can be quite unexpected.'

Since Bobbie had not found life recently to be at all funny, or to be anything except expected, she was, to say the least, unimpressed by Beatrice's warning, but eventually a woman had been found to teach her to type and to take down a form of shorthand, very, very slowly.

'I don't think you are made for this work, dear, really I don't,' Miss King would mutter, sometimes as much as twenty or thirty times a day as Bobbie struggled with pencil and rubber to pick up the rudiments of Mr Pitman's shorthand. 'Really, I should be doing your job, and you should be doing mine.'

This was all too true, since Miss King, unable to find secretarial work in the country, was being employed to work in people's gardens. But of course there was no question of swapping occupations for they both knew that Bobbie was being kept as a secretary at Baileys Court simply and solely as a form of imprisonment.

'I think Mrs Harper is – how shall I say – very nervous about you, dear. She is prey to her nerves, I gather, and so you really are a victim, aren't you, of her nerves, I mean?'

They were walking round the gardens at Baileys Court as Miss King ventured this opinion, and Bobbie looked about her sadly. The whole fun of the garden had gone. It had disappeared overnight in a flurry of modish ideas. Italian garden to be here – Tudoresque there – everything tidied up to a point of readiness. And soon, they both knew, it would all be planted out by people who would not care for it, who, once their job had been done, would go away and forget about it, leaving it to other people, who would not care for it either, to look after it. Julian and she, the Major and Miss Moncrieff, they had rebuilt the walls, they had cleared and they had burned, ready to start again, but most of all they had loved it.

Of course, it went without saying that Beatrice had managed to wipe all that out in a minute. She had stared around her, on that first day, and of a sudden there had been no happy memories, no laughter, no fine times to remember, and all that Bobbie could see and hear were her restless unhappy eyes and her impatient perfectly shod feet echoing over the stones and her disapproving voice calling, again and again, for attention.

For Beatrice needed attention as much as other people needed oxygen. It was as if she was determined to draw everyone else's energy away from them and use it just for herself. She was the motor car and they were her petrol. She left Bobbie exhausted, so much so that by lunchtime, whenever Beatrice was down she would find herself walking back to the Sheds in a state of tiredness that she felt could only be normal after a twelve-hour shift at a munitions factory.

Once back in the Sheds she would sink down into

what had been Miss Moncrieff's chair and sit with a cup of Bovril just staring in front of her. Nothing in this life was perfect. Bobbie had always known that, but Beatrice Harper, unfortunately, did not. She aimed for perfection in everything and everyone around her. Nothing was good enough. If a room had been cleaned from top to bottom, or, more to the point recently, completely redecorated, she could be relied upon to find the one patch, perhaps only the size of a sixpence, that had been missed by the painters.

Now Bobbie came to realize, and all too soon, why poor Miss Moncrieff had taken to sipping Bovril in her lunch hour, and knitting endless stockings for herself. Why, until the Major came into her life, Miss Moncrieff had never laughed or smiled; why she had lived in a state of permanent dread that 'Mrs Harper' would arrive to, as it were, suck her dry. Bobbie now understood why it had always been, 'What would Mrs Harper say?' 'We must telephone to Mrs Harper and find out whether that is possible.' When Bobbie had first come to live at the Sheds nothing had been possible without Mrs Harper's first being mentioned. Bobbie had sometimes teased Miss Moncrieff that they could not even clean the bath without the say-so of Mrs Harper.

'Oh, no, dear. No, but you do see, I mean – you do. Mrs Harper is most properly exacting. It is her way. She is one of the old-fashioned sort, do you see, dear. She must have her way.'

How exactingly true that statement seemed now to Bobbie – as true as the fact that the sun came up in the morning was the fact that, come what may, do what anyone could, no matter what, Beatrice Harper must have her way. But until now, until she had been forced to confront the full power of her guardian's demanding personality, Bobbie had not been able to appreciate just how draining that personality really was.

There was something so ruthless about her that it left everyone else wrong-footed. And there was no-one within her entourage who was not paid, so it would seem that there was no-one who dared to risk their livelihood by standing up to her, or answering her back, or telling her that what she had demanded was truly unreasonable. Often, as they left her presence, they would look as if they had just been told bad news, before passing Bobbie with tired smiles, or the look of a person who felt that any minute now, if luck was on their side, something must happen to relieve them of the misery of working for her. Something must bring much-needed light back into their lives, because such egotism as she possessed blotted out the sunshine.

Sometimes Bobbie would wake in the night and dream of drowning Beatrice in the sea in front of the Sheds – either that, or drowning herself. And then in the morning, as she dressed, she would tell herself that it made no sense to feel like that. That she had to have more of what the Major would always call 'gumption' and, that being so, today she would make sure to try to change *something*. She would stand up to Beatrice, she would tell her that it was unreasonable to expect her to work until ten o'clock at night. That it was impossible of her to still be telephoning the Sheds and demanding that Bobbie go and play canasta with her at two in the morning; or make her a boiled egg at dawn; or drive to London with the chauffeur to fetch a certain dress – a dress which would subsequently be hung up in the wardrobe by the sighing maid, only to be given to that same maid a day later, because Mrs Harper had found that she did not like it after all, and had no idea why the chauffeur and Bobbie had gone to London to fetch it for her.

Oh, but how Bobbie, as the time went by, realized that life around Beatrice Harper was *bleak*. Even the news of her arrival cast a long shadow, as everyone prepared for the sound of her voice, sometimes frantic with gaiety, sometimes almost guttural with fury.

And how everyone's eyes took on fixed looks, no-one smiling, except with a kind of forlorn tiredness. People new to her service, who had arrived in a flush of goodwill, grateful and willing, and *full* of energy, soon slowed up. Where before they had walked quickly and eagerly, at first seeing only the fun and the hope that a place like Baileys Court even in autumn or winter held out to the uninitiated, they soon changed. It did not take long, sometimes only a few weeks, and Bobbie would see them, like herself, walking slowly towards the closed library door, their feet dragging almost audibly. Or she would watch them secretly as they crossed the garden to the house in answer to the incessant ringing of the staff bell, their shoulders hunched, dreading to hear what the next set of commands might be, realizing, all too late, that they had been trapped by the wonderful house and its setting, by the luxurious life, by the lovely autumn weather, by Mrs Harper's beauty and sophistication – trapped into thinking that they would have a happy time with her.

And suddenly it would seem that it was already too late to leave, to change their minds, because in a very short time, given that there was still rationing, they had become accustomed to being fed terribly well on food and wines smuggled from France. They had grown used to sleeping in cool linen sheets under thick blankets and goose-feather eiderdowns, and when winter came again enjoying the warmth of the endless heat upon which she insisted, somehow finding fuel supplies where no-one else could, or had. And too they became reliant upon the security she offered, upon the fact that she paid them all twice, sometimes as much as three times, what anyone else would think was sensible.

Bobbie, however, she did not pay. Bobbie was expected to live on her usual small allowance, and look after herself in the Sheds, and drink Bovril for lunch and make toast without butter which could be dipped in the Bovril, and rely on Mrs Duddy to bring her in the luxuries that she and Miss

318

Moncrieff had enjoyed before Miss Moncrieff had escaped the terrible servitude that Bobbie now disenjoyed.

'You are in my service now, Roberta. You are a very lucky young girl. In return for this you will jump around whenever I am down. You will learn to take dictation, you will learn to answer all the telephone calls that I might wish you to answer, you will be on call, but only when I am down. So, really, you are a very fortunate girl, because I shall not be down a great deal in the winter, so you will have the place to yourself. Liberty Hall it will be, no doubt, when I am away. There will still be some staff in the house – a cousin of Mrs Duddy, or two cousins of hers, actually – and you can eat with them in the kitchen. That will do you until I am down again.'

Well, winter had come, but Bobbie soon realized that she was about as welcome to Mrs Duddy's cousins as a common cold. They would stop talking the moment she came into the kitchen and ignore her when she spoke to them, or make faces behind her back, and so she would walk back to the Sheds, and make do with yet more Bovril and yet more toast, until such time as Mrs Duddy called again with eggs and butter and home-made bread which saved Bobbie having to go on the scrounge to the main house, and meant she could just stay staring at the sea, and typing the few letters that were required very, very slowly.

'It's so bleak here, for you,' the older woman said

one morning, and she stamped her feet and blew on her mittened fingers as Bobbie went to fetch the money to pay her for the groceries. 'Aren't you lonely, too?'

Bobbie smiled and shrugged her shoulders. 'Oh, people come down at weekends, you know. Mrs Harper, and so on. And of course there's the wireless, Mrs Duddy, I do know that.'

'What a thing, to be here all alone. And where's that young man you used to tell me about, the one you used to go bathing with in the summer, you know? That young man.'

Bobbie looked at the change in her hand, but this time she frowned, and after a few seconds she said, having cleared her throat slightly, 'He's – er – gone. He was just here for the summer, and then he went.'

'He sounded so nice.' Mrs Duddy nodded, non-committal. 'I liked the sound of him. We were all hoping, at the farm, that something would come of it and we'd see a ring on your finger by now. But there, I dare say you'll meet someone just as nice, one of these days. I dare say.'

Bobbie nodded, turning away, only to turn back.

'I dare say I won't,' she said suddenly, to Mrs Duddy's astonishment. 'I dare say I will never meet such a friend again, not ever.'

The weeks that followed were spent avoiding the thought that Julian might return, and everything would be as it had been. How many times Bobbie had turned round to catch his eye, wondering if he had seen the same thing and found it amusing or interesting, only to find that he had? A hundred, two hundred, a thousand times perhaps? What did it matter? What did anything matter once you were alone once more and unhappy again?

She knew why he had left. He had left before autumn became winter, and now autumn seemed to her, for some perverse reason, to be the loveliest season of the year, because she would always remember him standing among the early fallen leaves, few as there were of them on the lawns, and smiling at her. She would remember him saying, 'Come on, Roberta better known as Bobbie, follow me to the sea, where we will wallow in cool waters like so many hippopotami.'

And how he would lead her, and she would follow, down that stony Sussex beach, and how he would look at her suddenly and say, 'This is . . . this is the life that one always imagines, somehow, the life of the beach, the sea, and no-one around to tell us not to do anything.'

'Or worse, telling us to do *something*.'

Julian had the gift of making everything, even the dullest thing, into something exciting. Even walking into Baileys Green together would become an exercise in hilarity with Julian's commentary conducted always in the lowest of murmurs.

'First we will pass Mrs Duddy's washing line, and see if she is still the proud possessor of seven pairs of green ladies' directoires. After that glorious discovery, we will walk on to the crossroads, to count the number of cars that pass in five minutes – all bets laid must be honoured immediately to buy pints of beer or something similar. Then to the Dog and Dicky Duck to see if the Major's team won at darts last night, and if so, chalk up a pretend score and leave it there to make him fulminate tonight. Because he does love to fulminate. *Shut up, Gilbert!*' (Here Julian would do his statutory imitation of the Major.) 'And then on to see if Rene's mother has any new gowns displayed in her shop, and if so, guess the colour of them behind that yellow cellophane she hangs at her windows. And so home, after a long glass of lemonade and perhaps even something a little stronger at the said Dog and Dicky Duck.'

It was all that which Bobbie so missed from her life, now that Julian had left. More than the poetry and the evening walks, and the long talks with the Major, it was the endless invention, the ability to make something out of nothing, some fun out of what everyone else would either ignore or just leave lying about in an ordinary dull little way. Julian could make a great big pink cloud of the day, where everyone else would leave it to stand around being grey and drear.

And yet, even now, even then, she had quite understood why he had gone. There was no more innocence left at Baileys Court.

Julian had used to say, 'You can't transplant things, you can only plant them. That's really why the trees fell over.'

In a way, Bobbie realized now, she was just the same. She was just like the trees that had fallen over in the winds. She had been brought in, imported from somewhere else, which was probably why she sensed that she too might, like them, quite easily fall over, quite soon.

Dick Fortescue gazed down at the young girl he and Teddy had laid down on the bed, a puzzled look on his face. It really did not seem quite the thing to bring her back to a bachelor's flat, but if, as Teddy kept insisting, this was his long-lost sister, then so be it.

Nevertheless, having removed his navy blue beret, Dick scratched his head and stared across at Teddy.

'Sorry to say this, dear boy, but she don't look much like you, you know. I mean – she looks the spit of everyone else in the Blue Note, but not much like you at all, if you don't mind me saying so.'

'It's her hair. She's done something dreadful to her hair. Dyed it or something. Normally she was blond, like me. We were both the same colour. That's how I came to be her brother, as a matter of fact, because of our hair.'

'*Came* to be her brother? You must explain, dear boy. How could you *come* to be a brother to someone? Surely, you just are, or you just are not?' Dick looked understandably puzzled and scratched his head again.

'If I said it was a long story, would you make a

great effort to believe me, even so? Because it happens to be a true one.'

Dick sat down, waiting for the story to unravel itself, an interested look on his face, as always, unlike so many people. Dick was interested in everything. It was one of his great qualities.

'Miranda and I – well, we lost touch. Mostly my fault, I'm afraid. I lost her address. First of all we'd been evacuated, and then adopted – and then, you see, after the aunts – only they really weren't our aunts – after they were killed in the war, all their money was put in trust for us, and so on, and so on. But you see, we were never really brother and sister at all. I mean we were, but we weren't. What happened was that she, Miranda, took me along with her, and pretended I was her brother. As I just said, we were evacuees, and I was in the orphaned bit, due to be shipped off to some orphanage, and I was bawling my head off, so she took me under her wing, and I went along with the brother thing, and whether or not the aunts ever knew when they adopted us officially, I don't know. What I do know is that the aunts were the kindest people I'd ever had in my life, and Miranda . . .' he looked down at her suddenly with bewilderment, 'she was just the tops, you know. She really was, so beautiful. You wouldn't think so now, she's so raddled, but she was really beautiful. Come on now, Miranda, wake up and tell your brother what has happened to bring you to this terrible state. She really was beautiful, you know. It's her hair, that awful black, it makes her look like a witch.'

The body on the bed stirred after that, and then slowly, oh so slowly, sat up.

'Water, for God's sake. Bring me some water,' it demanded in English, and then, looking from Dick to Teddy, it burst into tears. 'What am I doing here? Why am I here? Why are you here? Where's Macaskie?'

'If by Macaskie you mean that man who was last seen pulling your hair to stop you singing, I think, dear Sis, we will forget all about him, don't you? Not a good type. Steer clear of him, I'd say, and this is, although you probably won't recognize me, your long-lost brother speaking, so I should know.'

Miranda took the glass of water and stared up at Teddy, sniffing.

'Teddy! My God! Teddy!'

She burst into tears once more, immediately flinging her arms around her brother's neck in such a fashion that he was forced to clear his throat several times as she went on sobbing.

'Thank God you're here. You've found me. I've found you.'

'Well, yes, indeed,' Teddy agreed affably. 'But you know how it is, Miranda. I may be here, but how and why are *you*?'

The story came out bit by little bit. Between long and grateful sips of water, Miranda began to explain her recent past, and how she had come to travel with the man who had discovered her – *this*

Macaskie fellow, Teddy kept on calling him – to Paris.

'Everything was fine between us until I flopped as a model.'

'Flopped? How do you mean, flopped?'

'You know, as in *I was no good*, Teddy. You know. No good as in can't do it, thumbs down, get the girl out of here, that's how I mean flopped.' She stopped, remembering. 'Everything was fine, until he had my hair cut off, and then . . . with my hair went my confidence. I don't know why he wanted to cut it off so much, or why the hairdresser had to cut it all off at once, but you know – it was going to be fashionable, but once it had gone, that was it. I just wanted to hide away from everyone and everything. I looked terrible. I felt terrible. I mean – you can't go to bed wearing a hat, can you? You still see yourself, when you're cleaning your teeth or something, without hair!'

'Bad as the army was eh?'

'It's growing again now,' Dick added as if she did not know.

'Too late. Really. Besides, who cares what it does. I don't want to be a model any more. That's why I dyed it as soon as it started to grow a little, so as to look like everyone else on the Left Bank. Because when I realized I was a failure, I came across here, and I – well, I earned my living as a waitress and so on, so I had to look like all the other waitresses, or I wouldn't get work, you know how it is. I was still hoping to be a singer, but Macaskie had invested a lot of money in me, apparently. Which is why he made me sign this agreement when we came here. And I owe him still, so that was why I had to be a waitress, and try to be a singer too. But you know how it is.' She gave Teddy a sudden wobbly smile. 'Aunt Sophie having taught me to sing Noel Coward numbers that's all I had in my repertoire. And, *figure-toi*, "A Room With A View" is not quite as popular in the Blue Note as it would be in Mellaston at the rectory. That's what's happened to me up to now.'

There was a long pause as Teddy and Dick stared at her, unable to quite believe what an idiot she was.

'And so you really and truly think you have to pay this fearful chap Macaskie back?'

'Of course I do, Teddy. I owe him so much. After all, he tried to launch me as a model. I am his first flop for years, and he hasn't taken it very well. I was not only camera-shy, I drank before my first show, and' – she put her head in her hands and sighed heavily – 'and worst of all, I fell off the catwalk.'

Teddy tried not to look at Dick and Dick tried not to look at Teddy, because to do so would mean they would start to laugh, and laughter was not going to be quite the right reaction, not when Miranda was looking like something that not even the cat would bring in, but would leave by the dustbin.

'Well,' Teddy said, having managed to control himself and starting to feel just the right amount of righteous anger, 'I think this Macaskie should make himself ready for his second damn great flop for years, don't you, Dick?'

Dick looked across at Teddy and suddenly felt terribly sorry for him. After all, it must be a shock to find your sister in such a situation, and even more of a shock to find she'd made such a mess of things. This chap Macaskie was obviously her lover, or had been, at any rate; but whether or not Teddy had guessed this he did not know. What he did know was that Teddy was quite right, they had to get out of the apartment and find him, and do what all good Englishmen would do in these circumstances – lay the man out cold.

'It's no good thinking you can take him on, Ted,' Miranda said suddenly from the bed, as both men moved as one to the door. 'It's no good at all. You see, Macaskie knows everyone in Paris, and if you go giving him a black eye he will have you drummed out of the Left Bank and on your way back to England within five seconds flat.'

'Oh, all right, I take your point. The *gendarmes* will take it badly if their friend is found with a bump on his chin, eh?'

'That's it. He knows everyone, really. He even knows de Gaulle.'

Teddy nodded at her, as if in agreement, and then he moved towards the bathroom door and his recently unpacked overnight bag, and brought back a pill and some more water.

'Take this. They're really for sea sickness, but they'll calm you anyhow. And then go to sleep. Try to get to sleep.'

Miranda sat, a tousled mess, on the edge of the

328

bed. 'I am such a mess, aren't I?' she asked of no-one at all, but they all knew that she was not referring to her frantic hair or rumpled clothes.

'Not any more you're not going to be,' Teddy told her. 'From now on you're going to be Miranda Mowbray, Teddy Mowbray's sister. And I won't allow my sister to be a mess, do you hear? Now be a good girl and hop into bed, get a good night's kip, and leave it all to your brother, would you?'

He gave her a quick hug, and then left her.

Miranda stared after him. Her head was so painful that she would have loved to end it all, if only to stop the pain. But somehow, what with the wine, and the pill, it did not take long for her to undress and crawl between the rough French sheets and fall asleep, waking only once when she heard Teddy's voice, and thinking for a few seconds that she was back at the rectory with the aunts, and they were reading to them all, before blowing out the candles and leaving them all to fall fast asleep, ignoring the sound of the planes passing overhead, or occasionally the sound of their wireless down-stairs giving out the news rather too loudly because Aunt Prudence always did like to have it turned up when she was in the larder sorting jam.

And so, with these vague sensations of having somehow come home, Miranda drifted off into the deep sleep of the rescued.

Chapter Ten

When the moment finally arrived Bobbie could not have truly said what had made her run away. Perhaps it was that Beatrice had confined her to the kitchens over Christmas. Luckily Beatrice, glorying in her usual ritual humiliation of her ward, could never have imagined it, but the fact was that Bobbie actually preferred to be in the kitchen with the staff rather than in the drawing room. She had far rather spy on Beatrice's smart friends through the green baize swing doors, far rather watch them through the half-opened drawing room doors, all puffing endlessly on their cigarette holders and shouting 'Darling, darling, hallo darling, how good to see you darling', than actually be with them.

In fact, that Christmas Bobbie heard the word 'darling' so often, and said in such an unaffectionate way, that when they eventually all returned to London Bobbie found herself thinking that she would be hard put to hear that particular endearment again without thinking that she had, at the same time, heard iron filings dropping to the floor.

Yet it had not been Christmas at Baileys Court, with its awful falsities, Beatrice's pretence of heading some sort of motley Christmas family, made up purely of people who had eschewed having children but now wanted to prove that they too could enjoy Christmas, that had determined Bobbie to run away. Nor had it been Beatrice's new butler trapping Bobbie behind a door and trying to drag her towards the mistletoe, his hot alcoholic breath making her feel quite faint. It had been none of those things, because in truth, once they all went away and the house was left with only the Duddys to look after it, and Bobbie was able to go back to the Sheds and lead her own life once more, Baileys Court became a kind of haven. The seas pounding, sometimes right over the Sheds, the winds whistling and circling round and round the old servants' quarters, the beach with its strange outlines from the war still left to rust, were all, as it happened, particularly pleasing to her.

No, it had to be faced – and since Julian had left Bobbie found more and more that she did like to face things, that she was not happy to pretend – she had to leave Sussex and go to London not because she was necessarily more unhappy than anyone else, but because, finally, she could not stand Beatrice and her empress-like ways any more.

She wanted to go away to a place where the telephone would never ring with Beatrice on the other end. She wanted to go away to a place where no letters arrived addressed to *Miss Roberta Murray* in

Beatrice's handwriting. She wanted to get away from her guardian so fast and so furiously that she actually thought she would not mind starving to death in preference to ever seeing her again.

And yet along with this desperate desire for escape came the inevitable self-accusations. How *could* she be so ungrateful to Beatrice Harper of all people, her mother's friend? She had found out Bobbie's whereabouts, never an easy thing during a war, and discovering that she was ill, had paid for the sanatorium thereby probably saving her life. Compared to Bobbie's, poor Miss Moncrieff's defection would be as nothing.

Perhaps Mrs Duddy had become more of a friend than Bobbie realized, for, on the morning following Bobbie's decision, as she put down the groceries on the kitchen table, and blew on the ends of her mittened fingers, her small eyes staring at Bobbie from a face that was made up of such hardened, reddened skin it was more like a piece of rosy leather than a face and her short-sided wellington boots stamping on the tiled kitchen floor, she announced, 'God forgive me for what I am about to say. But. You'd best be out of this place, love, really you would. You'd best be out of here, and off somewhere on your own. Somewhere you can be young again. This place is making you into an old woman, really it is. It is making you as old as me, and that will never do, will it?'

Bobbie stared at her. Was her misery and loneliness that obvious?

'I – er – I am fine. I mean, I'm very lucky really. So lucky. I have the sea. I have this house, and I hardly have to do much to earn my living.'

'That's jus' the trouble, love. You do hardly have to do anything. You're like a dog in a kennel. You've got a roof over your head. You're given a bowl of food once or twice a day, and occasionally there's a visitor and you can bark – show you're not dead by barking at someone arriving – but otherwise you might as well be. Dead, God forgive me. But. You might, mightn't you?'

'Well, I dare say it is rather quiet here during the winter—'

'And who'd choose to be a kennelled dog, love, ask yourself?' Mrs Duddy continued relentlessly. 'Better to be free and barking when you want, even if it does mean you've got less in your bowl. Now that'll be half a crown for the eggs and all that there, and sixpence for the two loaves, if you don't mind.' She took the money and gave Bobbie a look that was both kindly and firm. 'Believe me, Miss Bobbie, I am a mother and soon to be a grandmother too, and I *know*. Times is hard in England, course they are, but nothing's worse than being a prisoner. And nothing gives security except what's right down there inside of you. It's what's inside of you – right in there, in your heart – that gives security, not three meals a day and beef of a Sunday. Not that, not nothing, not at all, I know because I'm the mother of children, and that teaches you as nothing does. It teaches you what's what, really it does. Children teaches you what matters, and what doesn't matter any more than a fly on a cow. It's because I've had children that I can tell you that you could ruin yourself just sitting here, love. God forgive me. But. You want to get out of here. Go somewhere.'

Bobbie smiled at Mrs Duddy, who was turning away, putting Bobbie's money into a leather pouch that was strapped satchel-like around her. It was only as she smiled that Bobbie realized, with horror, that it was the first time she had smiled, *actually* smiled, for weeks and weeks and weeks. Probably since Beatrice had arrived, since Julian had gone, and a whole lot of other 'sinces'.

She had smiled politely, of course, when Beatrice had given her a truly fabulous coat and skirt for Christmas. But it was not the kind of smile that she was giving now. It was a polite smile, a grateful smile, but a smile that was 'on account', that was in part payment, as so much of what happened around Beatrice was on account. In contrast to the smile that Bobbie was giving now, it had been a *look I am being properly grateful for your present* smile. It had not held an ounce of warmth, any more than the bump on the cheek that she had given Beatrice had held an ounce of affection, any more than Beatrice's label on the present *To Roberta from Beatrice* had held an ounce of love.

'So.' Mrs Duddy turned back. 'I'll be saying goodbye then. And I hope to see you some time in the future. Hope not to see you here next week when I make my rounds. A girl like you, you've got a future. Get on a train. Get away. Go on. Get away. God forgive me. But. Take my advice. Free yourself.'

And of a sudden Bobbie was on a train and heading for London, passing each station with increasing excitement. 'Haywards Heath', 'Three Bridges', 'Crawley'. They could have been the names of battles fought across France or Italy for all she knew of them. The last time she had been on a train was when the Dingwalls had put her into the special carriage at Mellaston station, and the silent, frightened young nurse had accompanied Bobbie to the sanatorium, scampering off as soon as they arrived, terrified that with just one cough, just one sneeze, Bobbie would infect her too.

Almost mesmerized by the scenery that they were passing, Bobbie found it amazing to stare out of the window and see not just the countryside, but the houses when they approached the stations, and the people, still thin and white from the war, but making the best of themselves in their hats and mended gloves, their polished shoes, everything about them showing a cheerful determination to make the best of everything, and never mind that there was rationing and clothing coupons, and queuing. They would make sure they looked as good as they could.

And again, as the train approached Victoria station, Bobbie found it marvellous to stare out at the old abandoned train carriages they passed, carriages that were now converted into a form of eccentric housing for the desperate and the determined. They too looked as good as they could, despite the smog and the train dirt, set about with geraniums at gaily painted doors, with smoke curling upwards out of crooked chimneys stuck into the top. They actually looked so nice that Bobbie wanted to stop the train and go and live in one, and she could not help thinking that if Julian was with her they would have one of their endless discussions about them.

In her mind she smiled as she imagined Julian saying, 'Well, Roberta, it has to be faced, if there is anywhere that could suit you *more* than living in the Sheds by the sea at Baileys Court, it has to be a converted train carriage beside the railway. Just think, instead of the sound of the pounding sea there would be the sound of the Brighton Belle pulling past your window. It would suit you. Living in a converted train carriage would suit you. You should get one.'

She remembered that Julian was always saying that. *It would suit, you should get one.*

Part of Bobbie's determination to leave behind the past had meant that she had burned everything from her childhood. Made a big bonfire in the grate of the old fireplace at the Sheds. And then, of course, she had to sit down and write a letter to Beatrice.

It had been a strain, to say the least, as why should it not be? Doing what you wanted always required being brave. Being selfish, having your own way, was probably not good, probably not right, and it was definitely not proper, but – taking the gamble that Mrs Duddy was right – Bobbie knew it was correct.

And that was what she had written to Beatrice. That she was terribly grateful to her, that she would not hurt her feelings for the world, but that she could not stay any longer, living alone at the Sheds, as her country secretary, only waiting for her to come down. Bobbie tried to explain that while she was very grateful she had to make her own way. She had to find herself, if that was not too pompous a way of putting it, swim out into the ocean of life, on her own, stand on her own two feet. She would try to repay her for everything that Beatrice had done for her, and she had taken nothing that was not hers, except the coat and skirt which had been a gift at Christmas.

Even now that she was arriving at the great bustling, comfortingly crowded station, Bobbie shuddered mentally at the thought of what Beatrice would say when Mrs Duddy presented her with Bobbie's letter. Mrs Duddy had actually volunteered to take it to her guardian. She had wanted to have her say with Mrs Harper for some time, she had told Bobbie when she called to say goodbye to her.

And besides, Mrs Harper's manager had not paid any of the Duddys since before Christmas, which meant that they had been forced to buy everything on tick, which was not at all a Duddy kind of thing to have to do. They were a proud family, used to being paid, and it was not right to leave them without.

As Bobbie picked up her cheap suitcase, purchased from the village store, she contemplated the quite splendid notion of Mrs Duddy, her short flowered apron peeping beneath her milking coat, her faded leather satchel strapped across her, marching in her thick stockings and brogues across the stone-flagged floor of the hall of Baileys Court towards Mrs Harper's study.

Of course she would have to wait for Beatrice to ring the bell for her to come in, after which Mrs Duddy would pad across the floor unconcernedly, towards the dark oak Tudor table at which Beatrice would be seated with her telephone to one side, her leather-bound, gold-tooled writing folder in front of her. Beatrice would not anticipate it, but no sooner would Mrs Duddy fetch up in front of her desk than Beatrice would have lost. Beatrice was used to being like Cleopatra on a burnished throne, looking down from on high at folk like Mrs Duddy, but Bobbie knew that as soon as Mrs Duddy fetched up in front of her, she would have lost. For despite all Beatrice's stylish simplicity – her couture country tweed suit, her country make-up with its lips correctly bare of lipstick, her simple country pearls, one strand only, her thicker silk stockings and lower-heeled shoes, everything so perfectly correct, so perfectly beautiful, so perfectly in keeping

338

with her surroundings – despite all this there was not a whit of truth about her. Whereas Mrs Duddy, with her freshly flowered apron, her highly polished complexion, her deep commitment to work – she was real. Mrs Duddy had done battle with life where Beatrice had merely jousted with it. Mrs Duddy had rowed bare-handed across deep seas that had been rocked by storms and finally arrived at a harbour, whereas Beatrice wore white gloves for fear of contagion.

'May God forgive me.' That was how Mrs Duddy would probably open her maiden speech in Mrs Harper's study. 'May God forgive me. But.'

Bobbie stared around her from under her hat. May God forgive her too, but for the first time since Julian had left, she felt happy. She queued for a taxi, which was a terrible extravagance, but she had too much luggage for a bus or a train.

Having helped heap her suitcase and various bags in the front, the taxi driver opened the door into the cab and held it for her.

'Where to, miss?'

'Where to? Yes.' Bobbie stared back at him.

The man's face under his cap was creased with the kind of lines that can only come from many anxious hours spent working for someone else for too little money.

'Yes.'

He waited.

'Yes.' Of a sudden it came to Bobbie – the memory of Miss Moncrieff talking about her flat in London.

Ebury Street, was it? 'Yes. I know. How about Ebury Street?'

As she stared into the cabbie's kind, round, brown eyes, Bobbie saw a resigned look creep into them.

'Well, how about it, miss?'

'Well, let's try Ebury Street. Would they have letting rooms there, do you think?' She leaned forward to the edge of her seat.

'There's letting rooms everywhere in London at the moment, miss. But if it's Ebury Street you fancy, I'll take you to Ebury Street. If it's Soho Square I'll take you there.' He started to walk round to his side of the cab. 'Ebury Street, right-ho.'

Bobbie reddened, realizing at once that he knew she had no idea of where she was going, but then she leaned back against the leather seating and stared out of the window as the cab started up. Really, it did not matter. What mattered was that she had made it. She was in London. And as long as she never crossed the tracks and went near Mayfair and Beatrice, everything would be fine. She had, at last, arrived.

PART THREE

'Hey everybody, let's have some fun –
You only live but once – so let the
Good times roll.'

Sam Theard

Chapter Eleven

Miranda stared around her at the studio. She had just returned from Allegra Sulgrave's funeral, after which it had transpired that her beloved self-styled guardian had ordered that Miranda be left Aubrey Close in her will.

'Not that it was really hers to leave you, but nevertheless I must approve,' one of the relatives had told Miranda, with a wry expression on her face. 'As a matter of fact I still have no idea who you are, or indeed why you were taken on by Allegra, but the truth is you were a great comfort to her in her decline. We both know that she never got over the way Burfitt went downhill during the war. She loved the place so. Just loved the place. Loved Burfers much more than old Sulgrave. She did not love him much at all. Matter of fact none of us could understand why she married the old silly. But still, she did love Burfers. I think it was because it was a sort of daddy to her. She and her father, they were twin souls, you see, there was no getting away from that. They were never happier than when they were doing things about the place together. Nothing Allegra liked better than to be with him outdoors, and of course after her brothers were killed she quite took their place as far as he was concerned. In fact her mother always said, because of Allegra, he almost felt he had three sons. She was very much a man's woman, d'you see. Not the kind of lady who is always at the hairdresser or the dressmaker. And as you know, she swore like a groom, and could down as much whisky as a huntsman. All jolly good fun, until the second war, d'you see, and then the army ruined it, Burfitt that is, and now there are just no funds to do the place up. Nothing there. So all in all she was gathered at the right time. By the way, was your hair always that strange colour?'

Miranda blushed scarlet, so red that at least her hair, still horribly dark no matter how often she washed it, must look a little lighter in comparison.

'I, er, had to have it tinted to – I was made to have it tinted, er – for the Paris shows. And then of course it takes so long to grow out.'

'I tell you what, I'll send you to my hairdresser in Sloane Street. Andre. He is quite the thing, and much the best. He'll soon get you back to rights. Really, those Parisian designers, they must have a bit of a thing about dark hair at the moment. Really, when one thinks about it, it's a wonder they didn't decide to shave your head completely, like they did to informers after the war. Mind you, I always think people who do that kind of thing are usually trying to distract attention from their own awful wrongdoings. You know, like conjurors – they create some sort of diversion, so I've been told, to make us look the other way while they pop the rabbit down the hat. Head shavers are the same, I'd say. Busy distracting from their own nefarious goings-on.'

Miranda had not laughed at this. She did not like to be reminded of Paris.

'But never mind all that, for the moment anyway. We are all going to be part and parcel of the same struggle to hold on to those pieces of England which everyone else is so anxious to be rid of – I know, I have my own house to try to restore, so Burfers just has to go, I'm afraid. And Aubrey Close, where we all were young together – you can't imagine that, I know, us being young I mean – I shall make it yours, because that is what Allegra wanted, the ducky, and because you brought her great cheer, about the only bit of cheer in her last years that she didn't – like your hair colour, bless you – get out of a bottle.'

The funeral tea at an end, they had parted, Miranda not quite believing what she had just been told, but, as it transpired, it was more than the truth, it was reality. She had indeed been left Aubrey Close in Allegra's will.

And so there it was, and it appeared always would be, Aubrey Close lying up a broad tree-lined street, standing a little back from the road, a discreetly Bohemian air to it, as if it was half apologizing for being a studio as well as a house. And now it belonged to Miranda, and, what was more astonishing, everything in it now belonged to her too.

Miranda picked up the old pre-war telephone. It had the new number of WESTERN 1196 written on it. She carefully wiped its mouthpiece, and then dialled Teddy's London number.

'Teddy? Oh – Dick. I say, both of you, would you like to come round this weekend? Oh, fine. Next weekend then perhaps? No, don't bring anything. Just come round. You know, Dick, there are some pictures here that you may be interested in, and so many frames; you might like to have some for your paintings, perhaps? Well, yes, they are quite carved. Oh, I see. Too old-fashioned. Well, never mind. Be in touch. Don't forget, next weekend.'

She replaced the telephone with that acute sense of disappointment that always comes about when, having been thwarted in showing off a new possession, the person concerned suddenly feels that they are wearing a damp vest.

'Oh well,' she said, looking round the studio and talking out loud to it as if it were a person, which, in a way, she felt that it was. 'Oh well, if no-one wants to come and visit us, we will have to do the very next best thing and spring clean.'

With her usual flair for dressing up, Miranda now pulled on a pair of bell-bottom naval trousers, found in one of the old trunks, and a mustard-coloured shirt, with full sleeves and deep, tight cuffs. She turned and stared at herself in the full length mirror in what she had now designated

346

as her bedroom. She looked satisfyingly eccentric, most particularly since she had topped off the whole outfit with a pair of black satin ballet shoes, and tied her now, thank God, nearly blond hair into a silk scarf.

'I just need a long cigarette holder, and a song, and I could appear in a review,' she told her image, and smiled, before kissing herself tenderly in the mirror.

She walked carefully down the stairs into the large studio room again. It did not really matter that neither Teddy nor Dick was coming round, not now she was dressed up, for the truth was that the studio was still so dusty that they would have been hard put to find anywhere to sit that was not touched with the grime of the past years.

She took an enamel bucket from under the sink in the kitchen. It was so lacking in chips, so really new-looking, that she knew at once that Allegra and her sisters could never have used it. She filled it with hot water from the Ascot, topped it up with cold water from the single cold tap that dominated the centre of the old stone sink, and turning with it and a packet of flakes headed back into the studio room. There was only one way to play the cleaning up game, and that was to make a party of it. She knew this from living with Allegra.

She put the bucket down on the wooden floor, and before starting to clean she hurried over to the old wind-up gramophone. Putting on one of the old 78s she started to sing along with Gertrude

Lawrence: 'He Never Said He Loved Me'.

She must learn the words. And soon. She must learn all the words of all the songs that she had ever heard, and then she must sing them, over and over again, to drown out the memories of the bad days. Most of all she must drown out the memory of Macaskie. Of his sadism. Of his fascination. Of his having taken her, and then laughed at her constantly, mocked her, reduced her in her own eyes in a way that she would never have thought possible.

The record came to a close, but just as soon as it had Miranda hurried over to the gramophone and inexorably the song started up again, each verse ending with Gertie's husky voice filled with the sound of pre-war charm, singing, *'But he never said he loved me!'*

No. He never said he loved her. Not once. What a fool she had been, an utter, utter fool.

Bobbie had arrived in Ebury Street, and in the charge of the kindly cabbie had cruised slowly up and down it until they had at last spied a notice written in wobbly red capital letters: ROOMS TO LET. APPLY WITHIN. Bobbie knocked on the door.

'What-you-want, love? A room, is it?'

A kindly face beneath a scarf tied at the top of her head, a pair of specs, and a vivid pair of red lips in a white, white face peered at Bobbie.

'It says rooms to let, here.'

The face pulled another face, half comical, half tragical, and turned to stare at her window.

'Oh, that's what it says, do it? Imagine that, and all this while I kept wondering why people will come knocking at the door. Wanta hand, love?'

'Well, I rather wanted a room, actually,' Bobbie joked back.

'Course you did, love,' the woman agreed, as her slippered feet joined Bobbie beside the suitcase and the bags. 'Well, you've only gone and found one, and in't that the truth?'

Bobbie smiled at the cabbie and gave a thumbs-up sign to him, before hurrying back to the taxi and helping him with her suitcases.

'Thank you for all your help.' She paid him off with a too-large tip, which he promptly gave back to her.

'No need for that, miss. Really. You're new to London, you'll need every penny, believe me.' He touched her lightly on the shoulder before moving off and smiling back at her. Bobbie too smiled, at the same time feeling strangely homesick for the taxi and its driver, wanting in some mad way to stay in the cab and just drive round and round, blocking out the sudden feeling of loneliness with which she had been left by his driving off and leaving her in Ebury Street.

'You want a room, and I got one, so that's satisfactory, if you like. The room'll be clean, but it ain't the Ritz and I don't want nothin' in advance, understand? No gentlemen callers after ten, but beyond that your life's your own, and no questions asked. Cooked breakfast at eight, no lunches under any circumstances, not even if you was Royalty, but tea's at six, and dinner if you're a snob at seven, but don't matter because the food will be just the same, whatever time you takes it.'

Bobbie said nothing, too busy dragging her suitcase into the narrow hall to reply. The house smelt clean, of polish and carbolic, so that at least was reassuring.

'Come into the parlour, love, and I'll give you a nice cup of tea. You look as if you could do with one, dear, really you do. Long journey? Up from the country? First time you've left home, I expect. I know. I've seen it all before. Now sit down, and I'll bring you a cup.'

She hurried off leaving Bobbie in her sitting room, a brightly painted apartment filled with the usual pre-war respectable furniture, the beauty of the plain rust-coloured upholstery carefully covered with lace-edged antimacassars at the head and mats on the arms, but the real interest of the room lay neither in the furniture nor in the china arranged on the mantelpiece – plates with the familiar bright gold lettering of souvenirs declaring that they were presents from Margate or Brighton, cups and saucers that were faded and perfect, but obviously not for everyday use – but in the ceiling, from which hung every kind of bird cage filled with every kind of bird. Canaries, budgies, parakeets, cockatiels sang or danced about her head. Bobbie stared at them. Their colour was fantastic, their songs quite perfect. They were as beautiful as anything she had ever seen.

'By the way, love, my name is Mrs Pond, but everyone calls me Dill. It's short for Dill-is. But we don't bother with the bottom bit. Too grand, I say. Dill does me. Like the herb, you know. Although I never did know what that looked like neither. Still. Here you are. The cup that cheers.'

Bobbie raised her china teacup to her mouth. 'You're being awfully kind, er, Dill.'

'Course I am, love.' Dill smiled at Bobbie. 'I know a stray lamb when I see one, and if you're not a stray lamb what has lost its sheep, I wouldn't care to say who is.'

Because young men gossip as much as, if not more than, young women, Dick Fortescue was now talking about Miranda to Teddy.

'I can hardly believe the story you are telling me, even though I've heard it before,' he confessed. 'You say that because you had matching blond hair Miranda said you were her brother, and brought you to the rectory, and the old ladies adopted you, and have left you with an old house in Mellaston as a result. Not to mention a stunningly beautiful sister with the longest legs I have ever seen.'

Teddy nodded. 'I know, it does seem just slightly too much, like some sort of Greek fable, I do agree. But the truth is she did adopt me, and the aunts did adopt me too, and although the rectory has tenants in it the truth is that it is all true. But the war is full of such stories, isn't it? That sort of thing. A lot of

351

us evacuees became more real to the families that took us in than their own, and of course the aunts had no-one else but themselves, so that explains why they were so keen to adopt. That and the fact that Aunt Sophie wanted someone to sing to her endless piano playing, and Miranda sings like a bird, I will say that for her.'

Dick stared suddenly at Teddy, his eyes widening. Teddy, although he was not Miranda's real brother, was speaking of her in precisely the way that brothers usually do speak of their sisters, either lightly mocking or deeply disparaging.

'Miranda, dear boy, is *beautiful*. Whether she can sing a note or nine don't matter three damns, she is *beautiful*.'

Teddy frowned. 'Now you're going too far, Dick. I know she's tall and all that, and her figure's quite good, but she's no more beautiful than you or I.'

'What is she, then?'

Teddy thought for a minute. 'Well, she's Miranda. You know. *Miranda*. Nice enough and all that, but you know, hardly an egg, Dick. Now some of those women we saw in Paris, wow! You've got to see some of my pictures, I've just had them developed. They make Madame Yin and her Society beauties look as insipid as a glass of soda water.'

Dick nodded. He had thought as much. It was obvious. Teddy simply could not see Miranda as being anything except his *sister*. Someone to walk either in front of him and take all the brickbats for him, or behind him to pick up all the pieces. He had always noticed at school that if boys with sisters were not busy taking them for granted, they were just as busy disparaging them.

'We've got the Winter Ball at the art school coming up pretty soon. I shall ask Miranda to accompany me.'

'Very kind of you. She's lots better now she's back in England, of course, but if there's someone else you'd rather, I'm sure she'd understand. I mean, Dick, you know and I know, Miranda is such a mess. She says so herself. I mean, to keep paying that fellow Macaskie. What a mess! To sign that piece of paper, and then keep on paying him. She needed her poor old brains examined.'

Dick downed the rest of his beer. 'Give me the tangle that is Miranda Mowbray, Teddy old thing, give me Miranda Mowbray above all the perfect flowers that do adorn the restaurants and cafés of Chelsea, dear boy. Give me her wild ways and her trapped heart, give me her gypsy soul, any old day. Who wants a girl that is perfect? Who wants Miss Average un-cracked nail varnish, never a hair out of place? Not me. No, Miranda is the perfection of all that is imperfect, which is why – she is perfect.'

After which he left the pub to go back to class, leaving Teddy staring after him. Dick had Miranda all wrong. Miranda was a *mess*.

Bobbie had found that Ebury Street had housed everyone in the world, at some time or another. Dill was a source of fascination as far as the history of

Ebury Street was concerned. She had even known Noel Coward's father and mother when they ran a lodging house in Ebury Street before the war. This was immensely exciting news to Bobbie, because the idea that she was living in a slightly Bohemian street was strangely satisfying. Besides, she knew that Julian would approve.

'Oh, there are lots of people like you, dear, really there are.'

'Like me?'

'Yes. Not ordinary, not like the rest of us. No, there are a lot of different kinds of people in this street, and of course there are actresses from the Royal Court Theatre in Sloane Square, and all sorts. Just along the way there is an old painter, newly moved in, I think. I see him quite a lot in the green-grocery, the one on the corner. He's one of the posher lot from opposite. They're a lot posher opposite. Although I will say next door has the aunt of a member of a ducal family, and three down has the old Countess of Ardingley. Never stands on her title, though, I will say that for her, calls herself "Mrs", but the trouble is that since she sends for all her food from Harrods and Oakeshotts, it rather gives the game away. You know how shops do like titles more even than money, I always think.'

Bobbie nodded, only really half listening. She knew that she had to get out and get herself some work, and she also knew that this was not going to be easy. There was not that much work for which she could apply, most especially since she had no reference, and was not likely to get one either. She could type, oh so slowly, and she could, thanks to her teacher from Baileys Green, take down short-hand at about the same rate. Borrowing Dill's newspaper from her she set about looking for some sort of temporary work.

After five minutes Dill looked over her shoulder and shook her head. 'You don't want to look there, dear. No, where you want to look for temporary work is here.' She pointed to a small agency adver-tisement. 'Always look for the one that can't afford nothing, because they'll be able to afford you, see? Their ad's the worst, so stands to reason they'll even take you on, see?'

Bobbie smiled at her landlady. She was off.

The letters on the door were sign-painted on the glass, but behind this particular door there was no sound of ancient typing machines being pounded, or indeed of any goodly industry, only the dreadful silence of failure.

Bobbie sensed this as she pushed open the door. She smelt it as the dusty, smoky atmosphere assailed her nostrils, she saw it as her eyes took in Mr Dudley and his partner Mrs Griffin. They were careworn by too much time spent with each other and, doubtless, judging from their flushed faces, in the pub on the corner of the street; and the hands that shook Bobbie's had index fingers that were stained yellow by nicotine, and shook a little when, to their evidently mutual astonishment, the telephone rang, and Mrs Griffin picked it up.

Having seated herself on the one rickety chair provided by the company for interviewees, Bobbie proceeded to evade the truth in the same way that Mrs Griffin – she could not help overhearing – was now lying to the company who had evidently just telephoned the agency with a request for a temp.

'We have just the person here for you, Mr Singh, a Miss . . .' Mrs Griffin's hand sought and found Bobbie's name in the otherwise empty diary in front of her, 'yes, Miss Roberta Murray. *Very* experienced, yes. *Very* suitable. *Yes*. And very reliable. *Yes*, she has worked for us before, and *yes* she is completely trustworthy.'

Mrs Griffin replaced the telephone and, interrupting Mr Dudley's desultory interview with Bobbie conducted between puffs of his untipped cigarette, she scribbled a name and an address on a piece of paper and handed it to her.

'Here you are, Miss Murray. Hop along there, it's not far. There's a good three weeks' worth of work waiting for you, I should say, and believe me, when I say work I do not mean it. They really only want someone to look after the office when they go out for their shopping or for lunch. Suit you down to the ground, my dear. But don't forget, you have been working for this agency for months and months, never stop. Don't let me down, now. Oh, and by the way, the money's good – religious organizations don't know any better, dear, really they don't.'

356

Bobbie smiled her thanks to Mrs Griffin, shook hands with both her and Mr Dudley, and flew back down the black lino stairs again and out into the street, and so to the King's Road. Because she did not know London she was once more forced to take a taxi, on the sound assumption that, unlike herself, cabbies did know their London, but then had to suffer the acute embarrassment of discovering that the address Mrs Griffin had scribbled on the back of an agency card was only two streets away from the agency itself.

This time Bobbie mounted a shorter flight of stairs, wider and much smarter. A good thick carpet covered these treads, and she did not pass other offices on the way up to the first floor, but arrived, quite soon, at a wide landing. This was a precursor to Mr Singh's office, itself guarded by double doors with large brass handles. In the forlorn hope that she might recognize some figure from the Old Testament – for since most of the staff at the sanatorium had been French she had never so much as opened a Bible her whole time there – Bobbie walked slowly past the sacred pictures that decorated the cream-painted walls, but none of them reminded her of anything she might know about – such as Moses and the tablets – so she now pulled at one of the impressively large brass handles, and walked into the office of the current London Director of the Holy Bible Company.

Mr Singh was small, bespectacled and smartly suited – almost over-correct in his dress, his suit an immaculate Prince of Wales check, his tie of woven silk polka dots, his shirt impeccably cut, his silk handkerchief spilling, just so, from his top pocket.

'Miss Murray, how do you do? I am Mr Singh. Do, please, sit down, and make your own choice of chair. There are several very comfortable chairs here, but you choose, you choose.'

In contrast to her recent interview at the Tee Dee Agency, faced with Mr Singh's meticulous presentation Bobbie now felt shabby to the point of shame. Her coat and skirt, the famous Christmas gift from Beatrice Harper, were still more than a little creased from the train journey and the lack of a travelling iron, or – as Beatrice would put it – *looked badly in need of one's maid, Roberta, my dear*.

'Miss Murray – we are in a hurry.' Mr Singh paused. 'I say, Miss Murray, I'm a poet, though I don't know it!' He began again. 'Yes, as I was saying, Miss Murray, we are badly in need of a replacement for poor Mrs Yates, taken ill and had to have her appendix removed, a very tender operation when it comes down to it, I believe. We still have Mrs O'Brien, of course, but she is not conversant with shorthand and typing, only answering the telephone and greeting visitors. But, as I understand it, you *are* first class at typing and shorthand.'

Bobbie was glad that the hat she was wearing partially hid her face. Before the shining goodness in Mr Singh's eyes, the lies that she had heard Mrs Griffin tell on behalf of the Tee Dee Agency and herself now seemed more like serious crimes than lies.

'Mr Singh, I must confess, I am not as, er, fast at shorthand and typing as you might perhaps wish. Certainly not as fast as Mrs Griffin made out, I am sure.'

'Modesty is very, very acceptable at the Holy Bible Company, Miss Murray. Wholly acceptable!' Mr Singh smiled. 'Whatever your speeds, Miss Murray, comfort yourself, you will have to be faster than Mrs Yates. She took her typing at what I believe is called a *Connemara clip* – that is to say, like the rain in Connemara, very, very steady indeed.'

Of course that made Bobbie feel better at once. And she could see, too, that Mr Singh's humorous attitude towards office life was bound to be most reassuring when she was seated in front of him, or Mrs O'Brien, taking dictation.

Except, as she subsequently discovered in the days that followed, there was no dictation; and certainly not on a daily basis. The wholly wholesome Holy Bible Company was London based, but essentially non-active.

The staff, once again consisting of three, including Bobbie, dutifully arrived every morning, hung up their overcoats, sat down in their various offices – large, spacious and beautifully furnished – and then waited to see whether any persons who, having received a Holy Bible (sold to them by one of a huge army of salesmen making their slow way around the country), might have found it wanting and, spurning the truths inherent in the sacred volume, sent it back.

It had to be said in praise of the continuing popularity of the Holy Book that very few people did seem to find it lacking. Or as Mr Singh once remarked, a little wryly, to Bobbie, 'I don't think they all get very, very far with it, Miss Murray. Certain it is, they do not manage to read it all at one *sitting*.'

The quiet tenor of their office lives meant that Mr Singh, Mrs O'Brien and Bobbie all became great friends. Such friends that very soon Bobbie found that she positively looked forward to coming to the office in the morning, and started to dread the day when Mrs Yates might recover from her appendicitis.

Part of the joy of the life at the Holy Bible Company was that at coffee, lunch, or teatime they all talked together so amicably. In the mornings, over chicory coffee and small finger-shaped biscuits, they talked about their families, their children, their pets – if any – and Mr Singh and Mrs O'Brien sometimes brought in snaps to show Bobbie. At lunchtime they brought out their newspapers and ate in steady silence before once again resuming the only slightly accelerated pace of office life. At teatime, once the newspapers had been duly digested over lunch, their conversations centred around such things as fashion, and the King and Queen.

Once or twice, but only during office hours, they

might actually talk about a Holy Bible that had been returned by some unhappy recipient who had usually found it *to long and the payments are to much* (sic). But this was more than usually unusual.

On receiving such a momentous communication, Mr Singh would immediately summon Bobbie to his office and, having cleared his throat, and placed his long fingertips against each other, began dictation.

'Are you ready, Miss Murray?' he would ask her quite excitedly, before clearing his throat again. 'Are you quite sure you are ready, Miss Murray?' Again the throat would be cleared. 'Good, then we may begin. Please, tell me at once if it is too fast, if my dictation is too fast, won't you? One must always, my father told me, speak very, very slowly to secretaries and waiters.'

And so he would begin his dictation, carefully enunciating each word with clarity and precision, while watching Bobbie's shorthand notebook with paternal concern.

Dear Mr Pope, We, at the Holy Bible Company, are most regretful at receiving the return of your Holy Bible. The Holy Bible as you know is a most beautiful testament. We are distressed that you find it too long. We will therefore ask our representative to call upon you personally and demonstrate the abridged edition with illustrations. The payments can be monthly on this edition too. However, since you are having difficulties, allowances can be made. Please fill in the form enclosed. We would recommend the *'penny a week' scheme*. It is most efficacious, and will not strain the family income while bringing enlightenment for many years to come.

We sign ourselves with God,
The Holy Bible Company

Both Bobbie and Mr Singh found this letter immensely satisfactory, and part of the satisfaction for each of them was that Mr Singh always dictated the letter as if he had just thought of it, and Bobbie took it down, in by now quite perfect shorthand, as if she had never taken it down before. And when Bobbie brought the letter back to Mr Singh, carefully placed in a leather folder, and held the pen for him to sign *On behalf of the Holy Bible Company, J. Singh*, they would, for a few seconds, stare in mutual admiration at this new epistle, before Mr Singh remarked with quiet satisfaction, 'Your spelling is quite perfect, Miss Murray. You must have had a very good education.'

Dill had something a little different to say. She said Bobbie was very lucky to have found work so quickly and so near, no bus fares, nothing, she said, marvelling at the luck of it all.

Bobbie could only agree. It seemed to her that at last her life had taken an upward turn, the first since the end of that idyllic summer with Julian and the

Major. Nowadays she made sure to live only from day to day, and never for tomorrow or yesterday. It was difficult sometimes – particularly if she saw a painting of the sea, or the blue sky of an early summer evening brought back voices from another time – and yet it had to be done. She had to forget.

And so spring cantered into a new summer and still Mrs Yates seemed not to have recovered from her appendicitis. Indeed, she had been away so long that her name was hardly ever mentioned, except by Mrs O'Brien who was knitting her colleague a blue cardigan in a very fine angora wool which shed hairs with monotonous regularity on the knitter's skirt.

'You know, Miss Murray, you are far too pretty to be always in an office,' Mrs O'Brien announced one day, looking up briefly from her knitting, which by now was assuming almost alarming proportions.

The three of them were seated in the tearoom, a large panelled area hung about with yet more illustrations from the Bible. As was the custom, and in keeping with their different status, they always sat at separate tables, but talked across the room at each other while enjoying buns filled with shredded coconut, and sardine sandwiches, and other delicacies sent in from a local café.

Bobbie had never thought of herself as pretty, far from it. It was something to do with having been so ill as a child, everyone fearing to be near her, not realizing just how much she needed them not to look repulsed by her. As a consequence of this, it was difficult for her not to look astonished at Mrs O'Brien's sudden observation, coming as it did after the deep peace and content that always followed their tea and biscuits.

'Don't you think that Miss Murray is too pretty to be always in an office, Mr Singh?' Mrs O'Brien asked, half accusingly.

'Of course she is too pretty to work always in an office, Mrs O'Brien. I have been saying that to you, Mrs O'Brien, for many, many weeks now. Miss Murray is wasted at the Holy Bible Company with us. She should be a fashion model, or a famous woman, not taking dictation and eating coconut buns with you and me. My wife said the same when she saw the office photographs that you took of us all at Easter, Mrs O'Brien. *A beautiful girl like that should be a fashion model or a famous woman.* That is what my wife said. *What a waste.* She said that too.'

Bobbie was blushing now, and at the same time feeling both helpless and a little suspicious. 'Do you want me to leave, then? I mean, does this mean that you think that I am not suitable?'

From their separate tables Mrs O'Brien and Mr Singh stared across at Bobbie, managing to look both horrified and hurt.

'Why, not at all!' Mrs O'Brien protested. 'Not at all. No, it is not that, Miss Murray. It is something quite other.' She turned to Mr Singh. 'Shall I?'

He nodded, gravely, solemnly, and the tips of

his long fingers met as they always did when he dictated a letter. It was that serious.

'Tell her, Mrs O'Brien. Please, tell her.'

'Miss Murray, Mr Singh and I were wondering if you would pose as a student of the Bible, for our advertisements on the undergrounds and the bus shelters and so on? That is what we were *really* wondering. Mrs Singh came up with the idea when she saw my snap of you at the office Easter luncheon. That is what we're on about, Miss Murray, our advertisement. Rather an embarrassing way of putting it, I know, but there. We mean well, really we do. But seeing as you have no family who might object to this on religious or any other grounds, it seems to us that you'd be an excellent choice. In fact, it seems to us that you are ideal. You have this, if we may say so, innocent look. You look as if you might really read a Bible, not like famous actresses or fashion models who would look like Jezebel or Delilah, more suitable for inclusion in the abridged version with illustrations than believable as having read the Holy Book.'

'Or worse,' Mr Singh added darkly, staring fiercely at the plain white tablecloth in front of his cup of tea as if an army of Jezebels and Delilahs was marching across it towards his plate.

'I should be quite happy to pose for you,' Bobbie agreed slowly, 'just so long as it does not mean giving up my work here.'

'Your work here is too important to us. We would not dream of asking that. Happily, Mrs Yates is still enjoying a long recuperation, for which the Holy Bible Company is more than happy to pay if it enables her to recover in every way, allowing her whole body to return to complete and commonplace fitness, and *you*, Miss Murray, to stay in your wholehearted occupation of your desk.'

Mr Singh's brilliant smile seemed to light up the tearoom, and then they all returned to work, Bobbie to sit patiently behind her large Edwardian typewriter waiting for, indeed sometimes longing for, a letter to type, and Mrs O'Brien to knit. It was so peaceful at the Holy Bible Company that of an afternoon, shortly after tea, Bobbie often mused to herself, as she practised very slow, comfortable typing, that she might have actually found a sort of paradise.

For a few seconds she pondered on the whole idea of posing with a Bible for a photo, but then, thinking that no-one would really notice, no-one like Beatrice would ever be on an underground, or waiting for a bus, never likely to see some obscure advertisement for a Bible, she relaxed.

Besides, it did not mean that she would have to give up her job. That was all that really mattered to her. Staying as she was, as happy as she had been these last weeks and months. Nothing to interrupt the quiet tenor of her days, strolling back from the office to Dill's lodging house in Ebury Street at night; and then in the morning, after a shallow bath of warm water in Dill's proudly smart bathroom with its new wallpaper in purple and yellow, strolling back to the King's Road and the Holy Bible

Company. Everything seemed to be pretty perfect in Bobbie's life at that moment.

She said as much to Dill that night, but Dill only looked at her, and for the first time Bobbie saw a worried expression coming into her landlady's eyes.

'Look, dear, I don't know much, but when my life is too quiet I worry, really I do. If the basement's flooded and one of me parrots is sick, or a canary hasn't sung that morning, then I feel fine. It's when the fire's lit and the tea's on, and I'm saying to myself "This is good, Dill, this is the life", *that's* when I get the collywobbles, and start looking behind me. It's the quiet times. I think that's why we were all so happy in the war.' Dill paused to wag her finger at one of her canaries as if to warn it to keep quiet during the rest of her speech. 'Yes. If you ask me, because there were no quiet times, because the bombs were dropping and we was always digging our loved ones out of somewhere, or something, or *someone*, it kept us fighting on. Now – well, now, it goes quiet, and we all start worrying, really we do. That's the trouble with peace, it's too . . . peaceful, if you like.'

Bobbie only half listened to what her landlady was saying, only half heard her words. She was feeling so hungry that she suddenly knew that Dill's six o'clock tea of chips and bacon, and a cup of tea, was not going to be quite enough. She just knew that as soon as she had finished it she would spring out of the door and down to Sloane Square where she would buy herself a proper dinner at the Royal Court Hotel, or some place like that. She would stare up at the new photographs outside the theatre, and find herself wondering if she would ever be able to spare enough of her 'rainy day' money to go to a performance there, in the theatre that had, she knew from Dill, been the first to show plays by many famous men, George Bernard Shaw included.

She dressed up in a new skirt that she had bought with a colossal amount of coupons, put the coat that Beatrice had given her over her cotton blouse and cardigan, and having slipped into some incredibly expensive stockings, only recently purchased, along with some shoes with a wedge heel, with some of her wages and another vast outlay of coupons, she started to walk, sedately and enjoyably, towards Sloane Square once more.

Long before she reached the Royal Court, Bobbie realized that she had been all but stalking the Bohemian figure in front of her. She thought he must be an older man, for his tread was heavy and his gait slightly lopsided, as if he had been wounded in one of his legs, or some such. But his costume – no-one would call what he was wearing 'clothes' in the conventional sense – was what had really taken Bobbie's interest. She always did like people who dressed differently, and it seemed that this man, whatever his age, was decidedly individual, for he was wearing a jungle hat, a belted safari jacket, knickerbockers to the knee, long socks up to the knickerbockers and leather shoes with tasselled fronts such as are worn by golfers.

He was walking slowly, as happy people do, really strolling more than walking, and on the busy pavement at first Bobbie too was forced to walk slowly behind him, all the way up to Sloane Square and the more crowded region of that particular part of town, deciding eventually that rather than strolling he was walking with great contentment, taking in everything, while over his shoulder, slung easily, and quite obviously filled with books or notebooks – at any rate with things that he must like or enjoy – was a large old-fashioned fishing bag.

Following him now, Bobbie stopped when he stopped, leaving some few paces between them and pretending to look down at something in her bag, and then as he began to walk, fell in behind him again, pacing her steps, for no reason she could really think of, to his. This sequence took place some half a dozen times, until their progress had turned into a polite kind of Grandmother's Foot-steps. Once the man lit a cigarette, but continued on without turning, now smoking in the same leisurely way that he was walking.

They had reached the top of Sloane Square when he started to turn, and Bobbie stopped a few yards behind him, leaving him a few seconds to get ahead. But he continued to turn, until she found herself face to face with the man she had, in essence, been tailing.

'Never stalk a man who has lived by his wits in

the jungle, old bean, do you hear? It's a sixth sense one develops, d'you see? Being stalked is a feeling, you don't have to see or hear anything, but you know you have someone behind you—' The man stopped talking abruptly, and his eyes filled with emotion. 'Oh, but my dear, you dear, dear old bean! Dear, dear, you dear old bean!'

Bobbie stared up at the face under the hat. If she had not recognized the face she would have recognized the voice at once, but as it was she recognized both at one and the same time, and her heart sank and rose simultaneously, because staring at her from under the jungle hat, the wearer of the fantastic costume, was that dear person from the past, from the summer idyll, from Baileys Court – the Major.

'I thought I might meet you again,' Bobbie told him excitedly as, having shaken each other's hands almost to pieces, they headed together for the Royal Court pub. 'In a way that was why I made for Ebury Street when I came to London, because I so hoped that I might find you and Mrs Saxby. I remembered her mentioning that she had a flat in Ebury Street, all that time ago, when we were first in the Sheds, but I had no idea of the number.'

'Well, you did very well, dear old bean, really you did. Because we are here, and you have found us, although not living in a flat any more. Myself and the second Mrs Saxby have bought the whole house. What number are you?'

Bobbie told him, and the Major gave a deep sigh of satisfaction.

'So near to us, and on the opposite side of the road. You must cross over. What will you have?'

'Oh, you know – a dry sherry, if that is all right. How is your pug, how is Boy?'

'Such a tyrant. Such a tyrant. You remember what a tyrant he was, I expect? And a notice box! Such a notice box. Imagine you remembering Boy, imagine you remembering him.'

'Of course. Who could not remember him?'

'In that case then you will remember that he was always such a snob? Still is, I'm afraid. And of course the second Mrs Saxby insists on letting him have his own way, not once or twice a day, but all day. She even puts on the wireless for him. Now, drink up and I'll take you back to Saxby Hall, as we call the old place. We take in paying guests, in fact, if only to pay for Boy's extravagant taste in foodstuffs, but we wouldn't poach you from your place, of course we wouldn't. On the other hand if you've a mind to come and lodge, we wouldn't stop you, of course. As a matter of fact, it would be quite like old times, wouldn't it? If you came to lodge with us, with the second Mrs Saxby and me?'

'Oh, but I couldn't leave Dill.' Bobbie looked at the Major, suddenly shocked.

'Fair enough, old bean, then don't leave Dill, whoever she is – and she must be a dear bean to elicit such affection – but at least come in and have a drink with myself and the second Mrs Saxby. Oh, but you must. I can't tell you, the excitement is going to be tremendous.'

But although Bobbie felt she could not leave Dill, it seemed that Dill could not wait for Bobbie to leave her.

'You got old friends across from here? Well, in't that splendid? Then I do beg you, Miss Murray, I do advise, you must go opposite, really you must. If they are on the other side of the road they are bound to be more your sort, and you won't get woken by the canaries and that.'

'I'd rather not go and lodge with them, actually, Dill. Really, I'm quite happy here with you. In fact, I prefer it, you know, really I do.'

'Course you do, dear, but remember I may not always *be* here. As a matter of fact, I have been meaning to tell you – I was going to get round to it – I have only been hanging on here, if the truth be known, until the lease falls in, which it does soon, and then I'm off to Torquay.' She smiled happily, as if Torquay was a dear old friend. 'I always did plan on Torquay for retirement. And the birds, you know – they'll be happier for the sea air. Sometimes I think one more winter of this London smog and they'll pass out, like what the poor creatures used to down the mines before the war and that.'

'Please don't go to Torquay, Dill. Please. Stay here. It's been so nice.' Bobbie sounded so emotional that Dill frowned and looked cross and embarrassed at the same time. But she was silent as Bobbie continued, 'You see, I don't really want to go to live with the Saxbys, precisely because they *are* my sort of people. They won't be nearly such fun as being here with you and the canaries. They'll stand on form all day long, I dare say, and then where will I be? I might as well be back with my guardian in Sussex. Really, I like being here with you, Dill.'

'Kissed the Blarney Stone you have, Miss Bobbie. Look, don't look a gift horse in the mouth, will you? Things have a way of working out, one door closes and another door opens.' Dill held up a stern finger and wagged it at Bobbie. 'And that's just what I heard a minute ago – the sound of one door closing, and another door opening. So. Just you be thankful. Instead of moping about and getting sentimental over my high teas, you be thankful for that opening door, Miss Murray. Be thankful, and do as I say, go through the open door, instead of moaning and feelin' sorry for yourself.'

Bobbie started to say something, and then stopped.

It was true. Dill was right. And what was more, if she was being truthful, Bobbie had heard that sound, too, even as Dill was lecturing her. The clear sound of one door closing, and another door opening.

Chapter Twelve

Miranda stared at herself in the full length cheval mirror that filled one end of her bedroom at Aubrey Close. Having spent some days in and out of Andre's famous hairdressing salon in Sloane Street, she was once more completely blond again. But it was not just her hair; the truth was that she was blond again inside too. With the return of her natural blond flaxen hair, which somehow seemed to emphasize the colour of her pale English skin as well, the real Miranda had also arrived back once more. There was now no trace of the awful '*Randy Darling*', the creature Macaskie had invented, and then discarded, but forced to pay him her pitiful earnings as waitress and sometime singer, by way of some sadistic recompense for letting him down.

Of course, since the terrible night in the Blue Note, she knew that she must never touch drink again. She knew it without being told by either Teddy or Dick. She herself did not want to touch drink again. She actually found it boring and dull. Neither did she want to smoke any more. The memory of Allegra's Passing Clouds in their pink boxes now made her feel vaguely sick. No, nowadays, when she awoke in the morning, her first thought and her greatest delight was to look forward to a cup of coffee and that most magic of all magical accompaniments, a real French croissant from a real continental bakery that she and Dick had found hidden away a few streets away from Aubrey Close. It was full of secret gourmet delights, apparently enjoyed only by the residents in the locality. And there had been other discoveries too for Miranda, of course, other delights – not least of all Teddy.

He was about to come round and show her his new photographs. Teddy was so awfully pleased with himself at the moment that she and Dick Fortescue had to keep working terribly hard to bring his head down to a normal size. Dick had even invented a trumpet sound which he now made every time Teddy took too long to tell them some new, usually fairly involved story about his latest shoot. Of course he devoutly imagined, indeed he was convinced, that he had actually invented a new style of photography, in which everything was to be photographed 'on the hoof'. *Movement, nothing but movement*, was what Teddy was always going on about.

He kept trying out things in the studio – cups suspended on threads, stuffed birds eating crumbs; his enthusiasm for action photographs seemed to be unlimited. The previous week he had Miranda directing a hair-dryer towards a line of washing which he had strung across the room, while a model he had hired for half a day stood in one of the costumes from Miranda's precious studio trunk and held a cup whose saucer, seemingly caught in the air, was suspended underneath it on a piece of invisible pale pink cotton.

'You must remember that there is nothing new under the sun, dear boy,' Dick would try to keep reminding him, as he picked up one of Teddy's new photographs. 'We are fools if we think we have arrived at anything new. Only God does that, and sometimes even He must regret a few of His less bright notions – such as that awful chap Macaskie that had poor Miranda blinded by his sadistic ways. And wasps. And the present and past British governments who hate art worse than sin.'

Since Paris the three of them, Teddy and Dick and Miranda, had become inseparable in their spare time. And most of their spare time was spent at Aubrey Close where Miranda, once recovered, set about doing what all single girls in triangular friendships always do, namely – cooking for the boys.

In truth Miranda knew very well that this was really why Teddy and Dick came round so often, and stayed for so long. It was for her food rather than her company, but Miranda did not mind. It was one of the many miracles of her life that she had long ago learned to cook, self-taught, for herself and Allegra. It had really been a form of self-defence, for Allegra's idea of eating had been a cigarette and a margarine sandwich, usually consumed alternately. But now, with fewer restrictions on foods, and less need – for those in the know anyway – for coupons and queuing, Miranda was able to start to experiment.

Paris had taught her about the need for fresh ingredients, and so, long before the boys stirred, she would take the Underground to Covent Garden in the early morning and return with pâtés and cheeses and fresh fruit and vegetables. Happily, speaking both Cockney and *café French*, as Dick and she called it, Miranda had been able to make friends with many of the stallholders. Weaving among their newly arrived produce she never forgot, before judiciously squeezing their pears, to ask after their wives, their children, their illnesses – anything and everything about them was of interest to her, so that they in their turn obligingly directed her to the best of their produce, which was immensely satisfactory to all concerned.

And then there would be the inevitable early morning taxi ride home to Aubrey Close, for much of what she wanted had to be bought in whole boxes, and in far larger quantities than she would really wish.

'You should start a restaurant,' Dick suggested quite casually one day as he finished a more than satisfactory bowl of soup, pushing Miranda's home-made bread in flamboyant French style around his soup plate to finish and savouring every mouthful of what it mopped up.

Miranda at the kitchen sink, busy washing up, alone, turned and stared at him. 'I don't think I am talented enough to run a café, Dick.'

'I do – and what is more I know someone very nice who will back you.'

'You do? Who? Who would back someone like me?'

'Me, dear girl, me. Dear old Dick here.'

Dick stared up into Miranda's beautiful face as she bent carelessly over him to place cheese and grapes in front of his place. Naturally, because he knew himself to be in love with her now, Dick was hoping against hope that she could not hear how hard his heart beat, despite his best efforts, when she was so near to him. He never would say anything to her, of course, that was not his way. Ever since, when he was a small boy, his mother had mocked his love for the beautiful girl next door, Dick had dreaded that more than anything in the world.

The awful shame of hearing his mother's voice saying, *What do you want to go and see her for? I suppose you have a crush!* And along with the shame the dreadful, painful inability to understand just why she should wish to mock him. Now of course he could not even remember the girl's name. He frowned. He could only remember her long, blond plaits, nothing else, not even her first name.

'You?' Although she had actually spoken quite quietly Miranda's voice seemed to explode around Dick as he tucked into his cheese and fruit, and at the same time tried to avoid noticing the incredulity of her tone, or the surprise in her eyes, as she stood back wiping her hands on her apron, not seeing him at all really, only gazing ahead of her at what might be some kind of new future.

'Would you really, Dick? I mean really, would you really be able to back me, if that is the right word?'

'Of course, dear girl. You were not to know that I have a little inheritance, from a great-aunt. Wonderful woman, upright and tenacious. She left us all, myself and my two brothers, a small sum, in the devout hope that we would make it larger. A large sum would, she always maintained, be bad for us. A large sum would make us lazy, a small sum would make us work.'

'Well, but – a café. Dick, do you think that I could run a sort of café-restaurant?'

'Not the Ivy, dear girl, no, you could not do that. But yes, you could easily run a small French-type café cum luncheon place. After all, you're more or less doing that now, aren't you? Forever in the kitchen making soups and pounding garlic in that old mortar of yours. You could call it Chez Miranda. And it would have checked table cloths, and – well, you know the sort of cafés you find everywhere in France, but not in England. Nice places that cook for the table and do those thin French chips that arrive all salted and hot at your place within seconds of being fried. You know. And delicious soups. Like what you just served up to

379

moi.' Dick ran his fingers through his thick curly hair and smiled, suddenly quite openly shy, so much so that he went on quickly, 'Nothin' more an' nothin' less, dear girl. *Savez?* Soups, French bread, croissants, coffee, the continental style, wine by the glass, the perfect tomato salad, the perfect crème brûlée, the perfect egg mayonnaise, perfection in every way for very little outlay and maximum pleasure. We might call it not Chez Miranda but the Café Perfect. We might call it that, think you?'

But Miranda had stopped listening to him some few seconds before and was staring past him. 'There might be somewhere near here, do you know that? A small place, where we could put out tables in the summer – chalk up the menu, that kind of thing. Oh dear.'

'Why the *oh dear*? Has my favourite cook thought of something bad?'

'Not *thought*, no, I have just *seen* a rather tall interruption.'

Dick stood up, all concern, longing to take Miranda in his arms and just hold her, if nothing else. She was so very beautiful now she was blond again, and somehow so touchingly determined to reform after what she now saw as being – she had confessed to him now many times – her terrible past in Paris.

To think I was bought for a pair of gloves!

She sometimes said that when they were all sitting up late at night drinking coffee and listening to Dick's new jazz records, and it fairly broke Dick's heart to hear her. She had not been *bought*, he always insisted, she had been young, she had been deceived, and that was quite different.

Same salad, different dressing was her statutory reply after one of their reruns of this conversation.

But now Dick saw that she had, all at once, stopped dreaming and turned hastily back to the kitchen.

'I see what you mean.' Dick strolled towards the outer studio doors. 'I see what you mean,' he repeated. 'Oh dear indeed. Enter our very own genius, fresh from the fields of photography, standing four square against oncoming fame. Come in, Teddy Mowbray, and tell us, do. Although before you do, please tell me first, has your hat size grown from seven and three-quarters to eight and a quarter, as rumour now persists in saying it has?'

Teddy nodded, hardly listening, waiting only to begin.

'Quite right, quite right,' he called out gaily, 'and when you see my pictures you will see why. It is true what they are all saying, I am the Michael Angelo of the camera. The day before yesterday I took a shot of two models skating, and just-wait-till-you-see. I have suspended them in the air. Just-you-wait-till-you-see. You will gasp, boys and girls, you will gasp, and you will know,' he added, calling to Miranda who was already heating up some soup for him, 'you will acknowledge that your brother, Teddy Mowbray, is something other. I have to be. Just look at these pictures. And although they will always bear the illustrious name of that old devil Stanis that I slave for on the bottom, although he will always claim them as his – tell me, am I or am I not just as evil a genius as him, to produce such work? Tell me. You have to admit it, I am!'

Miranda and Dick stared at the photographs which Teddy generously spread out on the large oak side table with its vast, almost clumsy carvings of grapes, and its heavy legs, purposeful and Tudor-type. As Miranda peered at the pictures she kept wiping her hands on her apron, and as Dick stared, he could not help darting little sideways looks at her. Seeing such high fashion pictures, rather different from the others that Teddy had brought back to the studio before, he worried that Miranda would once again be reminded of the dreaded Macaskie, and the not so recent, but still very painful, past.

But Miranda did not seem to mind looking at other models. She peered intently, even critically, at the photographs, and then, realizing that she was not seeing them in their full glory, went quickly to fetch her new glasses, a necessity nowadays, since whatever had happened to her in Paris had caused her, of a sudden, to become short-sighted.

'They are beautiful, Ted,' she told him, when she saw them clearly.

Dick noticed that Miranda always called Teddy *Ted* nowadays, and, knowing their past, he occasionally wondered if it was Miranda's way of keeping Teddy's head down to size. As if in some sisterly fashion she was trying to keep his feet on the ground by reminding him that he was still Ted Darling to her, whatever Teddy Mowbray might be, or want to be, to the rest of the world.

In fact, although the pictures were in actuality photographs, they might just as well have been paintings that had been arranged, expressly, to be photographed. And that was what was so clever. The women in the photographs were ostensibly modelling evening gowns, but of course they were not doing that at all, they were modelling the beauty of an age. At long, long last the great couturiers, numbers of whom had designed stylish utility wear to take women through the terrible years of the recent conflict, had been thankfully able to return to the grandeur of the past.

And so there, in a large ballroom, most decorously lit, were beautiful women modelling beautiful clothes, and the result, not unexpectedly was quite, quite beautiful.

Some of the women were leaning against a piano, very distantly seen. Some, seen only in head and shoulders, were looking towards others, nearer to the camera. For the most part, those in the foreground wore strapless satin dresses, some with matching stoles, and their hair, in contrast to what Macaskie had done to Miranda, was knotted into their necks, or arranged behind their ears to show off small diamond earrings and delicately fashioned necklaces. One young woman had her back to the camera, one shoulder bare, her short hair showing off a marvellous pair of shoulders, not sloping but slender and straight, her dress falling from the waist in satin circles and then caught up to the side in a full drop to the floor. To the right of her were other young women dressed in pale blue or pale lemon satin, and they too had hairstyles that showed off slender straight shoulders, and long evening gloves which covered elbows. It was a picture of an era which was still looking back. And yet, what a picture.

Teddy himself was so pleased with it that he stood looking at his own photographs, lost in admiration for them, long after the other two had moved away.

Miranda waited for him in the kitchen, slowly stirring the soup, making sure that it did not boil. She stirred it so long and so patiently that Dick did not understand why, after Teddy had finally finished praising his own work, she did not, quite frankly, throw it at him. But the fact was that she did not. Not only did she not throw it at him, she placed it most carefully in front of him, poured him a glass of wine, and then, to Dick's amazement, sat down and listened to the charming old bighead with the most meticulous attention.

Of course, Dick reasoned to himself, as he quickly wound up the gramophone and started to listen to a great new Louis Armstrong All-Stars record, that was what sisters did, even if they were maybe not sisters by blood – they cooked for their brothers, and listened to them.

'So, there we are. And I was allowed, by the great man, to actually press the trigger myself today. I took the picture, Sis, not him. Press, bang, it was me.'

'But I read that apparently Stanis never does take the picture, Ted. He has always insisted that his assistants take the picture. So it's not that much of a compliment.'

Teddy laughed at that, but he still would not be put down. That was not his way.

'Touché, Sis, touché, but I don't believe you.'

'And what will tomorrow bring, Ted?' Miranda stood looking down at Teddy, taking his soup plate away, and carefully placing some fruit and cheese in front of him.

'Oh, say not to reason why, and don't ask me about tomorrow.' Teddy gave a small groan, before reaching hungrily for the cheese and French bread. 'Talk about from the sublime to the ridiculous. I mean.' He shook his head as Miranda passed him some more of her precious supply of butter. 'I mean talk about the sublime to the ridiculous,' he said again. 'Tomorrow I only have to photograph some religious nut with a Bible, of all things.'

Bobbie had moved in with the Saxbys only a fort-night after re-meeting the Major in Sloane Square on that summery evening. It was, quite frankly, bliss, after Dill and her canaries. Not just because it was the opposite, smarter side of the road – Bobbie really did not care very much for such things – but because they had more hot water, and the beds were old and Edwardian and the moment she stepped up into hers she slept so soundly that it was difficult to wake without the aid of a borrowed alarm clock.

This particular morning, however, she had woken without its help, simply because she was feeling nervous. She had no idea of how to model or act, and yet she knew, in a way, that both might be necessary. She had no idea what sort of clothes to wear, and yet they too, she realized, were equally necessary to making the photo session a success. The previous evening she had laid out what she had imagined were the sort of clothes that a young woman who was devoted to her Bible (and knew her Jezebel from her Delilah) might wear. Full black skirt, plain white shirt, borrowed from the second Mrs Saxby, and dark stockings and buckled shoes.

The French student look, Bobbie called it, but the former Miss Moncrieff, now Mrs Saxby, disagreed.

'No, Bobbie dear, not French student. French students look a little louche and such like. No, with your long brown hair and your English rose complexion, you have the look of a girl who has been brought up to go to prayer meetings. You have the natural look, I am happy to say, nothing artificial about you. Quite appropriate. I'm glad my stockings fit you all right,' she added.

'They're just a bit, well, itchy,' Bobbie confessed.

'I'm not surprised. I knitted them in the war, but I never got round to wearing them.'

They both stared down at Bobbie's legs. Her legs did actually look what Mrs Saxby called 'quite appropriate' in the former Miss Moncrieff's fine hand-knitted stockings.

'Well, top marks, Roberta. And never mind what anyone else thinks about posing for photographs, dear, there is nothing that I know of in the Bible to say it is wrong. Provided, of course, that it is decorous. I just hope my stockings will stay up. I mean that is a worry, dear, for you are yards thinner than I am, or was. And though they are not fashionable at the moment it has to be said that they might one day be modish.'

She left Bobbie to finish checking her appearance in front of the mirror, brushing her hair for perhaps the hundredth time. Staring yet again at her own image, hating it, and yet not knowing what to do about it. The fact was that she was far too thin, and she and Mrs Saxby both knew it. They had even talked about it the previous evening, both coming to the inevitable conclusion that it really did not matter. Or, more to the point, that there was very little that either of them could do about it.

'The Duchess of Windsor is very thin, dear.'

'I am afraid I do not look like the Duchess of Windsor, Mrs Saxby. She scares me. She reminds me of the bad queen in Snow White.'

'I expect you'll put on weight soon,' came the encouraging remark.

'Yes, Miss M – I mean, Mrs Saxby – but not, it has to be said, by tomorrow. That would be a Biblical miracle on a vast scale, wouldn't you say?'

They had both laughed at that, and as she watched the former Miss Moncrieff laughing Bobbie had wondered, for perhaps the hundredth time, at the change that marriage had brought about in her. Gone were the cardigans with the moss-stitch cuffs and collars, gone was the hairstyle drawn to such a tight conclusion at the back of her neck that it would make Bobbie wince just to look at her. Instead, like the Major, Mrs Saxby had turned quite Bohemian, affecting floral blouses with elaborate shoulder gathers and billowing sleeves caught up in deep cuffs. Her long silver or gold earrings rang and sang as she moved about their sitting room, and her long grey hair was worn in a vast plait around her head, round and round, giving her face the inevitable plump look of a happy Victorian lady. Her watch strap, which used to leave a mark whenever she took it off to type, had been replaced by an old fob watch on a bow which she pinned to the front of her blouses, she wore large rings, and you could always hear when she was coming into a room because the charms on her gold bracelet announced her arrival long before she was seen.

She once referred to her sea change when she was watching the Major from their first floor sitting room window, remarking gaily, 'We just wish, the Major and I, that we had become Bohemians before, Bobbie dear, we do really.'

*　　*　　*

And now the car was there and everything was happening very fast as everything always seems to when you are nervous, Bobbie found.

And the driver, a professional chauffeur from some hire car firm, was bowing, and the front of his cap was catching the sun, so he looked, just for a few seconds, to Bobbie anyway, as if he might have been sent down from Olympus to fetch her, and somehow it made her nerves worse, and she minded more than ever that she was too thin and had never posed for photographs before. She found herself wishing, again and again, that the chauffeur would get lost, or that he would be found not to know the address, or that the place where the photographs were to be taken – a deserted building in the middle of Kensington Gardens – would be found to be full of other people, all busy taking their photos, so that the whole thing would prove to be a complete fiasco.

Unfortunately the driver proved to be entirely competent, and he delivered Bobbie to the deserted building with time to spare.

It was, or had been, an old orangery, but was now wrecked by the bombing, and yet to be restored. Clutching the Holy Bible supplied by the Holy Bible Company, courtesy of Mr Singh, Bobbie in her black clothes and home-knitted stockings moved slowly and reluctantly towards the group of people she could see standing about with cameras and lights, her face alternating between scarlet and

389

quite white with nerves, her teeth chattering.

'Yes, the electricity is still working, would you believe? Not even Hitler's bombing was that accurate. So that is fine. Hold that there! No, not like that – like this! Oh, and be a good fellow and go and fetch us some coffee from the back of the car, would you? Could someone tell me when we are to be blessed with the presence of the blasted model?'

There was something about the owner of the voice that Bobbie, long before she saw him, knew, for absolute certain, was familiar. Long before she saw his bright blond hair, or noticed how tall he had grown, or anything else, Bobbie just knew it was Teddy. But whereas before, when she had first seen Julian at Baileys Court, she had hoped so much that the man with the fascinating smile would turn out to be Teddy, now she found her heart sinking. Teddy of all people! Here and waiting to photograph her, of all people! It was almost a nightmare to find Teddy waiting to take a picture of her, Bobbie Murray, who when he last saw her was looking like Milly Molly Mandy, fresh from the caring hands of Mrs Dingwall. Of all the bad luck. As if it was not bad enough never to have done this sort of thing before, but to find that the photographer was Teddy Mowbray of all people! Teddy, who was always so dreadfully spoilt by the aunts and Miranda, to be fetching up photographing her, Bobbie Murray, with a Bible of all things. He would laugh his socks off.

Before she opened her mouth to say, as coolly as

possible, 'Here is the blasted model, Teddy Mowbray. The model, so-called, is behind you,' Bobbie was quite sure that she already hated the grown-up Teddy.

For his part, hearing her words, Teddy turned round slowly, and Bobbie stared up at him. At first he did not even recognize his fellow evacuee, but Teddy being Teddy, as soon as he did his face lit up, and he positively jumped across the room, whooping and seizing Bobbie's hands to swing her round and round, finishing by sweeping her off the ground and hugging her in front of all the amazed people standing around with the permanently bored expressions of people who are waiting to work.

'Bobbie, I can not believe this is true, I can't believe it's you,' Teddy kept saying. 'Is it really you?'

'Well, it is true, and it is me,' Bobbie kept replying, with her usual pragmatism. 'And frankly, I don't see why it shouldn't be, why it's so surprising. Why wouldn't it be true, for goodness' sake? England is not such a big place, after all. Not so big that people like us would not find each other again, is it? In fact, we were really rather doomed to meet again, when I come to think of it.'

'Still the same old crusty Bobbie, thank heavens. Gracious, you have not changed at all!' Teddy put his arm round her and hugged her again.

'Thanks.'

'Except goodness me, you are so much prettier.

My God, the last time I saw you, frankly you looked too terrible to contemplate. I would not have known you. Now. Well. Wow! I really never would have thought it. I mean when we were at Mellaston, it was always Miranda who was the beauty, not you.'

He stood back, finally staring at Bobbie with professional detachment, and then gave a satisfied grunt. 'When we were at Mellaston, you were quite the ugly duckling, you know.'

'Oh, Teddy, do stop! Talk about not changing, it's you that hasn't changed at all. Still putting your foot in your mouth, or someone else's.'

But Teddy went on blithely, 'And guess what? I have found Miranda too – my long-lost big sister, who adopted me. So now we have found you, we are a threesome again. How about *that*?'

After this news of course Bobbie just had to give in and come off it, and join in the general Teddy-type enthusiasm, because it was one thing finding Teddy, but if Teddy had found Miranda, then that really was too good to be true.

She stopped in her tracks, suddenly realizing something for the first time, the thought only slowly dawning, as it always did with her.

'I say, Teddy, do you realize – I mean, I've suddenly realized we might, after all these years, the three of us might be together again?'

'Yup, Bobbie, I do.' Teddy gave her another quick hug, and his eyes were so genuinely warm, it was suddenly all Bobbie could do not to burst into tears with the relief of suddenly finding him again, with the whole fantastic marvel of it all. It might be that now, at last, they would be safe again, as they had seemed to be at Mellaston, all those years ago.

'Now. To work. I have to create such a shot of you with the Holy Book that people all over London will be talking about it. Now how do I do that, I wonder? No, don't tell me. I have all sorts of ideas. I say, so much better being out of doors, don't you think?'

He gestured around him, appreciating the early morning summer light, the odd jagged landscape that bombed, abandoned, and broken buildings create, and then looked down at Bobbie.

'Destruction is the setting, d'you see? And you are in the middle, but holding the Holy Book, the symbol of hope, of goodness.' He paused, looking around him as if inhaling the atmosphere. 'Of course, although we will put you over there in the middle, we will fill in the spaces around you. Such things as, say, a robin pecking at some crumbs on the ground over there – not a real one naturally – and then this side a hothouse flower, I thought, sort of stretching up towards where the roof used to be. Meanwhile—' He clapped his hands. 'Meanwhile, Ruth! I say!' He turned and grinned back at Bobbie. 'How very biblical to be clapping my hands and shouting for Ruth. RUTH! Ah, there you are. Ruth, clothes please. Costumes. And in three seconds flat. None of your moaning, please. Good, now hold them up against Miss Murray, would you, Ruth? Hold them up and I will choose.'

Ruth had arrived on the shoot with a suitcase full of clothes. Odd clothes, crazy clothes, every kind of clothes, but all in black or white.

'Come on, Bobbie Murray.' Teddy tugged at her hand again. 'Time to dress you up as a young, pure, but voracious Bible reader. We are going to wow the billboards with these shots. Everyone is going to want to know who – but who – is that girl reading the Bible. Maybe you will even set a fashion for holy ways and Bible readings, who knows?'

Bobbie smiled back at Teddy. He was as irrepressible as ever.

And of course, she did not believe him.

The reason she was smiling was because she had suddenly remembered just about everything about Teddy. It was as if she had been handed a parcel with a label that said *Teddy* and quickly unwrapping it had found the contents exactly as she had remembered, an old present re-gifted to her.

She remembered how he was always eating things that he should not, and how the aunts were always having to make him sick with one of their odd mixtures that they kept for such exigencies on the larder shelf. She remembered how often she and Miranda had to rush him to the bathroom. She remembered too how much he had hated Mrs Eglantine because of how tactless she had always been about him, and how he would narrow his eyes behind her back, trying to make sure that she felt his loathing of her, and how Miranda and she would laugh, silently but hysterically, at the sight of this small boy with his flaxen hair, willing the Billeting Officer to feel his hatred. And now, looking as if he had just parachuted in, here he was, just the same old Teddy really, but wearing a smart straw hat, sleeves rolled up, building a set to photograph Bobbie, the ugly duckling of Mellaston, with a Bible.

Finally Bobbie remembered Dill saying, 'Well, dear, that's the war, throws up all sorts of stories you wouldn't believe, else you wouldn't be here with me now, would you, dear?'

The costume which eventually satisfied Teddy – and it was some time before he really was satisfied – was shockingly opulent. He did not have to announce that this was actually quite purposeful, because, after all that time choosing, everyone on the set that summer morning knew, without any doubt at all, that it had to be.

The costume included a vast, black ball skirt, made of masses of black satin, atop which Teddy wanted Bobbie to wear a Quaker shirt, plain to the point of absurdity, white and starched. Indeed the collar points were so rigid that an onlooker might imagine that to brush against them would be to hurt herself.

Finally, as he stared at her through the camera lens, Teddy called to Bobbie, laughing, 'You look like a member of some new and very opulent order. The Order of the Terribly Righteous.'

For the photograph Bobbie wore little to no

make-up, certainly not discernible. To add emphasis to the overall naturalism Ruth put a little mascara on her eyelashes and a light application of lipstick on her mouth. Her hands were left free of nail varnish, and her long brown hair was wrapped around something that Ruth called a 'mouse' – a piece of thick horsehair which when set under the thick coil of shining brown hair bulked it out and gave it huge emphasis. In this way, Bobbie found, when she saw the photographs for the first time, Teddy had made her neck look longer and more slender, 'gazelle-like' was how he put it, and reduced the size of her features, while somehow emphasizing her eyes.

The session was an immediate success. It just felt so right somehow, as things that happen easily and quickly often do, and a week later found Teddy staring proudly at the photographs.

'Am I a genius, or am I a genius?' he asked of his two adopted sisters. 'Is your brother not a genius? Of course he is. Your brother is going to be more famous than any photographer you care to name, if you could, which neither of you can, because neither of you knows the slightest thing about photography.'

Miranda, who had just finished recounting to Bobbie her terrible years with Allegra and her drinking in Norfolk, now remarked wryly to Bobbie, putting on an over-classy accent, 'Still the same old modest Teddy-bags, what?'

But of course, placed carefully on the floor of the

studio in Aubrey Close, with all of them staring down at them, under the brilliant lighting that the Victorians created for themselves to work in and under, the photographs did seem suddenly to have something. Certainly they did to the three joyous friends, now reunited under one roof, feeling as if they had never been apart, and at the same time knowing that because they had been separated they now appreciated each other, as Miranda said, 'lots more'.

'I can't get over how you have changed. She has changed so much, hasn't she? She has really changed.' Teddy would keep saying that as he stared down at his photographs, but Miranda would have none of it.

'She is still *Bobbie*, Ted. No matter what. I would always know that to be Bobbie. Just as you are still Ted, and I am still Miranda. We are still the same inside, it's just the outside bits that have become different. You know, grown up, and in your particular case terrifically bumptious.'

Teddy turned round. 'Stop giving out opinions, Miranda, and concentrate, will you? Concentrate on my genius, on the genius of your brother, your soon-to-be-famous brother, and your soon-to-be-incredibly-famous sister here.'

Obediently the two girls stared down once again at their brother's photographs. He had arranged them in order of his own preference, and now they all began to discuss the varying merits of each photograph, eventually arriving at the one they all considered the best, their voices blending and murmuring as they had done when they were children, years before, at the old rectory at Mellaston, their eyes going from each other's faces down to Teddy's work, to the pictures which were, they all knew, going to be sensational, as why would they not be? And when all was said and done Miranda and Bobbie wanted those photographs to succeed for one reason only – for *Ted*.

They told a story, and that was what Teddy had wanted to achieve. He had not wanted to photograph just a girl with a Bible, as Mr Singh and the advertising company had ordered him to do – just a simple photograph with the Bible posed on the lap. No, he had wanted to make a statement, send a message that would be, of itself, in a way biblical. And it had to be admitted that he had succeeded magnificently. He had succeeded in taking a photograph that was more than arresting, it was memorable. It made you want to return to it over and over again. Even Bobbie, who could scarcely recognize herself, would stop by the old oak table where Teddy eventually placed them, and stare for a few seconds. The session with Bobbie and the Bible had, for some reason, worked, and in no more than a matter of minutes. That was, Teddy said, how everything good happened. In a matter of minutes, it was just a fact.

Three months later found Mr Singh re-reading the company press cuttings out loud, to a hushed, silent

398

and appreciative audience. He was just about to start reading out his favourite, from one of the chicer glossy magazines.

'All London is talking about the new advertisement for, of all things, the Holy Bible. That, in this day and age, an advertisement for the Good Book could create so much discussion says much both for the model and for the photographer.

The advertisement shows a young girl, in this case the newly fashionable model Bobbie Murray, set against the backdrop of a bombed Victorian conservatory. The whole effect is sumptuous, superb, and she an innocent caught in the maelstrom, with only her Bible as solace, a large black leather Bible with gold lettering placed fantastically against a voluminous, black satin skirt.

Everywhere the advertisement is featured crowds gather to stare up at the billboards above them. It seems that the Holy Bible Company of all companies have a hit on their hands to rival *Oklahoma*. They are to be congratulated.'

When he had finished reading this press cutting out loud, and after a short reverential pause, during which he himself shook his head from side to side in silent amazement at the turn of events, Mr Singh looked across at Mrs O'Brien.

'I keep thinking, Mrs O'Brien – just imagine if we had not taken the Easter photograph of the office luncheon? And then again, just imagine if I had not taken it home to Mrs Singh? Miss Murray might have languished in terrible obscurity, her beauty for ever hidden beneath some kind of blackout. As it is, she is now famous. The advertisement is to be taken up by ten different countries, did I tell you? Ten different Bible-reading countries, and it is rumoured that the Bible belt itself is rioting over editions of the papers that carry the photograph. How can this be? How can this be? It is too heart-warming to be understood fully by me. My heart is full to bursting, I am quite sure.'

Mrs O'Brien nodded in silent agreement, smiling at her knitting as she always did, but not taking her eyes from it, not wanting to drop a precious stitch.

'Imagine that,' said the newly returned and now quite healthy Mrs Yates, and from behind her usual tea table she shook her head at the other two. 'Imagine, as you say, if you had not taken that snap, Mrs O'Brien. Or just imagine if I had not had me appendix out so bad.'

'God moves in mysterious ways, and none more mysterious than this last one, surely?'

'No, indeed, perhaps not, Mr Singh. Most mysterious.'

'And now Miss Murray is to become a fashion model, and the photographer turned out to be her brother, and her sister is found too, alive and well. It is like a story from the Bible itself, is it not?'

The two ladies nodded across at him from their tables. It was true, it *was* just like a story from the Bible.

'But then,' Mrs Yates went on, the expression on her good-natured, round face more than usually solemn, 'I suppose many of the Bible stories were based on true life stories, weren't they? So it stands to reason, doesn't it?'

'Not reason, no, Mrs Yates.' Mr Singh's head was still shaking in amazement. 'It has to be said that there is nothing reasonable about the success of this advertising campaign. All over the world people are staring up at our advertisement. The Holy Bible Company is set to become more famous than the Holy Bible, it seems. It is indeed a miracle to end all miracles. And Miss Murray is famous overnight.'

Bobbie did not feel famous. She felt infamous, which was just a trifle clammy, really. She had not wanted to pose for the photograph, but Mr Singh had been so sure that she would be perfect for his advertisement, he had insisted, and of course, as it had turned out, from his point of view he had been right. For the terrible truth was that not only was Bobbie now out of a job – Mrs Yates having returned post-haste as soon as she saw the photographs pasted on billboards all over London – but she had become instantly recognizable the moment she walked into a shop, or hailed a taxi. The frequency of recognition from complete strangers had become so monotonous and so slowing that Bobbie had started to wear dark glasses, and was careful to keep her eyes down whenever she hurried past anyone in the street. But it was no good, they always knew her.

She had to face it, while the posters were still up, albeit soon to be doubtless peeling around the edges, she was temporarily famous and the subject of so much press interest that the Saxbys had cause to change their Sloane telephone number not once but twice and that was not all.

'I think he's gone away now, Bobbie dear,' Mrs Saxby remarked, peering out of her window, her clean, white net curtain slightly held back so that she could see down into the street below, or rather across the road to the so-called pedestrian standing staring up at them from the opposite pavement. 'What I keep wondering is why these photographers do it? I mean surely, dear, they'll only end up with a photograph of you walking along with your head down, and what is the use of that? What is the use? I asked the Major yesterday the self-same question and he said it's *prestige*. That they can go back to their bosses and show them how diligent they've been in making our lives a positive misery. Isn't that a thing? And I mean to say. What a strange world we are all growing older in, to be sure. Why, the Major and I were at dinner the other day and no-one left the table. The ladies *stayed*. The Major was astonished. He kept asking me if I could imagine such a thing before the war.'

Mrs Saxby stared at Bobbie, momentarily, and

then the former Miss Moncrieff laughed, delight-edly, as if the new, shocking trend of things, while not being condoned, could not either be wholly condemned, certainly not by a lady like herself who, upon marrying very late, had embraced such new and outlandish ways most heartily.

'Major Saxby and myself, we had such a laugh afterwards, but the Major, you can imagine, was quite put out, and his cigarettes – well, they very nearly burnt a hole in his pocket, so much was he dying for a puff, but of course he never would have a cigarette in the dining room with ladies present, that would be beyond the beyonds. Dear me, how life gallops on, does it not, leaving us all behind by at least what the Major calls *two horses' lengths*. It does, doesn't it? Just gallops on ahead of us, wouldn't you say?'

But Bobbie was not saying because she was not really listening. She was wondering how on earth she could get past the photographer in the street, and how or when she could get her life back to normal again. It just did not seem possible that simply saying yes to Mr Singh and his invitation to pose with the Holy Bible for what had seemed such an innocuous advertisement could have so changed her existence.

Everywhere she went now, no matter how she dressed or looked, she seemed to be recognized. It *should* be most enjoyable and she was doubtless being stuffy, but at that particular moment she would, as it happened, have given anything to be back sitting quietly behind the Edwardian type-writer at the Holy Bible Company typing very, very slowly. As it was, she was not only a little bit famous at that moment. She was something much worse and perhaps even more alarming – she was discovered.

She had come to realize this at last, because even after some weeks the telephone never stopped ringing, and it was nearly always Teddy with another offer for a photo session. Everyone wanted to know the name of the waif with the Bible in the long ball skirt and the white Puritan blouse. Everyone, up to and including, worst of all worsts, Beatrice Harper.

And that was finally the real reason why Bobbie was not enjoying her new and wholly strange fame. For Beatrice, recognizing her ward on billboards all over London, the airport, everywhere, had rung Teddy's office at once, and warned him, and the advertising company, that she might be taking proceedings against them. She told Teddy that Bobbie was under age, and that they needed her permission to photograph her ward, and that they had done something illegal, and actionable.

It was all too terrible. In short, Beatrice had started to make trouble of a kind that Bobbie knew only too well that her rich and powerful guardian could and would make, trouble of a kind that might have unending repercussions. Beatrice knew everyone. She could, with her money, literally move mountains.

Worst of all worsts, she had left a message at the advertising company commanding Bobbie to appear at her London house the following week, on the dot, naturally. Ever since, Bobbie had felt, and on occasions been, quite sick. She would not be able to sleep or eat, drink or think until the interview – for she knew that was what it would be, not a meeting but an interview, such as you would have with someone you employed – was over. And after that, it was quite likely that, being under age, Bobbie would find that her life in London was over too, because that was how powerful Beatrice was, or could be, if she felt like it.

At night, when she turned her light off, all Bobbie could see was Teddy's career ruined and herself back in some sort of sanatorium, or at the Sheds with the seas pounding and only Mrs Duddy coming to find out whether she was alive or dead, or somewhere between the two.

The truth was that she did not really mind if she herself was to have her life ruined, but she minded terribly for Teddy. He had only just started. And he really loved his photography.

Only Miranda remained sanguine. She was, as always, to be found in the kitchen cooking, but also full of the kind of sound common sense that often results from having been there and back, at least as far as scandalous behaviour is concerned.

She said to Bobbie, looking up briefly from arranging some delicious-looking *plats du jour*, 'Best thing when someone's gunning for you, old

Allegra always said to me, was to gun for *them*. And without any delay. If they are suing you, for instance, you find something to sue *them* for, and so on. I bet if you ask that old secretary bird that you lodge with – what's her name . . .'

'Miss Moncrieff. Well, she's Mrs Saxby now.'

'Yes, her. I bet if you ask her she'll have something on this fearful Harper woman. Bet you anything. Secretaries, they're like nannies, Allegra always said. They know everything, and sometimes it doesn't take much squeezing to make the pips pop out,' she added, squeezing a lemon and making its pips do just that. 'Old Miss M, she'll have something on her boss, you wait and see.'

The sun was shining so brightly that Bobbie would have normally felt as happy as the proverbial clam. Instead she felt as if she was going for trial, as if a Black Maria was about to come for her, instead of Beatrice's car, which she could see from the first floor window at which she was standing was even now arriving. It was black, and it was gleaming, and it was arriving very slowly, nosing its way down Ebury Street as if it could hardly believe where it had found itself, as if finding themselves in such a place was a nightmare for both car and chauffeur.

'Miss Roberta—'

Davis held open the door, and Bobbie climbed into the back. She was wearing a new, sophisticated outfit, which she hoped might make her feel braver once she reached Grosvenor Square and Beatrice's palatial apartment. Teddy had gone to great lengths to borrow the outfit for her from one of his currently favourite models, a stunning creature by the name of Mary-Louise Brown-Finchley – known affectionately in the fashion world as the Double Hyphen or by Teddy as Ma-Loo-Boo-Fincher.

It was without doubt the most beautiful coat and skirt that Bobbie had yet tried on, and just lately she had tried on quite a few. It was not just fashionable, it was beautiful, but best of all it made Bobbie look a great deal older. Cut from grey flannel with a waisted jacket, a long pencil slim skirt and worn with a matching hat, more like a cap than a hat, tilted forward over her eyes, it was more than stylish, it was stunning. And to add to the whole air of sophistication there was a matching stole which draped gracefully across her back and down her arms, so that its very formality was emphasized, as if it was asking the wearer to be even more languid than she might wish.

Bobbie had not wanted to wear the stole as well, but Teddy had insisted on it, even going to Ebury Street and draping it around her himself, so that it looked quite perfect.

'If this woman, your guardian, is as frightening as you tell me, Sis dear, then you must look much older, and utterly different from the 'Bobbie' that all of London is seeing in my brilliant photograph. You must wrong-foot her, so that you are in the catbird seat when you go in. It is important. And anyway, it's fun. You will look so different, she will hardly recognize you.'

As Bobbie stepped into the back of the Rolls-Royce that had been sent for her, she could not help smiling to herself at how right Teddy was. Never mind Beatrice – it seemed that not even Davis now knew her.

'Miss Roberta?' he said again, peering at her from under his cap, but this time he said her name with a question mark in his voice, and he hesitated before he closed the door of the Rolls-Royce – a discreet black affair with the famed winged lady on the front, but no picnic baskets or flasks set about in the interior as they would be if they were on the way to the country.

'Hallo, Davis,' Bobbie said, and she shot him a brief glance from under her grey hat before indicating with an equally brief nod of her head that he could shut the door. 'I know what you are thinking – is this really me – and yes it is.'

'I never would have known you, Miss Roberta.'

'No, I know,' Bobbie agreed, and she leaned back against the leather upholstery and readjusted the grey stole around her jacket, and once again waved one gloved finger to indicate that he could shut the door, and his mouth.

As the chauffeur drove her slowly through the traffic towards Grosvenor Square, Bobbie determined that she would start to enjoy herself. Whatever Beatrice had to say to her, whatever reprimand she was about to administer, the fact was, as Miranda kept saying, *There's no need to worry. She can't cut off your head, Bobbie, really she can't. She just can't.*

But then Miranda had never met Beatrice, and if she had, it occurred to Bobbie as she watched London floating slowly and almost dutifully past the windows of the luxurious motor car, she might not have been so sure about her ability to punish those who she had decided were her enemies. What people like Miranda did not understand was that Beatrice was not just wealthy, she was insuperably rich. And she knew everyone from prime ministers to heads of foreign governments and members of European royalty.

As Bobbie viewed London from the Rolls' window she remembered that Beatrice had a way of saying to her friends, 'I know just the person who will do that for you, leave it to me. He will do just as I ask. I know just the person to help us.'

And not only did she indeed know just the person, but she had a habit of making sure that he jumped to and did as he was told, and when he was told too.

'I told that flunkey he had better do as he was told, or else.'

No-one had ever, as far as Bobbie knew, found out what the *or else* might entail, but the implications were such that it had always seemed to Bobbie that it might mean *anything*.

But worst of all possible worsts, Beatrice was always, always right in her own eyes, and occasionally in other people's too. That, it seemed to Bobbie, was what was so frightening about her, her self-belief. As far as self-belief went Beatrice possibly came second only to Hitler. And if a silly little man with a Charlie Chaplin moustache and a parting on the wrong side of his head could bring most of the world to its knees, having Bobbie's head cut off would mean nothing to Beatrice, surely?

'Roberta?'

For the first time in her life it seemed to Bobbie that she had wrong-footed her self-appointed guardian. In Beatrice's eyes she saw a mixture of total incredulity and a strange kind of affront. Incredulity because she simply could not believe that this tall young woman in her pencil-slim grey flannel coat and skirt, with its matching hat and stole, was actually Roberta, whom she had last seen crouching over the fire at the Sheds, long woollen socks up to her knees, a long woollen pullover stretching down to meet the socks, and only her head and the tips of her fingers peeping out from her mittens to bear witness to the fact that there was a human being nestling between all the layers of wool.

'How nice to see you again, Beatrice.'

Bobbie removed her elegant glove expertly from her right hand, and determinedly reached forward and shook her guardian's limp, ringed hand before either of them had time to realize that they should

410

really be kissing each other. Instead they were shaking hands as if they were strangers, only just meeting each other.

As Bobbie saw the effect this had on the astonished Beatrice she could only give silent thanks to Teddy for not just his expert costuming of her, but his help rehearsing her in her every move. The removing of the glove, finger by finger, the looking around the room to make sure of a chair that was higher than, or as high as, that which her guardian now chose to sit upon. The careful stretching out of her long, stockinged legs, feet together, ankles the same (never crossed) – it had all been carefully rehearsed by Teddy, and Bobbie had remembered his every instruction.

Most of all she had remembered his last warning, that whatever happened she must not become aggravated or defensive. If she did, Teddy had warned, if she betrayed any impatience, she would be lost.

'So this is how you have repaid me, Roberta Murray. This is how you have repaid all my kindness to you over the years, by running away to London, and becoming some sort of cheap billboard model!'

Bobbie was silent at this. Not feeling in the least 'cheap' she did not feel goaded by this salvo, nor indeed could she quarrel with the adjective 'billboard'. Beatrice began again.

'You do realize that you have made yourself the laughing stock of London? That this advertisement,

411

this posing with a Bible of all things, has become a talking point of *every* dinner party in Society? And, what is worse, that you have now been identified as being connected with my family, with the Harper family, and so the press are now determined to make more of it, if possible, than they have already done? You do realize this, don't you, Roberta?'

As a matter of fact Bobbie did not, but she was not going to tell Beatrice so. She had tried to carry on her life as normal, in that she had tried to keep working just for Teddy and his friends, like Dick, all of whom seemed, for no reason she could think of, more than eager to use a model so much in the news – the model who had become, according to the papers, the New Quaker Girl. According to Dick – whom Bobbie never quite knew whether to believe or not because the expression on his face was always so awfully wry – it was now being rumoured that Bobbie was to be as famous as Bubbles, the little boy in the Pears soap advertisements.

But Beatrice was continuing, inexorably. 'You have let down your whole background with the vulgarity of your ghastly, ghastly – we shall not dignify it with the word fame – with your ghastly *notoriety*. You have let down your poor dead parents. You have let down myself and my staff. You have let down the people who nursed you through your wretched disease. There is no-one I can think of, now I do come to think of it, whom you have not *let down*.'

There was a long silence, which Bobbie, remem-

412

bering Teddy's advice to her, was quite determined not to break. But then a terrible thing happened. She suddenly thought not of Teddy, or Dick, but of Julian, and how he would laugh at such hypocrisy and cant. He would double up with laughter at the thought of Beatrice making such pompous speeches, just as he had rolled about in the sand that enchanted summer, saying over and over again, 'Human beings, aren't they pathetic, so pathetic?'

Which was probably why Bobbie heard herself suddenly saying, in an innocent voice, 'Davis? Do you think I have let down Davis?'

'I beg your pardon? What has Davis got to do with anything, Roberta?'

'I just thought I might not have let Davis down, that's all. You know, that he might not feel let down, because he didn't even recognize me when he picked me up this morning, so he obviously doesn't know anything about my posing with the Bible and being on billboards, and so on; so I might not have let him down. At least I might not have let Davis down.'

Beatrice's eyes were hard and unmoving, as hard and unmoving as any eyes that Bobbie could imagine. And seeing their look, directed straight at her, it seemed to Bobbie that that was how the Jesuits' eyes during the Spanish Inquisition must have looked; brown, hard flints, with not a flicker of humour or humanity.

'I suppose you think that what you have just said was funny, Roberta?'

'It could have been funny, but it was obviously not.'

Taking the risk that her hands might shake, and her guardian notice it, but determined on her next course anyway, very deliberately Bobbie opened her chic leather handbag and took out a cigarette, which she fitted slowly, oh so slowly, into a holder, lit and inhaled. She had practised the lighting of that cigarette all week, knowing that if she could bring it off it would be more than a statement of independence, it would be taken by Beatrice as a positive insult.

As soon as she replaced the lighter and cigarette packet in her handbag Bobbie saw that she had succeeded in what she had set out to achieve, and now all there was left for her to do was to pray that she would not cough, that after all those long hours of hideous practice she was going to be able to smoke a cigarette, in a slow and leisurely fashion, and make a smoke screen from behind which she could view Beatrice Harper.

'No, actually, I did not think it was funny, what I thought was that I might lighten the moment, as the Major would say. That was all.'

'What major?'

'The Major that your former secretary, Miss Moncrieff, ran off and married.'

Beatrice did not bother to reply to this. She too lit a cigarette, with the result that within a few minutes there was a very satisfactory smoke screen hovering between them, and a casual observer might have thought they were just two sophisticates meeting to have a smoke and a chat on an early autumn morning in London.

'Roberta.' Beatrice gave Bobbie her blackest and most commanding look. 'I can promise you one thing. I can bring pressure to bear in certain quarters to bring your fame to nothing – or, to put it another way, to *de*-fame you – if you do not give me your word that you will toe the line, give up this inanity, and return to Baileys Court, take up your secretarial duties, and lead a properly quiet life.'

Bobbie had been waiting for this. The veiled threat at which her guardian was so very expert. The hint that she could and would do anything she wished, with or without the help of governments, democracies or even monarchies. She was rich, powerful, and what was more she was Beatrice Harper, and if Bobbie did not believe her now, then she would live to regret it.

'Well, I will of course, if that is what you really wish. But,' Bobbie paused. 'But you must explain to me. I simply do not understand what it is that I have done that is so wrong? I left Baileys Court because I did not want to be a burden on you any more, and besides that there was nothing to do, and now – well, now that I am independent, and will never again have to lean on you for anything, you want me to go back there and be dependent on you again.'

'I want you to be properly grateful for what I have done for you. You are still a minor, until you are

415

twenty-one, you must remember this. I am your guardian. Your mother left you in my care, for my sins.'

Bobbie sighed inwardly, but remembering all her friends back at Ebury Street, and all their advice, she said, 'But that is not true, and you know it. You are not my legal guardian. You just decided to make me your sort of ward, to help me when I was sick, and I am truly, truly grateful, but I don't really have to do everything you tell me. There is no legal reason. I am actually an orphan, not really your ward, and while I am sorry if I have disgraced you and been ungrateful, I realize I owe my life to you, and that is, after all, a great deal.'

'Your poor mother and I were the greatest friends, remember that, Roberta. She and I shared some of our happiest times as girls before the war. Your father too was one of my oldest friends. I will not stand by and do nothing, watch you drag your family name, your association with me, through the mud, to the delight of every newspaper in the land, reading material for every housemaid and boots boy in any backroom or bar.' She stopped suddenly, frowning. 'What is it they are calling you now?'

'The New Quaker Girl. It's only a bit of fun, actually, you know, and really it was just because Mr Singh did not want some Jezebel letting down the Holy Bible Company. I mean you can see his point, can't you—'

'Fun!' Beatrice stubbed out her cigarette in the silver ashtray on her leather-topped and gold-

416

tooled desk, and stared at the young woman in front of her. 'Fun! You call having all London talking about you, this kind of press fame, *fun*! It is appalling. Nice people are not seen on billboards all over London! Nice people do not let down their background in this way. Nice people behave themselves.'

'But it is not a nude picture or anything.'

'Nude it may not be, but it is large and vulgar, and you are posed trying to sell the most sacred book ever written, in a large satin skirt with the *Holy Bible*. It is appalling. Only last night at dinner Lord Holbrook made fun of the advertisement and you in that large satin skirt, to me, to my face. He knew I had something to do with you and he could not wait to mock me.'

'He was probably just joking.'

'He was making fun – that is not joking, Roberta. That is making fun at my expense, and you are responsible for my discomfiture. You and you alone. Ever since the newspapers picked up my connection to you, God help me, my life has been hellish, completely hellish. I am just waiting for questions to be asked in Parliament. That will be the final humiliation, a question asked in Parliament about the Bible and the Quaker Girl, or whatever they are calling you.'

There was a long silence while Bobbie tried her hardest to appreciate her guardian's position and think of a practical solution.

'Well, can't you just disown me? I mean,

wouldn't that be the answer, don't you think, to disown me?'

'Is that all you can say? After all the time and money that I have spent rescuing you from your wretched disease . . .'

'My *incipient* disease . . .'

'All you can say is *can't you just disown me*. What do you think your poor mother would say if she were alive now? What could she say? A heroine, a perfect heroine, in her own right, she would hang her head at your infamous behaviour at my expense.'

Bobbie stood up. It was all becoming too dull. She had to go. Beatrice had gone too far. Anyway, when all was said and done, she suspected that Beatrice was merely an older woman who was jealous. Her nose had been put out of joint by being connected to Bobbie, instead of the other way round. She had probably wanted to be a model or an actress or something herself. She had probably wanted to be someone like Vivien Leigh, and failed.

Besides, it was not Bobbie's fault that she had gone to work for Mr Singh. It was not Bobbie's fault that some ferret in the press had found out Bobbie's connection with the Harper fortune and Baileys Court and all that. It was no-one's fault. But there was one thing that was at fault at that moment and that was Beatrice Harper. She had gone too far, and as a result Bobbie was determined that she would finally end the whole hypocritical charade. She could hear Julian, sitting somewhere at the back of her mind as he always did, laughing and saying,

'Go on, Bobbie, tell her what you know. That *will* be funny; that will be *so* funny.'

'I am sorry you feel I have let you down, but I must tell you that I do know that your kindness to me has very little to do with my "poor mother" as you keep calling her, and everything to do with your own guilt. Miss Moncrieff has told me everything. She told me that you had an affair with my father, and that they were both killed before you could ask her forgiveness, and that was why you have looked after me all this time. Nothing to do with your friendship with my mother, but everything to do with your affair with my father long before the war. I will pay you back for everything you have done for me, every penny of the cost of my time at the sanatorium, and I have to say that I am in a far better position to do so than I would ever have been had I stayed down at Baileys Court. We had better say good morning now, and as I say, I do thank you. But you must realize, besides what I owe you, you have no further hold over me.'

As Bobbie walked back to the door, in her imagination she could hear Julian laughing and cheering, but in reality what she actually heard was Beatrice's hard voice saying, 'Don't think this is the last *you* will hear of this, Roberta, because if you do, you are even more naive than even I realized.'

Chapter Thirteen

Dick and Miranda had found the ideal site for the café cum restaurant on which they had both set their hearts. It was at the top of Kensington Church Street, but set back, in one of the many side roads threaded through endless square-fronted cottages that wound up and down behind the main thoroughfare. The cottages had been built for railway workers employed on the tunnelling needed for the London underground trains. They were substantial cottages, and now, a hundred years later, actually pretty and quaint, and largely occupied by artists and writers, the overspill from the older Bohemian areas of streets such as Aubrey Close, clusters of studios built for artists with grand ways and even grander ideals.

Miranda enjoyed walking in London more than she had ever done in Norfolk. She realized now that it must be her Cockney upbringing that made her love cities so much. It was because she was at heart a Cockney that the migrating of birds held no real interest for her compared to the occupants of those cottages. She was far more intrigued by seeing Augustus John walking about town in his black velvet, or a famous actress stepping from her open-top Bentley, than she was by seeing a migrating Bewick's swan, or an incoming swallow. Besides, it was the human beings that she hoped to attract to her café.

In the middle of the night, if she could not sleep, she liked to lie awake and imagine that, in time, she would attract famous people to her café, and as a consequence by the time she was old she would have many anecdotes to recount to friends about them. She thought of herself not as being the star of her premises, but the quiet listener, for if there was one thing of which she was quite sure it was that she never, ever, wanted to be the centre of attention again. The night when Dick and Teddy found her in the Blue Note, singing like a drunken sailor and looking like a tart, had ended all her notions of becoming a singer, or anything like it. Now all she wanted was to be quiet, cook, and become prosperous. Even her fascination with clothes had come to a shuddering full stop. Nowadays she found that she was far more interested in what dear Bobbie was wearing than in how she herself looked. It was as if by caring too much about her appearance she might be led back to be the person that she had become in Paris.

Of course she made sure that she washed her hair every morning, and following that, in order to be quick and get out to the café site, or to the market at Covent Garden, as fast as possible, she had designed herself a kind of uniform of navy blue jumpers and skirts, dark stockings, flat shoes, and a pony tail. Then she forgot about herself and how she looked until evening, when she bathed and changed into yet more navy blue.

'You don't have to look quite so boring,' Teddy kept complaining when he came home to yet another of her fabulous suppers. 'Does she, Bobbie? Not every day, surely? Not Sundays as well? You've become a sort of culinary nun.'

'No, I don't have to. I just want to, that's all.'

She could not explain to Teddy, of all people, just what it had done to her to be found by him, of all people, her sometime young brother, in that most terrible of positions for a young woman, a positive slave to a man who was using her when and how he wished. To be found in the thrall of a man who had delighted in humiliating her, who had somehow caught her in the headlights of his personality, who had so scared her, finally, that she would do anything and everything that he wished.

How could she explain that to Teddy of all people? Teddy who was as innocent of such ways as Miranda was now conversant? Teddy who, spiritually at least, had never really shaken off the influence of the aunts at Mellaston, who loved to see life as full of the kind of beauty that he was determined to photograph, who was incapable of hitting a woman, let alone pulling her hair? Teddy whom she loved with all her heart. She could not

422

begin to explain to him how someone like Macaskie could get a hold on you, whittling away at your confidence to such a degree that you no longer knew who you were, or cared.

'I like navy blue,' was all she said, before asking, 'Coming to the fun fair tomorrow, Ted? Dick and I are longing to go on the bumper cars and behave like the great Fangio. Would you like to come?'

Teddy turned to Bobbie. 'Coming, Bobbie?'

Bobbie nodded, and Miranda turned away, not wanting to see the look of delight in Teddy's eyes that Bobbie had decided to go with them.

She knew that she should be pleased that her brother was in love with her best friend, yet all she could feel was jealous. She loved Teddy. She had picked him up from the orphan section at the school, adopted him for a brother, and now she wanted no-one to love him as she did. He was hers.

Dick was full of the rumour that there was going to be some sort of festival for Britain. As it happened both Teddy and Dick had heard about it quite separately, and both were enthusiastic. After all those dreary years, it seemed that at long, long last the skies over Britain were lightening, and people were longing to celebrate the fact that the war and its aftermath might finally and actually be over, and there were young people and middle-aged people still alive and dying not to die but to live their lives and show that they were talented, that England was still full of invention, and flair.

They were all walking briskly along talking about it, on the way to the fair, and in great spirits although it was late and autumn. But the weather was fine, and the leaves on the London trees were still green in places, as if they too were hanging on grimly, longing to help enliven the post-war scene.

'Of course there would be an artistic point to absolutely everything in the festival,' Dick announced, as they grew nearer to the fair, almost as if he was warning them not to be complacent. 'I was talking about it to someone in plastics, would you believe, in the pub the other day. Of course the Labour government is not in the *slightest* bit interested. Too arty sounding for them, but you know it could be fantastic, really. It could be a sign-post for everyone to realize that we do have a future, that England *can* be great again. Certain of the press are getting a sniff of it, they can see what us arty types are on about, it's just the politicians and people who need convincing.'

It was early evening by the time they arrived at the fun fair, and all four of them could feel their hearts rising with the excitement of seeing such a medley of lights and colour. What with Dick's chatter and the feeling that there might, soon, some-time, be perhaps a great and colourful rainbow over Britain, a great arc of colour; that the death and destruction of the last decades might at last be over, perhaps even for ever, they all started to run towards the various attractions, towards the music and the fairy lights. They were grown up, of course, but they were still young, they could climb on the horses going up and down, or pile into the dodgem cars and ram each other's vehicles and laugh – and forget. Forget about the bomb sites and rationing, about coupons and bad food. Just for a few hours they could be as their parents might have been before the war, carefree and happy.

Bobbie's favourite attraction turned out to be a miniature railway.

'It's because it's like Mellaston.'

'No, it's not at all like Mellaston.' Bobbie shook her head at Miranda, frowning. 'No, it's more like the station at Baileys Green, where I was a few summers ago.'

'Oh, yes.' Miranda looked at her briefly. 'Of course. Where you met the Major and all that.'

'All that, yes.'

Miranda stared at her suddenly, her eyes narrowing, something of the old Miranda coming back into her expression, and she pulled Bobbie ahead of the others so that she could hear the answer to the question she wanted to put to her before the boys were tempted to eavesdrop.

'You were in love with someone at Baileys Court, weren't you, Bobbie? Tell, oh do. You fell in love with someone when you were there. A man, you fell in love with a man. Did you have an affair with him?'

Bobbie managed to look both shocked and affronted at Miranda's mockery, and Miranda started to laugh.

'It's not so shocking, Bobbie, really. Other girls do have affairs nowadays, you know, not just me. I am not the only damaged goods around this city. So long as you don't – you know – become *enceinte*, well, that's all right, isn't it? No babies please, we're not married.'

Bobbie's face had become scarlet with embarrassment, not for herself, but for Miranda. How could she sound so sort of careless about love, of all things, as if the act of love meant nothing? Love was for ever. There was no *so long as you don't – you know – become pregnant* about it.

That was not how she and Julian had been. They had been twin souls, seeing everything the same way.

'Oh, I know.' Miranda shrugged her shoulders, reading Bobbie's reaction at once. 'You think I am one of those girls who have had it, and I expect you're right. Not many men want to marry damaged goods even nowadays, do they?'

Bobbie sighed. 'Oh, come on, Miranda, don't let's talk like this. We're at the fair, we're here to have fun. Let's do just that. Besides, the way you talk – it's so grown up, and who wants to be that? At least not tonight. As a matter of fact I never want to become a grown-up.' That was something else that she and Julian had promised each other – never to be imprisoned by hideous maturity, never to stop finding life amazing and ridiculous, never to become solemn and incurious, their minds solidified by attitudes arrived at by someone else.

Of a sudden Bobbie threw off her hat and the wind caught it and tossed it about for a bit before landing it back at Teddy's feet.

'Bobbie's dotty.' Teddy laughed and picking up the hat he carefully, with great finesse, placed it back upon Bobbie's thick, brown shining hair, and as he did so he looked down into her large eyes, and Miranda's heart seemed to stop for those few seconds.

It was true. Teddy was in love with Bobbie for ever and ever, probably.

Now she too started to run, away from Bobbie and away from Dick, too, towards the merry-go-round that was about to crank slowly into life, away from all the realities. Bobbie was right. Everything else besides tonight, love, everything – it was too grown up.

After that it was as if they had all taken a vow, to be in love with whoever they wished, but no-one to tell anyone. They must have all known anyway that it was just as well, at that moment in their lives, to set love aside, for Miranda was too busy setting up her café with Dick, and Bobbie was too busy 'being famous' as Teddy liked to call it.

She had now been made even more comfortable in a suite of rooms in the Saxbys' house in Ebury Street. Her present money-earning status meant that she could afford to rent three rooms and a bathroom from the Major and Mrs S, three rooms which she and Teddy immediately set about decorating, in between visiting Miranda and Dick at the studio in Aubrey Close. Teddy, having found that he could not make enough money from photography alone, had started to design clothes privately for various top fashion models who were more than happy to wear them, but he was having no luck with any of them. They seemed to look brilliant on the girls he designed them for, but they did not translate, so that if Bobbie or Miranda tried them on for him they looked strangely dated.

'Maybe it's because you're not being inspired by your own ideas. Maybe it's because they're asking you to design things for them, rather than for you, as it were, and maybe, once you've had them made up for them, they just lose their impact.'

Teddy was lying full length on the floor of Aubrey Close, and Miranda, Bobbie and Dick were carefully walking around him as he groaned out loud at his lack of success as a designer, his failure to make any impression even on his friends.

'And maybe you're right,' he shouted from the floor, 'but how else do you design clothes, except by making them up and fitting them?'

Miranda paused on her way back to her kitchen to experiment with a new recipe for chicken liver pâté with herbs and cream.

'There was a designer I knew in Paris, in the bad old days of my bad old past. Unfortunately he killed himself over a girl, but before he did, well, he used to—'

'Silly fellow!' Teddy moaned from the floor,

interrupting as usual. 'Kill yourself for any reason but that. Not for a girl.'

Miranda stared down at him for a second before continuing. 'Yes, well, he did. But I did actually know him for a few weeks before that, and he used to design straight onto my body.'

There was a long, long silence, during which Teddy sat up, brushed back his long, bright blond hair from his eyes and stared ahead of him, a blank look in his eyes.

'He designed straight onto your *body*?'

'Yes. I'd have nothing on except – you know – my thinnest underwear, and he would mould the material onto my body. He was getting some terrific effects when, um, he took this overdose. Not because of me, poor ducky, because of a beautiful married woman known only as *La Contessa*. But, you know, he was that sort. Very inspired, and at the same time hysterical. There was nothing to be done. But I have one of his designs, somewhere, up there in one of the trunks. He himself thought it was a terrible flop, but you can see it, if you like.'

There was another long silence as Teddy, his eyes narrowed, started to walk about the great studio room in which they now all lived almost full time at weekends, sparing only enough time to earn their living, or, in Bobbie's case, to return to Ebury Street for what she called 'a spot of sleep', which meant that she could rest and think without Teddy coming over all enthusiastic, or Miranda insisting on her trying a dish, leaving Dick to play some jazz piano which never shut any of them up.

'Get the dress,' Teddy commanded. 'At once.'

'Not until I've whipped these precious eggs, Ted. Stay awhile while I am cruel to these eggs.'

'No, no, no, big Sis, you go and get that dress pronto, and leave the eggs the way their mother laid them for a little minute. This is my living we're talking about. I can't just photograph dresses, I have to make 'em, too. I am going to be the first to make the cross-over between photography and high fashion, and the effects will be spellbinding. You will see.'

Miranda did as she was bid, almost as a matter of course, because somehow, when Teddy wanted something, she always found that she sprang to attention.

Bobbie leaned towards the piano, which Dick was playing with wonderful lightness of touch, and murmured above the sound of his playing, 'Teddy commands and big Sis runs. It's not good for him, really it isn't. Miranda must stop kowtowing to him, before he starts crowning himself the King of Aubrey Close.'

Dick looked up, briefly raising his eyebrows to the ceiling, but he never stopped playing for a second. 'You noticed, Bobbie dear,' was all he said, and his playing at once took on a melancholy sound, as if from that moment a little of the joy had gone from the day.

Of course, when Miranda reappeared in the dress, it turned out to be nothing short of stunning, and for one moment, as she stood at the top of the studio stairs and raised her long arms above her head, not only did Dick stare up adoringly at her, they all did, even Teddy.

The dress was an inspired spiral of material that looked as if it had been literally moulded to her body, as indeed it had been, and now that she was out of her navy blue clothes Miranda's body could be seen to be well worth moulding silk to, or anything else, for that matter. The space between the bottom of her bust and the top of her waist was longer than on most ordinary people, and as well as being slender to the point of looking as if it might snap, the waist itself too seemed longer than normal, so that her long slender hips did not look exaggerated, but merely extended the same long slender line. In other words, she was all woman, nothing of the boy about her, and quite perfect in outline.

The cloth that the designer had used was a new mix, something that Teddy had not come across before, some new kind of thinner and more pliant silk, and the colours were shot together, apple green with a mauve mixed into it somehow. It positively glowed under the lights of the studio, and when she turned at the bottom of the stairs to reveal a vast bow knotted across her hips at the back they all found themselves applauding spontaneously.

'Why was Miranda not a success as a model,' Bobbie demanded when Teddy called round the next day to help her with yet more wallpapering. 'She should be far more famous than all of us. She should be on every billboard and magazine cover. She is stunning.'

Teddy shrugged his shoulders. 'Because she allowed herself to be picked up by this nutter called Mac something. I mean typical Miranda. And don't tell her I told you, but she was a disaster because she actually fell in love with him. That was her mistake. If she had just modelled and made a success of it, and come home, that would have been that. But she wanted him to love her too, and you know that kind of man – they're usually half sadist and half businessman.'

'No, I don't actually.'

'And you've got to remember, too, they despise women for having ambitions about anything, either themselves or anything else, really. They only really worship their mothers – women who will take care of them and their needs – and just want to make money from the rest, the beautiful young girls they meet. Just money, money, money, that is all that kind of relationship is about. And of course as soon as Miranda realized this, being Miranda, she started down the rocky road.' Here Teddy mimed knocking back a drink. 'Anise, I think she said was her Parisian tipple. But really, what does it matter? By the time we stumbled across her in the Blue Note she was just one great horrible mess. She's all right now, but – oh God. I mean we all love Miranda, but that night, I thought I would be sick when I saw her.'

'Poor soul.'

'Poor *soul*? It was her own fault. She should have had more horse sense. Falling in with a man like that.'

Bobbie put down her wallpapering brush, and frowned across at Teddy. 'Just you be careful, Teddy Mowbray. One day *you* will fall in love with the wrong person, and you will then see how chaotic love is, how terrible, how you suffer for it. Believe me, you do. You suffer as much as the damned are meant to suffer, perhaps more.'

Teddy stared at her from the top of the ladder where he was perched, suddenly realizing that Bobbie of all people, Bobbie whom he now thought of as the most beautiful creature in the universe, was speaking from experience.

'You have been in love.'

Bobbie frowned, and quickly turned away. 'No, of course not. But, you know, I do believe in what the Easterns call "karma" or something like that. That everything you do wrong, or that you despise in someone else, will turn back on you. For instance, if you are so busy making fun of poor Miranda for that beastly love affair in Paris that went so wrong, the same thing will happen to you. You will fall in love with someone who will hurt you. It will happen, Teddy, really it will.'

Teddy laughed. 'I am not the type to fall in love, Bobbie. You know me. Carefree Ted. Ambitious Ted. I do not fall in love. Women to me are there merely to be used. Like the dreaded Macaskie – that was his name – I will use women for my own purposes. Mould materials onto their divine bodies and sell them all, dresses and bodies and all, to the highest bidder. That is what I shall do,' he finished gaily.

So Bobbie said 'Humph' and went off to make them both some much-needed coffee, but first she made a speech to Teddy, wagging her finger up at where he still sat at the top of his ladder.

'The trouble with you, Teddy Mowbray, is that your head is too big. You will fall in love when you least expect it, you'll see. You will fall in love with a girl who won't care a silly little damn for you, and you will suffer tortures, you'll soon see. Just you wait.'

Teddy turned back to the wall and leaned his head against it and shut his eyes. He did not have to wait. He already had fallen in love with a girl who did not care a silly little damn for him, and she was making coffee and humming *Music while you work, Hitler is a jerk*', and she had a small yellow handkerchief tied round her rich brown, shining dark hair, and a pair of Capri trousers that ended halfway down her legs displaying slender ankles. Frankly, he thought miserably, if he did not love her so much he would hate her for never, ever noticing what was there in his eyes every time he looked at her.

'There.' She put down the coffee tray, and stared up at him, 'Quaker Girl makes perfect coffee for old bighead.'

She smiled up at him, and Teddy felt like pulling

434

her up his ladder and kissing her until she fainted, but it was just not him to do such a thing. No, he knew his place in life, and that was to go on being Teddy Mowbray, the old carefree bighead.

'Now, Bobbie,' he said, and he looked at her reproachfully, 'how can you call the man who has made you famous "old bighead"?'

'Because,' Bobbie said, biting into a biscuit and for no reason at all waving it about, 'I am cruel, Teddy Mowbray, don't you remember that? When we were at Mellaston, it was always Miranda who was kind, and I was always cruel.'

'That is not true, you were both darlings and you know it. Tell you what, let's go down to the old place, to the old rectory, at the end of next week? As a matter of fact, we could shoot that gumdrop advertisement there, couldn't we? An old rectory, a clergyman, and you, the Quaker Girl, in something perfectly outrageous chewing a gumdrop. Oh, God.' He leaned back against one newly papered wall and, determined to go on over-acting to make Bobbie laugh, he shut his eyes again and groaned. 'Oh, God, why am I such a genius? That is so beautifully brilliant. Oh, but guess who will take all the credit for it? North and Ryland. As soon as they see the pictures they will preen themselves in front of their clients, and the ad will take off and you and I will be paid in buttons, as always. Buttonholers is all we are, just like the buttonholers in the sweat shops at the back of the garment industry. We do all the work, and they get paid for it.'

'Yes, but . . .'

'Yes but what, Roberta Murray?'

'Yes but . . .' Bobbie waved another biscuit above her head, this time as if it was a fan and she was doing a fan dance. 'But we, don't forget, are having all the fun, and fun is better than money any day. I know. I have seen rich people, and I will tell you something – they never smile. And shall I tell you why they never smile? Because they are rich. No, we are having all the fun, and we must not spoil it by becoming rich too. Money ruins everything. I know. I have seen the unsmiling rich, always suspicious and worried that someone might sit down next to them who is not rich, who is only going to be interested in their money, who-whoo!'

Bobbie ended by making an owl sound through her closed hands, after which she climbed up her own ladder again and they continued wallpapering to the sound of the new wireless programme being listened to, rather too loudly, by the second Mrs Saxby, and Boy the pug, of course.

But Teddy, being Teddy, could not understand what Bobbie meant.

Chapter Fourteen

Dick was allowed to come with them for the duration of the shooting of the gumdrop advertisement, and of course Miranda had to come, and once Teddy had decided that Miranda could come it occurred to him that she might as well be in the advertisement too.

'It's not as if the two of you are in any way alike. Besides, it might be good to put Bobbie in the middle and then have you somewhere in the background. I'll work out the story behind it. Anyway, it means that we all get our expenses paid, and that is good.'

Miranda did not really want to leave London at that moment, but the temptation to return to the old rectory, and to Mellaston, was too much. Besides, if they brought Dick along with them it would, she imagined, prevent their all becoming too sentimental. That is what she hoped, anyway. After all, Dick and she were now partners, and that was something really.

She looked at him, driving them all along in his

brand new Morris Oxford to their first stop, for dinner. They would stay the night, and complete the journey to Mellaston the next day. Compared to Teddy – who was seated beside him, his feet up on the dashboard, his hat pulled down over his eyes, a cigarette in one hand, its smoke drifting out of the window – it had to be said that Dick, despite being a painter, was the acme of reliability. Not only was he never late or boastful, but unlike Teddy he was completely and utterly content. He was not like herself and Teddy and Bobbie; he had none of their restlessness, none of their huge ups, or fearful downs. But then again, despite his painterly background, Dick was unlike all of them in another way. Dick was a touch patrician. And not just because he had the good luck to have private money, and the talent to pursue what he loved to do; he was always at pains not to show his feelings, in case they affected someone else, which, Miranda realized suddenly, considering how they all were, was probably just as well, really.

However, patrician or not, Dick was not averse to making a speech once they arrived outside the Dog and Pheasant.

'England has the greatest tradition of coaching inns in the world. When they became popular in the eighteenth century they became the envy of Europe, did you know that? Great welcoming log fires, beef roasting on a spit, smiling ostlers rushing out to welcome you – it was one of the greatest boons of being an Englishman, travelling around this exquisite island of ours, to arrive, cold, tired, and travel-stained, at one of our coaching inns.'

It transpired that the Dog and Pheasant was in just such a tradition. A real English inn of a pub with a vast log fire burning in the hall, and that slight smell of wood ash mixed with lavender furniture polish and pot pourri which is so comfortingly English. There were fires in all the rooms, although it was still only early autumn, and the logs in the grates hissed and spat, and sometimes seemed to be declining to leap into life in a Christmassy fashion, but that did not matter. There was a spark and a flame here and there, and above all, through all the rooms, the delightful smell of wood smoke, an aroma which turns an arrival from the dullest journey into an event of warmth and delight.

Upstairs the rooms were small, the floors uneven, and the flowered curtains already drawn against the darkness outside. Bobbie and Miranda shared a double room, as did Dick and Teddy, with a bathroom somewhere down the corridors, which had to be scurried to, back and forth.

Every now and then, of course, because he simply could not bear to think that they were not talking or thinking about him all the time, Teddy knocked on the door and shouted some inanity into the girls' room, at which Bobbie and Miranda would groan and call, 'Go-away-Teddy! At-least-until-dinner-time,' which to their great surprise he eventually did.

Bobbie knew that Miranda had been reluctant to

come on the long journey back to Mellaston, not because she did not want to see Mellaston again, but because, as she had confided to Bobbie several times, she did not want to model anything for anyone, ever again. She feared that just standing about in a model gown, as she had done in Paris for Macaskie, might bring back memories such as no-one would want to revive.

'Was it that bad? I mean Paris, with that man, was it that bad?'

Bobbie suddenly found that she wanted to know everything, that, for some reason she could not name, she was overcome with an intense curiosity. Before, whenever the subject of Macaskie had come up, she had always turned away from Miranda's memories of Paris, and, most of all, their truth.

At her question it was now Miranda who turned away, frowning and shaking her head.

'You wouldn't know how bad.' She started to brush her hair. 'It's just a little pathetic, but I realize now that Macaskie, he – I – that I was never even in love with him. I mean I know – well, you think you should be, but it was nothing like that. He became a – well, a *challenge*. It was far more that than love really. You see, right from the start, he really did not want to know about me, as a person. To give him his due, he always made that quite plain. And so I made it my business to make sure that he *did* know about me.' She paused, the expression on her face one of resignation. 'You know how I've always been, part show-off, and – well, all push.' She turned from her mirror and looked sadly at Bobbie who was sitting on her bed pulling on her stockings, and clipping her suspenders to their tops in a precise, almost military fashion. 'Remember? At Mellaston? I always was a bighead, a bit like Teddy is now. And of course, being sent to stay with Allegra made it worse, really. She was always and forever urging me on in the wrong ways. I mean. She had me smoking, for goodness' sake, and for no better reason than because, she always said, if I smoked *she* would not feel so bad about smoking in front of me. She hated to drink and smoke on her own. I even used to have to pretend to drink in front of her, but then I would hide the glass when she wasn't looking. But of course, once in Paris, I really did start drinking wine, if only to keep up with the rest of them. That is how it is when you're someone like me, I'm afraid, with more front than Selfridges. And then of course he cut off my hair, and suddenly I was like Samson – lost me hair, lost me confidence, drank half a bottle of wine before going on the catwalk, and blow me if I didn't fall straight off it.'

Bobbie looked across at her. Although they both knew the story, and only too well, of a sudden at that moment it stopped having any tragic value whatsoever, and became more than funny, it became hilarious.

They started to laugh, and they simply could not stop, but every now and then between the gasps of laughter came a small strangled sound which was Miranda saying over and over again, 'I only fell off the catwalk! Oh God, I only fell off the catwalk! Oh God, I only fell off in front of the world's fashion press. Oh God! I would, wouldn't I?'

Finally Bobbie sobered up enough to say, 'Actually, it's a wonder you didn't hurt yourself, Miranda.'

'I did. As a matter of fact I was in bed for a week afterwards. The bruises, well, you can imagine, and that was before Macaskie – well, we won't go into that. He drank, you see. Not just a little at a time, either – when he drank, he drank a lot. It was all or nothing with him. He was all right to start with, laughing and talking, you know, and fun – and then that funny thing would happen, that switch-over that comes about with alcoholics, and boom – he'd lay into me, and that would mean another set of steak to go under the eyes. Or – well, he would start to make fun of me about, well, you know, intimate things, in front of everyone, mocking me, and of course I'd cry, and he would get such a thrill from that, from my crying. The times I cried in Paris. I reckon the Seine rose half an inch from my tears, I do really.'

'Why did you stand it? I mean – why?'

'I was lost, wasn't I? I had no-one to pull me out of myself – you know, the way we all need someone to pull us out of ourselves?'

Bobbie frowned. 'That is too awful to think of. I mean, maybe if we had all found each other before, it would never have happened.'

Miranda shrugged her shoulders. 'Don't feel too

sorry for me. As a matter of fact, I can hardly remember those days, or those nights, thank God. I drank so much it was a wonder I lived at all, that I didn't break my neck or something. I can hardly remember anything until, you know, Teddy and Dick found me in the Blue Note, and that was that. They brought me back to England with them, and really – I've never looked back, have I?'

'I know Teddy nearly had a heart attack when he found you. He told me that, only the other day. I mean there he was in the Blue Note, not doing anything but listen to the music, and then this girl with dyed black hair and a white face stands up. You can imagine how he felt when he realized that it was you. He could hardly believe it *was* you. I mean he worshipped you as a child, he really did. He worshipped the ground you trod. So you can imagine. He could hardly believe it was you, his Miranda.'

'I know.' Miranda's expression was suddenly curiously closed, and she turned back to her mirror. 'It was awful for him, poor Ted.'

'Especially since he thinks of you as his sister,' Bobbie continued inexorably, in her usual tactless fashion. 'Big sisters don't go down the drain, do they? I mean not in the minds of their younger brothers. Which is ridiculous really, because we're all human for heaven's sake.'

'Yes, I know.' Miranda took up her hairbrush and dragged it forcefully through her blond hair again. 'I say,' she said, staring at herself determinedly in the small mahogany mirror, 'I could eat the side of a house, I'm so hungry. Let's zip downstairs and order dinner before the boys. That'll put us in the catbird seat all right. I believe they are cooking roast pork for the first time. Hush, hush, whisper who dares, there is a piece of crackling cooking under the stairs!'

Bobbie nodded, not noticing anything different about Miranda, having her back turned to her as she pulled an evening top over her head. Which was just as well, really, because whether it was the self-inflicted pain caused by the hairbrush, or whether it was the fact that she was fainting from hunger, Miranda looked suddenly pale and drawn. She hurriedly applied some rouge to her cheeks to bring colour into them, and then, seeing how the rouge stood out against her pale skin, she pinched them hard, making two high-coloured spots she had to give time to calm down before turning to face the now waiting Bobbie.

'I feel like a cigarette,' she said, standing up. 'And a drink. A large drink. A very large drink.'

Bobbie frowned as she followed her down the wide shallow stairs of the old inn to the hall, and from there into the dark-walled bar. She could not quite remember, but surely Miranda had not drunk or smoked since Paris, had she?

They were too late to triumph over the men, however, for Teddy and Dick were already ensconced in the bar, enjoying both a drink and a cigarette, and perusing the dinner menu, which thankfully did not make mention of anything like Spam or Snoek, or even chopped cabbage.

'As soon as I see an old inn sign,' Dick confided to Miranda, as they shared the reading of a menu, 'I feel like Dr Johnson's hungry man who could eat a cow.'

Miranda smiled, and, taking one of his cigarettes from the packet laid out on the bar, said, 'Never mind the cow, just order me a gin, Dick, would you? And you don't mind me pinching one of your cigarettes, do you? Been dying for a fag the whole journey.'

Both the men stared at Miranda as Bobbie climbed onto a bar stool and ordered herself a lime juice with water.

'I know, I know!' Bobbie shook her head and at the same time shrugged her shoulders towards Teddy. 'It's not my fault. She just announced upstairs that she had reformed her ways, and would now, if you please, resume better habits.'

'Do you think you should, Miranda?' Dick frowned and lightly tapped her on the top of her head with the menu.

'Of course. You are, aren't you? Why not I, for goodness' sake? I am not a child.'

Miranda smiled, and Teddy saw, of a sudden, and with alarm, that Miranda's smile was the sly one she used to have when they were little and she was just about to chase him and Bobbie with a dead mouse, or push wet leaves down the backs of their pullovers.

445

'Come here, Miranda, come with me.' Dick pulled at her arm suddenly, succeeding in making her slide off her bar stool and marching her outside into the hall where he squared her up in front of him. 'About smoking and drinking, if this means you're going to end up trying to sing "Parisian Pierrot" at the top of your voice, I beg you, put out that fag, change your tune, and drink a tonic water as you normally do, Miss Mowbray.'

Miranda pretended to give a tired smile. 'Dick, dear Dick. I am not a Mowbray. I am a Darling.'

'Very well, Miranda darling,' Dick said pleasantly, taking her cigarette and throwing it into the hall fire. 'Very well, Miranda, please just stick to your guns and drink tonic water. You've done so well since Paris, really, it would be so tiresome for you if you slide back to your old ways. Besides, you know you will get tight if you so much as sniff the barmaid's apron. That is really your problem. You can't drink at all – not many women can. It is nothing to be ashamed of, really.'

'Who are you, Dick, please, who are you to tell me what to do? Please, tell me – who?'

'I am your business partner, and what is more I am your friend. And I love you,' Dick said simply. His large eyes were honest with the emotion of the moment. He did love her – even if she did not love herself. And anyway, it was such a relief to say the words 'I love you' – more than he could ever have known. He was experiencing a sense of simple

446

relief hearing himself say those deceptively complicated words.

Miranda laughed, not really understanding at all
and really rather determined on continuing with
her boring little performance. 'Oh all right,' she
murmured, suddenly giving in. 'Oh, all right, but
you *are* being just a little stuffy. I am sure I would
have been fine with just a little drink.'

'And I am quite sure you would not.'

After that she let Dick walk her back to the bar,
where she sat down almost meekly. 'Dick is being
strict,' she announced as the others rejoined them.
'He does not want me to have the gin, just the tonic.'

Teddy nodded. 'Dick's right. You're rotten on
drink, Sis. You should be like Bobbie here, just have
lime juice. Women aren't good on drink.'

'That's the whole point, you idiot.'

Both the men stared at her suddenly.

'Women are bad on drink. That is the whole point
of women and drink, isn't it, that it makes them
bad?'

Miranda picked up her menu, and fell silent,
perusing all the dishes, and still feeling sulky.
Bobbie. It was always 'Bobbie' with Teddy. Anyone
would think that Bobbie was Teddy's real sister, the
way he went on, instead of just a rescue case, like
herself – an orphan. As other voices blended into
Miranda's conscious mind, making that particular
sound that is so English, and fills and warms an
English bar on a cold autumn evening, she realized

that despite her jealousy over Teddy, she was happy.

Feeling Dick looking at her, waiting to hear her choice from the menu, she looked up and smiled at him.

'Thanks, Dick. You know. Thanks.'

'Friends again?'

'Of course. With such a friend, who even needs a brother?'

At that she smiled sweetly, nodding towards Teddy, but he did not even notice, too busy telling Bobbie how brilliant he was going to be on the morrow, how he would set up the camera at just the point where the old rectory gates still stood, how he would shoot through some smoke – lighting a bonfire to the side of the camera – and, and, and . . .

Miranda leaned forward and kissed Dick on the cheek. Not to annoy Teddy, but because she wanted to, and after that she found that she did not care to either smoke or drink. She cared only to wonder how Mellaston would be, if it, like them, had changed?

No-one said anything, they were all so afraid that what had been there would have gone away completely. Reassuringly there were the old gates up to which Aunt Sophie's pony Tom Kitten had trotted with Aunt Sophie click-click-clicking behind him in the pony trap, where Miranda and her new brother Ted huddled together in a frozen heap. And although the drive was now grassed

448

over, as so many drives had been during the war, and Dick had to park the Morris Oxford outside the gates in the small country road, the old house, Teddy's house, was there all right.

The tenants who had been living in it up until the past month were now flown, gone back to their own house in London, relieved to put the quiet life of the country and the small church-going society of Mellaston behind them, eager to take up the reins of city life, the hubbub and scrum, the hurly burly of the metropolis. In their stead, living over the stables, where the three of them had used to sit in the straw silently worshipping Tom Kitten as he, equally quietly, ate his hay with a steady chomp, chomp, was Mrs Dingwall.

Bobbie knew, because Teddy had told her, that Mrs Dingwall was now looking after the place for him, but what she did not know was how she would feel when faced with this former guardian to whom she owed, through no-one's fault, the legacy of her former illness.

Again Julian's voice, teasing her, came back. *Let's call ourselves The Incipients, like an American jazz band.*

Mrs Dingwall had not aged well. Bobbie realized as she greeted her that it would have been something of a surprise if she had done so, for with the life she had led, and Mr Dingwall now, alas, deceased, day to day existence in downtown Mellaston, on the other side of the tracks, could not be expected to be anything but harsh, as it was

Bobbie had never thought to see her again.

'Miss Bobbie! I would not have known you, except for that you're still needle thin. Really, I would not have *known* you, dear. You were such a plain girl, really, weren't she, Miss Miranda? Plain as a pig in a sty, and nothing *to* her. I used to put your hair in papers and dress you up in our poor daughter's clothes. I did what I could, but you still stayed as plain as a pig, but looking at you now – why, you're as pretty as Miss Miranda here, now. I'd say that was a turn up for the books, all right, I would really. Oh, but I do wish Mr Dingwall could see you now, dear. He never would have believed it possible, he never would. He always thought you'd end up on the shelf, as an old maid with a parrot for company, but he got that wrong, didn't he, dear? I would never have thought it possible, really I wouldn't.'

Nor would Bobbie have believed it possible to feel such a surge of revulsion at hearing from this well-intentioned old woman, in her flowered blouse and cotton scarf still knotted in the appropriate wartime fashion on the top of her head, how plain Bobbie had been. Standing beside her, listening to her running on about her looks, and how hard she had worked to put her hair in papers, Bobbie remembered the terrible day of the party when Mrs Dingwall had walked her up to the rectory and announced her in a special voice, and how Miranda and Teddy had stared at Bobbie in silent horror, and the aunts too.

It had been a nightmare. Worse than Teddy wetting himself in church that time; worse than when Mrs Eglantine had announced that the committee was insisting on splitting them all up and the aunts had decided that it was better if Bobbie went with Mrs Eglantine because she could 'cope better'; worse than all of that was standing here now while Mrs Dingwall blathered on about how plain she had looked. Of a sudden Bobbie was again that skinny little girl with the dreadful Milly Molly Mandy hair and the secondhand cardigan, and the silver shoes that held the shape of a dead girl's foot and chaffed a little at the sides. She had not realized until that moment how far she had come, or, really, from where.

'Bobbie? Bobbie? Come on!'

At the sound of Miranda's insistent call Bobbie turned away with relief from Mrs Dingwall's too interested expression.

'That's right, dear, you go along with the posh children. But you know, I never would have believed it, not never, that you would have turned out such a beauty, and famous too, you know that? That picture of you what's on the station at Mellaston, well, the dean, he's retired now, you know, he never would have known you, he never would. He said as much to me when I saw him outside the Co-op the other day. He'd read all about you in the newspapers, of course, but he never did recognize you, not until I pointed you out. He was that pleased that I had pointed you out, because he would never have known you, he said. Never would have known you! Not ever. Have you still got that teddy bear I gave you, dear? That was our Marion's, but once she had gone there was no point to keeping it.'

'Bobbie! Come on, tea and biscuits!'

This time Miranda was calling from the door of the rectory and beckoning too, so that Bobbie had a good reason to move out of the way of Mrs Dingwall's grasp, smiling as she did so.

'I say, I am sorry, they do keep calling me, Mrs Dingwall. I'll come up and see you in the flat, later, if that is all right with you?'

'Yes, you go along with the posh children, Miss Bobbie, that's right. Give yourself a bit of a leg up. Not that you need it now that you're on the posters and all that. Honestly. My Bert, he never would have believed it, really he wouldn't. Such a plain child! Like a pig! He always said that. "Poor Miss Bobbie, plain as a pig!"'

Bobbie started to walk away from her erstwhile foster mother, slowly at first, smiling grimly back at her, and waving a little, her breath starting to make little circles in the air as she gave a small cough.

'Something the matter?'

Miranda frowned, first at Bobbie's irritating little cough, and then at the now disappearing Mrs Dingwall, at whose retreating figure she pulled a little face.

'God, Mrs D! I don't know why Teddy thought of her as a caretaker. I'd forgotten all about her. She always was such a bloody old bore, wasn't she? Remember that time she sent you to the party looking like Milly Molly Mandy? That was so awful. I wanted to scratch her eyes out for you. You poor thing, you looked sick for the whole of the party. And then you ran off home and we never saw you again, Ted and I, did we? We never saw you again, until now. Bloody woman. She did it on purpose I always thought. Tried to make you look like one of them – you know, a Dingwall – on purpose. My grandmother had more taste in her little finger than the whole of Mrs Dingwall's body, and she was a Cockney. She knew not to make you look like a freak. She just wanted to make a point to the aunts. Like "She's one of us now, and nothing you can do about it." Just a cunning old woman, that's what she is.'

Comforting as it was to hear Miranda talk that way, the feelings that Mrs Dingwall had brought on would not go away, those feelings of being not just ugly but repulsive. Of being not just a plain little girl, but a girl from the other side of the tracks, none of whose friends and family would ever want to know her again. Bobbie gave another little cough.

'Anything the matter?'

Bobbie shook her head, but taking out a handkerchief she wiped her mouth with it and then stared down at it.

'Is that blood?' she demanded of Miranda suddenly.

Miranda, her hand on the door of the old rectory, turned, horrified.

'What did you say?'

'I said *Is that blood?*'

'No, of course it's not blood, Bobbie. For goodness' sake, what's got into you? That's your lipstick, you fool. Remember, you wear lipstick now?'

Miranda snatched the handkerchief from Bobbie and waved it in front of her.

'Oh my God.' Bobbie's eyes filled with tears. 'Oh my God,' she whispered, as Miranda took her in her arms and hugged her, 'for one terrible moment, I don't know why, I thought it was blood. I thought I had coughed up blood.'

Miranda patted her back and Bobbie stepped aside from her arms.

'God, Miranda, I am so sorry. It's that woman.' Bobbie blew her nose now on the lipsticked handkerchief. 'It all came back, the hell of that place – Rosebank, and Bert, and all that. My God, it was such hell. And really, how they hated me, poor things. Not on top hatred, nothing like that, but underneath hatred, because I was different from them, and they knew it, and I was not their beloved Marion. And, God, the ghastliness of the outside lavatory, and the attic with the rats. It all came back when I heard her voice.'

'Maybe it was a mistake—'

'You bet it was a mistake – I'd rather have someone strangle me and throw me in the river than ever go back to those days.'

'No, I mean coming back here, to Mellaston. Maybe we should never have come back. Going back is always meant to be a mistake, isn't it? Do you think we shall start looking for the aunts everywhere? Shall I start singing in a small reedy voice, and look for Aunt Sophie to play for me? Should we really not open this door, stay on this side, leave the past to be the past? Should we?'

Bobbie did not answer Miranda but gave another little cough, after which she took a lipstick and her compact from her handbag and repaired the damage done by her tears.

'I don't know, Miranda. I really don't know. But I have a feeling—' They both turned as they heard Teddy's voice calling them from inside. 'I have a feeling that it is too late to wonder what we should be doing, because, let's face it, we have done it now, and nothing to *be* done, really, is there?'

'It won't all be bad, surely. Will it? It won't all be bad and sad? There will be other bits, bits we have forgotten, behind this door, and we will remember them, and the aunts. Above all we must remember the aunts.'

Bobbie nodded, her eyes not meeting Miranda's, turning away from the pain of even hearing the aunts mentioned. The truth was that she had learned to hate the aunts, and Teddy and Miranda, and that was why she had never tried to meet up with any of them again. Once Beatrice had appointed herself Bobbie's guardian she had not thought to see anyone from the Mellaston days again, but she could not say that to Miranda who had suffered enough already, what with Paris and Macaskie, and now the expression on her face was so eager, hoping against hope that behind the door she was now opening would be some of the gaiety and the happiness of 'their war'; some of that time when they had all felt so oddly secure – that it would all come back to them, and the pain that had come after it all would recede, perhaps even fade to nothing.

'What's best, Bobbie?' Miranda's voice was low and urgent, almost panic-striken.

Bobbie shook her head. 'I don't know. I don't know. I wish I did, really I do. I wish I knew.'

Teddy was in his element. He was back at the old rectory, his house now, and the four of them were all together.

'It's just the same, isn't it? It's all just the same,' he kept saying to Miranda.

Miranda, following him, and in her turn followed by Dick and Bobbie, nodded. 'Of course it's just the same, Ted. But it's not the same either.'

Teddy stopped. 'I've kept it just the same as they left it,' he said, sounding indignant. 'Just the same. I had that old building firm in Mellaston – what are they called – Greenstones – I had them come in and wash the place down with sugar soap. None of the paint has been changed, all the furniture's been kept in the same place. I wanted it to be a shrine to the aunts who saved us from

456

whatever it was that they saved us from—'

'Hitler—'

'The bombs—'

'Our families,' Miranda said, giving a sudden rippling laugh. 'Ted doesn't even know who his family is,' she told Dick. 'Not a clue, have you, Ted, thanks to me and the aunts.'

'Lots of kids like me got swallowed up in the war,' Teddy told Dick with a queer kind of pride in his voice. 'And there we were and people took us on and changed us for ever. It happened a lot. Anyway, I don't care,' he called back to Miranda, who had stopped to peer into a cupboard. 'I don't care who I was, Ted Darling, Teddy Mowbray, anyone, I don't care, Sis dear. You took me on, the aunts adopted me, and that's enough for me. I mean it. I just count my lucky stars that I don't know *who* my mother was, because whoever she was she didn't want to know about *me*, did she? Or my father, whoever *he* was, and if that's the case I don't want to know who *they* were, and that is that.'

Dick, who was an emotional outsider at this point, and intended to remain very firmly as such, now murmured in a pacifying voice, 'Quite right, old thing, quite right. You don't want to go delving about in some bit of your life that don't matter and never will. It would be like trying to find out why you came about. Appalling thought. Although I say that, but I know from an uncle that I was apparently the result of too much gin at a cocktail party, on whose part, mama's or papa's, I could never find out, nor indeed cared to really. They never had much to do with me. The only love I had was from Nanny, and since they've all passed on, what does it matter now? I have a few letters from my father still – used to sign himself "Yours faithfully" . . .' As Miranda started to laugh, he turned back to her and said, 'No, don't laugh, really, he did. As a matter of fact for a long time I never could differentiate between letters from him and ones from the bank, since they both typed on rather similar paper and signed themselves in black ink too!'

'Well, there you are, you see,' Teddy too turned back to Miranda. 'There you are, Sis. Things are as they are, aren't they?'

Miranda stared at him for a few seconds. 'Yes, they are, Ted, aren't they? Now go on, let's get something together in the kitchen, shall we? I'm starving.'

She suddenly ran ahead of them all, and as she did she started to whistle, and instantly Teddy and Bobbie remembered that Miranda had always done just that, run ahead of them both, whistling some Cockney song that her 'nan' had taught her before the old woman had left her at the school to join the throng of evacuees from London. Some song like 'Roll Out the Barrel' or 'Knees Up Mother Brown', one of the old East End favourites. Aunt Sophie had never liked her to sing them, so Miranda had always got round that by whistling them instead.

*   *   *

As soon as they reached the old kitchen, still with its blue and white china on the dresser, and its large scrubbed table in the middle, a kind of reverent calm settled about them all. Even Dick, who had never been fed blackberries and cream around the table, nor run out from the back door to the scullery to pull on wellington boots and gallop off to the stables to see Tom Kitten, fell silent.

For a couple of minutes, standing in the old room with its now old – once new – cream-coloured Aga, none of them spoke. It was as if they were all overcome, so redolent of past times enjoyed was the old room. And not just their past times, but all the past times ever enjoyed in that room, which was now, it seemed, just resting, as if, like some old, beloved, and much polished piece of farm machinery, it was only waiting to be started up again, perhaps longing for someone to cook on its Aga, hoping that there would be other generations to sit around the table and eat and laugh. Or, as Miranda and Teddy had done, merely grow up surrounded by its welcome homeliness.

In the end it was Bobbie who broke their trance first, moving into the scullery to stare at the carefully labelled jam jars, still declaring in Aunt Prudence's clear, rounded, almost childish writing, 'Raspberry Jam, 1942' or 'Apple Chutney, 1943'. And too, alongside the now really rather too old preserves, all carefully sealed with wax and topped tightly with frilled hats and tied about with kitchen string, were tins and jars from before the war, obviously only recently dusted by Mrs Dingwall, who would, Bobbie knew only too well, disdain to eat such things as Patum Peperum or Cods Roe, or even sardines (*can't even bear fish paste, dear*).

'I don't suppose,' Teddy said, eventually, after he had joined Bobbie in the scullery, followed by the others, 'I don't suppose even Miranda could cook this lot up into something approaching a meal, could she?' He looked round slyly as they all stared in some fascination at the ingredients that had been left so untouched.

Miranda frowned, and turned back towards the larder shelves. Given some eggs and a packet of fresh flour, and various other things which she hazarded a guess even Mrs Dingwall would be keeping in her flat above the garage, she certainly could cook up something from what Teddy called 'this lot'. She turned to Bobbie. 'You and Teddy go and get some eggs from the old bag over the stables, and scrounge some flour from her, if you can. And Dick, you could drive into Mellaston and get me some bread, and some potatoes from the greengrocery and whatever fresh vegetables you can find, and – oh, some cider. Get some cider, would you? From the George, on your left as you drive out down the main street. I saw some apples in the garden, and some pears, and there'll be blackberries still in the hedges, won't there? Good.'

'I'll get the old Aga going, if you would like something roasted tomorrow.'

Teddy and Miranda stared at each other for a few seconds, silent again, until Teddy said, 'I say, just like the old days, isn't it?'

Less than an hour later they all returned from fulfilling their various commissions to find Miranda with one of Aunt Prudence's old cookbooks propped up against a jam jar, her hair tied up on the top of her head, and an old apron with lace frills on the bottom tied around her dress.

Teddy nodded at her briefly, much more interested in seeing what she was cooking than how she was looking. Only Dick stared at her, thinking that really the sight of a young woman concentrating on her cooking was one of the more beautiful domestic scenes, and how he would like to paint her, exactly as she was in the half-light of the old kitchen.

Turning to Teddy he said, 'Why don't you photograph Miranda like that, in the kitchen, with Bobbie as the hostess, standing by in that ball dress you were talking about and handing Miranda a fruit gum as an encouraging gesture. It would be great, wouldn't it?'

Teddy shook his head, staring at Miranda without much interest but considering the idea none the less, despite its having come from Dick. 'Not bad, actually. Miranda cooking and Bobbie standing by with the gums. Not bad.'

Dick stood further down the kitchen, still imagining his painting, but unlike Teddy thinking how beautiful Miranda looked when she was

461

concentrating, not paying much attention to anyone, really in another world, probably imagining how good the dish she was about to cook would be. Perhaps seeing in her mind's eye too how they would all look when they had eaten it, appreciative and smiling, perhaps hoping that they would all love her just a little more for providing them with such pleasure.

Not that he himself could love her more than he did at that moment. He really did not think he could. It was as if by taking her out of Aubrey Close, and the affinities of their life there, he was able to appreciate the whole of Miranda, Miranda in the round as it were, not just little bits and pieces of her.

He sighed inwardly as Teddy's voice came back into his consciousness, as the voice of a person who is climbing the other side of a hill on which you are standing comes to you, increasing in clarity, little by little.

'Actually, Dick, that's not a bad idea. I mean Miranda makes really quite a striking cook, and Bobbie is looking ravishing, isn't she, so that – as far as the advertisers are concerned – we could sell them the idea that there is something in the picture for everyone, couldn't we? The cook that no-one can find nowadays, even to marry, on one side of the frame, and on the other, with the kitchen table between, set with the blue and white china, the hostess that everyone everywhere always longs for their wives or girlfriends to be, cool, beautiful, slender and pure.'

Perhaps because Bobbie was not in the room at that moment Teddy stared back at Dick, who was still standing behind him. As he did so, he suddenly saw what was in Dick's eyes, and if he had let it his mouth would have dropped open.

Surely not? Surely Dick could not be in love with his sister? Not with old Miranda. *Never*. Miranda was just old Miranda. She was beautiful, OK – well, everyone knew that. But, well, she was *damaged goods*, for a start, and then she was – well, she was – Miranda. She was just – well, *Miranda*, for God's sake. No-one fell in love with *Miranda*.

He left the kitchen in a state of confusion, almost panic, and went in search of Bobbie.

'Bobbie?'

Bobbie had been sitting for some time quietly in the drawing room, on her own, thinking over the evenings they had used to have there, before she had been sent off by Mrs Eglantine to live with the Dingwalls, before all her happiness and security ended. She was enjoying the silence of the room, finding that the good memories were really very healing, when Teddy interrupted her, and walking noisily across the old wooden floor sat down beside her, seeming much larger and heavier to Bobbie than he actually was in reality because she had just been remembering him as a small, curly-haired boy, her brother who always needed protecting and looking after at every turn.

'You were always in such a pickle, did you know that, Teddy?' Bobbie said dreamily, but Teddy paid

463

no attention. He was far too alarmed by what he had just seen, Dick of all people, his friend, in love with Miranda, his sister.

'Bobbie. Doom. Bobbie? *Bobbie?*'

'Yes?'

'Didn't you hear me, *doom*.' Teddy looked at Bobbie, the expression in his eyes deeply troubled. 'I mean it, doom.'

Bobbie did not seem terribly impressed, just anxious to return to her memories of the happy times they had enjoyed in the drawing room. Her unspoken thoughts prevailed for a while, but finally she turned to him and without her saying a word Teddy knew that he was at last allowed to speak, that she had finished tripping down memory lane and was now prepared to listen to him.

'Bobbie.' Teddy dropped his voice just as he had used to do when he was a boy and did not want the aunts to know that he had swallowed a button and thought he might die, or that there were mouse droppings in the pony's food because his tame mouse had escaped from its cage. 'I think that Dick is in love with *Miranda*. I do. I think he's only fallen in love with her.' His voice rose slightly under the pressure of his emotions as the thought once more made itself plain. Dick was in love with Miranda, of all people – his sister, Miranda.

Bobbie leaned back against the old window panes before giving a small cough or two, and then with closed eyes she whispered back, 'Stale news,

Teddy old thing, very stale news indeed.'

For a second Teddy felt so grateful to Bobbie for not calling him Ted the way Miranda did, which was so *putty downy* always, that he did not take in what Bobbie was saying. 'What?'

'I said stale news,' Bobbie told him, suddenly opening her eyes and smiling.

'But Dick, of all people. I mean he's a nice man, he's far too nice for my sister. Miranda's – well, she's a good cook, but you know – that *Macaskie* thing. *You* know. She's not quite what she should be, is she? I mean living with someone like that – he used to beat her up, and everything. It's not as if Miranda is, well, the person she used to be.'

'Which of us are, Teddy old bean?'

Bobbie was really just imitating the old Major back in Ebury Street, but somehow because she had chosen to be lighthearted and facetious at that moment Teddy felt desperately wounded.

'There you are, you see. I never could talk to you half as well as I could to Miranda,' he said, hoping to hurt her. 'Out of the two of you it was always Miranda who listened to me, finally. I could never talk to you.'

Bobbie put her head on one side and smiled at him, realizing at once that she had offended him but unwilling to make a great show of apologizing because Teddy was always so protective of his own rather than other people's feelings.

'No, of course you could never talk to me, Teddy, which is why you've come all this way, right from the kitchen to the drawing room, to do just that.'

Bobbie closed her eyes again and breathed out. She hated complications. Who could talk to whom, and why. Or why people could not talk to whom, and if not. Because of her complicated childhood Bobbie had become almost determinedly uncomplicated. She liked to *do* things rather than to talk, and she liked other people to do the same.

'Play me something, Teddy. You know, like the old days. Play me one of Aunt Sophie's old songs. There's sheet music on the piano over there, and I know you can play just a little, and I'll sing just a little, and we might bring Aunt Sophie back into the room, imagine.'

And so Teddy sat down at the piano and, after shuffling through some of the old music on the lid, propped up something against the stand and began to play.

'It's hopelessly out of tune,' he said, but he played on. 'The soft pedal's gone.' But still he played on.

Bobbie walked across from the window seat and joined him at the piano and sat down beside him, which was where Dick found them. Teddy of all people singing and playing to Bobbie of all people.

Dick stood still, listening to them, singing 'If You Were the Only Girl (in the World)'. They looked like a couple suddenly, Bobbie and Teddy. And as they sang artlessly together, smiling despite the haunting sadness that the song's lyric seemed to hint at, Dick thought of crowds on newsreels

466

during the war, and people in pubs that he had passed with his uncle of a gentle English evening, those same words floating on the air, and then drifting down the village street towards the farms and the cottages in the distance where so many *only girls* were still sitting waiting for so many *only boys* who had not finally come back to them.

And yet here it was still being sung by the new generation, by two young people who had somehow survived to live and laugh again, despite everything. As Dick stood and listened, his tall figure framed in the doorway, unmoving, and unwilling to break the moment, the dust caught in the evening sunlight that span a length of light across the piano with the two young heads, so close and so suddenly intimate, he found himself realizing something that he should have realized weeks before. 'Good God, Teddy's in love with Bobbie, of all people.' That was the first thought, and the next was, 'Dear Lord, I wonder if Bobbie knows that Teddy is dotty about her?'

Feeling somehow as if he was intruding on a very private moment he backed out of the drawing room and into the kitchen, where he started to whip some eggs for Miranda very fast indeed.

What on earth would happen to Teddy? After all he knew, as well as anyone, simply because she never spoke about it at all, that Bobbie had been passionately in love with some man in Sussex. Poor Teddy probably did not have a chance with her, any more than Dick possibly had a remote chance with

Miranda. Suddenly everything seemed a terrible mess.

He stared at his eggs, unable to go on beating them with quite such vigour. Miranda looked round briefly from the Aga and smiled.

'Oh, Dick, be an angel and find some candles for the table, would you?'

As Dick did so Miranda gave a sudden sigh.

'It was good that we came back, wasn't it, Dick? It makes sense of everything that happened to us afterwards, you know – when we all became separated and Teddy never bothered to get back in touch with me after the aunts were killed. It now all makes sense, because we're together again, and it's even better – because you're here too.'

Dick smiled and as he always did when he felt shy and pleased at the same time, he ran his hands through his hair.

'Dear girl, dearest darling Miranda,' he said, softly, but quite to himself, alone in the old larder, as he searched for candles.

They all ate Miranda's sumptuous supper in a spirit of joyous festivity, after which the girls left the men to go to bed early, ridiculously happy at being able to fall asleep in their old beds, while Teddy and Dick walked round the garden, smoking and looking at the stars and wondering silently about each other, Dick thinking *Poor old Teddy, I don't suppose he has a chance with Bobbie* and Teddy thinking *Poor old Dick I don't suppose he has a chance with Miranda*.

Upstairs the objects of their thoughts fell asleep, laughing and remembering, because, together in their old room again, it was as if all the memories of the in-between years had been sent off to bury themselves in the distant hills and Aunt Sophie and Aunt Prudence had just been in to check the blackout and wish them a crisp goodnight, which was probably why they both slept without dreaming.

Bobbie's rooms at Ebury Street were finished and there was little now for her to do but enjoy them. It was, as always when the busy times of redecoration are over, an almost languorous moment, so languorous that it was verging on the dull, Bobbie found suddenly. It was not just that everything in her rooms was finished and perfect, it was not just that she now had a comfortably plush bedroom, it was not just that her sitting room was everything that she could wish it, painted in a decorous lemon, with brown tweed furniture and one of the newest styles of coffee tables on spindly legs; it was, she knew, because Teddy no longer had an excuse to come round, and so as a consequence life was dull.

What was more, if she wanted to see the others she had always to go to Aubrey Close, because Miranda only ever left the old studio to go round to the Café Parfait, as she and Dick had christened their tiny new café. So, when she was not working, or 'posing' as old Major Saxby always called it, in front of cameras for Teddy or some other photographer, Bobbie tended to feel left out by the other three.

Of course she said nothing about this because, it had to be faced, if she was one thing and one thing alone, Bobbie was proud. She stared up at her newly painted eau de Nil bedroom ceiling. She did not really, really miss Teddy exactly, but she did not *not* miss him either. Teddy was such a bighead always. No-one had ever yet praised Teddy more than Teddy himself – but, even so, when he was not around talking about himself, and jumping on and off ladders, there was no doubt about it, he left a bit of a gap. And it was not the same when they were working together, as subject and photographer, because, well, work was work, and it had to be admitted there was only a limited amount that you *could* say to each other when, as Bobbie had been last week, you were dressed as a clown and being made to sit on a trapeze for half the day.

It was at the precise moment that Bobbie had quite made up her mind to telephone to Miranda and Dick and ask them round to *her* rooms for dinner, a meal which she had already planned to be quite definitely Indian in flavour – the Major and Mrs Saxby having taken to cooking Indian cuisine had interested Bobbie in curry powders and rice and the use of coconut and chutneys, which was all rather exciting, to Bobbie anyway, and quite certainly exotic – when there was the sound of a modest knock on Bobbie's sitting room door.

As she heard the knock, Bobbie felt a surge of relief, and at once threw back the blankets and jumped out of bed. The truth was, she realized, long before she had thrown on her new oriental dressing gown, bought in a flurry of excitement from Fenwick's the previous week – the truth was that she was not bored with life, she was actually bored with *herself*. This was a shaming sort of truth, because people who are bored with themselves were *boring*, the aunts always said.

As she hurried to her sitting room door Bobbie realized that ever since going back to Mellaston she had felt a strange sense of dissatisfaction. It was as if she either needed to go back to live at Mellaston again, this time for ever, or should never have gone back there at all, because going back had reminded Miranda and herself of their marvellous days at the rectory. Days when they had only the aunts to look to, and no-one else in the whole world had seemed to care about them, and as a consequence they had been strangely free and unfettered and the rectory and its garden a paradise for children.

'Bobbie—'

Mrs Saxby – it was still strange to think of Miss Moncrieff as such, but there – stood at Bobbie's sitting room door, and her earrings and charm bracelet seemed to be ringing out not the kind of pleasant notes for which they had been made, but a very different sound, the sound of fright and alarm.

They seemed, as she swayed forward, the fingers of one hand pressed to her lips, to be pealing out a warning such as medieval bells must have rung, summoning everyone to the town square to help avert some fearful danger.

'Bobbie, oh Bobbie, the most terrible thing has happened.' Mrs Saxby waved a stiff piece of paper, closely typed and largely headed by a black print. 'The most terrible thing. The poor Major, he is destroyed. I cannot understand it. Trumped up, of course, the whole thing, but real none the less, we must realize, real, real, and terrible too.'

Bobbie took the piece of paper, suddenly feeling calmer and more grown up than Mrs Saxby. Probably because she had been so ill as a child she had a kind of ability, at moments when everyone else panicked, to stay quite calm. It was as if a voice inside her was saying, 'Well, you're still alive, and they're still alive, so there is still hope yet.'

She frowned now, as Mrs Saxby sank down in one of her new tweed chairs, and started to read the closely typed nonsense that was on the piece of paper.

Eventually, having digested the un-plain English, she looked up from the paper – no-one could call it a letter – and said, 'What on earth . . . who on earth . . . I mean to say, I never read such nonsense.'

She should not have said *who* on earth, for as soon as she said it she knew, and Mrs Saxby knew, *who* on earth could have perpetrated the trumped-up

472

charges written in that piece of official nonsense.

Beatrice.

'Mrs Harper. She is behind this, dear, isn't she?'

Mrs Saxby stared across at Bobbie, and Bobbie nodded slowly, her hands, which had been warm in a just-out-of-bed state, now ice cold as she re-read the letter, more slowly this time, quite unable to believe what she was reading, and yet quite able to believe it too.

'It is Mrs Harper, isn't it?'

Bobbie stared at Beatrice's former secretary and nodded again. 'Of course. Who else could it possibly be?'

'I should never have told you, should I, dear? About her and your mother. But really, dear,' Mrs Saxby took out a handkerchief and wiped her eyes, first one and then the other, 'I had to, dear, really I did, for it was so hard on you, always thinking that you had to kowtow to her, that she was your real guardian when she was no such thing but merely your father's ex-mistress. But don't think badly of your poor father, only of Mrs Harper, for any young man would have had his head turned by such a glamorous creature as she was. All furs and French scent, and lace insets in her underwear deeper than on a vicar's surplice. So no blame to him. These women, women like Mrs Harper, they must have their own way, dear, it is just a fact. And now she is to have it again, it seems. I can see that, after all these years, no-one better, believe me.'

At this point Mrs Saxby gave way completely,

and tears streamed down her face, and her own handkerchief was not enough to stem them, so Bobbie had to go quickly for one of her own, not a fine affair at all, left over from her childhood at the sanatorium, only made of cotton, with a rather shaming bunny rabbit embroidered in the corner.

'We must think clearly and coldly,' she told Mrs Saxby when the poor lady had finally stopped crying, and Bobbie had handed her a cup of strong tea, not at all the sort of tea that she liked but probably more the thing when it came to pulling them both together.

'We have no defence against Mrs Harper.' The ex-secretary's voice was suddenly as factual as it must have been when reading out to her old employer the day's projected engagements. 'She knows everyone from the Prime Minister to the bootboy at the Ritz. There is no-one she does not know, no-one she will not be prepared to lobby, no stone she will leave unturned until she has revenged herself on me, and the Major. By putting the Major behind bars on these ridiculous smuggling charges, she will be, more than likely, satisfied. At least we must hope so.'

Bobbie walked about the room a bit, sipping her tea, and then coming back and standing in front of Mrs Saxby, as if the sight of the lady who had, in former days, driven her quite dotty in the Sheds, would now bring about a sudden burst of inspiration.

But of course it did not, for the truth was, and it

was the truth, Beatrice *did* know everyone. And those whom she did not know she could pay, and those whom she could not pay would do what she wished anyway. There was no way around someone like Beatrice. There was no-one big enough or grand enough in spirit anyway, with enough courage to stand up to her. Somehow or other, and it was awful to think how, Beatrice had managed to find out that while restoring the garden during that idyllic summer, Major Saxby had flouted the currency regulations and infringed some other footling customs and excise law. It was pretty good detective work, in a footling sort of way, for, after all, the climate of the times being what it was, any infringement of the regulations meant that you were a cad, and there was nothing to be done.

'Of course it's not true. The Major never flouted the currency laws. How could he? But if he accepted some bottle of gin or something that Mrs Duddy passed on, well, how would he have *known* that it was smuggled? Of course he wouldn't, no-one would have. It was not possible to know. He some-times did use bricks and things that came in via the back door, but then everyone did. The building regulations were so complicated and those councils so narrow in their attitudes.'

'It was Mrs Duddy, was it, who – you know – told on him?' As soon as she finished speaking Bobbie thought dully it was a stupid thing to say. *Told on him.* It was the sort of thing she and Teddy would have said to Miranda in the old days at

Mellaston. Such a childish way of putting things.

'What could Mrs Duddy do against such a person as Mrs Harper?' asked Mrs Saxby, her voice of a sudden sounding harsh and bitter. 'She is Mrs Harper's tenant, for goodness' sake. What on earth could a poor widow, struggling to bring up a family and feed everyone by hook or by crook, do against her? Nothing. There was nothing she *could* do. Except confess, as it were, and hope that the whole thing would go away and she would be allowed to go on living at the farm. You can't blame Mrs *Duddy*.'

'No.' Bobbie stared at her feet. It was true. She could not blame Mrs Duddy, but she could feel like throwing a vase at her, if only to relieve her own feelings of frustration. 'Oh, for goodness' sake, this is ridiculous. There must be someone we can turn to for help, surely?'

'The Major is being very brave, dear. Really he is. He knows he does not stand a chance against her, and he is just trying to work out how many months he will be sent down for.'

'He's not going to go anywhere, not down, not nowhere. We absolutely won't have it. What we're going to do is think of a way to force Mrs Harper to make the customs people drop the whole thing. There must be a way. There's always a way.'

'She's a hard and horrible woman, and hard and horrible women do not go away, Bobbie, I'm sorry to tell you. They do not even fade away, dear. They live to make havoc of everyone's lives for ever and ever, amen.'

Mrs Saxby, despite the strength of the tea, started to cry again as Bobbie frowned. She could see only one way out, and that was for her to go and beg Beatrice to make whoever had trumped these charges up drop them, at once.

'The Major has been through so much, Burma, the war, everything. And now here he is in the October of his days, happy and at peace, and he has to go and face prison all because of me. He says it will be nothing after the railway, but I have heard dreadful things about men's prisons. He is not the right class for prison in England, dear, really he isn't.'

Bobbie stared at the carpet, trying to imagine the Major in prisoner's garb calling all the warders 'old bean' and generally being the gentleman that he was, and she suddenly felt like bursting into tears and at the same time laughing too. She remembered how good he was at forgiving his old enemies, and how he used to tell her and Julian off for not having more belief in humanity. The memory made her heart swell with indignation, and of a sudden she wanted to take a gun and shoot Beatrice who was just playing about with people's lives for the fun of it. For her own gratification and to assuage some petty feelings she nurtured about her past she was pulling the wings of people who had only just managed to learn to fly again after the horrors of the war.

'Leave it to me.'

'What's that, dear?'

'I said leave it to me. I am determined that the Major will never be taken to court. We will make them drop these charges, we will fight it all, we must do. He deserves his little bit of happiness, enough to make a sailor three pairs of trousers, as a matter of fact.' Bobbie patted Mrs Saxby briskly on the shoulder. 'You are not to worry about another thing. Tell the Major that I have friends at Court, and that I will speak to the King if necessary. We will find a way. You would be surprised at how many people I have met in the last months. Influential people, people who will be quite prepared to help the Major. It will all be all right. Tell him that from me. Just give me a few days, a week or so, and it will all go away, and don't you yourself, or the Major, give it another thought. Not even a tiny one, because it is not something that people like you should be bothered about. Besides, I hired the Major, in place of Mrs Harper, if you remember. So, really, it should be *me* who is put up on the charges. In fact I shall make sure it is me that they charge, if they do. So, away with dull care . . .'

'What, dear? What was that you said, that last bit?'

'Nothing. I was just being foolish. Just believe me. I will take care of everything, and if you don't mind I will keep the letter.'

Bobbie shut the sitting room door behind the now smiling Mrs Saxby, and went back to her new armchair, into which she had no hesitation in sinking.

It was all too awful, and the truth was that she had no more hope of being able to defend the Saxbys from Mrs Beatrice Harper than she had of forcing the Pope to get married.

If only Julian were there, if only he had not gone off, disappeared into the wide blue yonder, she could have gone to him and they could have done something together. Made some plan. But she had no-one. No-one who had really known them at that time, except the landlord of the pub in the village, and that too was owned by Beatrice.

'Oh God.'

Bobbie put her head in her hands and felt how hot her face had become. Her head was throbbing. She could see no way out, and in a way it was all her fault. If only she had not used the information that the poor woman had given her about her parents. She should never have faced Beatrice down with it, it was just a fact. She should have simply told her to go jump, and that would have been that. She was not her real guardian, anyway. But as Teddy always said, that was the trouble with Bobbie.

'You're so aggressive, that's your trouble, Bobbie.' He had often said it. 'It's because you were so ill as a child, I think. And being put with the Dingwalls who didn't understand you didn't help either. Now stand still and let me take the picture without you coming out with some statement liable to inflame.'

'I'm only ever aggressive with you,' was Bobbie's

479

statutory retort. But it was not true, as it happened. She was aggressive with a lot of people besides Teddy. She had been aggressive with Beatrice that day. She had said the *extra thing* that had brought about the Major's downfall. The Major of all people, someone, like the nurses in the sanatorium, who had been more kind to her than anyone, except the aunts.

She picked up the telephone beside her. It was quite new, and in keeping with her equally new status as a fashionable person, it was really rather stylish.

'Teddy?'

At the other end Teddy's heart fairly zipped about in his chest and started to resound in his ears at the sound of her voice. 'Bobbie?'

'I am afraid so.'

'Your usual dry self, so that is all right.'

'No time for jokes, Teddy. I am in such trouble. At least I am not in trouble, but I have got someone else into trouble. Two other people, Teddy, and it is *all* my fault.'

'Don't tell me, the Holy Bible Company is suing you because the designer has sold more copies of the skirt I put you in than they have of their Bible? Dick has painted a nude of you and been arrested for obscenity? Um. Let's see. The Major has left Mrs Saxby because he's in love with you?'

'No, Teddy. This is serious.'

'And that wouldn't be?'

Bobbie was sure that she could hear Teddy eating

his usual late breakfast of a baked bean and bacon sandwich at the other end.

'No, Teddy, this is *très, très* serious. My sort-of guardian, that Mrs Harper person, you know, the one who paid for me to be in the sanatorium, you know, I told you about her?'

'I think it was an asylum and they didn't tell you, you know that?'

'Teddy, please. She's had someone throw the book at the Major.'

'Not the Holy Book?' Teddy started to laugh. 'Not even your Mrs Harper could authorize that, surely?'

'No, Teddy, not the Holy Book. The Customs and Excise one. You know when we were in Sussex, by the sea, and we were doing the garden all that summer? Well, it seems that the Major, without realizing it of course, used to accept gin and other things, sometimes bricks for the garden, oh, I don't know – just things that were in short supply, or rationed, or had been smuggled from France, although of course he did not know about it. Well, they all did. We all did. Julian used to—'

'Ah yes, the sacred man in your past – the great *Julian*.'

'Julian used to laugh about it. We both used to tease the Major that he was breaking the law – but it was nothing. Just some bricks we needed to repair walls, and everyone bought gin from under the counter at the pub, and wine from Mrs Duddy at the farm, but now, guess what, because I'm living with the Saxbys she's got someone to charge him with smuggling and those sorts of things.'

'You must be joking.'

'I wish I was.'

'I will be round in the next two hours, just as soon as I have thrown out the dancing girls and put on a clean shirt.'

Miranda stared across the newly laid café table at Dick. 'You think Teddy is in love with *Bobbie*?'

'Yes, I do. In fact, I am convinced of it.'

Without realizing it Miranda found her hands rubbing themselves over and over on her checked apron. As soon as she saw Dick staring at them she stopped, but not before he had observed her reaction.

'And, er, I mean, do you think Bobbie is in love with *Teddy*?'

'She might be. She might be, and not know it, yet. That sometimes happens, you know. Sometimes a person has fallen in love but the penny hasn't dropped,' Dick finished, wistfully.

'I don't think so.' Miranda's mouth set in a really firm line as she thought about it. 'Bobbie's always had this sort of crush thing about Julian – this young man she knew in Sussex before she came to London. She still talks about him sometimes. I think you will find that he is who she is thinking about more than anyone, she will be thinking about "Julian".'

482

'Don't you like the idea of Bobbie and Teddy? Big Sis not approve?'

'It's none of my business,' Miranda snapped. 'Anyway, he's not really my brother, he's my wartime *adopted* brother.'

'He's your brother, dearest girl, really he is.'

Miranda stared at Dick. 'How do you mean?'

'Because that's how he thinks about you, that's how he talks about you. I know, believe me. You are as much his sister as anyone could ever be. Even if you had shared the same parents you could not be closer, and that's a wonderful thing. Not everything that came out of the war was bad, you know.'

Miranda opened her mouth to say that they were not really close, and that she and Teddy were as different as they could possibly be, and then shut it again. It was true. All the time that they had been back at Mellaston that was what had occurred to her, over and over again, although she had not wanted to admit it. She had tried to block out the thought, but it would not go away – Teddy and she were like brother and sister, more like brother and sister than maybe any brother and sister could ever be, and while she had thought that now they were grown up she loved him in a quite different way, it was not true, and going back to Mellaston had proved it to her. She could no longer think of Teddy as anything except a brother, all the rest was just a kind of ridiculous fantasy. She had chosen Teddy, the pathetic little boy with the half-torn label, standing wetting himself with fear in the orphans' section of the school, to be her much longed for younger brother, and although they had spent years apart that was what he still was, in essence, her much longed for younger brother. She could not love him as a man, and to think that she could, or might, was perfectly ridiculous.

Miranda looked up at Dick. 'Yes, you're right. I am Teddy's sister, and he is my brother, even though we're not related. That is how we are, and always will be. It is a fact.'

Dick lit a cigarette and blew the smoke out slowly. 'Good,' he said. 'So now that we've got that cleared up, and since there are no customers to speak of, shall we go along to the Odeon cinema and see the complete programme, including the intermission, and up to and not forgetting the cartoons?'

For the first time since they had worked alone together, starting the café and becoming not just close friends, but partners, as they walked along, Miranda slipped her arm through Dick's. Of course he pretended not to notice. Nor did he look anxiously down at her as if to reassure himself that she was really there. Rather they walked along in that contented silence that is brought about by a growing intimacy, leaving the café locked up behind them, and a great deal else besides.

Chapter Fifteen

How Bobbie and he laid their plan Teddy would never know, nor indeed would he care to remember. The fact was that they made the plan together, and as crazy conspirators always do they both thought that it would be easy to accomplish, was perfectly brilliant in conception, and would leave them unscarred and carefree.

Teddy knew that Bobbie did not love him, at least not at that point. In fact he would always know and accept that at that moment in her life she definitely was not in love with him. So there was no question, he knew that in order to win her he had to do something very special and very brave, and since there were no longer any Nazis to shoot down, or dragons to slay, and since the far flung Empire no longer wanted to be conquered, it seemed that the only way he could try to win her was to seduce Beatrice instead.

'Oh God, oh God, do you think it will work, me taking her to bed?'

He had actually said that, he had actually uttered

those words, and more than once, to Bobbie.

What he had not said, what he had not dared to tell her, was that he was not just not very experienced when it came to women, he was not experienced at all. He had just been, finally, up to then, well – just too busy.

Dick was older, and he was experienced, Teddy knew that. But he could hardly ask Dick since Dick was in love with Teddy's sister, and might tell her. And Miranda would, in the way that women do, immediately go round to Bobbie and tell *her*, and he would end up by being the laughing stock of everyone they knew. Or worse; if there was a worse. Out of all four of them he, Teddy, the great bighead, the Mr Toad of Aubrey Close, would be discovered to be wanting in an area where, it had to be faced, young men never, ever want to be found wanting, or worse ignorant, namely, in the bedroom.

From the moment that he and Bobbie had finally decided that it was the only possible way, since Beatrice Harper's two acknowledged weaknesses were herself and sex, Teddy had not hired a model, nor passed a beautiful woman or a pretty girl in the street, without wanting to stop her and beg her to help him gain experience of some kind, somewhere, so that he would not find himself hopelessly at sea with the beautiful Mrs Harper.

The trouble was that there was not much time, certainly not enough for a whole, big relationship. Not the kind of time that was needed to gain the sort of experience that would make Beatrice

Harper's body sing with delight at Teddy's prowess in the bedroom.

Unsurprisingly, since agreeing to accept his strange mission Teddy had found that he could neither eat nor sleep. He kept wondering why he had agreed to anything so foolish. Inevitably even he had to come to the sad conclusion that it was purely and simply so that he could look bigger in Bobbie's eyes. He loved Bobbie. More than anyone in the world he now knew that he loved spiky, droll Bobbie, with her skinny figure and her inevitable way of putting him down at every turn. Meeting her again on the shoot at the bombed-out conservatory, it had been as if he was meeting one of his oldest friends, and one of his newest. Compared to Miranda then, Bobbie had seemed so confident, so proud, so dismissive of him. Not at all like other girls or women, who, because Teddy was Teddy, always behaved as if they were determined to make themselves available to him, something which always seemed to have quite the opposite effect on him. He had always walked away, or been too busy for them. Making love had been something Teddy had told himself he would make time for very soon, after this shoot, or the next.

But then he had met Bobbie, and boom – that had been that. There was no longer any time that he truly wanted to spend with anyone else; every other girl or woman seemed dull beside her, beside Bobbie.

'Oh God, oh God!'

The thought of this Harper woman even haunted his dreams, nightmares where women turned into monsters with heads of eagles and bodies that evaporated the moment he went to touch them. Or he would find himself tearing down a black tunnel towards some light or other with some unknown figure pursuing him, until, at last, he woke up to the real world, and what to Teddy was rapidly becoming a worse place to be even than his dreams.

And yet it was easy enough to be introduced to her. Teddy might, in his agonized mind, have potential problems looming as far as his prowess as a lover was concerned, but being a photographer of beautiful women he had none in the social area. He only had to pick up the phone and make sure that some friend of a friend knew that Teddy Mowbray was yearning to photograph the beautiful, famous, wealthy Beatrice Harper, and all doors would open immediately to him. That part at least of the plan, his and Bobbie's plan, was easy.

He saw it all before it happened.

He knew that when he was ushered into the Grosvenor Square apartment, or taken down to the Sussex house, there would be the sound of servants running to and fro doing whatever servants seemed to have to do a great deal of within the hearing of the very rich. And seeing and hearing them hurrying about Teddy would know that his luck was in, that his whole career was going to take off, because that was the effect that being taken up by one rich woman could have on the life of one young man.

And yet, what would happen to him? What would happen to his soul, if he still had one? That was what worried Teddy. What about his integrity?

'Don't be silly, Teddy. You haven't got any integrity, at least not to speak of.'

That was what Bobbie had said as soon as he had mentioned it, hoping against hope, naturally, that Bobbie would come to the firm conclusion that now she had come to think about it, and seeing it from his point of view, to seduce Beatrice would be to endanger his soul.

'I have some integrity, Bobbie, really I do. As a matter of fact—'

'I tell you what. If you find your integrity does not allow you to get your wicked way with Beatrice, if you find you simply can't, well, we'll just have to think of something else. But I don't see how you can get her to get the *authorities* to drop the charges, I really don't, unless she is mad for you, and you're – you know, holding out, as it were.'

Bobbie was always very vague when she came to the logistics of their plan. Teddy had already noted this with some trepidation. He remembered it, suddenly, as he faced Beatrice Harper, standing in the very same place where, although he could not know it, Bobbie had stood some time before, facing her too, but for very different reasons.

What he had not counted on was her inestimable beauty. He had not expected to look across the room at her and have his breath taken away by a middle-aged woman.

For the truth was that hateful though she might be Beatrice Harper was still beautiful, and once he stood opposite her Teddy was left behind and the photographer took over, and he knew at once that he had to snap her. She was sensational. Such cheekbones. Such a marvellous head of hair, black, thick and sleek, and above all there were her grey eyes – so cold, so somehow unmoving, watching, always watching – for someone to deceive her, for someone not to pay her homage, for someone not to want to do as she wished.

'Mr Mowbray.'

Her voice was strangely deep for a woman, and terribly attractive. As soon as she had finished saying 'Mr Mowbray' Teddy knew himself to be in love with her already. He had dreaded this moment so much, and yet now he was here in his best suit, with his best shirt, his most charming smile, Teddy's poise deserted him, and he wanted neither to run forward nor to run back, but to stay quite still, staring at her across the thick, rich carpet that lay between them.

'Mr Mowbray?'

She smiled as she repeated his name as if to wake him up from some sleep into which she could see he had fallen, and her smile was the smile of a goddess, and he saw that she knew he had fallen for her, there and then, that instead of fearing her, he was adoring her.

'Mrs Harper. It was so kind of you to see me. I am so glad that you are here – I mean I am so glad to be here. And it is very kind of you. To see me. That is.'

'Mr Mowbray, why don't you sit down and I will ring for drinks for both of us? Would you like a glass of champagne? Would you like that? I know I would.'

As she rang the bell to the side of her desk she gave a rippling throaty little laugh that made the necklace of minute sapphires and diamonds at her throat seem to move in a shared moment of enjoyment, and sent Teddy's blood racing round and round his body more like a lasso around a cowboy's head than a human pulse.

'You are so beautiful.'

It was his voice saying it, no-one else's, and he knew that he should not have said it, not just like that, as if he was some kind of schoolboy. It was so unsophisticated to blurt out something like that. He should have waited at least five minutes before he told her what she already knew.

But it didn't seem to matter, thank goodness. Not at all. It didn't seem to matter one whit. She sat down opposite him and continued as if he had not blurted out his admiration.

'I gather you would like to photograph me, is that right?'

Teddy nodded.

'Let us talk about it, after you have drunk your champagne, and *I* have drunk my champagne. We will talk about it, and then perhaps you can come

491

back tomorrow and we can talk about it some more. I have to go out to the ballet in half an hour, but that does not mean we can not at least discuss some ideas.'

'No, of course not.'

'How would you like to snap me?'

She looked so interested in him. He breathed in, and then out, and then taking a sip of champagne promptly choked on it and she immediately went to him, laughing, and patted him on the back.

'Thank you.'

It was her almost roguish use of the word 'snap' that had done it. He knew that she had said 'snap' because it was up to the minute and almost risqué in its casualness, most particularly in the great, grand surroundings of her Grosvenor Square house. The word snapped and whizzed around the room, bouncing off the silk-covered walls, and nestling behind the plumped-up cushions on the great grand sofas with their golden colours flowing and glowing in the growing twilight. She wanted to be snapped by Teddy. He half closed his eyes. He would snap her all right. He would snap her until *she* snapped.

'I would like to see you in a vast ballroom lit only by candles, in a gold dress which shone under the warmth of the candlelight, and wearing what would look like live snakes in your long black hair.'

She considered this notion quite quietly for a moment, and then, having taken a sip of her champagne, she nodded.

492

'I have done something like that before,' she said, at last. 'Although not with snakes.'

He did not know from her expression whether she was teasing him or being serious, so he began again.

'I would like to photograph you in a sari, sitting on a great mound of cushions, with bare feet, and Nubian slaves kneeling before you holding up a bowl of fruit.'

'Now that I have *not* done, yet, at least I don't think I have. No, I haven't, I really have not.'

Teddy had no idea what Nubian slaves would look like, but he counted on the fact that he could rush to the library and find out long before he himself was found out.

'Continue, do. Your ideas are getting more and more interesting.'

'I would like to stand you by the sea with the waves coming up to your bare feet, in a white towelling dressing gown, your hair quite loose, blowing in the breeze, the clouds above you scudding by, a shell necklace around your long neck, a goddess stepped out of the waves to give us a new world.'

'Such a pity I have sold my beach house,' she murmured. 'But do go on.'

'I would like to photograph you in a great black velvet opera cloak with a great gold clasp, wearing nothing at all underneath.'

'That would be, artistically speaking of course, that would be very much to my taste—'

493

She was much nearer to him now, and her scent was quite exquisite. He knew that women like Beatrice had their own scents mixed for them, that not to do so would be considered vulgar, and that they disdained to wear other people's. Now that she was so close, coming to sit beside him, Teddy was glad he knew this, because it meant that there was some excuse for his feeling so dizzy and lightheaded.

He drained his glass of champagne, far too quickly. She drained hers, at a leisurely pace. She filled both their glasses up again, and in seconds was back beside him, making him once more feel dizzy and faint.

'Now, where were we?'

'I was putting you in a great black cloak—'

'That is right, you were, weren't you? You were putting me into a great velvet opera cloak. I have just the thing, as a matter of fact. I was going to wear it this evening. For the Wagner, or is it Mozart? But instead, I am thinking we could both go upstairs together and I could try it on for you, and it would be deliciously soft against my skin, wouldn't it?'

'I suppose so.'

Teddy said this against her soft lips and suddenly it was behind him, this thing that he had always had about not wanting to take a woman to bed, not wanting to make love with someone until the perfect moment, because suddenly he knew that this was the perfect moment, and they were both running up some stairs, and through doors, and

494

their clothes were not being taken off but mutually peeled off, and they were kissing and touching each other in places where he had only ever dreamed of touching and kissing a woman, until finally they were on what he imagined, indeed devoutly hoped, was her bed, a great gold-caparisoned affair with feathered eiderdowns and bolsters propping up countless pillows, and Teddy was entering the exquisite kingdom of love, and thinking that he surely would die from the pleasure of it.

Bobbie was standing by the window, for no reason that she could name feeling rather as she had done when she was a small child in hospital waiting for some pronouncement from a specialist or doctor.

'Well?'

Teddy stared at her, and then frowned. 'What?'

'Well, I mean, did you do it?'

Teddy went such a colour that Bobbie knew at once what the answer to her question was, and then, which was ridiculous, she too went scarlet, and they both stared at each other, feeling idiotic, no longer friends or conspirators, just heartily embarrassed by and with each other.

'Oh, for goodness' sake, let's just get on without telling each other any beastly details.'

'Yes, well, she is actually leaving England, pretty soon, I gather.' Teddy stared at Bobbie. How could he tell her that he thought he was now passionately in love not with Bobbie, but with Bobbie's hated guardian. How could he tell her that?

The truth was that he could not, and would not. But then, seeing her looking at him in that sudden sharp way that Bobbie sometimes had, he realized that she had arrived at something like the right conclusion. He did not *have* to tell her. She had already guessed.

'Oh, Teddy!'

'I know, I know. I didn't mean to, but she is so beautiful, you know. And, and, she has a way of being – I mean she really *listens* to me, really, really listens. She is interested in everything I do and everything I say, and that is such a change.'

Bobbie snorted lightly, knowing that this was an overt criticism of Miranda and herself. 'All older women *listen* to young men, Teddy.' She managed to look both impatient and worried. As if Teddy had made himself ill, as if he was the patient and she was trying to decide which doctor to take him to, which remedy might cure him. 'That's their *trick*, that's what older women *do* with younger men. They always listen to them, to take their minds off what they really want from them.'

'Which is?'

'Their bodies, Teddy. She just wants your body.'

'So what?' Teddy suddenly kicked the side of one of Bobbie's new chairs, which made him look quite the old Teddy, spoilt and childish, which was sort of reassuring and not reassuring at all, because it meant that he was still so easily gulled.

'Teddy.' Bobbie walked across to him and took one of his hands. 'Teddy, you have forgotten the

496

real reason why you decided on this – why we *both* decided on your doing this. It was to rescue the Major and Mrs Saxby, make sure that the Major is not had up on these stupid charge things about bricks and gin, and heaven only knows what. That is why you went to photograph Beatrice and seduce her and all that. You weren't meant to become besotted about her, Teddy, you were just there like – you know, like a wartime sort of spy, that sort of thing.'

'Look, you won't understand this, Bobbie. But she listened to me. She really listens, she's interested in my talent. I think she really loves me, actually,' he added dreamily.

Bobbie felt a sharp sensation and knew at once that it was jealousy – and over Teddy of all people.

'She's no more interested in your talent than Mrs Dingwall. She's interested in your bo-*dee*. You know, the bits of you that are young and vigorous. Didn't you know that was the older woman's way? To listen to young men and assume soupy expressions, and then lure them into beautiful love-making? That's all Beatrice wants, you to make love to her, because you're young and stupid and trying to make your way, and she knows she can help you and in return she can enjoy your body.'

'She has helped me already with my work. She has talked to *Vogue*. She's thrilled with my photographs. I took her in a marvellously beautiful black velvet cloak with a great brass clasp—'

'Brass is a very suitable material to go with Beatrice.'

'Don't be so utterly cynical, Bobbie! I am besotted with her. I really am, I am wild about her. I . . .' Teddy was just about to say that he loved Beatrice but he stopped, frowning momentarily. 'I – er . . .'

Bobbie sighed and frowned back at him. 'What, Teddy?'

'I – er – I think she's beautiful.'

'I can't believe you are saying these things after all I have told you about how appalling this woman is, how she seduced my father, and oh, what's the use?' She turned away.

'You're right, Bobbie. What is the use? There is no use when it comes to love, it's so utterly, utterly other, so amazing. It makes everything in life brighter and more radiant, the paint on the walls of a room, the colour of the trees outside the window. Everything becomes brighter and more brilliant when you are in love, believe me. You don't really know, but it does.'

'As a matter of fact – no, well, what's the use.'

There was a long silence after that during which Bobbie managed to look fed up and furious and sad at the same time, which made Teddy feel sad and furious and fed up too, but neither of them could think of a thing to say to each other. Bobbie thought she might be bleeding inside, she hurt so much, because she knew what Teddy did not. She had truly loved Julian, but Teddy would not understand because Teddy was in *physical* love.

'Do you want to see the snaps I took of her?'

'Oh, all right.'

Teddy brought out the contact sheets and spread them out on Bobbie's brand new pointy-legged coffee table, and almost dutifully handed Bobbie a magnifying glass. 'I've circled the ones I think are pretty good.'

'Yes, I can see you have.'

With a great effort of will Bobbie stared through the magnifying glass at the pictures in front of her. They were, she realized, really quite good. Once she had detached herself from the fact that it was the hated Queen of Baileys Court, the cold-eyed woman of many of her nightmares, who was the subject of the photographs, even Bobbie could see just how good they were.

In fact they were not just good, they were brilliant.

'Well, Teddy, I have to say, they are marvellous, they really are. You've somehow managed to make her look majestic. And her hair – that black hair with that black cloak. These photographs are really good. They are your best, I think.'

They had always had this professional thing, that when they worked together, they were honest and straight. The other bit of them could be as crooked and dangerous as it liked – the relationship bit – but the professional bit was always straight, and now Teddy was grateful for it, because he knew that Bobbie always told the truth. He also knew that telling the truth about these particular pictures was very difficult for her.

'I wanted to snap her by the sea, but it wasn't possible. So many beaches are not back to what they should be still, and the bit of beach that she used to own, apparently, in Sussex, where you were, she's sold that.'

'She's sold Baileys Court?'

'Yes, to some rich family who are going to restore it all. She never liked it, she said, which was why she agreed to drop the charges, or rather made the local authorities drop the charges against the Major and his wife. She was fed up with the whole Sussex bit anyway, and really, as she said, who cares what the wretched Major did, or you for that matter.'

'Well, I must say, that is Beatrice Harper all over. I mean to say, what price—'

Bobbie had continued talking for a few more seconds before she realized that the Saxbys were going to be all right after all. The Major was not going to have to go to prison with a lot of men who would not understand his calling them 'old bean', and their life would go back to being normal and nice and they could resume their roles as a couple of old Chelsea-ites pottering down the King's Road in their funny clothes and not caring too much how many old beans, or any other kind of bean for that matter, made five.

'Oh, Teddy, you are such an *idiot*! Why didn't you tell me they were going to drop the charges?' Bobbie stopped suddenly, and her eyes narrowed. 'Hang on. No, tell me. No. Did you get it in writing?'

'Better than writing. I saw her telephone to the appropriate people. It only took seven telephone calls and that was that. She was very good at it, really, I mean the telephone calls and influencing people, and all that, and she was fine about knowing that you wanted it, and so on. It just took a few telephone calls and it was all done, really.'

He stopped, remembering how Beatrice had stood there in her sumptuous bedroom in front of Teddy, looking so alluring with hardly a stitch on, and yet managing to laugh and saying, 'You little devil, so that is why you came here to make love to me, is it? So that I would let the Saxbys out of their cage, to fly free? Well, very well, I will do as you wish, but on one condition only – that you repay me, in every way, every day, for my great compassion and sweetness – agreed?'

Of course Teddy had willingly agreed, and of course he had repaid Beatrice in the way that she understood and enjoyed most, but he could not tell Bobbie that, and certainly not at that moment, not when she was so thrilled about the Saxbys.

Once Bobbie had finished celebrating with the Saxbys, she had actually woken up the next day not with just a colossal headache, but with that particular feeling of dull, gloomy cloudiness that comes from the start of a cold, or too much to drink the night before, because she now knew that she had not only lost Teddy, she had lost Baileys Court, and with it Julian.

'You're looking rather down in the mouth, Bobbie dear.' Mrs Saxby smiled.

'I am not just looking it, Mrs Saxby, I am down in the mouth. Teddy told me yesterday that Baileys Court has been sold, so that means we will never be able to go there again. Not that I particularly wanted to go back, but in another way I did really want to, you know. I mean I never thought Mrs Harper would sell it, just like that.'

Mrs Saxby shuddered. 'You are quite alone in wanting to go back, Roberta, I am afraid, for I am sure neither the Major nor I ever, ever want to return to that place, nor see anyone at Baileys Green or the Court again.'

Bobbie nodded. She could see Mrs Saxby's point, and of course it was true. None of them *should* want to go back to Baileys Court, not with the kind of understandable but nevertheless undeniable treachery that had occurred. Mrs Duddy, the landlord, everyone had finally given in to Beatrice Harper and her power, Beatrice and her money. And yet, Bobbie still could not help longing to return, in some secret way, somehow thinking that everything would be just as it had been.

Of course she realized that her particular longing at that moment was not based on anything except a resentment of Teddy. The moment Teddy had said that Bobbie would never understand *love* she had known that he was wrong. It was not true. She *had* understood love, that summer – great love – with Julian. And more than that, she had been, for once in her life, blissfully happy too.

Her summer with Julian had made her happier than at any other time in her life. They had been soulmates. She had hoped to forget him, but the fact was that she had been quite unable to do so, simply and solely because no-one had come along to take his place. Teddy could never do that, not now anyway. He was besotted with Beatrice, and Bobbie was quite sure that she could not love someone who loved Beatrice. It was not possible. She had loved Julian, her 'wretched boy'.

It was as a result of her honesty about this that Bobbie at once set about planning how she could visit Baileys Court again. It was winter now, and there would be no trees in leaf, but she could see the garden, and the walls that she and Julian and the Major had built. She could too, for once, be on her own with her memories, without Teddy to interrupt and trample about talking, talking, talking.

For the truth was that after all the guilt she had suffered over the Saxbys, over making Teddy seduce Beatrice, only to find that it had been really more than a pleasure for him to do so, she felt foolish, and in some ways put upon, as if *she* had been used, and not Beatrice. She had so hoped that Teddy would come back revolted by what he had done with Beatrice, but far from it; he had, if anything, come back elated to the point of bliss. Which was good from his point of view, she supposed, over and over again, but whether it was reasonable or not to feel as she did, the realization that Teddy was in bliss made Bobbie wish most heartily that she could get away from everyone and just be on her own.

It was difficult to find out who exactly had bought the house from Beatrice, but since, it seemed, it had changed hands some months before, Bobbie decided to take the train to Baileys Green and put up at the Dog and Duck, because, as she well knew, if you ever needed to find out anything in England all you had to do was visit the local pub, buy yourself a drink, sit on a bar stool, and soon, without any problem, whatever was new in the neighbourhood would come to light.

Just taking the journey down to Sussex, seeing the names of the stations – Crawley, Turners Green, Three Bridges, all those dear familiar stops – was like being pulled nearer and nearer to where Bobbie truly wished to be. She really, now, only wanted to be in Sussex, on her own, by the sea. To sit listening to the tide coming up the beach, or receding down it; even the memory of the sound of the waves crashing on the pebbled shore during a storm seemed to be drawing her back to her past. Drawing her away from being the Quaker Girl, and temporary fame, away from Teddy and his ego, his camera and his ambitions, most of all from his restless mad love for Beatrice.

Away from Miranda and Dick who were, nowadays, anyway only interested in each other. At that moment in her life, Bobbie knew absolutely that she just wanted to be on her own, quite quiet, with nothing to do but think about Julian, and how they had been together, to remember how idyllic that summer had been, and how the happiness had washed over them both, in just the same way that the waves sometimes washed over the Sheds.

The Dog and Duck was unchanged from the outside. Bobbie stared up at it as the station taxi deposited her outside its mild English exterior. As always, the village shop was shut, despite its being well past the time when a shop should be open. And as always the notice on the door declared that it was shut even for the sale of Bovril.

She was dreading seeing the landlord again, knowing that he would know that she knew all about the nearly terrible scandal concerning the Major. But, when she dragged her suitcase into the pub doorway, and banged the brass bell on the small inside desk, and he appeared, as soon as she saw him it became quite clear that it was not the same man.

Bobbie could hardly stop herself from looking relieved. It was partly that she did not have to feel embarrassed for the other man, knowing his treachery as regarded the Major, but it was also relief that she had, after what now seemed a long journey, arrived. She realized that on the journey down she had almost dreaded reaching Baileys Green, that she had wondered, over and over, if it would still be there, or if it would be so changed that she would not know it, or would not want to stay.

Having signed the book, and taken a key, Bobbie followed the landlord down a newly lino-ed corridor to a back room with its own, brand new bathroom.

The new host of the Dog and Duck was obviously very proud of both the bedroom and the bathroom, and having pointed Bobbie towards the equally new back luncheon room, which was still open for sandwiches, he brought back her suitcase, told her to let him know if she needed anything further, and left.

Bobbie sat down suddenly on the bed. What on earth was she doing in the Dog and Duck on her own? As she listened to the hushed sounds of a village pub, suppressed laughter from somewhere in the kitchens at the back, a bird singing outside her window, and the sound of a stream rushing, gushing, full of winter rain, down the bottom of the short garden with its single bench and its new swing, she wondered at finding herself in such a situation, back at Baileys Green, alone, staring at the new patterned carpet, listening for something of interest to happen, and all the time knowing that nothing would, until opening time. There was no real reason for anything to happen until then.

Finally she lay down full length on the bed, and fell asleep. It was the best thing that she could think of doing, but also there was nothing else for her to do. Not until, and unless, she could find out who now owned Baileys Court, and whether or not they, he or she, would allow her to see round it again.

*   *   *

In the bar that night there were a great many jokes being made around the village policeman.

"Is 'andcuffs,' one of the locals told Bobbie, ''is 'andcuffs do up 'is garden gate. 'E 'as so little use for them, that's all they're really 'andy for, doing up 'is garden gate.'

The policeman, a large red-faced man of great height, laughed heartily, and wiped his handlebar moustache against the back of his hand. Despite his purposeful off duty uniform of a fisherman's sweater and corduroy slacks, nothing could disguise the fact that he was indeed the village copper, because the authority of his policeman's uniform seemed to have seeped through his skin into his personality, so that with or without it it was evident to everyone, even in his corduroys, that they could still look to him for protection.

'I always know the bad ones, you know that?' he told Bobbie once they had struck up a conversation. 'And do you know why I always know the bad ones? Because I was at school with them, that's why. They don't change. Small people grow into big people, and bad small people grow into bad big people. That is the long and the short of it.' He laughed. 'Handcuffs. Who needs handcuffs when you can put their heads under your arms and march 'em off to the station without the bother? That is the good thing about the English police. We stay in our own villages, and so we know the rotten apples. We don't need to be told who to look out for, we know.

507

We've come up against them in the school playground.'

'Would you like another pint?' Bobbie pointed to
his glass. The policeman nodded.

'Very well, miss, even though it don't seem quite
right, somehow, taking a drink off a young lady.'
There was a small silence before he added, lowering
his voice, 'Are you a journalist, miss?'

Bobbie shook her head, and then, having ordered
fresh drinks for them both, she asked, 'Why? Why
would you think I was a journalist?'

The policeman kept his voice at the same level.
'Because it's usually only journalists from London,
we find, down here, who pay for men's drinks. You
know, young women like that, professional young
women.'

'Well, I am not a journalist, but you're right, I do
want to know about something. And since you
have always lived in Baileys Green, and know
everyone – well, I wondered if you knew who
might have bought Baileys Court. You *know* Baileys
Court, of course? It's been sold, apparently, so I
wondered if you could tell me who owns it now.'

'Certainly, miss.' He nodded towards a group of
people by the window. 'It's been bought by some
people by the name of Hartwell. Nice family. Only
young, you know. Want to bring up their children in
the fresh air. That's them over there, behind you,
in the window seat. That's Mr and Mrs Hartwell.
They come in here a great deal, and will go on doing
so, it seems, till they've finished doing up the place.

I'll introduce you to them, if you would like? I kept an eye on the house for them before they moved in, so we know each other all right.'

'In a minute. It would be very kind if you could introduce me, in a minute.'

Bobbie smiled in gratitude, and as she did so she realized that it was the first time for days and days that she had really smiled. As a matter of fact she had actually begun to hate life, and herself. Worse than that, she had seen, all too clearly, that if she was unhappy and grim-faced and unsmiling, she had only herself to blame. The truth was that she had made all her own muddles, and that was so dispiriting. It was no good blaming Beatrice or Teddy, or anyone really, it had all been her own fault. Everything-had been. Everything that had ever happened to her had been as a result of some colossal blunder. Right down, perhaps, to contracting TB. Maybe even that had been, in some way, her own fault.

After all, if she had told the aunts that she did not want to stay with the Dingwalls, which was the truth, they would probably have found her somewhere else, but Bobbie being Bobbie had been too proud to admit to anyone that she was miserable. If life had taken a bad turn then she had been determined to let it, and not make a fuss, so of course she had, in a way, even caused her own illness.

'Very well.' She finally put her glass down and smiled across at the policeman. 'If you wouldn't mind introducing me to the Hartwells?'

Mrs Hartwell was one of those slender, blond Englishwomen who look as if they might snap in the wind, or succumb to the slightest change in the weather, but who turn out to be able to ride horses, bring up children and run an immaculate house and garden while giving the impression that even doing all that is not quite enough, and really if only they were not such gooses, and just a little bit more organized, they should be doing a great deal more than they already were.

'I really must get organized,' she kept saying to Bobbie as she showed her round all the work being done at Baileys Court. 'I really must. I am determined to put my best foot forward next week, and get really, really organized for once in my life. I really must get organized.'

She might not be organized, but she was certainly wise, for instead of altering everything that had already been done at the house, she had in fact changed very little. Beatrice had repaired the main house most efficiently, and had finally painted it to her own taste, but Mrs Hartwell had not seen fit to tear down all trace of the previous owner's influence. Knowing that paint can always be changed at a later date, she had merely toned down what she could not stand.

'The dark red in her bedroom, for instance. I could not live with that,' she confided to Bobbie as they walked round together. 'And those awful monks' cupboards in the guest rooms, I am afraid

510

we have put those in the Sheds. I mean I quite see the point of them, but they really rather frightened the children. Such strange shapes for children's rooms, don't you think?'

Everywhere that Bobbie looked now she saw how much, in just a short time, Baileys Court was showing increasing evidence of English taste at its postwar best, for Mrs Hartwell had used pale colours and chintz curtains, and silver rather than the pewter that Beatrice had insisted on at every turn. Of course Mrs Hartwell's ideas clashed a little with the dark Tudor wood, and as she had indicated she had little time for endless Gothic shapes, but nevertheless the whole effect of the interior of the house was now charming, and homely, and that after all, as they both agreed, was the main purpose of decoration, to make a home for a family, for friends, where people would come and feel better for having stayed.

At long last, after an exhaustive tour, together with a comprehensive conversational examination of how the house had been in Beatrice's time, and how it was now in the Hartwells' time, and how they hoped it would be in not a great deal more time, Bobbie was able to come up with the one question that she was really wanting to ask.

'Have you started on the garden wing yet?'

Of a sudden Mrs Hartwell looked considerably less composed. 'My dear,' she said. She paused. 'Why did you suddenly ask me that?'

'Oh, you know, because I thought it was

interesting, an interesting bit of the house, when Mrs Harper was here, but of course she never got round to it, in the end. I always had the feeling that she never wanted to go into it, that she was afraid of all the problems, you know, the damp and so on. But of course with that long corridor connecting the two, there's no doubt about it, it makes the perfect guest wing, wouldn't you say? After all, people can be quite separate there, and you will never hear them when they are staying. And they can be independent, which is an absolute boon for a hostess.'

As she finished speaking, Mrs Hartwell started to pull the cardigan of her pale blue twinset closely around her and her fingers went to her single string of pearls which she twisted around her fingers slightly too tightly.

'My husband's been in there, of course, only last weekend, as a matter of fact, but, you know, even he – well, even he is at a loss. We actually have made up our minds to let it until such time as we can afford to really have a go at it. It needs really pulling together, don't you think? What did Mrs Harper think, Miss Murray? She must have had *some* thoughts.'

'Mrs Harper never went to the garden wing, not in my time here, I do know that. She really only concentrated on the main house. The wing was left for some future date.'

'Well, who did? It had definitely been lived in at some point, I heard.'

'No-one but myself, and a couple of the people

512

helping in the garden. We were the only people to go there. Myself and the Major, and of course the young man who was helping us during the summer. He stayed there too, but only in the very large room upstairs.'

The pearls around Mrs Hartwell's fingers had grown tighter and tighter, and now they suddenly burst and sprayed all over the floor, around their feet. Both women scurried after them, Mrs Hartwell busily apologizing, Bobbie laughing and saying, 'Don't be silly, that's just the sort of thing I do.'

At last they had all the pearls together, and knotted up into Mrs Hartwell's lace-edged handkerchief, and she said, 'Look, it's nice and sunny now, so why not let's go into the wing anyway? You're obviously dying to see round it, and as long as you don't mind the chaos, you know, I don't mind, really I don't. But really, nothing's been done there, as you know, since the Duffs owned the place, and that is some time ago. Anyway, now that the sun has come out—' Her voice tailed off.

Bobbie had no idea why its being suddenly sunny outside, a cold wintry sun at that, had anything to do with going to the wing, and would have asked as much of anyone else, but she sensed that her hostess was more tense than she wanted to let on, and so she followed her, almost dutifully, towards the subterranean corridor.

'I am actually glad of your company, because I don't really like the wing, you see, Miss Murray,' she said at last as they reached what was to Bobbie a familiar door. 'I am sorry to say that I find it shivery, that is all I can tell you. When the estate agent showed us round, when we heard that Mrs Harper wanted to sell, I was really rather against buying Baileys Court, purely because of the wing. But we are so comfortable in the house now, and I have to take some swatches of materials and try them in yet more of the rooms – so many of them to furnish really, but I suppose they will come in useful, in time. Do you know, my husband is not very practical in that way. When we saw round the wing my husband kept murmuring for "maids' rooms. So useful for maids' rooms." But really, I didn't like to tell him, there aren't any *maids* any more, and it is difficult enough to get a daily person for the main house, let alone for the wing.' The young woman smiled nervously at Bobbie. 'It's the history of it. I gather that is the problem with the wing. Its history, do you see? It must be that which makes it so sort of shivery, wouldn't you say?'

They were walking down the underground passageway now and Bobbie nodded in agreement. Yes, the history must have been something to do with it, she murmured, but she could only think of the summer days she had spent running through from the main house to the wing to meet Julian.

Mrs Hartwell seemed to find it necessary to keep talking as they went along together, as if she was covering up her nerves by doing so. 'That poor Duff family, everything so tragic, wouldn't you say? Too awful for them, losing so much, just too awful.'

Bobbie kicked aside some autumn leaves that had floated down the passageway somehow, and said, 'Oh, I never knew about them. I was actually thinking about the poor Catholics – you know, the persecutions, and Tyburn Tree and being hung, drawn and quartered if you were caught saying Mass.'

Mrs Hartwell shook her head. 'I always think that the Papists really rather deserved everything that happened to them, didn't they? I have no sympathy for *them*, I am afraid. That ghastly Queen Mary burning everyone, I mean to say.'

'Even so.' Bobbie looked back down the corridor along which they had just walked. 'Imagine hurrying through here to hide behind some fire-place up there, somewhere in some eight by eight little hole, just because of your religious beliefs. Pretty brave, wouldn't you say? Someone in the village said they found many skeletons in those places,' she added ghoulishly, and as it happened untruthfully, because she rather wanted to punish Mrs Hartwell for her narrow-mindedness towards Papists. 'Bleached bones and skulls.'

Mrs Hartwell seemed really rather unimpressed by this piece of information, probably because she suspected that the bones belonged to the Papists for whom she had no sympathy.

'Here we are.' She pushed open a door which was all too familiar to Bobbie, but patently un-familiar to her hostess, because she turned and beckoned. 'Don't leave me alone,' she said,

515

laughing nervously. 'Please. I've heard too many things about the wing. I don't want to be left alone here, really I don't. I am not a great believer in things, not since the war, but I know an atmosphere when I feel it. And the wing quite definitely has it.'

'What have you heard? About the skeletons in the hiding places?' Bobbie asked, catching the door, and, since she had made up her story, feeling more than a little surprised. She remembered how she had felt rather afraid herself, when she had first explored the wing, and how when Julian had found her she had pretended not to be, but how she had, at first anyway thought he was some sort of ghost, and how they had laughed about it together. So she went ahead of Mrs Hartwell, talking all the time, and climbing the all too familiar dark stairs that wound round and round, and brought them first to one set of rooms, and then to another set of rooms.

Unsurprisingly Mrs Hartwell insisted on standing in every room and discussing, at some length, where the light fell, and which way the room faced, and making little notes in her small, blue leather diary while all the while holding up small pieces of material. This made their progress through that part of the house painfully slow, as it must be when there are *blue* or *green* or *grey, I think, with that wonderful red that Colefax and Fowler use, or is it Syrie Maugham? At any rate, it would be lovely, don't you think, with the sea beyond? In the distance. Goodness, the views are good from these rooms. Such a shame they have never been used* types of monologues to be listened to, and Mrs Hartwell insisted on yet more standing in every room and taking swatches of materials out of her handbag as she did so.

Bobbie listened and joined in politely, with as much interest as her impatience would allow, until at last they reached the landing which led to Julian's room. Here again, she led the way.

'This is a lovely room,' she told Mrs Hartwell. 'You'll love this room. It would make the perfect guest sitting room, I think, I really do.'

She pushed aside the red velvet curtain, and as she did so she felt a pang of sorrow. She remembered that Julian had always said that he owned the curtain, and she wondered, in that case, why he had left it behind. But then, remembering how careless he had always seemed of possessions, how free of all the usual considerations that preoccupied everyone else, she pushed aside the thought with the curtain.

'How strange.' Mrs Hartwell's voice floated past Bobbie as she followed her into the room. 'I always think it is really very strange, to find everything just as he left it. I don't think I could do that, really I don't, just leave everything. So haunting somehow – particularly all these years later, and with the mother no longer here.'

Bobbie nodded, absently. She was right, everything was just as Julian had left it. And it was strange. There were all his pencils and drawing books, covered in dust now. And over there his easel, with his single painting, a painting that she always teased him would never, ever be finished, which had used to make him laugh, and turn away. And the cloth that he had covered the table under the window with, that was still there, and the mirror on the wall in which Bobbie had used to quickly brush her hair before leaping down the stairs after him, and out to the garden, and on to the sea, the two of them talking, talking all the time, never stopping to think about how happy they were, just talking.

'Do admit, it is strange, isn't it? The whole room is so strange, staying like this, just as it was. It gives me the shivers, it really does.'

Mrs Hartwell was still insisting on the strangeness of everything, while Bobbie, feeling as if she was intruding on a private room to which the owner would very soon return, nevertheless could not resist turning the notebook in front of her staring at the black spidery writing, writing that she could not connect with Julian, but – she realized, of a sudden – then, that was hardly surprising, since she had never actually seen him write, or draw. Those were things he seemed to do in the still of the night when she knew that he suffered fevers, and coughing, and all those things that they both knew about.

'Luckily the women from the village who come to clean for us don't mind coming to the main house, but they still will not come in here, you know, since the tragedies of the Duff family, they just will not. And you can't blame them. It was Mrs

518

Duff, you see. When her last child was killed, her mind quite turned, it seemed. And she would never let the room be changed, nothing must be touched. She would always dust it and look after it all herself. I mean, the tragedy of it. Poor woman, the tragedy of it.'

Mrs Hartwell nodded over to the table where stood a newly placed but faded photograph of a fair-haired young man dressed in sailing clothes and leaning against a boat.

'That was her second boy. She didn't want him to go, after his brother was killed, but he insisted. You know how they all did, at that time, especially down here, in Sussex – the whole of the south coast clambered into boats and took off to rescue the British army in Dunkirk. It seems that this poor young man made three trips over to France, and on the last, he was finally lost at sea. They say he was a consumptive, so the cold must have got to him, or the boat turned turtle.' Mrs Hartwell shivered. 'In the village they still say, my cook told me, that of a dark night he can be heard coughing up here. That is what they say. Of course, I don't believe that, but I do know that I must call in the rector, to bless the place, because we can't leave it like this, can we?' she went on briskly, obviously determined to be practical. 'Can't leave it full of a dead boy's things. And now that Mrs Duff too is dead, really, there is no point, is there? No point at all. My dear, is there something the matter?'

Bobbie was holding the photograph out to Mrs

Hartwell, but she must have looked terrible, because Mrs Hartwell in her turn was looking at her, obviously quite shocked at what she was seeing in Bobbie's face as she pointed to the photograph.

'Are you sure this is Mrs Duff's son who was killed at Dunkirk, Mrs Hartwell? Are you quite sure?'

'Well, no, of course not, Miss Murray. Good gracious, I could never say that, no. But I know that these are quite definitely his things. I know that, because the ladies from the village told me. So I would hazard a guess that the photograph must be of him.' She shook her head. 'You see, that is the bugbear of this wing. I keep telling my husband, the bugbear is the village's absolute *refusal* to come in here to clean. And that is why I must call in the rector. He must bless the place, and that will help dispel the sense of tragedy, get rid of the ghosts, if there are any, don't you think?'

Bobbie shook her head, suddenly distraught.

'No, no, the rector mustn't be allowed here. You mustn't let him do anything of the sort. You must leave it all as it is. You must leave Julian here, where he's happy. Please. Please leave him alone.'

'Julian? Who is Julian? Oh, of course, yes, you're right. Julian Duff *was* his name. Imagine you remembering.'

'Of course this is Julian.' Bobbie stared helplessly at the older woman, who she could now see was backing away from her, probably because Bobbie

520

was still holding out the photograph.

'My dear, are you a member of the family? Are you – at least, were you a Duff?'

'No, no, no! But I knew Julian, I knew him so well.' She turned the photograph away from poor Mrs Hartwell, who was now looking panic-stricken at Bobbie's reaction. 'You can see, he was so handsome. You can see that in this picture, can't you?' Despite every effort Bobbie started to cry, tears rolling down her face. 'He was so handsome and kind, and the silly fool, he would, wouldn't he? He would go out in his boat over and over again and try to rescue people. He was like that, you see. People with TB *are* like that. They are always trying to prove, you see, that they are better than they look, because people don't like coming near them, they're so disgusted by us – by them. And Julian, well, he had incipient TB. Oh, the bloody, bloody fool, he would go out in his boat and die, wouldn't he?'

She started to sob uncontrollably.

'Wretched Boy!'

Chapter Sixteen

Dick and Miranda wanted to make love. Of course they had known they wanted to make love for some time now, but the how and where of it had not been discussed, or even talked about. They just both knew. It was Dick who finally brought Miranda to consider the question properly. They had been kissing and kissing, and feeling terribly faint as they did so, and now, somehow, it was really not, they both realized, going to be enough.

'It must be right.'

'Everything must be right.'

'Nothing must go wrong.'

'No. Exactly. Where the lips and the noses go, we've sorted all that kind of thing out. Now we must make love, and then if that's all right—' Dick stopped, frowning. 'Then if that's all right, I really think – well, I really think you must marry me.'

Miranda turned from the kitchen table. They were in the café, late at night. Her favourite time to be alone with Dick. All the customers had gone home – all eight of them, as it happened, this particular night – and Dick and she would share a glass of wine, talk over the events of the day, and then walk back to Aubrey Close, where he would leave her.

'Do we have to make love before we marry, do you think?'

Dick nodded. 'Absolutely. There would be no point in marrying if we did not make love first. It can all go disastrously wrong, the beddy-byes bit. I have heard that it can go terribly, terribly wrong. No-one should take that risk, not ever. It's too important.'

'I don't want to just go to bed with you, just like that.'

'Well, don't then.'

After that there was a long silence during which Dick lit a cigarette and smiled serenely through the smoke, removing a little piece of tobacco from his mouth before taking another sip of wine.

'It would seem so cold-blooded, somehow.'

'As a matter of fact I agree. It would seem cold-blooded. Too cold-blooded for words. You are right. What we should do is not go to bed together, and just get married. Take a risk. What is life without risk?'

Miranda nodded, smiling, and blew him a kiss. 'On the other hand, marriage is a risk, isn't it?'

'Huge and horrible.'

'So if we married and we were not suited, what could we do?'

'Get unmarried and return to being suitable.'

Miranda nodded again. 'That is what I like about you, Dick. You talk about as much rubbish as I do. I should hate to be in love with someone who did not talk rubbish. It would make me feel inferior.'

'Or superior, if they talked worse nonsense than you.' Dick took hold of one of Miranda's hands and kissed the palm before holding it to his face. 'Tell you what, let's get married anyway.'

'You know all about me. There is that.'

'And you know all about me.'

'But what about the other two? You know. We can't get married, just like that. Not without talking it over with Ted and Bobbie.'

Dick sighed.

'Mind you, no-one can talk to Ted at the moment.' Miranda sighed, suddenly remembering her unwanted guest. 'I didn't tell you. I forgot to tell you. Ted came round at about six this morning and he was still as tight as a tick.'

'Oh well, if the studio's occupied then we'll have to get married if only to get Teddy out.'

'It's all Bobbie's fault. Such a stupid idea, throwing him at the beautiful Mrs Harper. She was bound to break his heart.'

'That's the bit I can't understand.' Dick frowned. 'The fact that Bobbie threw him at that woman of all people. You would think she would – well, you would think that she might not want to do that, somehow.'

Miranda caught up their coats. 'Come on, partner, let's go and see poor old Ted. He's probably sobered up by now and calling for an aspirin and an ice bag.'

'My favourite game – doctors and nurses.'

But as soon as Dick saw Teddy lying white-faced on Miranda's sofa, half asleep and half not at all asleep, he felt sorry for him.

Because he was comfortingly a little older than the rest of them, Miranda found that Dick had a way of taking charge at just the right moment, and so without questioning she ran for some blankets and they gave Teddy something to drink and tucked him up and left him while they, still longing for each other, crept off upstairs to Miranda's room.

Hours later Teddy found himself waking up on Miranda's large studio couch. Despite the darkness he knew that there was a downstairs cloakroom, somewhere in the darkness out there. Somewhere very, very far away there was a bathroom, and if he was determined to he knew he could reach it, but it was finding that determination, finding that courage.

At last his eyes started to sort out the different pieces of furniture, large, thank goodness, and then where the kitchen was, and then he saw that there was a small chink of light that was catching its reflection in Miranda's old brass kettle which she kept on the great oak side table, and suddenly everything came back to him in that single second of seeing that tiny chink of light in that kettle.

Of course. He had made a fool of himself, and he had

been dumped back outside Aubrey Close by Beatrice Harper's doctor.

He could still hear her voice saying those words to her guests. Heaven only knew how many there had been, but he could still hear her friend, he had no idea who, saying, 'Beatrice, who is that *gorgeous* young man of yours?'

And then Mrs Harper's reply, 'Oh, just a bit of *young*, very *active* young. My new little toy, to pass away the time. You know how it is at the moment, what with London's being so dull. I am planning to go to Venice – Gloria's there, you know that, don't you? We are going to go and stay at their new hotel, all of us. Not him, of course. Can't take him, because of you-know-who busily swimming back into my life. But I will say for my little toy that he *has* taken some brilliant photographs of me. Did I tell you? *Vogue* want to do a cover, but I don't know. Might let them, might not. We'll see.'

Teddy always did have a weakness for listening to conversations. To his own detriment, naturally.

He closed his eyes shut, tight shut, and found himself groaning as he remembered yet more. Please God! He hadn't really rushed down her stairs to her drawing room and screamed at her, had he? Please God he hadn't done that, had he?

But God had no need to respond to his question because Teddy already knew the answer, and it was in the affirmative. He had indeed rushed down the stairs and screamed at Mrs Harper, at Beatrice; and tried to pull her back up them too, shouting that he was not just a toy, that he counted for something, that he loved her, that she had said that she loved him too.

After that, perhaps particularly after that last statement, her friends had no hesitation in calling her doctor, and who could blame them? No matter how tight Teddy shut his eyes again, he knew that he could not black out the awkward, terrible truth. He had not made an ass of himself over Beatrice, he had made a complete *idiot* of himself.

Since it was Beatrice's private doctor, he had come round instantly – hardly surprising after all since Beatrice probably had him on a retainer. Anyway, he had injected Teddy with something quite lethal to stop his hysterics, and then eventually driven him home and thrown him out of his car, in the early hours of the morning, back outside the front door of Aubrey Close.

Of course Teddy had not been at all himself that evening. He had already been ill, not feeling well, running a temperature. That at least was a small, vaguely comforting excuse, but only vaguely. To say that was not to excuse how he had been. But that was why he had been drinking, to keep going, through her early evening cocktail party, through till nighttime when he could lie in her arms again and make love to her passionately, adoringly, giving himself to her entirely – no – giving himself *up* to her entirely.

But that had only been part of the whole misery. The other part of the misery was hearing her voice, laughing at him, laughing against him, and in a way that someone who really did not care a fig for you laughed, with despite.

He groaned inwardly as he remembered Bobbie warning him, over and over again, or so it seemed to him now, about older women, about how they just used young men, and then threw them aside, about how they just pretended to love you because you were young and virile, but really had about as much interest in you as a fly, about how dull you were to them, really, and how they only cared for your body and not for you as a person.

'It's all been my fault, all my own bloody fault.'

He said this out loud to the room, and then he managed with great difficulty to crawl out of bed and towards the narrow kitchen at the back of the studio where he hauled himself up and, reaching for the cold tap, drank from it. After that it was back again to the studio couch, and falling asleep, still aching and hurting, everywhere, inside and out, but somehow comforted by this minor achievement of reaching the kitchen and drinking from the tap.

Upstairs in her bedroom Miranda thought that she heard something and because of that she stirred in Dick's arms. They had made love at last, and it had been mystical and intense, and at the same time warm and comforting, and with the lovemaking had gone the whole, awful past. Paris, Macaskie, the idiot that she had made of herself – it had all gone away.

That was why she felt so sorry for Ted, because

528

she knew without being told that somehow or another Ted had made just the same kind of fool of himself as she had done in Paris. Miranda had known for the past few weeks that he was being ravished by the brilliant and beautiful Beatrice Harper, but what she had not realized was that Mrs Harper was the female equivalent of Macaskie. She crept down the studio stairs and across to the couch. He seemed to have woken for a little, because she could see that the disposition of the blankets was not the same as it had been earlier in the evening, or rather late in the evening, when they had seen to him before creeping off to bed to make love.

Poor old Ted. Miranda stared down at him. Poor old Ted. He must have really done himself to pieces to end up this way.

'Ted?'

'Hallo.'

He smiled weakly, and then, to Miranda's horror, she saw tears slipping down her brother's face. Teddy never cried, not since – well, not since he had been with her and the aunts at Mellaston. She was sure that he had not cried since then.

'What a fool I've been, Miranda. To think that I could make love with the Snow Queen and her ice would not burn me.'

Miranda who, while not being as entirely pragmatic as Bobbie, was nevertheless also inclined towards the practical, frowned momentarily. But realizing, after a few seconds, that Ted was indeed referring to the fearful Harper woman, she nodded sympathetically.

'Yes, I know, Ted. Women like that. Mm. Well, you know. You can't win. Anyway, she's gone away now, so you won't have to think about her any more.'

He opened his eyes again and tried to sit up. 'Gone away?' he asked, and then groaned as he felt his backside where Beatrice's doctor had given him an injection surely more fit for an elephant. 'Where's she gone?'

'Away,' Miranda lied quite determinedly, relying on the fact that rich people were always going away. 'So you can put her right out of your mind, Ted, and get on with your life, can't you?'

Teddy shut his eyes. Yes, he could. But even as he nodded his head feebly, he felt an awful draining sense of hurt, of disappointment, of dull despair, and as he drifted back into a strange, feverish sleep he knew that he was still longing for the smell of Beatrice's scent, to feel her body, to see her cold, grey eyes laughing at him. He was sure now that he had not loved her, and at the same time if he had not loved her, why did he feel that he was drowning in such sorrow?

'I think you should come round and see Teddy, as a matter of fact. He is better, sitting up and making much more sense, but Dick and I are at the café most days, and I'm getting quite busy, because Dick can only do so much now he's been commissioned to paint the Thames by some Society of Bargemen, or something. At any rate, I do believe that you should come round to see him, really I do.'

Bobbie felt intensely irritated by Miranda's interfering maternal tones, most especially because she knew that Miranda was right, that she should go round and see Teddy. Yet she still put it off for over a week.

The truth was that she was ill, and not able to cope with seeing anyone, least of all Teddy. With her return from Somerset had come the return of her insidious little cough, and a feeling of fever. Deep down inside, and she could hardly bear to think it, let alone admit it, she feared that somehow or another her incipient TB might have returned, and she could not cough without finding herself staring immediately at her handkerchief.

'I'll try to come and see him, but I can't promise.'

Miranda had replaced the telephone and then turned away from the thought that Bobbie might be the kind of person who, once she had used someone, no longer needed them around to remind her of the favour that she had extracted, and so would not want to see Teddy at that moment, perhaps at any moment.

Days passed, days that Bobbie spent in her room with the curtains closed, speaking to no-one, not wanting anyone to do or be anything to her, feeling as she had done all those years before when she had become so ill at the Dingwalls', unwanted, despairing, and wishing only to hide herself away from everyone.

Mrs Saxby, perhaps having noticed the eternal gloom emanating from the first floor rooms, had, eventually, made it her duty to knock on the door every now and then, but Bobbie refused to see her, explaining only that she was not quite the thing, not wanting her to come near her.

Finally Mrs Saxby, instead of knocking and enquiring after Bobbie, had telephoned to her, and most politely demanded to come up and talk to her.

When she finally arrived in Bobbie's bedroom Mrs Saxby was wearing her usual carefree Bohemian clothes, and her earrings sang as she came straight to the point, which, in a way, was of some comfort to the utterly despairing Bobbie.

'The Major and I knew that you were in for a shock, when we heard you had taken it into your head to go back to Baileys Green. The Major actually said, "The dear old bean will find out everything and that will be a bit difficult." And obviously it has been. A bit difficult. But then a great deal has been a bit difficult these last years, and the war before that, that was difficult, and the war before this last one, and now we have Malaya and Korea and so on. So I thought that perhaps, and I might have been wrong, you could cope with it, because you always seemed so cheerful and practical really.'

Bobbie sank low in her bed, her Japanese kimono

tied tightly across her undressed body, and sighed suddenly and violently at that word *cope*.

That was the word that Aunt Prudence had used when she was sending her off into Mrs Eglantine's care. *You will be able to cope better than the other two, Bobbie dearest.* How she had hated Teddy and Miranda because of that word *cope*. And anyway, she had not been able to *cope* better than them at all, rather less well, probably, what with one thing and another. She started to cough, and Mrs Saxby saw her staring into the handkerchief afterwards, looking for blood, but she carried on determinedly nevertheless.

'You see, Bobbie, when you first were sent to the Sheds, you weren't a very well girl at all, you really weren't. It was my opinion that they should have sent you to another sanatorium, or to Scotland. But the whole set-up at Hazel Hill was just a wartime thing really, and the French nurses understandably wanted to go home. And no-one could blame them. It was just that Mrs Harper wanted to keep control of your life, that is the impression I had. And so she had you sent down to Baileys Court, and myself too, and there we were together in the Sheds, and really, you weren't at all well still. It was not that you were especially ill, but after all those years spent among dying people you were not like other young people at all. I promise you.'

Bobbie had no difficulty believing Mrs Saxby. She was sitting up a bit better, the older woman noticed, and staring at her guardian's former secretary with something close to interest.

'I could not say anything to you, but if you ask Mrs Duddy, she was always worried about you. You were so shy, so silent, as if no-one had really spoken to you much, or if they had, perhaps, it was in French, and you did not understand.'

'I had teachers – I did school work.'

'I know, dear, but that is truly not the same thing, Bobbie.'

Bobbie knew that Mrs Saxby was feeling sorry for her. At the same time she realized that by telling her all this the ex-secretary was putting herself in a position of some authority over her, as if she too had been a teacher at the sanatorium and visited Bobbie, known her and taught her, when she was so ill.

'We spoke about it many times, the Major and I, about your relationship with Julian, and we just felt it was better left.'

Bobbie climbed out of bed suddenly, and pulling the kimono about her started to walk about the room with its drawn curtains despite the daylight outside. What were they saying about Julian and herself? What was better left? What was Mrs Saxby about to say to her? Bobbie dreaded to hear, and yet she knew that she *must* hear, for she had to find out, in the same way that she had found that she had to return to Baileys Court, to the sound of the sea, to the memories of herself and Julian, always talking, always trying to make sense of what no-one else had ever been able to, trying to make the world brighter.

Mrs Saxby watched Bobbie pacing about her room, and in contrast to her young lodger remained calmly seated, waiting to start again. Finally Bobbie stopped but started coughing once again. Mrs Saxby waited until she had recovered herself before continuing.

'You talked non-stop to "Julian", you see, Bobbie. A bit like – a bit like a child. You know how children invent people, and they say things like *Don't sit in that chair, Barney's sitting there.* That sort of thing. One of my sisters used to take up two seats in a railway carriage on account of her friend and the funny thing is, such is the belief of the child, we all went along with it. Do you see? All the grown-ups, everyone, went along with it. It's as if, in the face of such belief, we all know that we must tread as softly as angels. We don't want to break the spell, or destroy the magic, in case there really are little people sitting there and we might harm them by sitting ourselves on top of them. It's the belief of the child that is so compelling. Such is the case, you will find, with everything to do with belief.'

At this Bobbie once more resumed her pacing. 'So you are telling me that Julian never existed, is that what you are saying?'

'No, what I am saying is that, as far as the Major and I were concerned, he only existed for *you*.'

'But don't you see – he did exist, he really did. He

went to the sea with me and we talked and laughed, and we ate lunch together, I know we did. You never saw him eating lunch or anything, but you would have done, if you had come with me, he ate lunch with me every day of that summer. And in the evening I used to walk with him to the garden wing, and then come back and roll about in the hay barn. All those things were true, and real, they were.'

Despite her best efforts Bobbie found that she was now wringing her hands, and she repeated her last words again. 'Those things were true and real. They were. They were.'

'Exactly, Bobbie, they were true and real. So much that we can't actually see is true and real. We can't take out love and put it on that table, can we? We know we can't do that. We can't point to it and say *There's love*. We know it won't be square, or round, or triangular, coloured pink or blue, yet we know it exists, don't we? And we can't take out faith and put it on that table either – faith in the goodness of people, of winning through as we did in the war. We can't take that faith out and yet we know it was real—'

In the state that she was in Bobbie did not think that she could stand yet another of Mrs Saxby's speeches so she interrupted at this point with, 'No, no, no. I understand what you're saying, but you have forgotten one thing.'

'And what is that?'

'Julian does exist, did exist. We *can* take him out

536

and put him on this table.' Bobbie banged her bedside table lightly with her fist. 'We can take his pictures out and put them on this table, and we can lay out his pens and pencils, and the painting he never finished, and we can see the boat that he sailed in the photograph. And we know that he was called Julian Duff and that his mother never got over losing him, and we know that he had TB like me. In the village, at Baileys Green, they say that he can still sometimes be heard coughing. People have heard him in the garden wing, coughing. Mrs Hartwell told me.'

She started to cough again herself, violently this time, but Mrs Saxby's face did not change its expression as she watched her calmly.

'Of course.'

Mrs Saxby stood up, and went over to Bobbie. Taking Bobbie's hands in her own very cool ones, she held them, and as she did so the charms on her bracelet rang out in the quiet of the room.

'The war was full of such stories, I promise you. And I do not believe they are apocryphal. The Major and I know, as you said, that the "Julian" with whom you spent that summer with us was real. He was not just real to you, he was real to us, he was real to his mother, and he was real to himself. But he was killed, and not buried, and maybe – maybe that was it, because he was not buried, because there was no memorial to him, he came back to be with you, a young person of his own age, to enjoy an idyllic summer, be happy and carefree, and now he has gone on at last, happy. You, in your innocence, put him to rest perhaps that summer. Rest in peace. We say that, don't we? Because we mean it, we want to rest in peace. Now, I truly believe Julian *does* rest in peace, because of that summer he spent with you. He will be with his mother, and they will be happy, and – at peace.'

Tears were pouring down Bobbie's cheeks now, and indeed down poor Mrs Saxby's, and they were both clinging on to each other in the way that women do who need to comfort each other.

'How will we ever know that this is so?'

'We won't, Bobbie, we will never know, and we should never know, because that would make us too – uppity, wouldn't it? What we do know is what we believe, and that is quite enough. I believe that Julian's unquiet spirit came back to be with you, to make you happy and whole again after your illness, and that once he knew that you were, he was too, and he was able to leave once more.'

Bobbie sat down suddenly again on the bed, completely spent. 'But I must have looked so stupid – going around yammering away to someone that no-one could see.'

'No, you didn't, dear. You looked like a poor thin young woman who was being made whole again. Goodness, the Major and I, we were so comforted by you and Julian. Being with you and Julian made us feel not that you were mad, far from it, but that we were all gloriously sane. The Major needed to be healed, after Burma and the railway – you can imagine. And I needed to be freed, and it all happened that summer, and nothing has been the same since, only things have become much better. Even my mother is better. Found herself a new friend, and moved out of Pinner. Things can get better, you know. And they sometimes even do.'

'For you, they have. But I shall always miss Julian. I know I shall. Even now I so long to hear him laugh and have fantasies with him. Do you remember how he could make anything and everything into a game?'

'I do, Bobbie. But shall I tell you something?'

Bobbie shook her head. 'No.'

Mrs Saxby stood up. 'No, you're right. I have said quite enough. I am going now, dear. And I hope you will now bath and dress yourself,' she added in a firm tone, 'and I hope we can expect you for drinks and dinner at seven tonight.'

She closed the door quietly on Bobbie, but Bobbie did not look after her. She remained where she was, thinking back to that summer, that time of idyllic laughter, and wondering if Mrs Saxby had been right.

She stayed like that for some long time, just staring ahead of her, until finally she went to the windows and drew the curtains, standing to the side and feeling the heavy brass ends to the curtain pulls of which she was so strangely proud. Outside the usual sounds of London rose up to her in the still air of the early winter evening, the sounds of taxis pulling up and down the street, a voice, louder than the light sounds of the traffic, calling to a child to *bloody well watch it, won't you?*

They were all real, those sounds, she knew they were, as real as Julian had been to her. He had existed, and they had loved each other, intensely, but now he had gone, and she had to learn to live without the thought of him.

She started to cough once more. She would never make it down the stairs for dinner. Not now that it was all over, and the reality of everything was facing her once more. Instead she climbed in between the sheets and lay propped up against her pillows, staring towards the fading light.

Teddy was arguing with Miranda over how much his heart had been broken by Beatrice Harper. The argument was desultory enough, more a discussion than an argument, and carried out as they both played solitaire.

'Beatrice did not break my heart. She did not. She just fascinated and overwhelmed me.'

'She made you grow into a man, that's what she did,' Miranda insisted, going back to her crossword, having signally failed to leave less than five marbles on the solitaire board. 'She did, she broke your heart. You have changed, you know, since she went away. Even your face has changed. You look quite different.'

'That's just your imagination. You're just hoping that I have changed because you're so complacent, as people who are in love always are. You want me to be the same as you.'

'Not true.'

Teddy sighed as he moved the marbles at fantastic speed around the board. 'But I have changed, I suppose. I don't feel happy like I used to, and I don't feel sad either, I just feel as if nothing is happening to me. As if I am made of—'

'Runny junket.'

'Yes?' Teddy looked across at the girl he thought of as his sister. 'Yes, you're right. That is exactly how I do feel. How did you know? I do feel just like runny junket.'

'No, that's the *crossword clue*, you duffer.'

'Well, never mind. I don't even feel like working any more. I don't feel like doing anything except staring at my feet. I've never been like this before, not since I was in short trousers, and you collected me at the school and pinched me black and blue to make me say I was your brother and they wrote "Ted Darling" on my new label for you because you had thrown away the other one, not since then.'

'I did not pinch you black and blue – ah-ha. I know, got it. A flop. A *runny junket* is a *flop*. I did not pinch black and blue. You're a liar, Teddy Mowbray.'

Teddy looked up at her and the expression in his eyes was sad.

'That's just it, Miranda. That is it. I am a liar because my life has been a lie. Ever since you made me be your brother, I don't really know who I am, do I? Whether I am Ted Darling, or Teddy Mowbray, or who? I have just been pretending to be first one person then another.'

'Oh, join the gang, little brother. Since the war hardly any of our generation *do* know who they are. It is just a fact. We know your people were killed and you have no relatives and all that, and we know about *my* mother and father, and really, it doesn't matter. What matters now is what we feel we are. Do you feel you are more Ted Darling, or more – you know, Teddy Mowbray?'

Teddy busied himself on the solitaire board, loudly removing yet more of the large marbles before replying. 'Since – you know, since the last few weeks, I really think I might be more Ted Darling than Teddy Mowbray.'

Miranda put down her crossword and smiled. 'Oh dear, oh dear, Bobbie won't like that. Bobbie only really likes Teddy Mowbray.'

Teddy's face fell. 'Bobbie. What has Bobbie to do with it?' He continued to play for a few seconds, and then finally added inconsequentially, 'She won't see anyone, you know. Bobbie. I ask and ask but Mrs Saxby just sounds her usual inscrutable self and the Major just "old bean"s me, because the fact is that, since she went to Sussex that time, she won't see anyone. She just does not want to know about any of us. Particularly me. She's always been all right with me, but now, she won't see me. I wrote her a card, everything, but she's just shut up shop.

Either that or the Saxbys are keeping her away from us all, or something.'

'I don't think the Saxbys are like that. No, it's Bobbie, she's depressed for some reason. She gets like that when she's not well. The Saxbys said she wasn't well, hasn't been for some weeks. At least, that is what they told Dick and me. But, I mean, it's different for you. Why not go round and surprise her?'

'I don't believe in surprises. They always go wrong. People have never had time to wash their hair or put out the cat, or whatever it is, and they get cross or tetchy if you surprise them. Do you really think I should surprise Bobbie? She wouldn't like that, would she?'

'No, of course not. I just wanted you to talk about her. Thought it might help. After all, who put you up to the Beatrice Harper escapade, but Bobbie? I mean, it is all because of her that you're like this now, all sane and serious, the old Teddy quite gone. You should go round and tell her off for what she did to you, making you have an affair with Beatrice Harper to stop Major Saxby going to prison. I mean to say, whatever next, eh?'

Miranda was joking really, but Teddy did not seem to think so, because he stood up suddenly, leaving only two marbles on the solitaire board, which was very nearly satisfactory.

'Yes, but I mean to say . . .' He stared across at Miranda. 'You have to hand it to Bobbie, because it worked, didn't it? So Bobbie was right in that way.

I was able to talk Beatrice out of that business with the Saxbys.'

'I don't think it was your *talking* that did the trick, Ted.'

They both laughed.

'Not even *your* gift of the gab could have had *that* much effect on Beatrice Harper, Ted. But you *should* go and talk to Bobbie, you know – because you could cheer her up.'

'I could, couldn't I? I could go round and cheer her up.'

'Course you could. Besides, I happen to know this would be a good time. The Saxbys are away for a few days, and their charlady's holding the fort. She'll let you up if you go round, I expect.'

Teddy put on his overcoat and wound his scarf around his neck, looking brighter than he had been for some time, Miranda was glad to note.

'Good. Yes, I'll go and see Bobbie and – cheer her up, or something.'

Miranda watched him let himself out of the studio with some satisfaction. She and Dick had hoped that with a bit of goading they could get him to go and see Bobbie, and really, in the event, it had not taken very much.

Bobbie had one great advantage over Teddy. She knew what it was like to be ill for a long, long time. She knew what the horrors of long hours spent on your own did to you. She knew how dark the nights were, endlessly dark, lying on your own, with no-one visiting you, no-one really caring if you lived or died, or so it seemed anyway. And then at last the daylight coming, little by very little, and the sounds of the sanatorium waking up and eventually a human face bringing tea, the very smell of which would make Bobbie feel sick and long for something else.

Even so Teddy was hardly through her bedroom door, where she lay in semi-darkness, the curtains that hung at her window half drawn, before he looked as if he too might have realized what real illness could be, as he stared across at Bobbie's pale face with its two black patches under the eyes.

He had been about to say, 'I've come to pick a bone with you, Miss Murray,' when he stopped, standing still and staring in such an obvious way that Bobbie sighed.

'I know, I look awful. That's why Mrs Perkins was not meant to let anyone in. I have to keep out of sight in case I give everyone a fright.' She tried to laugh, but coughed violently instead.

Teddy found himself feeling oddly awkward in the face of such illness.

'You really are ill, Bobbie,' he told her eventually. 'I mean you look terrible.'

'That, Teddy, is stating the obvious, don't you think? Anyway, you're not meant to be here, you're meant to be somewhere else, pursuing a thriving career. So, please, go, please!'

She pulled a pillow over her head and started to cough again. Watching her Teddy could only admit to himself that it was true, he *was* actually longing to leave her. He so hated to see Bobbie like that, he just wanted to run away.

'Go on, go on, go! Please!' Bobbie called to him from under her pillow.

Teddy sat down on the bed. 'No, I'm not going. I'm fed up with always being told to go away. I'm staying, here, with you. I'm going to help you get better. And nothing you say will make me leave you.'

He leaned forward and took one of her hands in his, longing now not to go, but to see his Bobbie, the one he had re-met that day in the old bombed-out conservatory, coming back to him, instead of staring miserably up from her pillows as she was now, the dark circles under her eyes making her face seem plain and wan.

Bobbie was about to open her mouth and say, as the Major would have done, 'Oh, what tosh,' when she started to laugh weakly.

'Oh, Teddy, if only I could snap your face!'

'Don't laugh at me. I'm like a dog, you can laugh with me but not at me.'

'Sorry.'

Teddy stared at Bobbie now as she moved restlessly against her pile of pillows. He stood up and went to the back of her.

'Sit up, while I do your pillows. I know how to do this. Two crossed pillows, hospital style, and now one straight one. There.'

He took up the folded newspaper from the table

beside her bed and looked at it. She had folded it into a square to do the crossword, except, because Bobbie had never been any good at crosswords, she had only filled in one clue.

She looked up at him defensively as he stared at it. 'It's probably wrong.'

'It is,' Teddy agreed absently. 'What was I saying?'

Bobbie frowned. 'I don't know. Something.'

She half closed her eyes, already tired out but still waiting patiently, as if Teddy was about to start reading her a story, and had just put the book down for a minute before continuing.

Teddy sat down again. 'Let's do the crossword together.'

'No.' She opened her eyes and looked petulantly at him. 'I don't want to do crosswords. I can't think at the moment. My chest hurts too much to think.'

'Very well, I'll read to you.'

'No, I don't want that.' She kicked out suddenly and restlessly at her bedding. 'Mrs Saxby keeps reading to me and it just sends me to sleep, and then I'm awake all night, instead of all day. Besides, I feel frightened at night on my own, I alway have.'

'Wireless then.'

Seeing her eyes close once more, Teddy tiptoed over to the wireless and, having switched it on, adjusted the sound to 'low' and prepared to tiptoe out to the shops to find her something tempting to eat, or a present of some kind.

'Don't go.' She opened her eyes again. 'Please, don't go.'

'I wasn't going to *go*, I was just going to go *and* – buy you something, a present, something cheerful.' Teddy took one of her hands, looking as calm as he did not feel.

As he stared into Bobbie's eyes, which were not at all like the old familiar Bobbie's eyes, but like someone else's, someone who was not really there, Teddy realized with sudden shock that he had never really seen death close to. People he had known had died, but he had never *seen* death. The aunts had died, and his parents had died, of course, but now it seemed to him that in reality, for the first time, he might be facing death, Bobbie's death, and it was as if there was only silence around him, and around her. People did die of tuberculosis, or whatever she had, and now it occurred to him that Bobbie might indeed be dying.

As this thought came to him and together with it the next one – namely that even he might not be able to *stop* her dying – it seemed to him that although the old big-headed Teddy would have been able to make instant decisions the new Teddy could only stare, and pray silently, *Please God, don't let Bobbie die!*

He went to the shops and came back again with a box of glacé fruits and a large jigsaw puzzle. Bobbie was so pleased that he was able to get her to agree to go with him to see a specialist, because, as Teddy said, 'Lying about being ill is not much fun, even if you are quite used to it.'

* * *

548

'Really Miss Murray should go back to a sanatorium, but—' the specialist hesitated.

It was that *but* that hung in the air and waved itself in front of Bobbie and Teddy, in the manner of an inn sign. Backwards and forwards that *but* swung before Bobbie's frightened eyes. She had known so much sorrow over her last years of growing up, she had known that there was so much of which to be frightened, that she had learned never to look ahead for more than a few hours. Even so, back to a sanatorium again, all those whey-faced nurses, all those other patients in various stages of their mutual illness. She looked quickly at Teddy, suddenly frightened.

'Miss Murray doesn't want to go back to a sanatorium,' said Teddy, speaking for her. 'And you can't blame her; she's spent half her childhood in one. Besides, I often think that when you're ill the last place you want to be is with someone *else* who is ill. No, there must be some other way. After all, it's just convenience that makes you lump sick people together under one roof with a whole lot of other sick people, it's just because you don't want the bother of them singly. But it's not like that for Miss Murray. She has someone who *does* want the bother of her, someone who can nurse her and look after her.'

The specialist managed to look both bored and irritated at this statement. 'Her mother or someone? I suppose some relative might be prepared to—'

'No, not some relative, me. Her—'

'*Brother!*'

Teddy and Bobbie stared at each other, momentarily embarrassed and confused at Bobbie's sudden interruption, but the specialist could not have been less interested if they had been married and divorced.

'Scotland is good,' he said in a voice of polite disinterest. 'Scotland is very good for incipient TB – plenty of mountain air. Or the seaside can sometimes do the trick. A lot of patients go to the seaside.'

'I was at the seaside before – in Sussex.'

'Well, I suppose that could be as good as anywhere. Sussex.'

'Very well, we shall take her to Sussex.' Teddy smiled suddenly at Bobbie, and stood up. 'I will take you to Sussex, and you will get better, see if you don't. You won't be seeing her again, Dr Larkman – not if I have anything to do with it.' He put his arm protectively round Bobbie. 'Come on, Miss Murray, bucket and spade time.'

Outside the door Bobbie looked up at Teddy. 'But what about your work, Ted?'

'My work can go fish. My work is you. You're much more important than my work.' He stopped suddenly. 'I say, I suddenly realized – you called me Ted. Is that how you think of me?'

'Course.' Bobbie leaned against him, allowing herself to feel suddenly affectionate for a few seconds.

'That's funny. Miranda said that of the two of us – Ted or Teddy – you would prefer Teddy.'

'As a matter of fact, *Ted* – I like both.'

'Both.'

'Yes. I like both of you.'

After that they walked on down the seemingly endless hospital corridor in silence, knowing that they had reached an understanding, although what exactly it was, neither of them could have precisely said.

Teddy was as good as his word. Within a few weeks of their visit to the specialist, he took Bobbie to the seaside. All right, it was the seaside in winter, but the seaside in winter was without doubt just as beautiful, if not more beautiful to Bobbie. Teddy had managed to hire a small house for her, in a quiet road on a private estate, and himself set up home for them both, living, as far as the estate agent, their landlady and their neighbours were concerned, as brother and sister – Mr Mowbray and his sister Bobbie Mowbray.

'Must preserve the proprieties!' Teddy liked to joke, while secretly thinking that 'Bobbie' and 'Mowbray' went together as if they were made for each other.

With the realization that Bobbie was so ill and needed him more than she would ever admit, Teddy found, to his permanent surprise, that not only was he able to run a house, quite effortlessly, but he actively enjoyed it. Day after day he meticulously observed the same routine. First he would rise early to make breakfast for them both, whistling and singing and going to the gate for the paper in a determinedly cheerful manner. Then he would run Bobbie a bath, and after she had washed and dressed, help her to the downstairs room where he would leave her to sit warmly blanketed with rugs in front of the open French windows giving onto the garden, which itself gave straight onto the beach.

And so, having breakfasted off fresh lemon juice ('the best drink for bad chests') and coffee and rolls, Bobbie would find herself warmly wrapped but breathing in sea air, listening to 'Housewives' Choice' to the sound of the ancient Hoover provided by their landlady being pushed with ferocious enthusiasm by Teddy all over the carpets, until she was sure that there could not be an atom of dust within miles.

The house they had rented was not big, but it was spacious enough, and the long room that was its feature overlooked not just the sea but the small garden as well, so that there was a square of green and some hedging before the beach began. As Bobbie knew only too well from her childhood, on a bad day the sky and the sea could seem un-remittingly grey without some green somewhere to relieve the depressing intensity. It was on this small, green sward that Teddy started to turn away from direct images. Unable to leave Bobbie for any length of time, and having found that he had tired of people and fashion, which nowadays seemed to him to be suddenly lightweight, he became fascinated instead by photographing the wonders of light reflected on water.

As his patient slept or woke fitfully all during the day and sometimes at nighttime too, only to sleep again, tired out from coughing, her hands clasping an unread book, the wireless playing endlessly, and sometimes, it seemed to her, quite pointlessly, Teddy worked on his pictures of sea and moonlight, sea and sunlight. Early morning, late at night, whatever the time, he found himself again and again drawn to the shore.

'I am in love with light on water.'

The results were so good that he sent some up to his new gallery in London. Happily the post brought back an enthusiastic reception and several commissions. It also brought an invitation to Dick and Miranda's wedding and ensuing reception at their café, which Teddy took at once to show Bobbie.

'I can't go, Ted.'

'Of course you can go.'

Bobbie shook her head, miserable but certain the way people with lingering diseases can be. 'No, I can't.'

'Dick and Miranda probably won't get married at all if you're not there.' But even as Teddy finished speaking he realized from the expression on Bobbie's face that she would not be moved.

'No, Ted. I am sorry, but I'm just not well enough.'

'You are better than you were. You know you are. You look better.'

'I know. I know I am better than I was, but if there is one thing that no-one really understands about this wretched disease . . .' She paused, remembering. 'Well, no, there was someone, once, who did,' she said, remembering Julian and their jokes about being The Incipients. 'At any rate, to put it another way, if you haven't had something like this, what you don't understand is that it fills you with a horrid sense of self-disgust. You hate yourself for being like this, and as a consequence you don't really like anyone else. It's just a fact, I am sorry to say.' As Teddy looked shocked, she shrugged her shoulders but went on, insistently, 'No, really. It does. This disease makes you hate yourself, and then you can only see the distress that it seems to cause other people, and so you end up not wanting to see anyone. Not anyone! Not even – well, you. No, I want to see you, but no-one else.'

Teddy sighed, the invitation still in his hand. Their two best friends, his sister, getting married and Bobbie was refusing to go, even for a few hours.

'Miranda will be devastated, you know that. I mean, Miranda, well, she sets such store by things – and Dick – they're so fond of you—' His voice petered out.

But Bobbie just shook her head and tried to smile in an effort to lighten the moment.

'Don't be dotty, Ted Darling. Can you imagine? I mean, really, just as the organist starts playing

554

"Here Comes The Bride" I'll start one of my marathon coughing fits, and everyone will stare and wonder why I bothered to come all the way up from Sussex just to cough at the happy pair. It'll seem more like sabotage than friendship, to go all that way to make everyone else feel uncomfortable, and you'll end up wishing I'd stayed at home.' She attempted to laugh at the idea, but then as always the coughing started again, and conversation came to a temporary end.

'Oh, very well. I expect they'll understand.'

Teddy wandered off looking morose, and during the following weeks Bobbie imagined that despite acceding to her wishes and writing to tell Dick and Miranda that she was still too ill to attend, he had not really understood how she felt. As he prepared to go up to London by the early train on the day of the wedding, leaving Bobbie in the charge of their landlady – a matronly woman in a navy blue coat which she never seemed to take off – Bobbie could hear him whistling and singing to the wireless as he dressed, and his very cheerfulness seemed to confirm what she had thought. Teddy was too insensitive to either understand, or care how she felt. How her self-disgust and embarrassment at her disease made her feel that everyone would stare at her and pity her, and how her sense of isolation from the world made her feel resentful that she was too ill to go, which in turn made her feel sorry for herself, sometimes finding herself crying miserably in the night, wondering if she would ever get better.

'I am on my way.' Teddy peered round the sitting room door looking extraordinarily smart for Teddy, and of a sudden extraordinarily handsome to Bobbie. She nodded, pretending cheerfulness.

'Send them my best love, Ted, won't you? Don't forget the present, and don't leave it on the train. And tell them I shall raise a glass to them at four o'clock when they should be cutting the cake.'

Teddy nodded, now walking down the long room to where Bobbie was stationed, as always, in front of the open windows. He bent down and kissed her on the cheek, and at the same time brought round a large box from behind his back.

'Wear this for me while I'm gone. Wear it for me, and for Dick and Miranda, pretend that you're with us in London.'

Bobbie opened the box and carefully undid the tissue paper. Inside was a hat, as it happened the prettiest hat she thought she might have seen in months, if not years. Having examined it for a few seconds in delighted silence she turned to thank Teddy, but he was long gone, and when she set aside her rugs and went to the front room window, he was already waving to her from the station taxi and leaving her to find a note at the bottom of the box.

Wear this and think of us.

Bobbie stared out to sea. The sea like the hat was blue. That was propitious. She thought of Miranda, and then of Dick, and she thought of their happiness, and she put on the hat, and went on staring out to sea to some indefinable moment that she imagined might never be hers.

In London Dick and Miranda's wedding was everything that a small wedding between two Bohemian young people should be, the church filled with friends and flowers and the café tables laden with as much food and drink as rationing would allow. But none of them could stop thinking about Bobbie, her absence having the effect of making her illness seem even more real, and of course in his anxiety Teddy could not help talking about her.

'I keep hoping that she will be better once the *spring* comes. At least she is not worse, at least she's still with us. I suppose that is something, isn't it, Dick?'

The bridegroom put a sympathetic hand on Teddy's shoulder. 'Just don't set too much store by her getting better quickly, old chap. Remember Bobbie's been ill since she was a child. I sometimes think that is what is so hard for her. I mean to have got better, and then suddenly to get the wretched thing again. Miranda thinks it was all to do with this Julian fellow and some sort of discovery that he died at sea, you know, rescuing people from Dunkirk, setting off again in his little boat and then being overcome by the sea, and all that. She thinks that in her heart of hearts Bobbie's still waiting for Julian, that she actually doesn't want to get over him. That she's still clinging to the idea of him, not really interested in anything or anybody else. But,

557

you know, it's anybody's guess whether her illness has made her think of sorrowful things or whether sorrow has made her ill again. Just a shot in the dark, I'd say, but for some reason Miranda's convinced. Just thought I'd tell you, you know. In case it helps.'

Teddy nodded, and as there was to be dancing and he had been asked to play the piano he put the matter out of his mind until he returned home when, having given a lively account of the wedding and all its gaieties to Bobbie, he suddenly announced that he had taken it into his head to buy himself a boat.

Chapter Seventeen

The day had been longer and sunnier than expected, as can sometimes happen in early spring, but now it was getting dark, and the sea was rough and the sky streaked with orange, alleviated now and then by clouds darker than its own reflection. Bobbie had been reading in front of the French windows as usual when she awoke to find the growing darkness outside was slowly becoming a reality. She closed the open doors and then stared through a side window. Normally Teddy would be home by now, but he patently and obviously was not, either home, or busy calling to her from the kitchen.

She vaguely remembered his telling her that he might be going out in his little boat, because it was such a fine afternoon that he might load it up with some cameras and try photographing the shore from the vantage point of the sea. But that was all she could remember now, having not paid much attention to what Teddy was telling her in his usual enthusiastic way, and now of course she had no idea of how long he could have been gone or even whether or not he might have taken it into his head to go on a longer trip than usual. She knew that the boat had an outboard motor and that there would be a flare on board, or something of that nature, and that he would be warmly dressed and in an oilskin, which he always was of late, but that was all that she did know.

'You'm do well to ring the coastguard, Miss Murray,' her landlady agreed when she came in to make Bobbie tea at the usual time. 'Folks is lost out at sea all the time these last years. But only to be expected, what with it being a Labour government, my husband says.'

Bobbie stared at the telephone. Somehow it seemed such a big thing to send people out searching for Teddy when, knowing him, he had probably just taken a longer trip, or was anchored somewhere trying to perfect a picture of the sun sinking below the horizon, or the moon climbing up to the stars. Of late he had been almost dreamy for him, not at all the same Teddy. Sometimes she thought he would rather not be with her, that he would rather be outside anywhere rather than inside with her, but the next minute he would start reading to her, or telling her some joke that he had heard in the pub, and she would realize that how she felt was nothing to do with Teddy and everything to do with herself, and they would start talking together, and as always their talk would be non-stop.

Of a sudden the unimaginable thought came to Bobbie. Supposing, like Julian, Teddy never came back? Supposing he had gone out in his little boat, like Julian, and, like Julian he never returned? She started to pace up and down the room feeling both desperate and stupid because she knew so little of where he had gone, or when.

'Sea's very rough tonight, miss. Your brother should have been back by now, I should have thought.' Still, as always, in her navy blue coat, the landlady, small and hatted, stared at Bobbie, a cup of tea in her hand.

'I think I will just go outside and down the beach and see if I can see him coming in.'

'That's said to bring bad luck that is, round these parts. Bad luck, a woman waiting on the shore. You want to bring him back safe to you, you must do like fishermen's wives, my dear. They light a candle in the window of their cottage, that soon brings them home. I have some somewhere, and a holder. I'll light one for your brother, and see if he don't come in safe and sound as soon as maybe.'

But Bobbie was not content to be a fisherman's wife and sit whey-faced in a window with a candle for help, and so she pulled on Teddy's old duffel coat and a pair of his gloves and, looking and feeling a little like a child wearing its parents' clothes, she stepped out into the cold weather and the realities that lay outside the window, inwardly cursing Teddy and his lateness.

Of course once outside she realized at once just

why the fishermen's wives never stood waiting on the shore for them, but lit a candle and placed it in their cottage window instead. It was surely less to do with superstition and more to do with the cold of the wind and the wet of the rain – both of which were now starting to blow towards the rapidly freezing Bobbie.

'Teddy! Teddy!'

If there was anything more useless than calling out to sea and waving a scarf in a growing gloom Bobbie did not know it. Yet it had to be done, for she could see that there was a small boat in the distance, and even hear its outboard motor, and although she doubted that it could possibly be Teddy's boat she felt a strange surging sense of release at just being able to call his name.

'Teddy!'

If only he had a more sensible name, she would probably feel less stupid. Given the shore and the shingle, the sea and the dark sky, calling 'Teddy' out to sea sounded somehow ludicrous.

'Ted!'

The boat that had seemed to be some distance away now grew nearer, and nearer, and nearer until at last, eventually, Bobbie heard the crunch of its bottom on the shingle and saw its single occupant jump out. For a few seconds it seemed to her in the dark of the evening that, despite its quite definitely not being Teddy's boat, yet the man in the boat might somehow, against all the odds, still be him. Perhaps Teddy might, for some reason that she would soon discover, turn out to have taken someone else's boat? As she slipped and slid across the shingle towards the figure that she found herself willing to be Teddy's, despite the fact that she could now see quite clearly that the oilskin was not Teddy's oilskin, and that the face under the woollen hat was not Teddy's face, somehow Bobbie was still trying to convince herself that it was going to turn out to be Teddy after all, because she so wanted it to be him.

It was only when the man who was not Teddy said 'No' in answer to her frantic, 'Ted? Is that you?' that Bobbie realized just how anxious she sounded. Yet her voice that seemed to her to be so loud must have been barely audible to the stranger above the sound of the wind and the tide that had now turned and was beginning to creep up the shore again.

'Best phone the coastguard if you're worried about someone, miss.'

'Yes, of course. I just thought you might be . . . Ted.'

Bobbie turned round and struggled up the beach once more, and along the path that eventually led back to the little rented house where a candle had already been placed in the window by her superstitious landlady, who would have long ago slipped back to her own house.

Bobbie was in such a fury of anxiety that she threw herself through the French windows and onto the oak parquet flooring as if she had been suddenly pushed from behind.

563

'I'll have to phone the coastguard. They'll have to send out a boat to look for him. Put up flares. He must have been gone for hours, but how many hours? I don't know how many hours!'

As she talked out loud to herself, like a mad person, Bobbie grabbed the first phone book that came to hand and started to flick frantically through it, not really knowing which number to call.

'Do you call nine nine nine for a coast guard? *Who* do you call? They *must* send out someone to look for him!'

She was practically shouting out her questions to herself, so busy searching through the various ageing telephone books that she failed to notice someone coming into the room, or see the man standing at the other end of the long room, stocking-footed, his handsome head of fair hair still wet with the rain.

'I say, Bobbie, you weren't worried about me, were you?'

Teddy stood at the door, hoping, so hoping that she had been worried out of her mind about him, for such had been his intention to steal away and see if, at long, long last, she might miss him.

'*Teddy!*' Bobbie flung herself against him, furious and yet at the same time faint with relief. 'Teddy! Where on earth have you been? God, if you knew how worried I was. I was frantic. I've been out there running about calling to you, I was calling to you and you wouldn't come back. You wouldn't come back!' She stopped, staring at him, and tears came

564

into her eyes. 'You just wouldn't come back, no matter how much I called to you, you wouldn't come back. Why didn't you come back?' she asked him, yet again. 'I was waiting for you, Teddy.'

Teddy looked down at her, his handsome face strangely emotionless as he saw the tears in her eyes.

'Yes, you were, weren't you, Bobbie? You were waiting for me, Teddy, and, look, I did come back, Bobbie, didn't I? I came back.'

Bobbie flung her arms round his neck. 'Oh yes you did, didn't you, Teddy? You did come back. Thank God! You came back!'

They hugged and kissed each other, filled with relief, and at the same knowing that it was something they had both wanted to do, no matter what time or when Teddy had finally appeared. After which Bobbie sank back into her old familiar position in front of the window, trembling with the relief and the happiness of the moment, before promptly falling into an exhausted sleep.

Watching her sleeping Teddy knew that there was still so much they had to say to each other, but he had no intention of saying any of it until he was quite sure that Bobbie was on the mend. Sometimes things were best left, and this was one of those times. He knew now that they had both turned a corner, and were facing a shared future of some kind, although not, he hoped sincerely, just as brother and sister. Exactly how it would be was something that need not be contemplated at that moment. But of one thing he was quite sure, Teddy paused before looking back towards the sleeping girl, Bobbie was going to live. Of that, at least, he was going to make quite sure.

Of course it was many months before Bobbie did finally throw off her illness and return to London to take up any part of her former life, and once she did it was only to leave it the following summer, again in the company of Teddy, but this time to be married to him from Mellaston.

Miranda and Dick followed shortly after, and the four of them set about making the old rectory look as festive as it had ever done, crowded with fresh flowers from the gardens of all their well-wishers, and although the wedding was small, and conducted at a side altar in the cathedral, there were enough guests to make their little party look the happy band that it undoubtedly was. Naturally the Major and Mrs Saxby were among their number, the Major giving away the bride to her groom in the appropriate manner, and Mrs Saxby obliging by crying into a small lace handkerchief.

Later, at the reception in the old rectory, the best man, before inviting the guests to rise and toast the happy couple, asked them, 'to always remember what has gone before, all those who gave their lives in the war, not for us to be unhappy, or without hope, but so that we could attempt to live sincerely, with grace and with kindness, or they will have died for nothing'.

The speech ended, Major Saxby and some of the other guests were heard to make *hear hear* noises, and other similar sounds, and of course everyone rose to their feet to raise their glasses to Bobbie and Teddy.

As they did so the bride was making her own silent toast, for she was quite certain that from behind her she could hear the sound of laughter, and she knew at once that it was Julian's laughter and that he was saying in his mock reproachful voice, *But I thought you promised me you would never become a woman, that neither of us would ever grow up?* and she could feel his arm through hers as they walked through the underground passageway at Baileys Court, away from the moonlight and the smell of fresh-cut hay and salty breezes, away from everything that was so redolent of a Sussex evening by the seaside in summer.

Bobbie turned, knowing that he was there, perhaps briefly visiting, seeing all the flowers, the gold threads in her veil, the cream of her dress, the embroidery of the old cloth set about the table, and she smiled back at him, understanding.

Wretched Boy!

THE END

Charlotte Bingham would like to invite you to visit her website at www.charlottebingham.com